Split by the Bell

By: Jessica Terry

Split By the Bell

Jessica Terry

Published by Jessica Terry, 2022.

SPLIT BY THE BELL

First edition. March 14, 2022.

Copyright © 2022 Jessica Terry.

ISBN: 978-0578393414

Written by Jessica Terry.

Chapter 1

"I LOVE YOU, DESIREE."

The post-coital sweat hadn't even dried from Desiree's brow yet and she was already wondering how she was going to get rid of this man.

Tobias was her man of the moment, and lately he had been talking like he wanted to be her man for life. *Instant* red flag. Desiree didn't do monogamy, at least not long-term. She just had her fun and moved on. And Tobias talking about love after only two weeks was a sign that it was time to pack it in.

"Hey, come here," Tobias ordered softly, pulling her closer. Her back was to him, but she allowed him to pull her bare body into his. The bulge against her backside let her know that he probably wanted to go another round. She would have loved how insatiable he was if only he could keep his mouth shut. "What's wrong?"

"Nothing."

"Mmm, you feel amazing." Tobias's hands roamed her hips and thighs as he nuzzled the back of her neck, burying his face in her hair. "What's that scent?"

"Brown sugar and vanilla."

"You always smell so good," he murmured. She felt his tongue glide across her skin. "It's one of the things I love so much about you."

Rolling her eyes, Desiree didn't respond. She didn't want to hurt his feelings, but he was sadly mistaken if he thought they were star-crossed lovers. Far from it. She enjoyed his company, she enjoyed his body, and that was as far as it went.

"You gonna stay with me tonight?" he asked her.

"Oh, I have some things I need to do, actually. I can't stay tonight."

"Aww, come on, babe...you know I hate when you leave me like that. I can order some of that chicken and sausage pizza you like and we can just watch some movies in bed. Then in the morning, I'll fix you breakfast..."

"I can't, Tobias."

"Please?"

"Don't beg. It's unattractive."

"What is it you have to do? It can't wait until tomorrow?"

Her patience fading, Desiree sat up. This was just another reason she knew it was time to end things with Tobias; he was too clingy. She'd been at his house for the past three hours and he was acting like she had just gotten there ten minutes ago.

"There's some work I need to do for my events this weekend. The parties don't plan themselves, you know."

"I thought everything was set."

"Promotion is never done. I want a full house."

"You know I've been spreading the word. I've told all my boys about it, and they're gonna try to bring someone."

"Have they bought their tickets yet?"

"I don't know. I can ask, though."

"Let them know it'll be twice as much at the door. And space is limited."

"I got you. Regardless, though, you know *I'm* gonna be there. Those Desiree Mashburn events are epic."

"Well, I don't know about *epic*." Desiree couldn't resist blushing.

"You're good at what you do, babe. I'm just glad I took my friend up on their offer and went to your end-of-summer bash a couple of weeks ago. Or else I never would have met you." He reached up and caressed her face.

"True." Desiree gave him a tight smile.

She remembered the night she and Tobias met. She threw a pool party/cookout to wind down the summer season. A pro football player that she'd grown up with agreed to let her have the bash at his mansion, with ample security, of course. So many people had shown up that they had to start turning people away. Desiree sauntered around in her iridescent pink bikini and gauzy white sarong, tending to needs and putting out proverbial fires, doing more than her fair share of flirting along the way. She even managed to sneak away for some heavy-petting action in the pool house with a hunk she'd been making eyes at all day. Her friend Lovey always teased her that she only became an event promoter so she could work and play at the same time.

Tobias had shown up pretty late into the party, but Desiree noticed him. He was pretty hard to miss. A tall drink of caramel latte, he pretty much stayed to himself, nursing a beer and occasionally talking to someone he recognized. Desiree hadn't been able to keep her eyes off his bulging biceps, which was one of her favorite features on a man. He had a calm aura about him. His eyes just took in everything as he stood there in his tank top and cargo shorts, not pressed to be noticed but not minding when he was. Desiree liked that.

Desiree had never been shy about approaching a man she was interested in, not bothering wasting time playing hard to get. She went over and introduced herself, and they hit it off quickly. Whenever she had to step away and deal with something, Tobias always waited patiently for her to come back. And when things started winding down, he stayed to help her get everything in order, and then saw her home. She invited him in. And now, two weeks later, here they were.

And Desiree was over it.

Tobias sat up and wrapped his arms around her, kissing her shoulder. "I'd really like it if you stayed with me tonight. I'll make it worth it."

"Oh yeah? Is your dick gonna update the social media postings and send out the reminder to my email list?"

"No, but it can mellow you out for when you can take care of all of that later. Plus, you never go anywhere without your tablet. Just do all that from here."

This man never gives up, Desiree thought to herself. The residual tinglings from the awesome bed-romping they just shared had already dissipated, replaced with an exhausting weariness. *Lovey would probably find this kind of thing flattering and romantic.*

"You know I'll take care of you," Tobias assured, his large hand smoothly sliding towards her moderate breasts. She shuddered, not being able to help it. Weak spots were called that for a reason. "I'm always gonna take care of you, babe."

He turned her face towards his and pecked her lips before laying a deeper one on her, sliding his tongue into his mouth as he simultaneously fondled her brown mounds. Desiree felt herself melting into him, giving in to his hands that had shown her what they could do on their very first night together. He had a way of making her forget and lose her head, which wasn't a good thing to Desiree. She liked being in control of things at all times.

Despite knowing this, she turned in his arms and returned his kisses deeply, sliding her arms around his neck. He lifted her onto his lap and grabbed a handful of her highlighted brown wig, gently pulling her head back so he could get full access to her neck. Desiree moaned, hating how much she enjoyed what he was doing. She knew they were going to have to have a talk, but it could wait for now.

Plus, if we're doing this, he's not talking about our future and crap, she silently rationalized.

They fell onto their sides, in full devour mode. Tobias retrieved another condom from the nightstand and plunged into her; Desiree didn't need a lot of foreplay. They went at it until their sweat was the only thing on them that could move. Tobias fell into a deep sleep, a possessive hand clamped to her thigh.

Desiree dozed off briefly, but she woke up, glancing over at her lover. He really was a good man. And if Desiree had been like most women, she would've been over the moon about him seemingly wanting to make her a permanent fixture in his life. But the idea of happily ever after bored her. She loved drama, and variety. And she liked being able to do as she pleased, with no one to answer to but herself.

Easing out of bed, she quickly got dressed and gathered her things. She scribbled a note on the back of their takeout receipt and left it by his side of the bed. With one last glance over her shoulder, she left.

A COUPLE OF DAYS LATER, Desiree was home working. She sighed as her phone chimed with yet another text from Tobias, probably with more whining about how she had left him in the middle of the night. Maybe it had been a little cold to break up with him in a note - *right* after sleeping together - but she didn't want him to try to dissuade her. She just wanted to make a clean break. It was better this way.

She was typing out an email when she heard Tupac's voice.

"*Dear Mama...*"

Smiling, Desiree grabbed her phone, always glad to talk to her mother, Elyse.

"What's up, Ma?"

"Girl, I'm out here trying to find the right pair of gold heels but can't seem to find anything satisfactory."

"What do you need gold heels for? You going somewhere?"

"Sure am. Right up to the top floor of the house to put it on your daddy."

"Ma!" Desiree laughed, shaking her head. She and Elyse had a very close relationship, often talking like sisters more than mother and daughter. Her parents had been happily married for over thirty-five years, and Elyse wasn't shy about the fact that she and her husband still had a very active sex life.

"What? Don't act brand new. You know what it is."

"I know *too much* of what it is," Desiree chuckled.

"Hell, you're thirty-two years old. I'm sure you've done everything you've heard me talk about and more. Speaking of that, how's Tobias?"

"Tobias is over."

"Damn, already?" Elyse was well aware of her daughter's short attention span when it came to men.

"You know how I am, Ma. Once your time is up, that's it. He doesn't seem to want to accept it, though. He's been blowing up my phone ever since I left his house the other night."

"Well, how did you leave things? You were polite to him, at least, right? You said he was a nice guy."

"Yeah, he is. And I admit I probably could have done better than leaving him a note and dipping out while he was asleep..."

"Desiree."

"Well! I had tried to tell him earlier than I needed to leave but he was being all clingy and stuff. That was the only way I could leave unbothered. You know he was already talking about our future together and stuff after two weeks?"

"So what's the problem? Hell, me and your father were planning our wedding on our first date."

"Your kind of relationship is rare, Ma, you know that. You and Daddy are some kind of anomaly."

"And what about your sisters? Dana, Diamond, and Dori are all in happy marriages with the men they knew were 'the one' immediately."

"Okay, well maybe *I'm* the anomaly, then. At least as far as this family goes. You know I've always been the rebel."

"Oh, I know. I just hope you don't miss out on something just because you want to be different. There's nothing wrong with being in love, baby."

"I know. For the people that want that. Super-serious relationships just aren't my thing. That doesn't mean I don't care about the men I date; I just don't want to get married or have their babies."

"Who said anything about babies? Diamond doesn't have any kids."

"It's the social expectancy. You know, 'first comes love, then comes marriage, then comes Desiree with the baby carriage.' Barf."

"For the life of me, I will never understand how you and Lovey got to be friends. You all are almost total opposites."

"In a lot of ways, yes." Desiree took a huge bite out of the honeybun that was sitting by her laptop. "If I had known he was going to turn out to be such a cling-on, I'd have introduced Tobias to Lovey first. She'd be on cloud nine right now."

"I do hope she finds someone, though; she's such a sweetheart."

"Well you know she's been dating that dude Evan. Things are going pretty well, from what she says. Hopefully this one sticks."

"I hope so. She deserves it."

"She really does."

"You do too, you know."

"I'm good, Ma. Really. I don't feel like I'm missing out on anything at all."

"Yeah, okay. The right man will change your mind. Watch what I tell you."

Chapter 2

THE PHONE HADN'T LEFT Lovey's hand for the past three hours. She and Evan had only been on a couple of dates, but Lovey's hopes were already embarrassingly high. The fantasizing and doodling of his last name on hers had already started.

She knew she had a tendency to fall hard and fast when she really liked someone, and this time was no exception. Ever since Evan had approached her at the grocery store, asking if she knew the difference between parsley and cilantro (because he didn't), Lovey had been smitten. And he seemed smitten with her.

So why hadn't he contacted her today?

Trying not to think the worst, she curled up on the couch and tried to focus on the latest episode of *Black-ish*. She laid her Samsung phone next to her, resisting the urge to check the ringer. It was driving her crazy, this waiting.

Her mind wandered to their first date. He had taken her bowling, and didn't seem to mind when she beat him two out of three games. They hung out, eating turkey burgers and beer, trading stories about their college days and laughing at each other's exploits. Lovey had never felt so comfortable with someone so soon, and had taken it as a good sign. They'd gotten so caught up in their conversation that they hadn't realized everyone around them had left; the employees were giving them that get-up-and-get-out glare. Not wanting to leave each other yet, they went and sat in Evan's car, picking right up where they left off. Pretty soon they were the only ones in the parking lot, talking (and eventually kissing and necking) well into the night.

Lovey smiled at the memory.

He'll call, she assured herself. *You can't fake the kind of connection we had.*

Feeling slightly better, Lovey turned her attention back to the television, laughing at the antics of her favorite actress, Tracee Ellis Ross. When her phone rang, she immediately snatched it up, only partially disappointed that it was her best friend, Desiree.

"Hey, girl."

"I think I need a restraining order," Desiree barked.

"What??"

"Girl, Tobias has been straight blowing my phone *up*. Ever since I broke up with him-"

"In a note..."

"Whatever! I never made the man any promises. We weren't in a *real* relationship. Hell, I just met him two weeks ago! What did he expect??"

"Um, maybe to be told to his face that you were no longer interested instead of you putting him to sleep with your punanny and then sneaking out."

"Well, I *did* try to tell him that I needed to go and he wasn't trying to hear it. So I don't know what else I was supposed to do."

"I'm saying, Desiree...did you *tell* him that you wanted to end things?"

Pause. "No. Not in so many words."

"Why not? It's not like you to bite your tongue."

"I guess I can admit I didn't want to hurt his feelings. It's not like I don't like him. If he hadn't started talking about forever, I'd probably be over there right now. But he's trying to jump the gun so I had to get out."

"Still. You should've just been honest."

"Okay, I acknowledge I could have handled it better."

"Just talk to him and explain yourself. At least give him that."

"He'll just try to convince me to change my mind. I wouldn't put it past him to pull the L-word out again. I just don't wanna go there."

"*Or*, maybe he'll respect your wishes and go away gracefully."

"I doubt it."

"It's almost not even fair. Here I am waiting on Evan to call me and you're complaining about a perfectly good man who apparently won't stop until he talks to you."

"You haven't talked to Evan today?"

"No. I sent a couple of texts this morning but he hasn't responded. I called once; no answer. I didn't want to seem pushy so I left it at that. But I can't help but wonder what's going on."

"I'm sure it's nothing. You two hit it off really well; I bet there's a perfectly good reason why he hasn't called yet."

Lovey bit her lip as she played with the hem of her sweatshirt. "You don't think he's fading to black, do you?" she asked, referring to their term for when a man's calls and availability steadily declined to nothing. It had happened to Lovey more times than she cared to admit.

"Nooo. I think he's just busy. He's *not* fading to black."

"I hope not."

"Why don't you go surprise him? You know where he lives, right?"

"Yeah, but I don't wanna freak him out. I've never been one for showing up at someone's place unannounced."

"Hell, I would," Desiree scoffed. "Throw on something sexy and show up at his door. I bet you money he won't turn you away."

"I don't know. I think I'm gonna just wait it out. I'm sure I'll hear from him soon enough."

"You will. In the meantime, though, quit waiting by the phone. Get up out of those raggedy gray sweats I'm sure you have on and go do something to take your mind off it. Don't let your whole existence be about waiting for some man."

Giggling, Lovey looked down at the sweats she loved to wear around the house. Desiree knew her too well. "I wouldn't say all that. But you have a point. There *are* other things I could be doing."

"There you go."

Feeling a little better, Lovey hopped off the couch and made herself keep busy by washing the neglected dishes in the sink, vacuuming her living room, and ironing her clothes for work the next day. She wrapped her long light brown hair before going to bed, not being able to resist sending a simple good night text to Evan before doing so. Lying down with a content sigh, she just knew she would have a message from him by the time she woke up.

She didn't, though. Lovey grabbed her phone and checked it as soon as she turned off her alarm the next morning, and there was still nothing from Evan. Worry was starting to creep in. They had only been dating a short while, but he usually at least texted her, if he couldn't call. It had now been a full twenty-four hours since she had heard from him, and Lovey was starting to get that bad feeling again.

"No, he wouldn't do this to me," she assured herself. "Maybe his phone broke or somebody in his family died. I'm not gonna think the worst."

Going on to work, Lovey tried to put Evan out of her mind, but it was futile. She could hardly concentrate on the numbers in front of her because her mind kept leaping to other conclusions about Evan's whereabouts. What if he had been in an accident? What if he lost all the contacts in his phone and hadn't memorized her number? What if he had met someone else?

That last one caused Lovey to gasp. What if he *had* met somebody else? For all Lovey knew, he could have been dating other women this whole time; they never discussed being exclusive. Lovey had kept all her attention on Evan since she met him, and the thought of him not doing the same to her was a little jarring.

"But that doesn't really explain him not getting back to me, though," she reminded herself. "How much time does it take to respond to a simple text?"

Lovey knew she was going to drive herself crazy if she didn't get some answers. Pushing her work aside, she closed the door to her office before logging on to Facebook. She frowned when she saw Evan had been active on there, posting a few times since she had last spoken to him.

"So he can get on Facebook but can't talk to *me*?"

She continued to peruse his timeline, her confusion multiplying with each passing minute. Why was he ignoring her? What had she done wrong? Had she been too pushy, too needy, too *something*? Evan had never given the impression that he was unhappy with her or their budding relationship; in fact, just the other day he told her that he liked her more than he had any woman in a long time. Why would he say something like that and then do this?

Clicking on his photo album, Lovey put her chin in her hand as she perused his pictures. She couldn't help but smile at how cute he was, with his reddish-brown hair and freckles splayed across his light brown skin. He seemed so adorable to her when they first met. And with each picture she clicked on, she felt that warm sensation she always felt when she was crushing on someone take over her. It happened every time; it felt like someone was slowly pouring warm liquid into her body, filling her from the bottom to the top. It's how Lovey always knew she was really into someone.

There was a knock on her door.

"Yes?" Lovey called out, quickly closing Facebook.

The receptionist, Tara, poked her head in. "Your next appointment is here."

"Okay thanks. You can send them in."

Lovey managed to keep her mind on work for the rest of the day. When her last client left, she logged on to Facebook again and noticed that Evan had checked in at the gym. Chewing her lip thoughtfully, she wondered if she should go by there and see him. She *had* to know what was going on; all this speculating was only going to drive her crazy.

Her sister, Liz, appeared in her doorway. "Hey, girl. You about done for the day?"

Lovey jumped slightly, having been lost in her own thoughts. "Huh? Oh...yeah, I'm done. I didn't know you were coming by."

"I was over this way running some errands and thought I'd stop by and see you, that's all." Liz entered the small office and took a seat in front of Lovey's desk. Her short black hair was shiny and chic, as usual. "You have a good day?"

"It was okay."

Liz eyed her. "Just okay?"

"I'm an accountant. It's not exactly exciting work."

"But you love it."

"Yeah, I do. I'm sorry, I just...I have some other stuff on my mind right now."

"I could tell. What's wrong?"

"It's Evan. I haven't heard from him in over a day. Something's wrong."

"Oh, honey, that doesn't necessarily mean anything's wrong...maybe he lost his phone or something."

"Maybe. But I saw he's been posting on Facebook pretty regularly. He could have at *least* sent me a message on there to let me know, if that was all it was."

Liz, having always been the more practical of the two, pursed her lips. She knew her little sister's tendency to dive in headfirst when she liked someone. Lovey was probably already picking out china patterns and wondering what she and Evan were going to name their kids. She was a huge romantic who wore her heart on her sleeve, and unfortunately it usually ended with her being heartbroken when the men didn't share her enthusiasm.

"Well, I'm not gonna try to sugarcoat it for you, then...it *does* sound a little shady," Liz gently agreed. "You've tried to contact him, I take it?"

"Yeah. I sent a few texts and called once yesterday."

"And he didn't acknowledge any of it?"

Lovey shook her head, her eyes still scanning Evan's Facebook page.

"Then he's avoiding you, it sounds like."

"But why would he do that? Everything was fine day before yesterday."

"If you ask me, it doesn't matter. There's really no excuse he could give that would be good enough. He's inconsiderate, ignoring you like that. Forget his ass."

"You know I can't do that. I really like Evan, Liz. Part of me still wants to believe there's a good reason I haven't heard from him."

"I hope the other part of you is the one with the common sense. Because, I hate to say it, but you've been down this road before. And it never ends well."

"Thank you, for reminding me of that." Lovey rolled her eyes and grabbed her purse out of her desk drawer. She took one last glance at Evan's profile picture before shutting down her computer.

"I'm not trying to be mean; I'm just saying...after a while, you need to start recognizing the signs. A man that was *really* into you wouldn't ignore you, Lovey."

Lovey knew her sister had a point. This certainly wasn't the first time a man had disappeared on her, and it usually meant that he had moved on.

But she was determined to stay optimistic. There was a first time for everything, after all.

"I have to go," she muttered, slinging her purse over her shoulder.

"Where?"

"L.A. Fitness."

"Really? I didn't know you had a membership there."

"I don't." Lovey looked at her sister pointedly.

"Oh no..." Liz stood up from her seat. She knew full well what her sister was planning to do. "Do *not* go over there trying to confront that man."

"It's not going to be a confrontation. You know I'm not into causing scenes. I simply want to know what's going on so I can stop driving myself crazy."

"Lovey, girl, you *know* what's going on...you just don't want to admit it. If he doesn't have enough respect and consideration for you to be honest, then you don't need him. Just put him out of your mind."

Lovey knew she would never be able to do that, just like she knew her sister would never be able to understand why. So she just gave her a quick hug and scooted past her towards the door.

"I'll call you later," she promised.

Liz just looked after her helplessly, hating that her sweet sister kept falling for these jerks. She wanted to hold out hope that Evan was different, but Liz knew this was just another fade-to-black fatality.

"Better go stock up on the ice cream," she muttered to herself, heading out of the office.

LOVEY SAT IN HER CAR in the L.A. Fitness parking lot, waiting nervously. She had been sitting there for close to an hour after driving around and making sure Evan's car was still there. Making sure she parked where she could see the front entrance, she tried to prepare what she was going to say when she saw him. Should she act like this was a chance meeting or be honest about waiting for him?

Unfortunately, since they hadn't been dating that long, she couldn't really predict how he might react upon seeing her. Would he get angry at her for ambushing him? She worried that he'd be so put off by the surprise visit that he wouldn't want to talk to her. Lovey started to rethink her plan, but knew she had to stick with it. Even though it had only been less than two days, and Evan never made any promises to her, she had to have some answers.

Desiree and Liz were always getting onto Lovey about her tendency to always think every man she met was 'the one.' She would be fantasizing about marriage and babies before either of them had even said 'I love you.' Lovey knew that she often let her heart run away with her, but she couldn't help it. Ever since she was a little girl, she dreamed about having the kind of long, loving marriage that she always saw in old movies. She imagined the perfect wedding, getting married to her dream man in a wedding dress so beautiful every woman would be asking where she got it, professing their love and devotion in front of God and all her friends and family. It was a fantasy she could never imagine letting go of. Her own parents had a wonderful marriage, having gotten married straight out of high school and staying married until they were both killed in a car crash when Lovey was almost thirty.

She smiled wistfully at the memory of her parents, as she always did. It had been almost five years, but Lovey knew that pain from losing them would never fully go away. They were her examples, in every way. Her mother, Stella, had been a romantic just like she was, and Lovey missed the talks they used to have. At times, Lovey felt like her mother was the only one who truly understood her desire to have the husband and family she dreamed of. To her, it represented beauty, security, and warmth. Stella had just been fortunate to find her knight early; Lovey sometimes wondered if she would ever find hers.

Lovey was so deep in her thoughts that she almost didn't notice Evan when he emerged from the building. She jumped, sitting up straight in her seat as she watched him pause for a moment to check something on his phone. Perking up slightly, she bit her lip.

Maybe he's just now seeing my messages, she tried to tell herself. *Maybe he's about to call me back right now.*

Her phone never rang or buzzed, though, and Lovey felt her heart sink just a little. She was trying her best to give Evan the benefit of the doubt, but she was starting to think that Liz might've been right.

Her nerves kicking into overdrive, Lovey quickly checked her appearance in the mirror and got out of the car, making sure not to lose Evan in the stream of people leaving the gym. She hurried over to him, waiting until she was fairly close before making herself known.

"Evan!"

He turned around, and she could almost see the color drain from his face. He glanced towards the gym before walking towards her.

"Lovey, what are you doing here?" he asked.

Lovey wanted to hug him but resisted; he didn't seem all that thrilled to see her. "I'm sorry to just show up like this but I was worried; I've left you messages and you haven't responded to any of them."

"Look, let's talk later, okay? I can't do this now," Evan suggested, his voice urgent. He glanced toward the gym again.

"You can't do *what* now? I'm not trying to cause any drama, Evan...I just want to know what's going on with you. It's not really like you to ignore me like that."

"I'm sorry about that, Lovey...I-I'll have to explain it to you later, though. Just go home and I'll call you later, okay?"

"Will you, really?"

"Yes, I promise."

"All right, but can I at least get a hug first? I haven't seen you in a few days and I've missed you."

Evan hesitated before giving her the lightest, quickest hug she'd ever experienced. "Okay, you get home safe and I'll talk to you later," he hurried, pushing away from her. "Where'd you park?"

"Over there. What's the rush?"

"No rush."

"Then why are you literally pushing me towards my car?"

"I told you I can't talk now."

"If you have somewhere to be, just say so. But you don't have to-"

"Evan?"

Lovey's head whipped around towards the woman's voice calling her man's name. Evan cursed under his breath before stepping over to the brown beauty who was looking at them curiously.

"Hey, I was wondering when you were gonna come on out," he said to her, kissing her cheek. "I was just walking my friend here to her car."

"Well, aren't you a gentleman?" the woman smiled, tweaking his chin. She held her hand out to Lovey, her dimpled smile flashing under the parking lot lights. "I'm Alexis, and you are? I love your hair, by the way."

"Oh, thank you...I'm Lovey."

"Yeah, Lovey is...she's an old friend of mine," Evan introduced, looking at Lovey pointedly. His eyes pleaded with her to play along. "She was over this way meeting a client and we ran into each other."

"Yeah? What kind of business are you in?" Alexis asked her.

Lovey wondered if her face was as red as she felt it was. It was times like this she wished her fair brown skin was darker. "I'm an accountant."

"Really? I need to get your card, myself. I'm kind of an airhead when it comes to numbers."

"Come on now, babe, you're not that bad," Evan said, putting his arm around her. "And anyway, I think Lovey has a full deck right now, anyway. Isn't that what you said the other day, Lovey? Got more business than you can handle, right?"

Babe??

The tears were already starting to tickle her eyes but Lovey knew she couldn't dare let them fall in front of them. She was humiliated enough. Finding her voice, she managed to say, "Yeah. I couldn't take any more right now if I wanted to." She shot Evan a look, and he turned his eyes away.

"Well, that's good that business is going so well for you, then," Alexis commented, not seeming to notice the tension around her. Her slightly messy high bun, makeup-free dewy skin and curvy body that was evident even through her blue tracksuit made Lovey feel slightly inferior, even though she knew that was just her hurt clouding her judgment. "I love seeing a smart sistah doing so well for herself. And here I am just a personal trainer. That's how I met Evan, here."

"Oh?" Lovey didn't want to ask, but she knew she needed to. "Are you two dating?"

"For a few weeks, yeah. But as of yesterday, I'm upgraded to 'official' status." She smiled up at Evan.

Lovey felt like she was going to faint. "Just yesterday, huh?"

"Yeah, we spent the day together and he went ahead and locked me down. Now he's all mine." She grinned. "Asked me to be his girlfriend while we were making out in the car at the bowling alley, girl."

"Alexis!" Evan chided. "I'm sure she doesn't want to hear all that."

"I don't see why not. Y'all are friends, right? Plus, I'm just so damn happy about it!"

Evan still wouldn't look at Lovey. So this was why he hadn't gotten back to her; he was too busy *making things official* with someone else. Lovey could tell Alexis had no idea that she was someone Evan had been seeing simultaneously. She figured he hadn't mentioned her to Alexis at all, since there was no sense of recognition when he introduced them earlier.

I can't take any more of this.

"Well, that's wonderful...I hope you two have the kind of relationship you each deserve. I need to get going...it was nice meeting you, Alexis."

"You too!"

Not having the stomach to say anything to Evan, Lovey turned on her heel and hurried back to her car, resisting the urge to run. Tears were already starting to stream down her face, and her body was burning with embarrassment. She got into her car and slammed the door, wasting no time backing out of her parking space. When she dared to look in the direction of Evan's car, she saw Alexis pull his face down to hers for a passionate kiss.

Feeling like the biggest fool, Lovey stepped on the gas, peeling out of the parking lot.

Chapter 3

DESIREE LOVED HER NIECES and nephew, but every time she babysat them it only reminded her that she didn't want to have any children of her own.

Her sisters and their husbands were all going to a Charlie Wilson concert and had roped Desiree into watching the kids. She made sure to wrap up her work early so she could devote all of her time and attention to them.

"When is the pizza gonna get here, Auntie?" Simon, her sole nephew, asked her.

"It'll be here soon, baby. The tracker says it's out of the oven so they're just checking it to make sure it's right before they bring it."

"You remembered to get extra pepperoni, right?"

"Sure did. I know what you like."

"Thanks, Auntie." Simon headed back to the game he had been playing. Her nieces, Candace and Roxy, were huddled over their tablets trying to beat each other's scores in Candy Crush.

Desiree checked some emails until the pizza arrived, and then they all sat down on the floor in front of the TV and pigged out. Candace and Roxy, her sister Dana's daughters, were within a year in age and often mistaken for twins. Simon was Dori's son, his lighter skin and curlier hair thanks to his Caucasian father, and he often stayed to himself. Desiree knew he wished he had a brother or some male cousins he could play with at times.

"You have a boyfriend, Auntie?" Roxy asked, her mouth full of pizza.

"Nope. And you know better than to talk with your mouth full."

"Why don't you have one?" Candace asked as her sister finished chewing.

"I don't really want one right now, that's all."

"Why not? You're pretty."

"Thank you, baby. But I'm just dating right now; don't want a boyfriend."

"Then how are you gonna get married? Aren't you over thirty?"

Desiree couldn't help but chuckle. "Yeah. So?"

"You're gonna be too old to have kids, if you wait too long," Roxy advised. "We want some more kids to play with. Mama already said she's not having any more."

Simon, as usual, just listened quietly while he ate.

Desiree tried to think of a tactful way to tell them that she had no plans of ever getting married or having kids. She didn't want to sour their ideas of what they considered to be happiness.

"People shouldn't have kids until they're ready," she finally said. "And I'm not ready for all that. Being a parent is a big responsibility."

"Is that why Mama said we should keep our legs closed until marriage?"

Desiree almost spit out her soda. She tried, somewhat unsuccessfully, to straighten her face as she grabbed a napkin and wiped her chin.

"Yeah, that's one of the reasons," she replied. "There are other ones too, though."

"Like what?"

"Well...getting pregnant isn't the only thing that can happen when you have sex. Sometimes you might end up with an STD."

"What's an STD?" Candace asked.

"Sexually Transmitted Disease. Someone could be infected and pass it along to you."

"Like AIDS?" Simon finally spoke up.

"Yeah, that's one of them. There are plenty others."

"So if you get an STD, does that automatically mean you're gonna die? I saw a movie where somebody had AIDS and they died," Roxy commented.

"No, baby, you don't die from all of them. Some of them can be cured. Some can't, but that doesn't necessarily mean you're gonna die right away...they have medication you can take to help you live longer."

"Like that basketball player? I saw on TV how he got infected a whole bunch of years ago and he's still alive," Simon said, popping a piece of pepperoni into his mouth.

"But he's rich, though," Candace jumped in. "He can buy a bunch of medicine. I bet if he wasn't rich he'd be dead by now."

"Okay," Desiree clapped her hands, wanting to change the subject. "Enough about that. Let's finish eating so I can whoop y'all's behinds in some Uno. I need to get you two back for cheating last time," she added, pointing at the girls.

"We didn't cheat!" they protested in unison.

"Uh-huh." Desiree winked at them as they all turned their attention to the television. Desiree was just glad they were no longer talking about dating, diseases, and death.

Desiree actually didn't have anything against marriage. She had seen firsthand how it could be a beautiful thing when you married the right person; her parents, her sisters, and even Lovey's parents before they died had all been great examples of how great marriage could be. But it just wasn't for her. Desiree didn't like the idea of being tied down to anything, no matter what it was. That's why she went into business for herself, that's why she rented instead of bought, and that's why none of her relationships ever lasted more than a few months.

And she *definitely* didn't want any kids; at least with marriage you could get a divorce. Kids were for life.

After they all played a few spirited rounds of Uno, the kids went back to entertaining themselves and Desiree decided to cruise around on social media. She curled up in the corner of the couch with her tablet, scrolling through Facebook, and was just about to respond to one of her friend's crazy updates when an instant messenger box popped up on her screen. When she saw it was from Cornell, she grinned.

What up, sexy

Grinning harder, Desiree glanced at the kids before typing her response.

Everything is everything, handsome. Good to hear from you

You know I'm gonna check on you. U busy?

Babysitting

Damn. Guess you can't give me a show like you did the other night then, huh?

Stifling a giggle, Desiree rubbed her legs together as she typed her response.

Check back with me later on

And you know I will

Cornell was someone she met in a Facebook group about a year before. They had hit it off and flirted heavily, but that was as far as it went. Cornell lived across the country, and neither of them had ever expressed any interest in getting on a plane to see each other in person. The instant messages and occasional erotic video chats were good enough for them.

Desiree continued to chat with Cornell while the kids played, only stopping whenever Candace and Roxy would get into one of their intermittent spats. When her phone chimed and she saw it was a text from Tobias, she sucked her teeth and dropped it back on the couch, ignoring it. She didn't know what else she could tell that man to make it clear to him that their little fling was over.

There was a knock on the door. Desiree checked her watch and put down her tablet, standing up from the couch and stretching.

"Who is that, Auntie?" Roxy asked.

"It's probably Auntie Lovey. I asked her to come by."

"Oh good. I haven't seen her in a while."

"I'll go with you to the door," Simon offered, popping up. Desiree smiled as he accompanied her, her hand playing with a few of his dark curls as they walked.

Desiree checked the peephole before swinging open the door, automatically smiling at the sight of her friend. "Hey girl!"

"Hey," Lovey droned with a half-wave. She hadn't wanted to come but Desiree persisted until she agreed, feeling she needed to get out of the house and stop crying over Evan. Desiree knew how much Lovey loved kids, and figured some time with her nieces and nephew would do her some good and take her mind off things, at least for a while.

"Hey, Auntie Lovey," Simon greeted her, stepping from behind Desiree.

Not being able to resist, Lovey smiled and opened her arms to him. He ran to her. She and Desiree had been friends for so long and were so close that she considered Desiree's nieces and nephew her own. And they loved her as much as they loved Desiree.

The three of them went to rejoin Candace and Roxy in the living room, and the girls were just as happy to see Lovey as Simon was. They almost forgot Desiree was there as Roxy started telling Lovey all about some boy she liked at school, while Candace played in Lovey's long hair, something she always loved to do. Simon just curled up under her arm on the couch, snuggling up to her like he always did.

"Dang, give her some room to breathe, Simon," Desiree joked.

"Hush; he's fine right where he is," Lovey replied, giving Simon a little squeeze. He smiled and buried his face in her arm, trying to hide his blushing cheeks.

"Auntie Lovey, you tell me what you think I should do," Roxy chattered on. "Should I sneak a note into Eric's backpack or send something to him on Snapchat? Snapchat, right?"

"I don't know...a note is more personal," Lovey replied. "Plus it's something he can keep."

"But it's something he can show other people, too," Roxy countered. "I don't want everybody in my business."

Desiree laughed. "Girl, you are twelve years old; you're not old enough to have any business."

"Mama always says that same thing," Roxy sucked her teeth. "Still, though. What you think, Auntie Lovey?"

"Hmm. What kind of stuff does he like?"

"He really likes football. That's all he talks about."

"Do *you* like football?"

Roxy shrugged. "It's okay. I don't know a whole lot about it."

"Well, why don't you ask him if he can teach you a few things about the game? Boys tend to like it when you show an interest in what they're into."

"Hmmm..." Roxy contemplated the suggestion, actually tapping her chin. "That's not bad. I could even cheer for him when he's playing after school, with his friends."

"Sure. But if you do that, though, everyone is gonna know you like him. So think about that part of it, too, since you're worried about people being in your business." Lovey looked at Desiree and winked, who just chuckled.

"Good point," Roxy mused. "So I'll just give him a note asking him to teach me about football. I'll make sure he follows me on Snapchat, too."

"Eric isn't even all that cute," Candace commented as she tried to pile all of Lovey's hair on top of her head. "He's got big ears."

"I like his ears. And nobody asked you, anyway."

They continued to plot Roxy's route to Eric's attention and play beauty salon until Desiree sent the kids to go lay down in her room until their parents got there. They dozed off almost as soon as their heads hit the pillows. Desiree and Lovey retreated to the kitchen, where they shared the rest of a carton of butter pecan ice cream.

"You know I don't need to be eating this stuff," Lovey mumbled, digging her spoon in for another bite. "No need in me being lonely *and* fat."

"You are nowhere near fat, and you don't have to be lonely, either. You have me, Liz, the rest of the fam..."

"You know what I mean. I love y'all but you can't do for me what a man does."

"Guess I can't argue with you there. But I keep telling you, you'll find somebody."

"When?" Lovey challenged, looking intently at her friend. "D, I'm really starting to feel like I'm going to spend the rest of my life by myself. I want a husband and a house full of kids...and I'm not getting any younger. Maybe it's just not meant to happen for me."

"Stop talking like that, Lovey. Don't speak it into existence."

"It's already existing, Desiree. My love life is a joke and you know it. I really thought Evan and I had something and he played me like all the others do. I just wish I knew what I was doing wrong."

"Who says you're doing anything wrong? Girl, men nowadays ain't shit. There are so many desperate women out here that they know they can get away with pretty much anything, because most women will put up with it just to have somebody. At least you're not like *that*."

Lovey shrugged. "I guess."

"Girl, believe me, there is nothing wrong with you. You're beautiful, intelligent, and you have a heart of gold. If they're too blind or immature to see and appreciate that, to hell with 'em. *Including* Evan's ass. I didn't like him, no way."

Lovey couldn't resist a chuckle as she looked at her friend appreciatively. "You always say that."

"Well. When they mistreat my girl, they're automatically on my shit list. Evan better hope I never see him walking these streets 'cause I will try my best to go Vin Diesel on him and run him down with my car. You know I can be fast *and* furious."

Lovey laughed, covering her mouth with one hand and hitting Desiree on the arm with the other. "Girl, you are a fool!"

"I meant it, though," Desiree said with a grin, happy to see her friend smiling. She hated when these men screwed Lovey over and left her doubting herself. Lovey had to be one of the most genuine, loving, give-you-the-shirt-off-her-back people Desiree had ever met. She didn't deserve to keep getting treated like she had been. Desiree had offered to set her up with someone several times, but Lovey always declined, claiming they didn't have the same taste in men. Desiree just didn't want her friend ending up with any more losers and figured she would be objective enough to make a good selection. When Lovey fell, she fell hard, and her rose-colored glasses stayed locked in place until they were knocked off.

They were just polishing off the rest of the ice cream when there was a faint knock at the door. Desiree checked her watch, frowning curiously.

"Is that your sisters to come get the kids?" Lovey asked.

"Shouldn't be; they texted me a little while ago saying they were just leaving the concert. There's no way they could be here that fast."

"Are you expecting someone else?" Lovey followed Desiree to the door.

"Nope. And could you fix your hair, please? I don't know what Candace was trying to do to it but I can't look at that anymore."

"Hush; my baby did this and I'm proud to wear it." Lovey lifted her chin and stuck out her chest.

"Whatever." Desiree checked the peephole, then cursed under her breath. "No this negro didn't..."

"Who is it?"

"It's mister can't-get-the-damn-message." Desiree yanked open the door, attitude all over her face and a hand on her hip. "Tobias, what the hell are you doing here?"

Tobias stood in front of them, looking contrite. He briefly nodded acknowledgement to Lovey before turning his eyes back to Desiree, the longing in them obvious.

"I'm sorry for just showing up like this," he began. "But you wouldn't respond to any of my messages..."

"Gee, most people would take that as some kind of hint," Desiree snapped.

"Desiree, come on...you left a note and dipped out on me in the middle of the night. That's no way to end a relationship. Can we just talk for a minute, please?"

"What relationship? We slept together for two weeks. Never *once* did we discuss anything other than that."

Feeling like she was intruding, Lovey gently cleared her throat and inched away. "Um, I'm gonna go check on the kids."

"You don't have to go anywhere. This won't take long." Desiree grabbed her arm.

"No, you two *should* talk. And I don't need to be here for that." Lovey leaned in and muttered where only Desiree could hear, "It's not gonna hurt you to talk to him. And *be nice*."

Sucking her teeth, Desiree sighed as Lovey walked off. When they were alone, Desiree looked at Tobias pointedly. "Okay. What is so important that you just had to come over here this time of night? I'm listening."

"Can I at least come in?"

"I'm babysitting my nieces and nephew. They don't need to hear our mess."

"I'm not trying to start any mess, Desiree. But I don't want to stand in your doorway, either."

Desiree wanted to tell him to kick rocks, but she remembered Lovey's directive to be nice. And she knew she should be, anyway...Tobias had always been good to her. And it *was* kind of messed up how she ended things. He deserved an actual explanation.

"Okay, fine," she finally acquiesced, stepping aside. "We can go in the kitchen."

"Thank you," Tobias replied, relieved. He stepped inside and followed her to the kitchen. Just as they were sitting down at the small kitchen table, there was another knock on the door.

"That's probably my sisters coming to get the kids," Desiree said, standing. "I'll be right back. Help yourself to something to drink, if you want it."

After quickly rounding up the kids and having a quick chat with her sisters Dori and Dana, Desiree trudged back to the kitchen. Lovey was in the spare bedroom Desiree used as an office, browsing on the computer.

"Thought you were gonna ditch me or something," Tobias admitted when Desiree rejoined him at the table.

"No. I know you don't deserve that."

"I didn't deserve that note and late-night skip-out, either."

Desiree sighed. "I know."

"So what was up with that?"

"Things...things were just getting a little too heavy for me, Tobias."

"What do you mean?"

"I don't really do relationships. Maybe I should have told you that up front, but I thought we were just gonna hang and enjoy each other...you started getting really clingy, wanting to be up under me all the time, and that's always a big red flag for me."

"Why didn't you just tell me that?"

"I don't know...I don't really do this kind of drama, either. Didn't want it to be a big unnecessary scene."

"So you just knew what I was gonna say and do, huh?" When Desiree just lightly shrugged and looked at the floor, Tobias sat forward and looked at her, leaning his muscular arms on the table. "Desiree, I like you. Like you a lot. But give me a little credit. The only reason I've been reaching out to you so much recently is because I wanted to know why you left the way you did. And the only reason I even give a damn is *because* of how much I like you. But if you had just been straight up with me, we could have avoided all of this."

Desiree knew he was right. She should have just been honest instead of expecting him to read her mind, and then just accept that she was done without explanation.

Holding her hands up in surrender, Desiree looked at him apologetically. "Okay. You're right. I could have handled this way better. My bad."

"Thank you for saying that." Tobias looked at her. "You look beautiful, by the way."

Not being able to resist, Desiree blushed. "Thank you."

Lovey sat in the office, the door only slightly ajar, reading articles on MSN and browsing around on Facebook. She could faintly hear Desiree and Tobias' voices in the kitchen, though not well enough to make out what they were saying. She just hoped Desiree was being nice to the man.

For the life of her, Lovey couldn't figure out how Desiree could treat men like that...a good man who treated her well and genuinely liked her, and who wasn't willing to give up on her so easily, and Desiree just tossed him out like he was nothing. Lovey would *love* to have someone be that into her. Most of the men she met lately didn't have the courtesy to let her know they were no longer into her...they treated her like Desiree treated Tobias.

Shaking her head, Lovey sighed. This was just another area where she and her best friend were complete opposites.

Lovey was looking forward to hearing how things turned out; she kept waiting for Desiree to come in and give her the rundown. But when she heard Desiree's bedroom door close, then very distinct moans and whispers shortly after, Lovey knew she would have to wait until the next day to get the details. Desiree and Tobias had apparently patched things up, and would probably be 'patching' the rest of the night.

Trying to block out the sound of Desiree and Tobias' bed-rocking and ignore the unexplained tears stinging her eyes, Lovey grabbed her purse and tiptoed out of the apartment.

Chapter 4

DESIREE SAT IN HER car in front of Barfly, a local club she was hoping to do business with. She had a meeting with the club owners in a half hour, and her head was killing her. Digging in her purse, she hoped she had some aspirin or something that would quell her throbbing headache.

She didn't know what she'd been thinking, allowing Tobias back into her bed. The night he showed up at her apartment and they finally talked, she started to feel herself like him again, and they ended up naked in her bed. Then naked in *his* bed the next night, after gorging on her favorite chicken and sausage pizza and throwing back Patron shots like they were water.

Now she was kicking herself, because Tobias was blowing up her phone again, now with messages of how much he can't wait to get between her legs again and what he plans to do to her during their next tryst. When her phone chimed with another message from him, Desiree rolled her eyes and ignored it. He seemed to accept that she didn't want a relationship, but now he was just acting like she was his personal booty call. It was just from one extreme to another.

"Uuuggghhhh..." Desiree groaned, letting her head fall against the headrest. She should have known better to drink like that and be up so late the night before a meeting, but Tobias' body could be addictive, despite herself. Regardless, she knew she had to get herself together or else she was going to blow this meeting. She was hoping to secure a contract with them to promote weekly parties in their facility, and with their club being relatively new and her popularity growing by the event, it could be very beneficial for everyone.

Checking her watch, she picked up her phone and tried to call Lovey. She hadn't spoken to her since she had come and hung with her and the kids at her apartment, and Lovey had been gone when Desiree emerged from her bedroom later that night. She hadn't been able to get in touch with Lovey since then, and Desiree was worried about her. She knew she was still bummed about Evan, and her love life in general, and Desiree hoped Lovey didn't do anything silly. Lovey was someone who loved hard, and needed someone to love her back. She craved it. Not having anyone to provide that for her was like a plant that wasn't getting any water; eventually it just withered and died. And Desiree could only hope that Lovey's heart hadn't reached that point yet.

Her call to Lovey went right to voicemail, and Desiree frowned. She left a message asking her to call her back, then checked her watch again before giving herself a quick-once over in the visor mirror. Taking a few moments to give herself a pep talk like she always did before doing business, she finally opened the door and got out, steeling her spine before strutting confidently into the building.

There were just a couple of people milling around when Desiree walked inside. One of them noticed her and walked over with a smile on her face.

"Hi, can I help you?"

"Yes, I'm Desiree Mashburn. I have a meeting with Mr. Bell."

"Oh, okay. Would that be E.J. or Roland?"

Desiree was stumped. She hadn't even been aware there was more than one, and that fact embarrassed her. When she spoke with the owner over the phone, he never mentioned his first name, since she had only addressed him as Mr. Bell.

Taking a guess, she just said, "E.J."

"Okay, he's in the back. I'll go get him. Would you like a bottle of water or something?"

"Oh no, I'm good, thank you."

"No problem. Be right back."

Desiree slowly paced around as she waited, taking advantage of being able to get a good look at the club while it was empty and well-lit. Her mind was already racing with the ideas for the parties she could throw there. She loved the exposed brick walls, the clusters of colorful couches, the exposed beams with attached platforms where people could place their drinks, and the vast wooden dance floor. She wandered over to the bar area, nodding her approval at the glass shelving holding the wide array of liquors and spirits, the shiny curved bar, and the cushioned wrought-iron stools.

"Ms. Mashburn?"

Desiree whirled around to greet the masculine voice behind her. A tall man the color of a Hershey bar stood before her, smiling.

"E. J. Bell?" Desiree confirmed, holding out her hand.

"That's me." He shook her hand firmly. "Sorry to have kept you waiting; I was wrapping up a phone call."

"No problem at all."

"Let's head on back to my office," he suggested. "Did Casey offer you something to drink?"

Assuming that was the young lady that greeted her when she came in, Desiree nodded. "She did. I'm good."

"Follow me, then."

Desiree tried not to notice how fine he was as she followed him to his office. He was dressed casually in a white Polo shirt and black slacks, and Desiree could tell that he spent a good amount of time in the gym. But she didn't need to lust after someone she was trying to do business with. And when he stepped aside and ushered her into his small office, she saw the flash of his gold wedding band. Even more incentive, since she absolutely didn't mess with married men.

"Have a seat, Ms. Mashburn," E. J. invited, rounding his slightly-cluttered black desk.

"You can just call me Desiree."

"All right, Desiree. I was intrigued by the proposal you sent over and your ideas when we spoke on the phone. I was talking it over with my brother and we both like what we've heard so far."

"I'm glad. Will Roland be joining us today?"

"He will, yeah. Should be here any minute, actually. I handle more of the business side of things, while he generally takes care of the front-end stuff. If we come to an agreement, you'll mostly be dealing with him, after we get the numbers portion squared away."

"Sounds great. Are you currently working with any other promoters, if I may ask?"

"We have here and there, but no one on an ongoing basis. We've only been open a little under a year, which is why we think partnering with you would be great to get more people in the door. I've been checking you out and you have an impressive following, for someone who's primarily working solo. Judging from the photos on your site and social media, not to mention the feedback I've gotten from the few people I've taken the liberty of reaching out to, your events are generally successes and very well-run."

Desiree grinned proudly. She had worked very hard at building her business, ever since she discovered her knack for putting together parties back in college. She was definitely a people person, and loved putting on events where people could just enjoy themselves and have a good time, and where *she* could have a good time, as well. Being a party promotor wasn't easy, but she loved it so much that it didn't feel like work to her.

"I appreciate that. I take a lot of pride in what I do," she responded.

"As do we. So what niche do you primarily cater to?"

"All of my events are for the over-30 crowd, grown and sexy, fun but still classy. Far from ghetto or hood while still not being bougie."

"Sounds like that will fit very well with the vibe we've tried to establish. We play some current stuff but our DJ primarily sticks to '90s and old-school R&B. It still amazes me how hyped people get when certain songs come on."

Desiree chucked. She could tell already that she liked E.J. "I know, right? Whenever E.U.'s 'Da Butt' comes on, that's an instant packed dance floor, right there."

"I'm sayin'. So you want to propose a weekly arrangement?"

"I do. Based off of feedback I've gotten from my regulars and followers on social media, as well as what I've seen when I've visited your club myself, I believe having a standing weekly event would be a great way to go. Something people can look forward to after work. And it would get them more familiar with your club, too."

"What day of the week were you thinking about?"

"Wednesday or Thursday, for the standing promotion. I have other ideas in mind for weekend events, should we get that far."

"Thinking ahead, huh?" E.J. stroked his chin, smiling.

"Always."

Just then, there was a knock on the door. Desiree turned to see another milk chocolate cutie walk in, eyes on her. Her breath hitched in her throat, and she hoped to high heaven it wasn't obvious. Every pore in her body started to sizzle with attraction. Even more so when she subtly glanced down and didn't notice a wedding ring.

"I'm sorry I'm late; there was an accident on 285." He reached out to bump fists with E.J. before turning his eyes back to her. "Roland Bell. You must be Ms. Mashburn."

It took a second for Desiree to realize he was holding his hand out to her. *Get it together, girl*, she silently admonished herself as she put her hand in his. "Yes. But you can call me Desiree."

"Desiree." His eyes lingered on hers, and she noticed that he didn't immediately let go of her hand. Not that she minded. "It's nice to meet you."

"You, as well."

E.J. eyed them both for a moment, clearly noticing the electricity between them. He cleared his throat. "Have a seat, man. Desiree was just telling me about her proposal for a weekly event here."

"You have the pull for that, getting people in here every week?" Roland asked, taking the seat next to her.

"Well, I can't guarantee anything or force people to come in, of course, but I have a successful track record with these kinds of things. I maintained weekly contracts with Club Vibe and The Mocha Room, each for the better part of a year." Desiree pulled some papers out of the leather binder she had brought in, handing them to Roland. "These are the numbers for each agreement, as far as average head count, bar and concession numbers, and admission sales, both online and at the door. As you can see, even on the months where the numbers are lower, they're still better than average."

Roland perused the paperwork with an intrigued brow, before glancing at Desiree and handing them to his brother. "I'm impressed."

"Thank you. I've been here several times and I noticed Wednesdays and Thursdays are your lightest nights. We could target the after-work crowd, maybe provide them with foods like sliders, eggrolls, maybe some kind of kabob...something that will satisfy them enough to where they won't feel the need to go elsewhere to eat first but light enough to where they'll still be willing to stay and party afterwards."

E.J. was scanning the paperwork, nodding slowly. She could tell he was interested.

"For me, promotion is everything. If we do a good ramp-up, about a month or so out, that'll give us time to spread the word and get people interested. And there might even be some weeks where I can cajole a celebrity appearance, since I know some people in the NFL and in the music industry. That always gets more people in the door." She pulled more papers out of her binder and handed one to each of them. "Here is a business plan I've come up with that includes what we've already discussed as well as some other things; budget and pricing techniques, financial breakdowns of my target goals, promotion strategies, and risk assessments. If I've left off anything or if you have any questions, please feel free to let me know."

E.J. and Roland exchanged a look, and Desiree could tell they were having a silent conversation right there. She felt like she had presented herself well, but there was still no guarantee they would want to do business with her. She waited patiently, hoping she didn't appear as anxious as she felt.

"Well, I definitely like what I've seen and heard," E.J. finally said, thumping the paperwork in his hand. "You've got your act together, Desiree, I must say."

"You definitely do," Roland agreed. Desiree could feel his eyes on her, and she tried not to squirm in her seat. His cologne was already making her want to bury her face in his neck.

"Could you give us a few minutes to look this over and discuss a few things?" E.J. requested.

"Of course." Desiree stood and couldn't help sauntering towards the door, in case Roland might be admiring the view. She stepped out into the hallway and closed the door behind her, taking a deep breath. She felt the meeting had gone well, and knew it was likely out of her hands now. She just hoped they were willing to take a chance on her.

While she waited, she pulled out her phone and checked to see if Lovey had called or texted her back. She frowned when there were no messages from her friend, but three new ones from Tobias. She was scrolling through some emails when Roland popped his head out.

"You can come on back in, Desiree."

Taking a deep breath, Desiree went back into the office and retook her seat. "So what's the verdict?" she made herself ask.

With a nod to his brother, E.J. said, "Let's make this happen, I say."

Not being able to help it, Desiree grinned. "Excellent!"

"Now let's get the fun stuff out of the way, and then we can talk about a preliminary schedule," E.J. announced, pressing a button on his laptop.

"Let's do it."

After they had discussed the financial particulars, they agreed to do an initial event in the next couple of weeks, with their weekly agreement beginning a month later. When their meeting was over, Desiree was as giddy as could be, her mind already running over with ideas.

Roland offered to give her an in-depth tour of the facility before walking her out to her car. They flirted mildly...giving each other lingering looks, walking or standing close enough to where their arms touched, smiles for no real reason that neither of them could seem to help. Desiree's body felt electric the entire time she was around Roland; she ached to touch him, or have him touch her. Several times her gaze fell to his lips, and she became consumed with how it would feel to kiss them. She was *definitely* attracted to this man. And she didn't think she was off base to think that he was attracted to her, as well. She saw the looks he was giving her, also, and the fact that he didn't seem to be in a hurry when they were touring the club. He took his time explaining everything, and Desiree's mind wandered to if he also took his time in the bedroom. She couldn't help it.

"Thank you for coming in," he finally said, as he walked her out to her car. His hands were in his pockets, as if he wanted to keep himself from doing anything inappropriate with them. His eyes roamed her face, like he was memorizing it. "I'm glad we were able to work something out. This is gonna be a good relationship, I think."

Oh, I'm sure it is. "I agree. I'm already so excited and can't wait to dive in."

"Me either. We're gonna be good together."

"We're gonna be *amazing* together."

The subtle double entendre wasn't lost on either of them. Desiree was actually surprised at how openly flirtatious she was being; she was usually very firm on not mixing business and pleasure. But there was something about Roland that grabbed her and held her in some kind of heart-stopping vice grip. All of her rules and good sense seemed to fly right out of the window. She almost didn't care about what effect it would have on their new working relationship; right then, all she could think about was just how much she wanted this man to grab her and kiss her until her lips went numb.

They gazed at each other for several moments, almost as if they were each waiting on the other to make a move, before Roland finally cleared his throat.

"So...we'll talk in the next couple of days about the first event, yes?"

"Um, yes...I'll be contacting you soon. Once I get the details of what's bouncing around in my head together, I'll send them over to you and E.J. In the meantime, I'll start announcing on my social media that I'm partnering with you to get some buzz going."

"Sounds good." He pulled out his wallet and pulled out a business card. "Call me if you need anything." His eyes bore into hers. "Anything at all."

Biting her lip, Desiree took the card without taking her eyes from his. "I'll definitely keep that in mind, Mr. Bell."

With that, Desiree made herself slide into her car and close the door, because with every second she stood in front of him, she felt her restraint weaken. He was getting to her without even touching her, and she knew she needed to make her retreat before she made a fool of herself in the Barfly parking lot.

"Lord, help me," she whispered to herself as she drove away, watching Roland as he watched her.

DESIREE ALWAYS ENJOYED visiting her parents; she tried to get over to their house at least once a week. By now they were like her buddies as well as her parents, and she loved their relationship. She always made sure to knock, though, because they weren't above having spontaneous quickies in random parts of the house, and catching her father bending her mother over the back of the couch once was enough to make her put away her key.

"Where's Daddy?" Desiree asked, after her mother let her in.

"Upstairs, knocked out." Elyse smirked at her daughter.

Not missing the implication, Desiree shook her head. "I swear...are y'all *on* something?"

"Of course not."

"Every time I turn around, y'all are gettin' it in. I love sex as much as the next person but that's just not normal."

"Who says?"

"Ma. That's all y'all do."

"Girl, hush. It is not *all* we do. But even if it was, so what? That's my husband. Once you find that man you can't get enough of, you'll see for yourself."

"I don't think there's a man alive that can keep me on fire for him like that."

"Uh-huh. We'll see. So I guess you're not bringing anybody with you to Thanksgiving dinner, huh?"

"Just Lovey. And Liz, if she wants to come."

"No date?"

Desiree's mind immediately went to Roland, and that surprised her. She hardly even knew the man, and they were going to be working together; there was no way she could justify inviting him to a family dinner.

"I'm not dating anyone at the moment. I finally talked to Tobias, by the way...granted, he showed up at my damn door so I was kind of forced into it, but I did it."

"Yeah? So did you apologize for leaving him hanging like you did?"

"As a matter of fact, I did. I knew he didn't deserve that. I just let him know I wasn't looking for a relationship and he seemed to understand."

Elyse eyed her. "Y'all slept together again, didn't you?"

It's like she has some kind of radar. "Okay, yes, we did. I thought that maybe since everything was out on the table, we could just enjoy each other with no pressure. But, of course..."

"Of course what?"

"Now that's all he's hitting me up for. Like I'm on-call booty."

"Quit answering him."

"Oh, I have. But he's a persistent S.O.B."

"You sure know how to pick 'em, huh? Well, hopefully he'll get the message if you just ignore him, since y'all have already had this talk before. And *quit giving in to him*." Elyse eyed her daughter pointedly. "But if he keeps bothering you, you know your daddy will handle that."

"Mama, please, I don't wanna kill the man."

"He protects his daughters like he's supposed to do. You know he generally stays out of y'all's business since you girls are grown now, but just say the word and he'll pull out the shotgun."

"Exactly. Which is why we don't need to tell him anything. I can handle Tobias; he's just annoying, that's all."

"If you say so."

Just then, Desiree's father Darius came into the kitchen. Desiree immediately wondered if he had just heard any of their conversation.

"When'd you get here, pretty girl?" he greeted Desiree, leaning down to kiss her cheek.

Desiree grinned, as she always did when her father called her 'pretty girl.' That had been his nickname for her since childhood and she'd always loved it. "Not too long ago. I've been here an hour, maybe."

"How come you didn't come upstairs and speak, then?"

"Ma said you were 'sleep." Desiree didn't want to mention that she knew he'd been in a post-coitus coma.

"Just a little catnap." He stepped over and swatted his wife on the butt before wrapping his arms around her from behind. Elyse giggled as he began kissing her neck, and Desiree shook her head. They were like two horny teenagers.

"What's for dinner, baby?" Darius asked Elyse. "Smells good in here."

"I haven't even started dinner yet."

"Hmm. Must be you, then." He growled as he went for her neck again, and Elyse squealed happily.

Desiree was amazed, as she always was, at how affectionate her parents still were with each other after so many years of marriage. They had gotten married young, while they were in college, and were barely twenty years old when they had Dana, Desiree's older sister. A couple years later, Desiree was born, then Dori, then Diamond. They were all two years apart. Ever since Desiree could remember, it had been the six of them, and Desiree never knew how good she had it until she got older and saw how many of her friends were in single-parent households, or whose parents were always at each other's throats. She could only recall a handful of times when she heard her parents argue; they'd done a very good job of keeping that away from their girls. All Desiree and her sisters saw was how much they loved each other, and the commitment they made to their family. Divorce simply wasn't an option, and whatever issues they did have, they worked through them. Desiree couldn't help but admire that, even though she was almost certain she would never have anything like that for herself.

After several moments of her father groping her mother, Desiree loudly cleared her throat. "So what *is* for dinner, Ma? My stomach is growling."

"I was just gonna bake some chicken and roast some vegetables. Something kinda quick."

"When are you gonna make some more fried pork chops? I love those things."

"I don't know. I'm trying to lay off the fried stuff."

"Aww, damn. Don't tell me you're trying to turn into one of those health nuts."

"No. But I *do* wanna take better care of myself. Gotta keep it tight."

"I know that's right," Darius agreed.

Elyse grinned at her husband before continuing. "You need to start watching what you eat, too. Every time I turn around, you're eating some kind of junk food. That body isn't gonna just stay in place like that forever."

"Please...as much as I run around town for work and dance at all these parties, I am not even worried about getting fat."

"It ain't just about getting fat. Thin folks get diabetes."

"I'm fine, Ma. When Thanksgiving comes around, you're not gonna be trying to serve us tofu and brown rice and nothing but fruit for dessert, are you?"

Her parents laughed. "*Hell* no," Darius mumbled, grabbing an apple from the bowl on the counter and rinsing it off before taking a huge bite out of it.

"Nah, I'm gonna make the same stuff I always make," Elyse confirmed.

"Good."

"Speaking of Thanksgiving, Lovey is coming, right?"

"As far as I know. She hasn't said anything to me about *not* coming."

"Tell her she can bring a date with her, if she wants to."

"I don't know if I wanna mention anything to her about dates. That's kind of a sore spot for her right now."

"Oh no. That Evan boy fell off?"

"I didn't tell you about that? Yeah, she had waited for him outside of the gym when she hadn't heard from him, and that's when she found out he was in a whole relationship with somebody else. I still don't think she's gotten over that; it was pretty humiliating for her."

"I sure hate to hear that. I swear, I am so glad that I don't have to go through the dating stuff you girls go through. I'd damn near kill somebody."

"And that's my cue," Darius muttered, strolling out of the kitchen, still munching on his apple.

Elyse and Desiree chuckled. "Maybe we should fix Lovey up with somebody," Elyse suggested, running her fingertips through her short chestnut brown hair. "She might have better luck if someone else does the choosing, you think?"

"Maybe, but good luck getting her to agree to that. I haven't even been able to get in touch with her since she came over to my place a few nights ago, the night Tobias came over. I don't know if maybe seeing him there with me made something snap for her."

"Could be. I hate that she's feeling so bad, though."

"Me, too. Which is why I doubt she'll wanna come for Thanksgiving...between you and Daddy, and my sisters with their husbands, I don't think she'll wanna be around so many happy couples. Might just be too hard for her."

"Hmm. I just hate the thought of her over there hurting because these sorry men don't know how to act. But I'm gonna think positively; Thanksgiving is still a little ways off. You never know what can happen between now and then. And Lovey is like one of my daughters...I want her here with the rest of us."

"I do, too. I guess we'll see."

After Desiree left her parents' house later, her mind was still on Lovey and her whole situation. She hated that her friend was going through this, and wished there was something she could do to lift her spirits. Her mother's suggestion of fixing her up actually wasn't a bad one, but Desiree would want some kind of guarantee that it would work out, which of course she wouldn't have. And if the guy ended up hurting Lovey like the others did, then she might end up blaming Desiree and Elyse, and Desiree didn't want that.

Her mind flashed to Roland, and a smile automatically curled her lips. He had been on her mind constantly since their initial meeting, and she could admit that there were a couple of times since then that she manufactured excuses to call him. He seemed like a really nice guy, and she began to wonder if maybe he would be a good match for Lovey. Sure, Desiree was feeling him herself, but she had other prospects; Lovey didn't. And something told her that Roland wouldn't do Lovey like all the other men had done her.

Desiree decided to invite Lovey to her first event at Roland's club, already knowing that she would have to practically bribe her to get her there.

Chapter 5

LOVEY DIDN'T KNOW HOW she let herself get talked into going to this party. Desiree had been on her back for days about getting out of the house, and Lovey eventually gave in just to shut her up.

"You have been moping around that apartment for too long, girl," Desiree had admonished her. "I get that your hurt about Evan and every other asshole that has dogged you; I really do. But don't let them have this much power over you, girl. Get back out there. You're never gonna meet anybody else sitting around the house."

"People meet online every day," Lovey disputed.

Pause. "Are *you* looking online?"

"No," Lovey responded in a low voice.

"Okay then, so that doesn't really apply to you, does it?"

"I just don't feel like partying right now, okay?"

"Well, if not now, when? What are you waiting for?"

Lovey sighed. "Desiree..."

"Look, I'm just gonna get on your nerves until you agree to come, so you might as well give it up. You never wanna hang anymore, you've stood me up the last couple of times we were supposed to meet up...hell, I'm surprised I was even able to get you on the phone now. You are too beautiful and intelligent to let yourself be defined by whether a man likes you or not."

"Who said all that? I know that."

"Do you? Because every time this happens; whenever you like somebody and they show their ass, you get all in your feelings, close yourself off from everybody, and sit around your apartment in those raggedy sweats pigging out. Any other time, you're all worried about calories and stuff, drinking green smoothies like they're going out of style."

"Well, excuse me that I can't just bounce back from getting dumped as well as other people can. I happen to take that personally."

"Okay, fine. I'll take that. But at some point, girl, you have to shake it off and keep it moving. *They're* the ones with the problem, Lovey, not you. *They're* the ones that didn't have the balls to be honest with you. Why would you want to pine over anyone who would do that, anyway?"

Lovey paused, giving some thought to her friend's words. When she put it like that, it *didn't* make a lot of sense for Lovey to get as upset and distraught as she did. It wasn't like she and Evan were in love; they had only been on a few dates. But the way he played her, making her think he was into her and then disappearing, ignoring her calls and messages while he was getting into a relationship with another woman...it burned her. That wasn't something she could just *shake off*. Especially since Evan wasn't the first one to do something like that to her.

"I get what you're saying. And on some level, I agree with you. But it's not so much about *them* as it is about what they did, and how they did it," Lovey explained. "Maybe something like this wouldn't bother you but it bothers me. We are two different people, Desiree, and I'm not going to react to things like you would. So I really wish you would respect that."

After a few thoughtful moments, Desiree spoke. "All right. I understand that. And I'm sorry if I seem insensitive; I don't mean to just dismiss your feelings. I can definitely see how getting treated like that would feel like a kick in the gut."

"Thank you."

"But still, though, girl...I still say you should get out of that apartment and try to enjoy yourself. You might just meet someone else that will make you forget all about those other assholes."

"I guess..."

"I know for a fact that there are going to be some *fine* men in attendance at this party. You know how I roll. You never know; you could meet the man of your dreams."

Lovey wanted to automatically doubt her friend, but she couldn't help being intrigued. It was true that some nice pieces of eye candy usually frequented Desiree's parties.

"Well..."

"There's one in particular I want to introduce you to," Desiree persisted. "I already know you two would hit it off. But you can't meet him if you don't show up."

Too tired to argue anymore, Lovey finally acquiesced, "Fine, I'll go."

"That's my girl!"

Now, Lovey tried to tell herself to think positively as she gently pulled the large magnetic rollers from her long hair. Part of her would still rather spend the evening curled up on the couch with a tub of sorbet and her remote, but the other part was mildly excited about the prospect of meeting someone new. She knew she needed to push Evan and all of the others before him out of her mind...they had made it clear they didn't want her. Lovey wanted to focus on finding someone that did.

She hurried to the door when the doorbell sounded. She had invited her sister Liz to join her, since Desiree would be mostly in host mode and probably wouldn't be able to hang with her that much.

"Well, aren't we looking glamorous this evening," Liz greeted when Lovey opened the door.

"Do you think it's too much?" Lovey asked worriedly as she closed the door. "I just took my rollers out; my hair isn't gonna be this big."

"No, you look hot. Husband-landing hot." Liz winked at her.

Not being able to resist the grin that shot across her face, Lovey shuffled back to the bathroom to finish getting ready. Liz followed her, leaning against the doorjamb.

"I've been hearing about this new place, Barfly, for a while now...I'm really curious to see what kind of crowd Desiree can bring in."

"Yeah, she said she's expecting a decent amount of people. She's been promoting hard for the past couple of weeks." Lovey finished applying her mascara and reached for her hairbrush.

"Well, I'm just trying to let off some steam after a frustrating work week." Liz smoothed the back of her short hair and adjusted her bustier top underneath her cropped jacket. "As soon as we get there, just point me to the bar."

Lovey chuckled as she brushed her hair until it flowed into smooth waves around her shoulders. She twisted around in the mirror to check the back of her knee-length, form-fitting light blue dress. "Do you think I'm showing too much cleavage?"

"I think you're right on that line between sexy and trying-too-hard," Liz informed her.

"Perfect. Let's go!"

ROLAND BOTH WAS AND wasn't looking forward to this party tonight. And both reasons were because of Desiree Mashburn.

He hadn't been able to get that woman off of his mind since he met her. She was stuck in his head, and just about every night when he finally got home after long days at the club, she would cloud his thoughts, making him wish he could conjure up a believable-enough excuse to call her. But they had only been in contact in a professional capacity, and regardless of how much his body wanted him to change that, he knew that's how he needed to keep it. It just wasn't a good idea for him to get involved with someone he was working with, especially with so much potential for his club's popularity boosting by being associated with her on the line.

But that didn't mean he didn't take extra care to make sure he looked irresistible when he knew he was going to see her, though. He spritzed on some of his most intoxicating cologne, made sure his all-black outfit was wrinkle-and-and-lint free, and brushed his fresh haircut until the waves flowed. He smoothed his goatee with his fingers as he checked his appearance in the mirror, reminding himself for the hundredth time to keep Desiree Mashburn at arm's length, because he had a feeling that she was going to try to entice him some kind of way before the night was over. He could see the desire in her eyes when he walked her to her car the day they met. If he was honest, he wanted to kiss her then...and he was convinced she wouldn't have stopped him if he had.

Even though he knew he shouldn't get involved with Desiree, Roland couldn't deny that he was looking forward to seeing her again. It had been a while since a woman had piqued his interest as much as she had. Running a nightclub was an occupation that caused a lot of women not to trust him very much, especially since he was so charming and engaging with the patrons, which was often viewed as flirting. Roland was and always had been a one-woman man, but he got hit on a lot, and the women he had dated in the past didn't seem to get that he wasn't trying to do anything to provoke it...it just happened.

Like the time when a bride was having her bachelorette party at the club not too long after it opened. Roland was standing at the bar talking to the bartender, when out of nowhere the drunken bride came over and grabbed his butt. She started dancing seductively on him, practically pinning him to the bar, and her friends all gathered around them, cheering them on. He wanted to push the woman off of him, but a couple of the ladies were recording the whole scene with their phones and he knew that would get misconstrued no matter how much he was justified. They'd splatter it all over social media and his business would be doomed before it really got off the ground.

He had no idea that the lady he was seeing at the time had come in, and was mortified seeing some other woman grind and claw on him like some horny alley cat. They had a huge argument about it later, with her accusing him of not doing enough to get the woman off of him and enjoying it a little too much. Roland actually hadn't enjoyed it at all, but nothing he said convinced her of that. She branded him a player and dumped him.

After a couple more similar incidents, Roland was now very particular about who he chose to date. Women were either overly-suspicious of him or of every woman he looked at, and he had just run out of energy for the whole thing.

But that didn't mean he wasn't curious about Desiree. Something told him that she was far too confident and secure to let random women giving him the eye bother her. If only he had met her outside of the club...

He and his brother E.J. got to the club early, as they always did, to make sure everything was in order and ready for the night. When they convened in the office, his brother gave him a warning.

"This could be a good thing for us, man," he stated, regarding their partnership with Desiree. "Don't mess it up."

"How would I mess it up?"

"I see how you two look at each other. Any idiot could see the attraction."

"Well, hell. She's an attractive woman."

"Yes, she is. But she's also now essentially a business partner, and we need to keep that relationship going. I've been getting a ton of calls about this party tonight so I expect a huge turnout. If she can bring in the people like that every week, we'll exceed our projections for this year."

"I know, man. I'm as excited about it as you are."

"So I'm saying...don't mess it up."

Roland sighed, throwing up his hands. "Damn, man. What is it you think I'm gonna do? I'm not some player, and you know that."

"It's not about you. All she has to do is *think* that you're dogging her and she'll take her parties and her people with her, and probably drag you on social media, to boot. We don't need that."

"Look..." Roland sat forward in his seat. "Am I feeling Desiree? Yes. I can't deny that. But I'm not stupid enough to do anything that would be detrimental to our business. As hard as we worked to save the money to buy and open our own spot? I'm just as invested in this as you are."

"Good. I just wanted to remind you. 'Cause I had a feeling that if I wasn't in the room that first day, y'all would have christened my desk."

"Man, stop," Roland chuckled, even though is stomach tightened at the thought. Desiree's toned body was one he had fantasized about several times, with her shapely legs and perky breasts. And don't even get him started on her backside. He wanted to ask if she spent all her free time doing squats.

The brothers chatted for a few more minutes, going over some particulars for the night before Roland stood to leave. His phone chimed in his pocket, and he sucked his teeth when he pulled it out and saw who it was.

"It's her again?" E.J. asked, recognizing the look on his brother's face.

"Of course." Roland stuffed his phone back into his pocket, ignoring the text. He wished she would take a hint and leave him alone. "I'm gonna go check on things out front. Desiree should be getting here any minute."

A COUPLE OF HOURS LATER, the party was in full swing. Desiree was thrilled with the turnout; the place was already almost full and the doors had just opened barely an hour before, and there was a long line at the door. She was in full planner mode, making sure everything was going smoothly and nipping any issues or potential problems in the bud before they got out of hand. Every now and then she would grab the mike at the DJ booth and hype the crowd, or just encourage them to mingle and enjoy themselves. This was the part of her job that she loved; when all her hard work came together.

When she saw Lovey come in with her sister Liz, Desiree squealed with excitement and rushed over to her, hugging her as if she hadn't seen her in months. Part of her wondered if her friend would actually show up, and she hoped that Lovey's appearance meant that she was feeling better about things.

"I am so glad you came," Desiree said to Lovey over the music, after giving a quick hug to Liz. "And you are looking *hot*, too!"

"Am I? It's not too much?" Lovey looked down at her outfit as she did a half-turn.

"You know not to ask me that. What is 'too much' for me?"

"True," Liz muttered.

Desiree cut her eyes at her, then chuckled. She and Liz had always had a kind of love/hate relationship.

"Wow, great turnout tonight," Lovey observed, glancing around.

"I know, right! I'm so glad this is getting off to such a good start...after this, those Bell brothers are going to be *begging* me to stay in business with them." She noticed someone across the room waving her over and she held up a finger. She grabbed Lovey's arm and said, "I have to go see about something but try to have a good time tonight, okay? And don't forget, there's someone I want to introduce you to, so don't be trying to sneak out when my back is turned."

Lovey looked at her skeptically. "Desiree, please tell me you're not trying to set me up."

"I told you the other night I wanted to introduce you to someone. He's real cool and I think y'all would hit it off. But if it'll put your mind at ease, it's not a set-up."

"Good."

"Well, I'm about to get acquainted with the bartender," Liz announced, adjusting her jacket.

Desiree frowned slightly. "Why? You think he's cute? I mean, he's aight, but..."

"Girl, he's the one pouring the drinks. That's all I care about." Liz began making her way over to the bar, with Lovey and Desiree giggling behind her.

Lovey followed her sister and Desiree went to see what this latest issue was. A couple of guys approached her, but she found herself not interested in them. After the whole Tobias situation, she wasn't too keen on getting involved with any of her party patrons any time soon.

When she happened to look up and see Roland, an automatic smile came to her face and her stomach did a little flip. There was just something about this man that woke up every nerve in her body. The few times they had spoken that night had been all business, and Desiree was proud of herself for keeping her composure as well as she had, considering she still wanted to jump this man like an Olympic decathlete.

And anyway, she was supposed to be introducing him to Lovey. Every time she started to do just that, she got pulled in another direction. She had to get them together before the night was over, or before Lovey got bored and left.

But leaving was the last thing on Lovey's mind. She had met Clay, and he completely captured her attention.

"I'm sorry if I keep staring," he said, leaning closer to her ear as they stood at one of the standing tables nursing their drinks, "But you are absolutely gorgeous."

Lovey felt her face immediately flush. "Thank you, Clay."

"I know you probably think I'm just trying to run game, but seriously...I haven't been able to take my eyes off you since I came in."

Never quite knowing what to say when people complimented her like this, Lovey flashed him a sweet smile. "I'm flattered; that's really sweet of you to say."

"I mean every word."

"You're looking awfully handsome, yourself," Lovey made herself reciprocate. She meant it, but she always felt rather shy when she first met a man she was interested in.

"I'm glad you think so." Clay winked at her as he took a sip of his Hennessey and Coke.

I'm gonna have to give Desiree a huge thank you basket for this, Lovey thought to herself. *She picked a good one this time.*

Lovey and Clay ended up never leaving each other's side the rest of the night. They danced together, drank together, and huddled up on one of the couches, getting to know each other. Lovey was thrilled when Clay asked for her number and promised to call her later that evening, especially since Liz was giving her that look that she was ready to go.

Desiree was looking for Roland. She stood on her tiptoes and tried to spot him over the crowd, and brightened when she noticed him near the bar. She made her way over to him, focused so she wouldn't lose him again. When another woman sauntered over and positioned herself in front of him, Desiree remained unfazed. There wasn't a woman alive that intimidated her.

"Excuse me," she said politely, placing her hand on Roland's arm. The woman glanced at the action with a raised brow and shot Desiree a look that would send most women running. But Desiree just grinned at her.

"Hey Desiree," Roland smiled, looking slightly relieved. "What's up?"

"I need to borrow you for a minute."

"Absolutely." He excused himself from the woman, who was looking like she had just been slapped in the face, and followed Desiree away from the bar. When they were a little ways away, he leaned down and said, "You showed up right on time."

"Another admirer, huh?"

"That woman is here every week. She hits on me more than Mayweather on Pacquiao."

"It must be hard being so irresistible."

"I didn't say all that."

"I know...I did." She winked at him, and thought it was cute when it looked like he was blushing.

"Anyway," Roland tried to suppress his smile, "Is something wrong?"

"Not at all. There's just someone I wanted to introduce you to."

"Yeah? Who?"

Desiree turned to where she had last seen Lovey, and spotted her practically hugged up with some tall, creamy-skinned cutie on the couch. He was whispering in Lovey's ear and Desiree could see that her friend was smitten from across the room. The smile never left her face.

Hmph. Well...so much for that, she thought. *Looks like Lovey doesn't need my help, after all.*

Realization stretched her smile. *Guess I can keep him for myself.*

She turned back to Roland. "You know what? Another time. They're busy. But there's something else I need to run by you and it can't wait...can we talk in private for a minute?"

Clearly curious, Roland nodded. "Yeah, sure. Come on."

Desiree turned and headed straight towards the offices, quickly running through her mind what she wanted to say. She'd never had an issue letting men know she was interested in them, but for some reason Roland made her nervous. Her palms were actually sweating a little bit, and she rubbed them on her hips when she stopped in front of his office, turning to him.

"Is E.J. still here?" she asked.

"Nah, he dipped out about an hour or so ago. Had to get home to the wife."

"Oh okay." She looked at him, and found herself mesmerized for a moment. Her eyes just roamed over his handsome face...the milky brown eyes, the slight bump in his nose, the goatee framing those moist lips...

"Desiree?"

Embarrassed, Desiree tried to play it off with a flirty giggle. "My bad...mind wandered there for a second."

"Yeah?" Roland stepped closer to her. He was looking at her intently.

"Yeah." Desiree bit her lip, immensely turned on. The look in his eyes, his cologne, them being in such close proximity to each other...it was all mixing into an intoxicating combination that was making her composure slip by the nanosecond. She wasn't used to this.

Roland's eyes were on Desiree's lips. Everything in him wanted to kiss her. And he could see the desire in her eyes for him, too. His hands itched to grab her by the waist, back her against the wall and kiss her until her lips screamed for mercy.

The plan had been to make some kind of small talk and then ease in to suggesting they hang out, but Desiree's growing desire for Roland was making her forget about all pretense. She wanted this man and, despite her head knowing it probably wasn't the best idea, she wasn't about to keep trying to act like she didn't.

"What are you doing later?" she practically whispered.

He stepped even closer to her. "Got something in mind?"

"I think we *both* have something in mind." She looked boldly into his eyes. "Why don't you come over tonight?"

The entire conversation he had with E.J. earlier evaporated from Roland's mind. It had been a while since he had been this attracted to a woman and he wasn't about to ignore it.

"I'm there."

Desiree was determined not to be the one to break first, but she was caught up in those eyes again. The slightly muted music from the club thumped around them as they stared at each other, their bodies close but not touching, almost as if they were engaged in a silent dare.

"Guess we'd better get back out there," she finally said, licking her lips.

She started to step away, but Roland grabbed her arm and pulled her to him, grabbing the back of her neck and bringing her lips to his. Her arms immediately encircled his neck in sensual relief, glad that they were no longer playing the coy game. He backed her against the wall, pressing his body into hers, letting it be known just how turned on she had him. Their mutual deep sighs and moans of pleasure filled the slightly darkened short hallway, and it wasn't long before the party they were both there for and so invested in was practically forgotten.

Several long minutes later, their kiss slowed down. Desiree's hands were clamped to the back of Roland's neck, her chest heaving. Fire burned her body. She wanted this man. And she didn't want to wait until the end of the night to get him.

Seeming to read her mind, Roland reached behind her and opened the door to the office. She grabbed his hand as they entered, neither saying a word. The door locked behind them as they proceeded to do what they each had been fantasizing about since they met.

Chapter 6

A FEW DAYS LATER, DESIREE and Lovey were hanging out in Desiree's apartment. It was their first time getting a chance to really talk since the night of the party at Barfly, and the best friends each had plenty to gush about.

"Girrrrl, when I tell you that Roland had me weak in the knees, I am not *playin'*!" Desiree tucked her bare feet underneath her on the couch. "I swear, I would've done anything that man told me to do that night."

"Wow, I've never heard you say anything like that before." Lovey grinned. "He had you open like *that*?"

"He had me open like *that*. The *only* thing that kept us from getting busy all over that office was that we didn't have any protection. That's it. And to be real with you, I was so damn horny for him that I almost didn't care about that."

"Thankfully you came to your senses...don't let your punanny cloud your judgment."

"I can't take the credit. He's the one that said we should pull back."

"I like him." Lovey reached for the bowl of mangoes and strawberries in front of her while Desiree grabbed a couple of chocolate chip cookies. "So what happened when he came over after the party? Did y'all get busy then?"

"No, damn it," Desiree admitted grudgingly. "I guess by then, he had cooled off 'cause he said he wanted us to get to know each other a little better first before taking it there. Can't say I was thrilled to hear that but at least we still kissed and fooled around some."

"Girl, that's a good sign. He's trying to actually get to know you instead of just jumping into bed the first chance he got."

"I don't need to know his life story. It's not like I'm gonna marry the dude."

"But remember what happened with Tobias...you slept with him on the first night and then he became a pain in your butt. It might do you some good to take things a little slower this time."

Desiree couldn't deny she had a point. Tobias was still constantly calling or texting her, wanting to hook up. The thrill had long since worn out since they had temporarily reignited their sexual relationship, and Desiree just wanted him to leave her alone.

Right on cue, her phone rang. When she saw it was Tobias calling, Desiree cursed so loud Lovey actually flinched.

Snatching up the phone, Desiree angrily shouted, "Look gotdammit, if you don't quit calling my damn phone I *will* have my ex-con cousins come and beat your ass to oblivion! I don't know how many times I have to tell your thirsty ass that I'm done with you but this will be the *last* time, you got it???"

Lovey couldn't resist giggling as Desiree practically jammed her phone between the couch cushions. "Girl, you got that man strung out. You must have some kind of coochie cocaine."

Despite her anger, Desiree couldn't resist bursting out laughing. "Shut up! You wouldn't be laughing if Clay was damn near stalking you. And the way he was looking at you the other night, I wouldn't put it past him."

"We're nowhere near that place yet," Lovey shook her head, though the smile on her face melted into a somewhat wistful one at the mention of her latest crush. "We haven't even kissed yet."

"What??"

"Nah, girl, just some really long hugs...he took me to dinner last night and everything in me wanted to invite him in, but I'm trying to take things slow this time. You know how I lose my head when I like somebody...I'm trying to avoid that with Clay."

"I guess I can understand that, but...not even a kiss? I don't know if I could've done that."

"It certainly wasn't because I didn't want to. Girl, he is so cute and fine and funny and just..." Lovey sighed like a lovesick schoolgirl. "He has me open. But I'm trying not to let him know that yet."

"Please don't tell me you're going to start playing hard to get and all these other little games."

"No, no games. You know that's not my style. I just mean that I don't want to make it so obvious just how much I like him already, which is a lot. Men tend to take advantage when they know you like them more than they like you."

"But how do you know it's more than he likes you? He could be feeling you as hard as you're feeling him."

"I have no way of knowing; at least, no way of knowing for sure. He could tell me anything to get me to let my guard down. And I've just been through that too many times. Different actions produce different results, right?"

"That's the word. So you like him that much, huh?"

"I really do...you did a good job this time."

Desiree frowned. "What are you talking about?"

"With Clay. You said you wanted to introduce me to somebody that night, right? Not too long after that, Clay had made his way over to me. I figured you sent him."

"Oh..." Desiree took a huge bite out of her cookie. She had forgotten that she was initially going to introduce Roland to Lovey; ever since they kissed in the hallway, Desiree had mentally claimed him as hers. At least, for the moment.

"Well, I'm just glad you're happy," she finally said. Desiree didn't want to lie to her friend, but she didn't want to admit the truth about Clay not being who she had been planning to set her friend up with. Lovey might think it was shady for Desiree to be all over Roland so soon after she was going to hook him up with Lovey.

"I'm *very* happy," Lovey grinned, her dewy skin glowing. "I know it sounds cliché, but I have a good feeling about this one."

"Cliché or not, it could be true. Just enjoy him, and don't expect too much or get your hopes up too high too soon."

"I'm trying."

"Roland and I are going on our first official date tomorrow night," Desiree announced with a smile she couldn't help. "Hopefully we've gotten to know each other enough and he's ready to give me some."

"Girl..."

"What? I'm attracted to him; what's wrong with that?"

"I'm just saying, I don't think it's just about sex this time. I can see the way your face changes when you talk about Roland; you really like him. Why not do something different, too, and actually see where a relationship between the two of you can go?"

"Because I don't *do* relationships. You know that."

"I don't know why you're still so jaded on love. Relationships are a beautiful thing. Having that union with someone, that bond...it's way more meaningful that anything just physical."

"It's just not for me, Lovey. I'm not anti-marriage or against monogamy, for people that want it. It's not like I don't have any good examples of happy marriages all around me. It's just...not something I desire for myself, that's all."

Lovey eyed her friend. She knew there was more behind Desiree's desire to remain carefree than she was letting on, but it was a sore subject among them and had been for years. Desiree refused to talk about it, and even though Lovey felt it was something she needed to deal with since it clearly still haunted her, she didn't want to push her on it. Choosing not to speak on it for now, Lovey just shook her head and stuck a piece of mango into her mouth.

"If you say so."

"DAMN."

Desiree grinned. That was the kind of reaction she'd been hoping for.

It was the following night, and Roland had just arrived to pick her up for their date. Desiree had taken great care in getting ready, wearing an almost-new yellow mini-dress and gold heels, and an extremely natural-looking dark blonde wig.

"Glad you like. Come on in."

Roland stepped into the apartment, and revealed a black plastic bag from behind his back. "I brought you this."

Desiree glanced at him before taking the bag and peeking inside. She squealed and pulled out the deluxe box of oatmeal pies.

"Figured you'd like that more than flowers." Roland chuckled.

"You hit that right on the head, 'cause I hate flowers. That's so cool of you!" She threw her arms around his neck and immediately closed her eyes, glad to be touching him again. When she pulled back, she couldn't resist grabbing his face and planting a quick kiss on his lips. "I see you were paying attention the other night when I mentioned how much I love sweets."

"I definitely pay attention."

"Good to know."

At that moment, Roland's phone buzzed in his pocket. He checked it, frowned, and stuffed it back in his pocket, ignoring the call. Desiree raised a brow but shrugged it off.

"You ready?" she asked.

"When you are."

"Then let's go," Desiree grinned as she grabbed her purse and keys.

They went to Bhojanic, since Roland also remembered that Desiree loved Indian food. He knew he had scored another few points with her when he was graced with yet another pleased grin.

"You really *do* pay attention, huh?" She grabbed his arm and snuggled closed to him as they walked into the restaurant.

"I try."

"You like Indian food, too?"

"It's fine. I can take or leave it, really."

Desiree's eyebrows shot up in surprise. "And you still brought me here?"

Roland shrugged. "Why not? It makes you happy, right?"

Her mouth falling open slightly, Desiree seemed rendered speechless for a few moments. Her eyes softened as they roamed his face, and she quickly looked away, as if catching herself. She cleared her throat.

"Well, I...wow," Desiree murmured softly. "Cool."

They had a short wait to get a table, then proceeded to have dinner, with Roland asking Desiree a lot of questions about herself and her background. She was very forthcoming and didn't seem to mind all of his questions, but he noticed that she didn't ask many about him. He tried not to think that was because she just wasn't interested in learning about him. The thought made him frown, but he quickly checked himself.

She's not Anna. Chill out.

His phone kept buzzing during their meal and he always ignored it, barely even acknowledging the interruption, and Desiree was growing more and more curious about who it was that was so eager to talk to him and even more so about why he tried to act like it wasn't happening. She didn't look at it as courtesy; she looked at it as denial. After the sixth buzz, it was on the tip of her tongue to ask him about it, but she stopped herself. It wasn't any of her business.

After dinner, Desiree could tell that Roland seemed a little annoyed; she attributed it to the constant phone calls he was getting. She wanted to suggest they go back to her place, but something told her he might not be in the right head space for that yet. She needed to get him to loosen up some first.

"Let's go out and do something fun," she suggested, sliding her hand into his as they walked back to his car. "I'm kinda wired."

"Yeah?" Roland subtly checked his watch. "I wouldn't mind a couple of games of bowling."

"I'm not exactly dressed for that," Desiree replied, looking down at her outfit. "Let's go dancing!"

"Dancing? Really?"

"Yeah. What's wrong with that?"

"I guess since I'm at the club so much for work, when I'm out and about I like to do things a little more on the chill side."

"Oh come on, please? I promise you'll have a good time. I know just the place to go." When he hesitated slightly, she reminded him, "You wanna make me happy, right?"

Roland looked down at her, and she batted her false eyelashes at him flirtatiously. She could tell he didn't really want to go, but she hoped he would concede and give in to her so she could take his mind off whatever it was that was bothering him. He seemed fine when he picked her up earlier, but those constant phone calls he was getting seemed to have dimmed his good mood.

With a heavy sigh, Roland just lifted his shoulder in a light shrug. "Yeah, sure. Okay."

Desiree grinned. "Great! Let's go!"

They ended up at Sanctuary, and Roland inwardly groaned when he heard Latin music. He liked it okay, but he didn't know how to Salsa or Meringue or any of that.

"Um, I don't know about this, Desiree," he hedged before they entered the building.

"Why? It'll be fun!"

"I'm just not comfortable dancing to this kind of music..."

"Nobody's expecting you to be an expert. We're just having a good time. Trust me, there are plenty of other people in here that don't know what they're doing, either. It's not a competition. Just relax and follow my lead. Okay?"

Roland still wasn't feeling it, but he acquiesced again. "Yeah."

They were too late for the dance class they offered for beginners (to Roland's relief), so they just joined everyone on the dance floor. Desiree immediately began moving her body to the lively music, looking like someone on *Dancing with the Stars*. She was certainly a natural. He couldn't deny he enjoyed watching her move.

Grabbing his hands, she showed him how to do some simple steps, and was glad when he started to relax a little bit and get more into it. She was surprised he was so reserved, seeing as how at ease he always was whenever she saw him among the patrons at Barfly. But then again, that was his spot, so of course he was more comfortable there.

They didn't do too much talking while they were there; with the music and all the people around them, it would have been almost impossible. There was a lounge area, but by the time Desiree had danced circles around him for a couple of hours, Roland was just ready to call it a night.

"That wasn't so bad, was it?" Desiree asked as they were leaving.

"Nah, it wasn't. I didn't hate it."

"Ease up on the enthusiasm, why don't ya," Desiree chuckled. She released a content sigh as she gazed over at him from the passenger seat.

"You tired?" Roland asked, glancing over at her.

"Not at all. Kinda wired still, actually." She bit her lip. "You?"

"I'm a little tired, yeah. It's been a long day."

Rubbing her legs together, Desiree tried unsuccessfully to quell the multiplying dirty thoughts she was having about this man sitting next to her. She had been fantasizing about what was underneath his clothes ever since he picked her up hours before. She didn't want the night to end with him just dropping her off at home with nothing but a goodnight and a peck on the forehead.

"Let's go to your place," she boldly suggested.

Roland glanced over at her. "My place?"

"Yeah." Her eyes narrowed slightly. "You don't have a roommate or some chick living there, do you?"

"No. I live alone."

Desiree breathed a small sigh of relief. "Good. I'd love to see where you live. And we can finally have some one-on-one time...I'd love to have you all to myself for a while."

Roland rubbed his chin thoughtfully, and Desiree thought she was going to have to talk him into it like she had to with Sanctuary. But to her pleasant surprise, he agreed rather quickly.

"Dig that. Sounds good."

Grinning, Desiree reached over and put her hand on his thigh, leaving it there for the rest of the ride to his Marietta townhome.

"This is nice," she complimented, once he had opened the door and ushered her inside.

"Thanks."

"How long have you lived here?"

"A few years. I bought it back when I was still in corporate America. Wanted to have something of my own after living in apartments since college."

"I feel you." Desiree wandered around, noting the open two-story floor plan, the dark hardwood floors, the sizeable kitchen, and the French doors leading out to a deck. "Rather large for a single guy, huh?"

"I don't plan on being single forever."

A wave of something Desiree hadn't felt in years washed over her, and she stopped in her tracks.

"You okay?"

Desiree whirled around, seeing the look of concern on his face. She tried to quickly shake off that jarring feeling and get herself together.

"Yeah, I'm great. Um, show me the upstairs?"

"Sure." Roland was eyeing her strangely, but he led the way towards the staircase.

He showed her the guest rooms, one of which had been converted into a workout room-slash-office, before leading her to the master bedroom. He stopped at the door with his hands in his pockets as Desiree strolled around like a potential buyer.

"Very nice," she murmured, nodding approvingly. "You decorated all of this yourself?"

Roland tried to keep the automatic frown off his face. "I had some help. But most of it was me."

"I love the colors." Desiree ran a hand over the green and beige comforter. She had kicked her shoes off downstairs and her red-painted toes dug into the Berber carpet. When she leaned over the bed, Roland bit his lip at the sight of her short dress rising and revealing more of her beautiful brown thighs. "You have good taste."

"I like to think so."

Desiree sauntered over to him and slid her arms around his waist. The look in her eyes blatantly displayed her intentions.

"Me, too," she drawled before rising onto her toes and pressing her lips to his. He responded immediately, opening his mouth to hers and gathering her into his arms. They both moaned as their breathing got heavier, and Desiree's desire for this man went from full to overflowing. She had just backed him against a nearby wall and was starting to untuck his shirt when the doorbell rang.

"You expecting somebody?" she asked breathlessly.

"No, I'm not." Roland looked frustrated.

"Then just ignore it." Desiree started to resume their kiss when the doorbell rang again, more insistently this time. The uninvited guest proceeded to continue to ring the doorbell, making it clear they weren't going to be ignored.

Cursing under his breath, Roland excused himself and hurried out of the room towards the stairs. Knowing her curiosity would not allow her to stay where she was, Desiree was right on his heels.

"Who is it?" Roland bellowed.

"You know who it is," a female voice called out.

"Son of a *bitch*," Roland muttered angrily. He glanced back at Desiree, who was hovering halfway down the stairs. "I apologize in advance for this."

"For what? Who is that?"

"As far as I'm concerned, nobody."

Before Desiree could ask what that meant, Roland swung open the door and a short, caramel-skinned woman with wide hips and waist-length cornrows immediately strutted inside with no invitation. A large orange leather purse was hanging from the crook of her arm. She either didn't notice Desiree or chose not to acknowledge her if she did; her eyes were fixed on Roland.

"It's about time."

Roland glared at her, and Desiree immediately wondered if this was the person who had been blowing up his phone earlier.

"What do you want, Anna?"

"You already know why I'm here. Don't play."

"How many times do I have to tell you not to come to my place unannounced?"

"Well, if you would answer your damn phone, I wouldn't have to."

So this is *her*, Desiree thought. She continued watching the scene before her, intrigued.

"I was on a date, Anna," Roland informed her pointedly. He swept an arm in Desiree's direction. "And it's not over."

It was then that Anna finally turned her eyes towards Desiree. Her facial expression went through a range of angry, to surprised, to worried, and finally, hurt.

Anna looked back at Roland, who was still standing with the door open. "So it's like that?"

"You made it like that. Now, I need you to leave."

"We need to talk, Roland."

"We don't have anything to talk about. And even if we did, now wouldn't be the time. As I mentioned, I'm busy." He held the door open wider. "So what you need to do is take a damn hint and leave me alone; if and when I decide to contact you, I'll do it on my own time."

Anna glanced at Desiree, almost as if she expected her help. Desiree just raised a brow at her and folded her arms.

She turned back to Roland, giving him a pleading look that Desiree was willing to bet worked magic once upon a time, but now, Roland was totally unaffected by it.

"Bye, Anna. Please don't make me have to ask you to leave again."

Looking like she was blinking back tears, Anna hurried out the door, her stride less confident than when she arrived.

Roland closed the door behind her and turned to Desiree. "I'm so sorry about that."

"Was that your ex?"

"Yeah." He ran a hand over his head wearily.

"I bet there's a juicy story behind all of this."

"I guess. But I don't wanna get into it."

Desiree held up her hands. "Hey, no problem. I don't wanna spend our time together talking about another broad, anyway." She began to descend the stairs, her eyes taking on that lustful slant again.

Roland raised his eyebrows in surprise. "You're not ready to leave?"

"Why would I be ready to leave?"

"Because of that whole scene, and just the implications of what could be behind it. I'm sure you've figured out by now that that's who's been blowing my phone up all night. I guess I figured you wouldn't wanna deal with the drama."

"I like drama. It's entertaining. Hell, we all have exes…I'm not tripping off that." She slid her hands up his chest before leaning in to kiss his neck.

Roland closed his eyes when he felt her tongue glide across his skin. "Yeah?"

"Of course." She grabbed his face and placed a wet kiss on his lips. "You're not getting rid of me that easily, sir."

Smiling, Roland leaned down and reclaimed her lips with his. They kissed deeply for several moments before Desiree resumed her task of untucking his shirt from his pants. She deftly undid the buttons, taking a moment to admire his strong chest before leaning down to slide her lips across it. She smiled when he moaned in pleasure, and eased down to her knees as she began unbuckling his belt, eager to turn those moans into screams.

"Desiree, hold up a second," Roland whispered, gently grabbing her hands.

She looked up at him. "What's wrong?"

"Not that I'm not enjoying what you're doing, but this isn't why I brought you over here."

"I know. It was my idea to come, remember?"

"True, but still. I'm definitely attracted to you, Desiree, but I actually like you and want to get to know you, too. It's not all about the physical with me."

Remaining quiet for several moments, Desiree gazed up at him. She finally replied, "And I appreciate that. I absolutely like you, too. We can get to know each other later but for now..." She finished unbuckling his belt and yanked down his pants. "The physical is all that's on my mind." She began massaging his manhood through his black boxer briefs.

Hissing in pleasure, Roland fell against the door, his eyes closed. He made no further attempts to stop her from her pleasure mission. When he felt her pull down his underwear and slowly cover him with her mouth, he released a string of long, drawn-out curses that had Desiree feeling like the queen of the world.

She gladly pleasured him, enjoying it almost as much as he did. They ended up christening several spots in Roland's place, ending up in his bedroom, spent and satisfied. As she dozed off in his arms, Desiree recalled his words about liking her and wanting to get to know her. She absolutely liked him too, but she hoped that he didn't turn into another version of Tobias.

No matter how much she was feeling Roland, she still didn't do relationships.

Chapter 7

"STOP IT!" LOVEY ADMONISHED herself as she hurriedly scratched out the mindless doodle of her and Clay's name on her notepad. They'd been seeing each other steadily for the past couple of weeks and this was just another time she caught herself fantasizing about him when she was supposed to be working.

She was determined to keep her head and not get too head of herself this time, like she did with Evan. But she couldn't deny that she really liked Clay. They just seemed so in sync; when it came to the important issues like family, spirituality, life goals, and other things like that, they seemed to be on the same page. Lovey's hopes rose with every interaction they had, and it was taking a lot of effort to keep a reign on her imagination, not to mention her hopes. Clay was turning out to be everything she wanted in a man, at least, so it seemed. It was hard for her not to look ahead to their possible future.

With a deep breath, she turned her attention to her computer and the inbox full of emails she'd been neglecting all morning. Her concentration had been shot all day; she and Clay had stayed up video chatting until almost one in the morning, and then he called her before she left for work. The smile never left her face, and she knew she was glowing like a Scooby Doo nightlight.

She was getting prepared for an upcoming meeting she had later that day when there was a light knock on her door.

"Yes?" she said, looking up.

"Sorry to interrupt, but you have a delivery," Tara, the receptionist, announced with a smile.

When Lovey saw the big bouquet of pink and yellow roses, she gasped, dropping her pen.

"Those are for *me*?" she confirmed, removing her reading glasses.

"They sure are." Tara entered the office and set the glass vase on the end of Lovey's desk. "You're on somebody's mind today, I see."

Lovey couldn't help but grin. She loved flowers, and she loved surprises like this. Before she even dug in for the card, she knew they were from Clay.

"These are gorgeous," she marveled, touching the petals with her fingertips.

"I wish you could see the look on your face right now," Tara smiled, a hand on her hip. "Somebody has you lovestruck."

Lovey wanted to wipe the grin off her face but she knew she wouldn't be able to do it. Not as long as she was able to see those flowers.

"I don't know about all that yet," she made herself say, even though Tara was right on the money. Lovey wanted to dish and gush all about Clay, but she would save that for when she talked to Desiree or Liz later. She and Tara were cool, but not *that* cool. "It's just, you know, a guy. Nobody special."

"Mmm-hmm," Tara winked at her before walking out of the office. Clearly, she didn't buy Lovey's blasé attempt.

Once her office door was closed again, Lovey excitedly searched for the card within what had to be at about two dozen roses, and bit her lip anxiously as she read it:

A beautiful woman deserves beautiful things.

I hope these make you smile as much as you've made me smile these past couple of weeks.

Can't wait to see you.

Clay

Not being able to help it, Lovey let out a little squeal and kicked her feet happily underneath her desk. Her body felt warm all over, and her heart was beating like the bass on a drumline. This wasn't the first time Clay had done something romantic to make her melt...he would try to call her when he knew she was leaving work and keep her company during her half-hour commute home; he brought her medicine when her sinuses were acting up one evening; when she had to cancel a date due to an emergency with one of her clients, he brought her dinner from her favorite restaurant; and he had yet to let a day pass without them communicating in some fashion, regardless of how busy either of them were. And she hadn't even known him a full month yet; he had already done more than the past three men she had dated combined.

She remembered him telling her that morning that he would be tied up most of the day, so she sent him a text to let him know she received the flowers, and to thank him. Roses might have seemed cliché to some people, but they had always been Lovey's favorite; they symbolized classic romance to her. That was another thing she loved about

Clay; he remembered little things she told him, and seemed to have an awesome sense for what she liked.

Not being able to resist, Lovey snapped a picture of the roses, then another of her happily smelling the roses, and sent them to Desiree. She couldn't wait to talk to her best friend later, but for now, Lovey tried to pull herself together and focus on her work. Every time she glanced up at those flowers, though, the smile was right back on her face.

Lovey knew she was falling for Clay, whether she wanted to or not.

"YOU WANT SOME HOT WINGS?"

"No, thanks. I have my smoothie, here."

"Girl, you and those green smoothies. I don't know how you drink that stuff day in and day out. I need some *real* food."

"This *is* real food. There's kale, green apple, celery—"

"You can go ahead and stop. You're not making it any more appealing." Desiree brought her plate of hot wings and fries to the table where she and Lovey were going over her books. Her face was makeup-free and her hair pulled back in an afro puff. She was shuffling around in a UGA sweater, short shorts, and fuzzy socks.

"I don't know how you eat all that junk and still stay so tight," Lovey commented, eyeing the food. "If I ate like you do, I'd be as big as a house."

"Dancing keeps me right, girl. That and just good genes." Desiree tucked a leg underneath her on the kitchen chair and munched on a French fry.

"I guess."

"And anyway, I think you obsess over your weight a little too much. You know you got that kind of body men break their necks over...big boobs, small waist, hips and a big booty. You're like a cartoon character."

"Yeah, but I have to *work* for it to stay like this, unlike you. Plus, you know I stress-eat. I just indulge every now and then. You indulge all day every day."

"Not *all day every day*; quit exaggerating."

"I don't even remember the last time you ate a vegetable."

"Don't I always eat the carrots and celery that come with my wings?"

"Doused in ranch dressing? Sure."

"Whatever. Still eat 'em."

Lovey chuckled as she turned her attention back to her laptop, where she was going over Desiree's business expenses. She had been keeping Desiree's books in order ever since her friend decided to go into party promoting professionally, and they met up every couple of months to make sure Desiree was staying on track.

"So how are things going with you and Roland? You're still seeing him, right?" Lovey asked as she entered some numbers onto the Excel spreadsheet.

"Yeah, we're still kickin' it."

"Yeah? Not getting tired of him yet?"

"Honestly? I'm not." Desiree moved her foot to the floor and sat forward in her seat. She looked thoughtful as she played with one of the carrot sticks on her plate. "I have to say, Roland is very different than any other dude I've messed with. He's not all about superficial stuff or just getting busy; he actually tries to get to know me while still giving me my space. I dig that."

Lovey looked at her friend. "You *dig* that?"

Desiree ducked her head as she smiled somewhat shyly. "Roland says that a lot. Guess I picked up on it."

"I see." Lovey grinned. "Looks like somebody's a little smitten."

"I didn't say that."

"You don't have to say it. I'm looking at you."

Desiree tried to wipe the smile off her face. "I don't know what you're talking about."

"You might as well give that up, girl. You like the man; just admit it."

"Okay...so?" Desiree looked slightly uncomfortable as she dipped her carrot stick in and out of the cup of ranch dressing. "So I like him. That doesn't mean anything."

Lovey couldn't help but chuckle. Desiree never liked to let on exactly how much she was into anyone; it was as if being into a man made her look weak. But Lovey saw the look that came on Desiree's face when Roland's name was mentioned. She didn't doubt it was along the lines of the same look that she got when Clay's name came up.

"If you say so," she finally said, turning her eyes back to the spreadsheet.

"What about you and Clay? You still on cloud nine?"

Lovey grinned again. "Something like that."

"And you talk about *me*."

"*I'm* not trying to deny it, though. If I'm fighting anything, it's to keep my imagination from running rampant and my hopes from getting too high too soon."

"Are you able to do that? I know how you get when you really like somebody. Making plans months in advance, stalking their Facebook page..."

"I do not *stalk* anybody's Facebook page. I only did that with Evan because he had fallen off. But I haven't had to worry about that with Clay because he always makes sure to stay in touch. Hasn't missed a day of communicating yet."

"Yeah?"

"Yep. And *he* usually initiates it."

"Wow. That's a change, huh?"

"It is. But, I'm trying to remember that it's still early on and men are usually on their best behavior during the first few weeks. I really am trying to keep my wits about me this time."

"Well, then good for you. I know how much of a romantic you are. This Clay seems to be a good dude, though."

"So far so good."

"When are you seeing him again?"

"Probably this weekend. He'll be out of town for work until then. But next weekend, we're going up to those cabins at Blue Ridge. Oh my gosh, I am *so* looking forward to it. I need to get away for a minute."

"Going away together already? You don't think it's too soon?"

"You know, I was worried about that at first, too, but actually...I don't. It just *feels* right, you know?"

Desiree smiled at her friend, glad to see her so happy. She just hoped this Clay guy was as good as he was portraying himself to be. "I think I do."

"We're gonna be staying in the Enchantment Cabin. Isn't that just delicious?"

Chuckling, Desiree picked up one of her wings. "Very."

"It has a fireplace, flat-screen TV, king-sized bed, a hot tub *and* a bedside Jacuzzi, girl. Just beautiful."

"Oh wow, that *does* sound hot. I've been wanting to go to one of those cabins."

"Maybe Roland can take you there," Lovey teased, twirling her pen.

"Hmph. We're nowhere *near* that level yet. I don't move quite as fast as you."

"What? Didn't you sleep with him on the first date?"

"Shut up. Sex is one thing; going to a cabin in the mountains where it's nothing but you, him, and your feelings is another."

"Well, we all know how you run from feelings."

Desiree eyed her, but chose not to comment. "Speaking of sex, have you and Clay...?"

"No, we have not. Not yet."

"But you're planning on it."

"It'll happen when it's supposed to happen. We both agreed not to rush into that. We want to let things progress naturally. We'll know when it's the right time, I'm sure."

"I've got a hundred bucks that says it'll be in that Enchanted Cabin next weekend."

"Uh, as your financial advisor, I'd advise against that bet," Lovey tapped her laptop screen with her pen and smiled. "And it's Enchant*ment* Cabin."

"Whatever."

"But for real...maybe when Clay and I get back, we can double-date with you and Roland. That'd be fun, huh?"

Desiree was about to agree, then she remembered that Lovey still thought she was the one that set her and Clay up. She knew she needed to go ahead and straighten up that confusion.

"Yeah, we can definitely do that but first, I need to admit something."

Lovey looked at her. "What?"

"You remember the night at Barfly, the night you met Clay?"

"Yeah..."

"And before that, I had told you that I had someone I wanted to introduce you to?"

"Yeah...that was Clay, right?"

"Actually, no...it wasn't. I've never even met Clay."

Lovey frowned. "Huh?"

"Girl, I was going to introduce you to Roland. But before I could, you met Clay and you two were so into each other that I just left it alone."

"Oh...and kept Roland for yourself, huh?"

Desiree couldn't tell if Lovey was being sarcastic with that question or not. "It wasn't like that..."

"Would you have said anything about this if Clay and I didn't work out?"

Desiree's mouth hung open. "I-I don't know..."

"I do." Lovey played with her straw.

Eyeing her friend, Desiree sat forward in her seat. "Are you mad?"

After a few moments, Lovey looked at her friend and sighed, pushing her cup away. "No, I'm not mad. A little surprised, that's all. Thankfully, I *do* have Clay so I'm not really worried about the 'what if' factor. Just don't know why you waited so long to tell me, though."

"Because I didn't want you to think what you're probably thinking now; that I was on some shady stuff and was trying to keep the good men to myself. You know I wouldn't do anything like that to you." She noticed Lovey's unreadable expression. "Don't you?"

"Yeah." Lovey gave her a tight smile before turning her attention back to the laptop. "Yeah, I know."

Desiree could feel the mood shift in the room, and something told her that Lovey wasn't as fine with everything as she let on.

LOVEY WAS EXCITED THAT her weekend away with Clay had finally arrived. She'd been counting down the days ever since they had made the reservation, and she looked forward to having some secluded, extended time with Clay where they could really get to know each other better and get closer.

And, it would help her take her mind off of the whole thing with Desiree and her admission about not having anything to do with Lovey and Clay meeting as she had initially thought. Lovey didn't know why, but that admission just bugged her.

She and Desiree had been best friends since they were teenagers, and she had been witness to how underhanded her friend could get when she saw something she wanted. Desiree hadn't been above stealing other girls' boyfriends, and would do things like start a scandalous rumor about the girl to get the guy to leave her, set something up where it would look like the girl was being unfaithful, or just straight seduce the guy. One time in particular, Desiree had her eye on a guy named Fernando, who was already in a relationship. Unbothered, Desiree snuck into his car while he was in the library one night, then had her friend who was working the front desk make an announcement that his car was about to be towed. When he rushed outside, Desiree was waiting for him in the backseat with nothing on but her favorite bra and panty set and some heels. Fernando didn't resist her. Men hardly ever resisted Desiree.

Desiree had calmed down since then, pretty much leaving her pursuits to unattached men, and Lovey knew this situation wasn't nearly the same, but for some reason it still bothered her. She couldn't understand why Desiree had waited so long to mention it. If there was one thing Lovey hated, it was secrets and dishonesty.

But she tried to remember that Desiree was her best friend; she wouldn't purposely do anything to hurt her.

Shaking off those thoughts, Lovey continued to pack for her trip with Clay. She was choosing between two different bikinis when there was a knock at the door. She hurried to answer and smiled when she looked through the peephole and saw it was her sister.

"Hey, girl," Lovey greeted her with a quick hug before heading back to her bedroom.

"What you doin'?" Liz asked, closing the door and following her.

"Packing."

"Still? You were packing when I called a couple of hours ago."

"Yeah, well...this is me and Clay's first weekend away together; I want things to be right."

"Well, I'm sure Clay will be feeling *right* if you wear this," Liz commented, picking up part of Lovey's mint green string bikini with her forefinger.

Lovey giggled and snatched the bikini top from her. "Shut up. This is for just in case we use the Jacuzzi."

"Girl, you know good and well y'all are gonna use that Jacuzzi. The only question is how soon and how often."

"Whatever." Lovey couldn't resist blushing.

"So," Liz leaned back on her arm as she sat on the bed, "Is this gonna be the weekend?"

"For?"

"Don't play. You and Clay haven't slept together yet, right? I can only imagine a romantic cabin getaway would be the perfect time to consummate your budding relationship."

"Well, you just said it right there; *budding* relationship. We haven't even declared being official or exclusive yet. And we both agreed that we didn't want to rush into anything physical."

"That's awesome. But make sure you take some protection, anyway, just in case. Just sayin'."

"I've already thought about that." Lovey reached into the side of her suitcase and pulled out a box of Trojans. "Even though I thought about not taking these."

"Why?"

"Because if I know I have them, I'll probably be more tempted to use them."

"I get that. But still, better safe than sorry. You both might decide the time is right while you're there and it would be a bummer to not have any protection, especially since you're not on the pill anymore. And I know you know better than to get some love without that glove."

"Absolutely."

"There you go. So go ahead and tuck those back into that suitcase..." Liz took the box from her and placed them back where she had taken them from.

Lovey giggled and shook her head as her phone rang. When she saw it was Elyse, Desiree's mother, she quickly answered it.

"Hey, Mama!" she greeted enthusiastically.

"Hey, baby. What you doing?"

"Just packing for my little getaway with Clay."

"Girl, I can hear the smile in your voice; this Clay must be your new man."

"Not officially yet, but hopefully." Lovey grinned at the thought as she stuffed both of her bikinis into her suitcase. Liz eyed her amusingly.

"I'm so happy to hear that. Does that mean that you'll have a date for Thanksgiving dinner this year? You know I need to see your face in the place."

"I'm not sure of Clay's plans for Thanksgiving but if he's able to come, I'll absolutely bring him. It'd be nice to have someone with me besides just my sister for a change."

"Hey!" Liz exclaimed.

Elyse laughed. "You know Liz is welcome to come, too. So you're really diggin' this Clay guy, huh?"

"Oh I *am*, Mama," Lovey swooned as she dropped down onto the bed, clutching the shirt she was holding to her chest. "He is so wonderful. I've been trying to keep my head and not get too ahead of myself, but I can't lie...I'm feeling him a lot. I mean, a *whole* lot."

"I am so happy for you, baby. And I'm praying that this one does right by you and doesn't fade to black like these other punk asses."

"You and me both. But he hasn't shown any signs of that so far so...I'm keeping my fingers crossed."

"I've got my fingers, toes, *and* legs crossed...until later on tonight, that is."

Lovey shrieked with laughter. "Mama!"

"Girl, you already know how I get down. My husband and I are still as hot for each other now as we were back in the day. Hopefully you and Clay will be like that."

"From your mouth to God's ears."

"You already know I'm praying for you, baby. Always are. You are too good a woman to keep getting dogged like you have been. But the *right* man will appreciate you. And he's comin.'"

"Thank you so much, Mama. I love you for that."

"I love you, too. Now if I could just get some sense into your homegirl's head..."

"Ugh," Lovey grunted. "You know how Desiree is. She has her fun and then she moves on. To her, men are like toys kids get on Christmas that they play with until they get bored and then toss them for something else."

Liz glanced at her sister, sensing the slight edge in her voice.

"Can't disagree with you on that one," Elyse agreed, not noticing. "I keep telling her that one day she's gonna come across that man that will change everything for her. She isn't trying to hear that, though."

"Oh I know, believe me."

"Well, I'm gonna let you go. Let me know what Clay says about Thanksgiving but regardless, you make sure *you're* here."

"Yes, ma'am."

"All right, baby. I'll talk to you later."

They ended the call and Lovey lightly ran her finger across the screen of her phone, looking thoughtful.

"Something on your mind?" Liz asked after a few moments.

"Not really." Lovey's voice was distant.

"You sure? Nothing going on between you and Desiree?"

Lovey looked at her. "Why would you ask that?"

"Because I know you and I know her. What did she do now?"

Lovey started to tell her sister about the whole Desiree-Clay-Roland situation, but decided against it. She already felt like she was making a bigger deal out of it than was necessary.

"It's nothing, girl," Lovey dismissed with a wave of her hand. "I guess I'm letting my nerves about this weekend get to me."

"Just relax. Enjoy yourself. Don't put any more pressure on this weekend than there needs to be."

"I'll try."

"Don't forget to text me the address and stuff, and you've got your stun gun, right?"

"Yes, Liz."

"Hey, you can't be too careful nowadays."

"I know. But now you're starting to freak me out in a whole other way."

"I'm sorry. I really do want you to have a good time with Clay. You seem to like him more than you've liked anyone in a while."

Lovey couldn't help the smile that revisited her face. "You're right, I do. And something tells me this weekend with Clay is gonna be special."

THE NEXT MORNING, LOVEY and Clay headed to the Blue Ridge Mountains for their first romantic weekend together. Lovey kept reminding herself to chill out; her nerves and anxiety were actually making her hands shake. She just wanted everything to go well.

"You all right?" Clay asked her, reaching over to clamp a hand on her thigh. "You seem a little nervous."

Lovey glanced over at him as she placed her hand over his. "Maybe I shouldn't admit this, but I am. It's just been so long since I've gone away with anyone."

"It's been a while for me, too," Clay revealed, glancing at her.

Lovey's eyebrows shot up. "Really?"

"Why do you look so surprised?"

"I don't know; I guess I thought..."

"Lovey, I can't tell you how long it's been since I've been with anybody I've even wanted to seriously date, let alone go away with. You're special to me; I can't help wanting to spend as much time with you as I possibly can."

Lovey knew her face was probably as red as the just-in-case pumps in her bag. She rubbed his hand affectionately. "I feel the same way."

Clay smiled at her, and Lovey felt something she hadn't felt in a long time spread throughout her body. In that moment, she felt closer to Clay than ever. She leaned over and rested her head on his shoulder, her nerves and anxiety suddenly eased.

Once they arrived at the cabins and got checked in, they took their time putting their things away and exploring their cabin, stopping for plenty of flirtatious neck-nuzzles and kisses.

"This is so beautiful, Clay," Lovey sighed, her arms around his neck. She gazed around the room before her eyes landed on his. He was looking at her intently already.

"So are you," he countered in a low voice before leaning in and kissing her. The kiss started off soft but quickly deepened, and their holds on each other tightened simultaneously. Lovey's body was screaming, and she loved the feel of Clay's hands languidly roaming it. She was glad Liz talked her into bringing those condoms, because she wanted to put them to use right then.

"Before we get too carried away," Clay panted when he hesitantly pulled back, "You wanna go get something to eat?"

Still kiss-drunk, Lovey pressed her body to his. "I'm not hungry," she murmured, leaning in to kiss his neck.

Clay moaned, biting his lip. He reached down and grabbed her ample backside with both hands, pulling her closer to him. "Baby..."

"You wanna lay down for a while?" Lovey whispered, her hands slowly easing underneath his shirt. She knew she should probably pull back but she couldn't help herself; the environment and his kisses were sending her arousal into overdrive, and she was reminded just how long it had been since she'd gotten any. She definitely wanted Clay to be inside of her before the night was over. Heck, before the next minute was over.

She boldly reached down and massaged his manhood through his jeans, and loved the grunt of satisfaction she was rewarded with for doing so. Her restraint was slipping fast and she almost didn't care to try to rein it back in;

in that moment, she wanted Clay more than she had ever wanted anything. Her hands wanted to rip off everything he was wearing.

Moaning again, Clay enjoyed the feel of her lips and hands for several more moments before taking her face in his hands and planting a deep kiss on her and stepping back. She looked at him, slightly surprised and disappointed.

"I'd love to lay down with you all night," Clay assured her, noting the look in her eyes. "And I plan to."

Lovey smiled.

"But I want our first time to be better than this," Clay continued, cupping her chin in his hand. "You deserve that."

Suddenly feeling like she had come across like some kind of harlot, Lovey blushed slightly in embarrassment, looking away.

"I'm sorry for coming on so strong," she said somewhat timidly, her boldness from just minutes before already practically evaporated.

"No, baby, come on; you don't have anything to apologize for," Clay quickly assured her, taking her into his arms. He looked down at her, the adoration in his eyes evident. "I was enjoying every second of that. And I love that you seem to want me as much as I want you."

Not wanting to admit out loud just how much she did want him, Lovey just grinned. "Good."

"And in the spirit of that, there is something I've been wanting to talk to you about."

A cold dart immediately shot to Lovey's stomach. "Yes?"

Clay opened his mouth to speak, but stopped himself. Now wasn't the time. "It can wait. Hey, there's a winery not too far from here; how 'bout we go do a little wine tasting?"

"Um, okay." Lovey tried not to think the worst as he took her hand and led her out of the cabin.

AS MUCH AS LOVEY LOVED wine and was enjoying the tour of the Habersham Vineyards, she couldn't help but wonder what it was that Clay was going to say to her before they left the cabin. It clouded her mind, and she couldn't help but conjure up all kinds of scenarios, most of them negative. Was he going to end things? Reveal he had a wife he was separated from or a girlfriend he was on the outs with? Did he have a bunch of illegitimate children? They had discussed all of this already, and Clay had assured her that he was single, never married and with no kids, but now Lovey was questioning everything. She hated that their first romantic weekend together was already being marred by something, and she didn't even know what that something was.

After the wine tasting, Clay suggested they go to the nearby Ann Ruby Falls, since it was such a nice day. Lovey mindlessly agreed, though she would have preferred to go back to the cabin and discuss whatever it was he'd been about to bring up earlier. He didn't seem to still be thinking about it, as he was just enjoying being in the beautiful environment they were in together, but Lovey wasn't able to enjoy herself as much as she normally would have. Lovey loved nature as much as Clay did, but all of the possibilities of what it was that Clay wanted to talk to her about ping-ponging in her mind was about to drive her crazy.

Before long, she couldn't take it anymore. They were strolling along the paved path hand-in-hand and Lovey stopped in her tracks.

Clay looked at her, concerned. "You okay? What's wrong?"

Trying to choose her words wisely, Lovey took a deep breath. "Clay, I'm sorry, but this is driving me nuts..."

"What is?"

"Whatever it is you were going to say before we left the cabin. I haven't been able to get my mind off of it."

"So that's why you've been so quiet all day?"

"I don't want to ruin our time together by being paranoid, but my imagination tends to do its own thing, and I've come up with a million things you might've been getting ready to tell me, and almost none of them were good. It didn't *seem* like it was going to be good news."

Sighing, Clay slid an arm around her and kissed her forehead. "I'm sorry for leaving you hanging like that."

"Can we please just talk about whatever it is now?"

Looking at her for a few moments, Clay stepped back and dug his hands into his pockets, suddenly looking at little nervous. He gazed at the scenery around them. "Okay. Now is actually a great time for this."

Swallowing nervously, Lovey could already feel the tears stinging her eyes. She just knew Clay was about to break things off with her. Why he would invite her on a romantic trip to do it was beyond her, but at least he was telling her to her face instead of fading to black like most other men did.

"Lovey," Clay began, "I've been doing a lot of thinking about us these past few days. And now more than ever, I'm sure that I know what I want, in regards to you and me."

Biting her trembling lip, Lovey fought to keep her tears from falling. She could almost hear her heart breaking. Of *course* he had been too good to be true; apparently Lovey didn't deserve a good man. That's what it was turning out to seem like.

"And what's that?" she made herself say with a feigned strength that actually took the wind out of her. She placed a hand over her chest, bracing herself.

"I want to be your man."

The tears already streaming down her cheeks, it took several moments before Clay's words registered with her. When she realized what he actually said, her head snapped to him. "Wh-what did you say?"

"I want to be your man, Lovey. I want us to be together, *really* together, exclusively." He stepped over to her and took her face in his hands. "You're all I've been able to think about since we met. I've never met a woman who got into my head and my heart the way you have. I need you in my life, Lovey."

Lovey's tears were now of relief and happiness, rather than the dread and sadness they'd been about before. Grinning harder than she ever had in her life, Lovey gripped Clay's shirt in her still-trembling hands.

"Yes, Clay," she responded, looking right into his eyes. "I definitely want us to be together, too. I've wanted that for a while now."

Grinning, Clay leaned down and kissed her. "You sure?"

"I've never been surer of anything else."

She squealed when Clay suddenly picked her up and spun her around, obviously thrilled with her response. They both laughed when Clay's foot slipped on a pebble and Lovey screamed, clinging to him as if fearing he would drop her.

"I got you, babe," he assured her. He set her back on the ground and looked her right into her eyes, hoping she knew how serious he was. "I would never let anything happen to you."

Her heart bursting, Lovey eagerly wrapped her arms around his neck and returned the deep, ecstatic kiss he planted on her. It was then that she realized they had stopped in front of the waterfall, the sound of the rushing water suddenly becoming clear to her, and the sun peeking through the trees and basking on them as if in approval. Lovey continued to savor the moment, enjoying the kisses that seemed new now that Clay was officially hers.

AFTER THEY FINISHED walking the trail at Anna Ruby Falls and had dinner at a nearby restaurant, Lovey and Clay headed back to the cabin. Both still floating on air, they cuddled up on the couch to watch a movie. They talked about Lovey's misunderstanding of what Clay had been planning to say to her, and had a good laugh about it. Clay insisted that parting ways with Lovey never crossed his mind.

"Hey, I wanted to ask you...do you have any plans for Thanksgiving?"

"Not really. I usually go see my folks in Virginia but this year they're going on a cruise, so I was just gonna chill this year. Why?"

Lovey nervously played with the hem of his shirt. "Well...I usually spend the day with my friend Desiree's family; my sister usually goes, too. Would you...like to join us?"

"Absolutely," Clay didn't hesitate to reply.

Smiling with relief, Lovey looked up at him. "Really?"

"Of course. Spending the holiday giving thanks with my woman beats some football and Waffle House any day. Plus, I'll finally get to meet the infamous BFF."

Chuckling, she breathed an inaudible sigh of relief. "She'll love meeting you, too. Since my parents died, her family has taken me in as their own. Just a heads-up, in case you get bombarded with questions; they can be kinda nosey when they wanna be."

"I can take anything they throw at me. Nothing to hide over here. I'm just looking forward to going with you and being around your people."

"I'm glad to hear it." Lovey snuggled closer to him.

Clay kissed the top of her head and lovingly rubbed her arm as they continued to watch the movie.

"You wanna get in the Jacuzzi?" Lovey asked when the movie was over.

"Hell yeah!" Clay quickly exclaimed, causing Lovey to laugh.

"Silly," she playfully admonished, hitting him lightly on the arm. "I'll go change."

Before she could get up, Clay grabbed her by the waist and pulled her back onto his lap, kissing her deeply as he caressed the side of her face. His other hand roamed to her breasts, and Lovey felt an immediate gush to her middle, her earlier arousal coming back full force. She turned in his lap to where she was straddling him, and they kissed fervently as her hips grinded against him. Clay's hands were going everywhere they could reach, and Lovey could feel how hard he was underneath her.

"Come on," she whispered, tapering off their kiss as she lightly grazed her nails down the side of his neck. "Before we get too carried away..."

"You caught me just in time, girl," he informed her, running a hand through her hair. "I was two seconds from tossing you on your back."

Giggling despite how intrigued she was, Lovey made herself push away from him. "I like how you think. Meet you at the Jacuzzi in five." She got up and started to walk off.

"The one on the deck or the one in the bedroom?" Clay called out.

Pausing at the door, Lovey looked back at him seductively. "The bedroom."

They shared a smile as Lovey turned to walk away.

"*Wow...*"

Clay seemed mesmerized by the sight of Lovey's voluptuous body in the mint green bikini. He couldn't take his eyes off of her as she slowly walked towards him, feeling an awkward mix of self-conscious and sexy as she noted the obvious approval in his eyes. She nervously bit her lip as she stopped in front of him.

"You like it?" she asked, referring to the bikini.

"I do." His eyes bore into her. "But I like the woman wearing it more."

Lovey couldn't help grinning. Clay had a knack for making her feel like gold.

He stepped into the Jacuzzi before offering her his hand as she got in to join him. They played around for a little while, lightly splashing each other in between kisses, before Clay pulled her to sit between his legs and wrapped his arms around her. Lovey leaned her back against him, closing her eyes and feeling more content than she had probably ever felt.

They sat like that for a while, neither feeling the need to say anything. They just enjoyed the soft jazz playing from Clay's iPhone as they reveled in the moment, each genuinely happy just to be there together. Clay would occasionally kiss Lovey's shoulder as he softly hummed along with the music, resting the side of his head against hers.

"Babe?"

Lovey opened her eyes. "Hmm?"

"Thank you for saying yes."

Feeling an automatic surge in her heart, Lovey turned in his arms, facing him as she wrapped her arms around his neck. Her hands caressed the back of his head as she gazed at him like the lovestruck woman she was.

"Thank you for asking me."

Clay looked anxious for a moment, as if he was working up the nerve to say something. "Lovey...I-I'm falling for you. I feel it with everything in me."

Lovey gasped, clearly caught off guard by that declaration. Her hand covered her pounding heart. "Are you serious?"

"Immensely. I don't wanna freak you out or anything, if you feel like it's too soon—"

"No, stop." Lovey placed a finger to his lips, shaking her head. "It's not. And if it is, too bad. 'Cause I'm definitely falling for you, too."

Clay's grip tightened on her as he grinned in relief. "You don't know how glad I am to hear you say that, baby."

He grabbed her face and kissed her intensely, which she eagerly returned. Their moans and sighs overtook the music and filled the room, the bubbling water in the Jacuzzi the only backdrop. As they looked into each other's eyes, they both knew they were starting something special, something neither of them had been graced with before. For Lovey's part, she knew she was going to do everything she could to preserve it and make it last. Because she already couldn't imagine her life without Clay in it.

Their kisses resumed, even hungrier than before, and it wasn't lost on either of them that tonight was gonna be the night. Clay's heated gaze bore into her as he slowly slid down the straps of her bikini. His hands cupped her luscious breasts, skin-to-skin for the first time, and gently but fervently explored and massaged them, his thumbs playing over her dark nipples like the strings of a guitar. Lovey's whimpers of pleasure were music to his ears. And when he leaned forward and teased her areola with the tip of his tongue, not being able to resist anymore, she clung to him, because she felt like she was going to faint.

"Please, Clay," she begged as he continued to tortuously pleasure her. One of his hands had drifted beneath the water to gently tease her womanhood, and he was driving her absolutely crazy. "I can't take this, please..."

"I wanna make you remember this, baby," Clay whispered, grabbing the back of her head and looking at her as his other hand continued to tease her under the water. "You're gonna remember this time with me; I guarantee you..."

"Aaahhhh..." Lovey couldn't even speak as Clay sucked hard on her neck, sending her body into overdrive.

"Whenever you're ready, baby. I'll get inside you whenever you're ready for me."

"Now!" Lovey knew she probably sounded eager, but she didn't care right then. She *was* eager. She wanted Clay; needed him. He was lighting a fire in her that hadn't been lit in over ten months.

"Whatever you say, love." Clay reached over and got a condom from the side of the Jacuzzi, and proceeded to make love to the woman that had taken hold of his heart since the night they met.

Chapter 8

"YOU WANTED TO TALK, so talk."

Roland leaned back in the chair in the Barfly office, sipping from a snifter of cognac as he braced himself for this conversation with his ex.

"It's about time. I thought you were never gonna talk to me."

"You can thank E.J. for changing my mind. 'Cause that was certainly the plan."

Anna sighed. "Can we meet somewhere? I'd really rather not do this over the phone."

"You're lucky we're doing it at all. So I suggest you take what you can get."

"Fine. But I don't know why it has to be like this, Roland. We used to be so close, and you act like you hate me now."

"I don't hate you. I'm not giving you that kind of power. But I certainly don't like you."

"Wow, really?" She sounded hurt.

"Why would you be surprised about that? Do you not remember stepping out on me with some random dude when you went with your girls to Essence Fest?"

"I told you that didn't mean anything. I was super drunk; I barely even remember it."

"Yeah, that makes it a whole lot better," Roland scoffed with obvious sarcasm. "You weren't even gonna tell me about it; I can thank social media for alerting me to that particular deception."

"You and I were high school sweethearts, Roland. Had been together for years and years. I guess I just needed to experience something else."

"Uh-huh. If you wanted to *experience something else* so bad, then you should have just ended things with me."

"I didn't *want* to end things with you! I loved you, Roland! I still do! And I also think all of that history should make me due for a second chance."

"I *gave* you a second chance. And you blew that by bringing some other man into my house."

"Roland, I explained that..."

"You *tried* to explain it. Not that I believed you."

"Keith was just a co-worker of mine that needed to come in and use the restroom after dropping me off. That's all."

"Sure."

"Roland-"

"I'm over this," Roland cut her off. His patience had run out. "We really don't have anything else to talk about."

"I think we do. I love you, Roland, and I *know* you still love me, too."

Roland sucked his teeth as his call waiting beeped. When he saw it was Desiree, he sat up in his seat.

"I've gotta go," he told Anna. "Got another more important call coming in."

"That woman that was at your house that night?"

Not bothering to answer, Roland clicked over to Desiree. "Hey, you."

"Hey." The smile in her voice was clear. "You busy?"

"Not right now. What's up?"

"Just out getting some stuff done and wanted to hear that sexy voice."

Roland couldn't help the grin that crossed his face. "You sure know how to flatter a brotha."

"Only those that deserve it."

"You wanna meet up for lunch or something?"

"Damn...wish I could but I'm gonna be running all over this city all day, doing stuff I've been putting off all week. How 'bout you come by my place later, though?"

"That'll work. What time?"

"I'll be home probably around eight, so just come whenever you're done at the club."

"Aight. I'll bring something to eat; I know you like that."

"I *do* like that." Desiree chuckled. "Food is an excellent way to get into my good graces."

"So I've learned."

"Just as long as we can work off whatever you bring later."

Roland instantly hardened at the seductive drop in her voice. This woman sure knew how to get to him. "No doubt."

They spoke for another few minutes before ending the call. Roland had a little extra spring in his step as he went about his tasks for the day, already counting down the hours until he could get to Desiree's apartment. It was actually the first time since they opened the club that he hated he had to be there. Desiree was slowly creeping her way under his skin, and he liked it.

When E.J. arrived, Roland went to meet him in his office. E.J. was also thrilled with Desiree, though clearly for different reasons.

"Man, have you seen these numbers since we started partnering with Desiree?" he marveled, looking at his computer screen. "Things are up thirty percent, and it's only been a few weeks."

"Yeah, she's definitely good at what she does," Roland agreed.

"She's damn good. Not to mention our social media channels have been busier lately, too. If things keep going like this, we'll be closer to being able to hire more staff and expand than we initially expected."

"I've already been getting inquiries about renting the club for private parties, which would be major. Especially if we can get some big names in here every once in a while."

"Desiree was talking to me about some reality-star friend of hers hosting something here. I tell you, that woman has been like mannah from heaven."

"Yeah, she's got it going on, all right."

E.J. eyed his brother, an amused smirk curling the corner of his mouth. "I'm sure *you* think so."

Roland tried to neutralize his facial expression but knew it was futile. "What are you talking about?"

"Brother, please. Let's leave acting coy to the ladies."

"Nobody's trying to be coy. I like Desiree; I'm not gonna try to deny that."

"I'd venture that you like her a lot. More than anyone since Anna."

Roland twirled his thumbs thoughtfully. "Maybe."

"I admit that I was wary of you two hooking up because I didn't want it potentially affecting the business, but it's good to see you open up to someone again. I was starting to wonder if you ever would."

"I didn't plan on it. But Desiree just...she put some kind of grip on me right from the beginning. I find myself wanting to do all this stuff to make her smile, and learn as much as I can about her. I just...like being with her. A lot."

"Sounds like you're smitten, little brother."

"Yeah," Roland admitted with a smile. "Yeah, I am."

"You going to be spending Thanksgiving with her? You know I'll be out of town with the wife, visiting her family."

"We actually haven't talked about any plans for that, yet...I don't know what she's gonna be doing. Probably with her family and her homegirl Lovey that she's always talking about."

"Well, maybe you can go with her."

"Ehh. I don't know. I don't get the sense that she's in any hurry to introduce me to her people. And I guess I can understand that. I'll just chill at the house and watch football and movies all day."

"Just ask her if you can hang with her. You shouldn't be by yourself."

"I don't mind. I'm around a bunch of people every day; it'll be nice to have a day to myself."

"If you say so."

Roland and E.J.'s parents were deceased; their father died of cancer and their mother had been the victim of a hit-and-run, and didn't survive her injuries. Sometimes Roland would join his brother and sister-in-law for the holidays, but he really preferred to be by himself. He did a lot of reminiscing about his parents that he didn't allow himself to do the rest of the time. Losing them had left a lingering burn in his heart that he knew would probably never be eased.

If he was honest with himself, though, he wouldn't have minded if Desiree had at least invited him to spend Thanksgiving with her. He had noticed during his time with her that she was eager to talk about a lot of things with him, but she never got too personal...he still didn't know a lot about her family or her past. And she still wasn't asking him a lot about his, either. He tried to convince himself that maybe she just took her time opening up about certain things, though there was a small part of him that felt like she was keeping him at arm's length. Whenever he would try to forge a conversation about anything deep, she would stick her tongue down his throat or climb onto his lap and grind on him until his train of thought was officially derailed. Seduction was always her method of diversion and Roland would be lying if he said he didn't enjoy it, but he had to wonder why it was she was so reluctant to really open up to him.

He vowed to himself that when he went to see her that night, he would ask her exactly that.

DESIREE MANAGED TO wrap up her errands a little faster than expected, and without even thinking about it, immediately got to work straightening up her apartment.

When she realized she was actually cleaning because a man was coming over, her actions stalled.

"What the hell am I doing?" she muttered to herself, glancing at the vacuum cleaner she had just pulled out of the closet. She shook the moment off, though, convincing herself that she wasn't doing anything for Roland that she wouldn't have had to do, anyway. It's not like she wanted her apartment looking a mess.

When she finished cleaning up, she sent a text to Roland letting him know she was home and ready for him. He responded that he would be another hour or so, so Desiree took a quick shower and then fired up her tablet. She was planning on checking her emails and social media accounts, but not too long after she logged on to Facebook, she got an instant message from Cornell.

> **Hey sexy**
> She grinned.
> *Hey there. What's up with you tonight?*
> **Hell, I'm trying to see what's up with YOU**
> *Just chillin right now*
> **What you got on? Somethin sexy?**
> *Maybe. Use your imagination.*
> **Oh believe me, I do.**

Ginning harder, Desiree burrowed deeper into the corner of her couch. She and Cornell proceeded to flirt and tease each other as they usually did, with things eventually progressing to them trading pictures of each other's body parts. Desiree had just slid her robe to the side to send him a picture of her breast when there was a knock on the door.

"Oh, crap!" she mumbled, covering herself and typing a hasty 'gotta go' to Cornell and scrambling off the couch.

Hurrying to the door, Desiree adjusted her wig and her robe to make sure she was showing a good amount of cleavage before greeting Roland with an expectant smile.

"There he is." She eyed him flirtatiously.

"Hey, babe. Sorry I'm running a little behind."

"Don't even worry about it." She didn't want to say that she had lost all track of time and had been so caught up in messing around with Cornell that she had temporarily forgotten that Roland was on his way over.

And since when did he call her *babe*?

"Come on in," she said, pushing those thoughts out of her mind as she pulled him by his shirt towards her. She pushed the door closed with one hand and pulled his face to hers with the other, laying a slow, deep kiss on him, pressing her body to his. Ever since they had started sleeping together, every part of her seemed to crave him. Just seeing him automatically turned her on.

"Glad to see me, huh?" Roland noted with a smile once the kiss finally tapered off.

"Very."

"It's good to see you, too. You're looking hot and fresh."

"Just call me Krispy Kreme. You don't happen to have any of those, do you?"

Roland laughed and slid an arm around her shoulder as they headed towards the living room. He loved that she made him laugh like she did. "I got you next time. For now, though, it's just some Chinese food from that place you said you liked."

"Ooh, yum!" Desiree clapped her hands like a kid who got what they wanted under the tree for Christmas. "Let's get our grub-on, then!"

They proceeded to have dinner on the couch in front of the television, while Desiree told him about some drama that popped off at one of her recent events. Roland listened, but waited for her to ask him how *his* day went and how things were going with *him,* but those questions never came. She just continued to talk about her own stuff, and Roland continued to wonder how long he was going to wait to point out this tendency of hers to her.

"I mean, you're a club owner; I'm sure you've seen your share of mess since y'all opened."

"I guess you could say that," Roland replied. It was the closest thing to a question he had gotten.

"If there was any part of what I do that I don't enjoy, it's that...having to deal with people who don't know how to act when they go out." Desiree reached for her soda and took a long sip. "That's why having good security is so important. As soon as it looks like something is getting ready to pop off, I give them the signal and they're on it. Gotta nip that kind of stuff in the bud."

"That's a good thing. Things can escalate quickly nowadays."

"You're right about that. That's why the security detail I have places people at the door, as well as a couple of plain-clothed 'roamers' that integrate themselves into the crowd so they can jump on things when they see it. I can't be everywhere, after all."

"True. You really know how to handle things; I dig that."

"I appreciate it." Desiree smiled at him. "It just comes from years of experience and lots of trial and error."

"Right."

"I could tell you some *stories* from when I started out, though," she continued. "Oh my gosh, some of those were just hot-mess fests. I usually got good turnouts since I was always pretty popular and had a little bit of a reputation as a party animal...I figured, since I loved to party so much, why not get paid for it?"

"I feel you."

"Why don't you come over here and do that?"

Roland almost didn't realize what she said, and his eyebrows shot up when she started easing her robe from her shoulders. He couldn't say he was surprised that she was naked underneath.

Despite his mind reminding him what he wanted to talk to her about, his body was telling him that it could wait. Without a word, he put his plate down, crawled over to her, and covered her body with his, temporarily forgetting about everything else.

After they fooled around for a while, Roland helped clean up their dishes before Desiree grabbed his hand and led him to her bedroom.

"Can I use your restroom real quick?" he asked her.

"Of course; you don't have to ask. You know where it is."

While Roland went and relieved himself, Desiree checked her phone. She saw a post from Lovey on

Facebook, checking in at Studio Movie Grill with Clay. Desiree smiled, thrilled that her friend had found a good man, finally. When Lovey had returned from her cabin weekend and told Desiree about him asking her to be his woman in front of the waterfall, them professing their love for each other and then making love in the hot tub, it *almost* made Desiree wish she had something like that for herself. Lovey had been walking on air ever since then.

"Hey," Desiree said to Roland when he re-entered her bedroom. "What would you think about going on a double-date with my girl Lovey and her man?"

"That'd be cool," Roland casually replied. "I'd like to meet Lovey, finally, since you talk about her so much."

"You're gonna love her; she's one of the sweetest people you'll ever meet. And she finally got her a man that treats her like she deserves to be treated. I'm thrilled for her."

"That's great." Roland eyed Desiree. "What about *you*, though?"

Desiree looked at him, confused. "What you mean, what about me?"

"Do *you* have a man like that?"

"Are you trying to ask me if I'm seeing other people? Because I haven't been."

"Okay, maybe I need to be more clear." Roland crossed the room and stood right in front of her, looking into her expressive brown eyes. "Am *I* your man, Desiree?"

Temporarily stumped, Desiree's mouth opened, but nothing came out. He had caught her totally off guard with that.

"Umm..."

"What's the problem?"

"I wasn't expecting this conversation."

"Some of the best things come unexpectedly."

"Roland..."

"I told you I was trying to actually get to know you. I didn't mean that casually. Are we not on the same page? If not, let me know."

Desiree looked at him, and his eyes were serious but still held a tenderness that displayed how much he was into her. She felt that *something* again, the same *something* that she was feeling more and more whenever she was with him. She tried to suppress it, tried to ignore it, but it just wouldn't go away. Roland had her open, whether or not she wanted to admit it to anyone out loud. She thought she had done a pretty good job of keep him from getting too close, but now it was looking like he was tiring of her forced distance. And something told her that if she said the wrong thing right now, he might just walk out of her life and not look back.

She didn't want that.

"Roland, I..." She paused, her earlier chattiness disappearing. Words tumbled around each other in her mind. "I do like you. A *lot*."

He eyed her pointedly. "But?"

"I'm just...I guess I thought were just getting to know each other still, you know? Just taking things as they come and whatever happens, happens."

"Do you think we're really getting to know each other?"

She frowned slightly. "Of course. You don't?"

"Not really. I know your body better than anything else I know about you, other than maybe your career. You were pretty open on our first date, but since then you've pulled back on really opening up to me about anything real."

Knowing he was right, she just bit her lip nervously.

"And I've also noticed that you don't seem that interested in learning much about *me*, either," Roland continued. "You almost never ask me anything about my past or my *anything*. Most of our conversations are about some general stuff, or you."

"Roland, I'm sorry..."

"If you're not as into me as I'm into you, just say so...I'm a big boy. I can take honesty. What I can't and won't take, though, is being led on."

"I'm not leading you on!"

"I'm not interested in a fling, Desiree." Roland's voice was firm. "If that's all you want, just someone to bring you food and sex you down, then I'm the wrong dude. I'm into *you,* and not just for your body. So, sorry if it feels like I'm putting you on the spot, but I need to know where your head is at when it comes to us. 'Cause I just don't have the desire for something that's not going anywhere."

Taking a small step back, Desiree ran her hands down the back of her neck, running his words back in her mind. She knew that he wanted to know more about her because he had told her as much on their first date. And he was too attentive and considerate of her to only be interested in her casually. But she hadn't been expecting *this*. And she honestly didn't know how to take it.

"So...you're saying it's now or never, when it comes to us?" she verified after several moments.

"Not necessarily saying that. If you're not ready, you're not ready; I can't force you into a relationship with me. But just know that I *will* be looking for someone else that's on the same page I'm on, even if you and I decide to keep seeing each other until then."

Well damn.

"This really isn't a hard decision, Desiree. Either you want to be with me, or you don't. Either you're ready for me to walk out that door, or you're not. It's that simple."

Desiree didn't think it really was that simple for her, but she *was* sure of one thing: she definitely didn't want to lose Roland. She didn't want him with any other women. And the thought of him leaving and putting her behind him made her stomach hurt. And there was no need trying to blame that on the Chinese food.

It freaked her out to like someone as much as she liked Roland. But she'd rather be freaked out with him than without him.

"I definitely don't want you to leave," she finally said. She placed her hands on his chest. "I admit, I'm not the best at this kind of stuff. But I...I *do* want to be with you."

"Really?"

"Yes, really."

"Okay, so I'm gonna ask you this again," Roland said as he took one of her hands in his. "Am I your man, Desiree?"

Only hesitating for a split-second, Desiree replied, "Yes."

Chapter 9

IT WAS THE NIGHT OF the double date, and the two couples were sharing a booth at Hard Rock Café. It was a beautiful night in Atlanta and Desiree, Roland, Lovey, and Clay were all having a good time together, with everyone having clicked pretty much right off the bat. Lovey and Roland seemed to have a lot in common, and Desiree totally approved of Clay, who was clearly into her friend. She almost didn't mind hearing, *again*, the story of how Lovey and Clay became official.

"I swear, I never get tired of telling this story," Lovey admitted, grinning as she placed a hand on Clay's thigh. "I'm sure Desiree is probably tired of hearing it by now."

"Nah. But I'll let you know when I am," she replied with a wink. Everyone laughed.

"That *is* kinda dope, though," Roland said, taking a swig of his beer. "Were you planning on doing it in front of the waterfall like that, man?"

"Not really, no. I was actually going to ask her to be my woman when we got back to the room. But she was so..."

"Paranoid," Desiree coughed into her fist.

"Shut up! But I kinda was, though, I admit it." Lovey shrugged.

"And I could understand why, with the way I had left her hanging earlier. So I just went ahead and got it off my chest, which I wanted to do all day, anyway. It just turned out to be a perfect setting by the waterfall. I couldn't have planned it any better than that." Clay squeezed Lovey's shoulder lovingly.

"It was so romantic!" Lovey gushed. "I'll never forget that day as long as I live."

"The way my brother E.J. proposed to his wife was kind of similar to that...it was under fireworks on the Fourth of July, though."

"Oh wow, I bet that was beautiful!"

"Yeah, it was. Someone had recorded it on their phone, so now his wife can look at it whenever she wants. I think the times she's watched that is up to about five thousand now."

The four of them laughed. "I bet Lovey would be the same way if she had a video of her and Clay in front of that waterfall," Desiree stated, devouring one of her plump fried shrimp.

"Probably, yeah. I'm a sap, what can I say?" Lovey shrugged again with a smile.

"That's definitely not a bad thing," Clay assured her with a kiss to her temple. Lovey blushed and tweaked his chin, clearly smitten.

Desiree smiled at them, loving seeing her girl so happy. Clay seemed like a really good and genuine man, and anyone could see that he was just as taken with Lovey as Lovey was with him. They were affectionate but not in a way that made the people around them uncomfortable. They had the rapport and comfort level of a couple that had been together for years, and Desire caught herself kind of gazing at them a couple of times, almost in awe of their chemistry. Then she would snap out of it and wonder if anyone noticed.

Roland noticed. He saw the look Desiree had in her eyes when she looked at Lovey and Clay, and then how sheepish she was when she caught herself. He couldn't help but wonder what was behind that.

It had been a couple of weeks since he and Desiree became a couple, and he could tell that there were some moments when she just wasn't quite all the way there. He would ask her what was wrong and of course, she would insist it was nothing...usually she blamed her distractedness on work or something in her family, none of whom he had met yet. He sensed that Desiree liked to go at different paces...when it was just about the physical, she was full steam ahead. But when it came to matters of the heart, she was a little quicker to pump the brakes.

Her friend Lovey seemed to be the opposite, which is one reason why he found their friendship interesting. Lovey was a warm soul who wore her heart on her sleeve, and who seemed to have an innate welcoming aura about her. When they all arrived at the restaurant, she had greeted Roland with a big hug that had Roland feeling like he was meeting a long-lost family member instead of his girlfriend's BFF for the first time. He automatically liked her.

"Roland, what are you going to be doing for Thanksgiving?" Lovey asked, sipping her margarita.

"Oh, nothing much. Just chilling."

"By yourself? How come?"

Roland shrugged. "My brother is going to be out of town with his wife visiting the in-laws. My parents passed away years ago, so it'll just be me. I don't mind, though."

"Awww." Lovey looked genuinely concerned. "I am so sorry to hear that; about your parents, I mean. Mine passed away, too, about five years ago."

"At the same time?"

"Yeah. A car accident."

"Oh man...I hate to hear about that."

"Yeah, the holidays are usually kind of a rough time for me, but thankfully Desiree and her family have long since taken me in as one of their own, so I don't have to be by myself, stuffing my face and crying."

"That's a hell of a club to be in...I don't know what I would do if I lost both of my parents like that," Desiree chimed in.

"Me, either," Clay added.

"I'm just thankful that I was blessed enough to have people who were there for me," Lovey said, smiling at her best friend. "Desiree and her family have been a godsend."

Roland looked at Desiree with a smile, impressed. "Dig that."

Desiree blushed.

"You have any more siblings, Roland, other than your brother?" Lovey asked. "Let me know if I'm asking too many questions."

"Nah, you're good. I just have the one older brother."

"Yeah, it's just me and my sister Liz, too. She's a couple years older than me."

"You usually hang out with her on Thanksgiving?"

"Well actually, she sometimes goes with me to Desiree's house. Clay is coming...why don't you come, too?"

Roland's eyebrows shot up in surprise. "Oh nah...I haven't even met Desiree's family yet. I wouldn't want to impose like that—"

"Please, you're Desiree's man; there's no imposition," Lovey waved off his objection. "I just can't stand the thought of you being alone like that on Thanksgiving. You should be around family. Right, Desiree?"

Desiree would have kicked Lovey under the table if she thought she could get away with it. She hadn't planned on inviting Roland to her family's house for Thanksgiving, even after he had told her he was planning on spending the holiday alone. He had insisted that he was looking forward to the peace and quiet of being by himself, and she accepted that, inwardly relieved that she wouldn't have to worry about family introductions just yet. But now Lovey was ruining that by putting her on the spot like this.

"Uh, sure, yeah," she made herself say. "You're more than welcome. Mama always cooks a ton of stuff and loves having a house full of people."

"And her cooking is awesome," Lovey added. "I'm gonna have to stop myself from gorging on her sweet potato pie."

"I haven't had some good sweet potato pie in forever," Clay said. "I'm already looking forward to all this home cooking."

"You won't be disappointed, believe me. Mama Elyse is a magician in the kitchen. Her cornbread dressing is enough to make you dance."

"Dressing has always been my favorite Thanksgiving side dish...my mama used to make some killer dressing." Roland gently bumped Desiree with his shoulder. "Do you get in the kitchen, too, babe?"

"Oh no," Desiree immediately shook her head. "I'm good at a lot of things, but cooking is not one of them."

"Come on, you can't be that bad," Clay replied.

"I mean, I've never made anyone sick or anything, but I won't be gracing Food Network any time soon, either."

"I don't know. They *do* have that *Worst Cooks of America* show on there," Lovey teased.

"Shut up!"

"Damn, babe, you're that bad?" Roland chuckled.

"No, I am not *that* bad. But thankfully, you didn't get with me for my cooking." She leaned over and pecked him on the lips.

"No disagreement there," Roland agreed with a wink.

Lovey grinned at them. She had been thrilled when Desiree told her that she and Roland were an official couple now, and she was impressed with Roland for basically telling her that he wasn't going to be her plaything. Desiree needed someone that wouldn't let her get her way all the time, but would still respect and pamper her. Lovey sensed that Roland just might be the one to do that.

Later that evening, the women were on the phone, discussing how the evening went.

"Girl, I *like* Clay!" Desiree informed.

"Do you, really?"

"Now, you know good and well I'm gonna tell you the real."

"Yeah."

"I think he's just the kind of man you need, girl; affectionate, considerate, charming..."

"Not to mention romantic, sexy, a fantastic lover..."

"Well, that's always a bonus." The women shared a laugh. "Where is he, by the way? Did he drop you off?"

"I'm at his place. He's in his office, doing some work. Is Roland over there?"

"Yeah, he's in the shower. We were gonna go to his place but the traffic over his way was ridiculous."

"I am so glad you two got together, D," Lovey said. "He seems like just the kind of man to balance you out."

Desiree raised a curious brow. "Meaning?"

"You know how you're kinda outspoken and can be rather wild at times. Roland seems like the laid-back, cool-headed kind of man that also won't take any mess. You need someone like that...someone that lets you be you but will check you when he needs to."

"I must say, I *was* a little impressed when he just told me to my face that he wasn't trying to just be my personal sex and food deliveryman. And I knew that if I didn't come correct, he'd leave my ass standing there. So I really had no choice."

"And *why* didn't you feel like you had a choice?" Lovey goaded.

"Girl..."

"Come on, I just wanna hear you say it out loud."

"Don't actions speak louder than words? Isn't that what folks always say?"

Lovey found it amusing how difficult it was for Desiree to just admit that she was feeling Roland. Amusing, but sad. "You have no problem going on and on when you're tired of somebody. Look at all that fussing you did about Tobias. But you can't do the same when you actually like someone?"

"Gushing is for blood and that candy with the juice in the middle."

"And for amazing orgasms."

"Fast ass."

"Whatever! I just don't get why this is so hard for you, that's all."

Sighing, Desiree ran a hand over her pulled-back natural hair and glanced towards the bathroom. She could still hear the shower running. "Fine," she grunted. "I like the man. More than I've liked anyone in years."

"Now, was that so hard?"

"Shut up. In fact, I like him so much that I almost don't mind you putting me on the spot like you did."

"What are you talking about?"

"About Thanksgiving? I hadn't exactly planned on inviting him."

"I don't see why not. He was gonna be all by himself on a day where he should be around loved ones. Plus, you'd be just about the only one there without somebody."

"Girl, since when has that bothered me? That bothers *you*."

"Well, thankfully that's not an issue this year. And hopefully next year and the year after that."

"I'm glad Clay is able to come. And you're right, I *don't* really like the thought of Roland being by himself on Thanksgiving, either, even though he had insisted he was fine with it. I was just gonna leave it at that, but then you nagged him 'til he agreed..."

"I did not!"

"I'll be honest with you, though, girl...I'm a little hesitant to introduce him to the family so soon," Desiree admitted, lowering her voice as she glanced towards the bathroom again. "You know it's been years since I've been serious about anyone."

"Yeah, I know. Not since—"

"You don't have to say his name," Desiree forcefully interjected. "We both know who the bastard was."

She still won't talk about him, Lovey mused silently. Opting to leave the sore subject alone as she usually did, she simply replied, "Yes, we do."

AS DESIREE AND ROLAND'S relationship continued, Desiree found herself falling deeper and deeper for him, despite her best efforts not to. She was getting increasingly used to spending her free time with him, and without even realizing it, looked forward to seeing him every night. The feeling of 'coming home' to someone was foreign to her, but if she was honest with herself, she liked it.

Roland treated Desiree better than any other man she had been with. He paid attention to her, listened to her and respected her, and was always putting her wants and desires first. At the same time, though, he didn't shy away from telling her when she was wrong. Desiree might have acted stubborn during those times because that wasn't something she was used to, but in all honesty, it was a huge turn-on. She liked getting her way, but she also didn't like weak men. And Roland was far from that.

But the closer the two of them got, them more apprehensive Desiree became. True, she liked Roland a lot, but parts of her still wished she didn't. She didn't *want* to be as into Roland as she was, and the powerlessness she felt over that was frustrating. She didn't know what it was about him that made him so different than other men, but she sometimes wished she could conjure up the courage she usually had with everyone else to keep a certain amount of distance. But Roland had already made it clear that he wasn't going for that.

And of course, now that she was in an official relationship, Roland was the number one topic of conversation whenever she talked to her friends or family. One of the first questions out of their mouths always had to do with Roland, and Desiree found herself becoming aggravated by that. It's not like her relationship with Roland was the only thing she had going on, or the only thing in her life worth discussing. But that's all folks seemed to want to talk about.

"Is Roland over there?" Elyse asked her one day.

Rolling her eyes, Desiree shook her head into the phone. "No, he's not."

"Where is he?"

"I don't know, Mama. I don't track the man's every move."

"I certainly know where *my* man is when he isn't here."

"Mama...you and daddy are married. Plus, I keep telling you that your relationship isn't typical."

"Hell, yours isn't, either. The fact that you're in one at all isn't typical."

"That's hilarious."

"I like this man already. Can't wait to meet him next week. I already met Clay."

Desiree frowned slightly. "What? When??"

"Lovey stopped by and he was with her. He's such a sweetheart; those two are getting married, mark my words."

"I'm sure Lovey would be on top of the world if they did. I've never seen her so happy."

"She definitely deserves it." Elyse paused. "What about you? You happy, too?"

"Sure, yeah." Desiree hoped she sounded convincing enough. "Business is going really well, so I'm over the moon about that."

"Is that all you're *over the moon* about?"

"Isn't that enough?"

"That's plenty, but you have a good man now, too."

"Okay? A man doesn't determine my entire demeanor. I was good before Roland and I'll be good after him."

"Oh, so you're gonna try to act like you wouldn't care if he weren't part of your life anymore, huh?"

"I won't say I wouldn't care, but I'd keep right on rollin'. No man is gonna stop this show."

"Still stubborn as hell, huh?" Elyse sucked her teeth. "All right then, girl. Hopefully you won't have to eat those words."

"IT'S ABOUT DAMN TIME! I've been trying to call you all day!"

Lovey took her time responding; she only answered because Desiree had already left her several messages and she didn't put it past her to show up at her place.

"Sorry."

"What's the matter with you?"

"I'm just a little bummed. Clay had to break our date tonight to go out of town for work."

"Aww...I'm sorry to hear that. Remind me what it is he does, again?"

"He's a mechanical engineer."

"Oh yeah. Well girl, you know he has to travel for work sometimes."

"I know. I was just really looking forward to seeing him tonight."

"Well, when is he coming back? I'm sure y'all will meet up then."

"A few days."

"Days? Is he gonna be gone for Thanksgiving?"

"No, he says he'll be back before then."

"Well that's good."

"Hmph."

"Cheer up, girl. Hey, why don't you come out with me tonight?"

"I thought you had a date with Roland."

"Yeah, I do. You can join us."

"Oh no," Lovey protested immediately. "I'm not tagging along on your date, D. Forget that."

"Why not?"

"Because I don't want to be a third wheel. And I'm willing to bet Roland wouldn't want me there, either."

"Girl, please, he wouldn't mind," Desiree insisted, although she knew Lovey was probably right. But Desiree wanted Lovey there because she was getting the sense that Roland was getting more serious about them, and Desiree wasn't ready for the conversations Roland was trying to have. She needed Lovey to be her buffer, because she knew Roland wouldn't get into all of that with her there.

"He would."

"Oh, so you think you know my man better than me?"

"What a convenient time for you to start claiming him out loud."

"What?"

"You've never referred to him as 'your man' before. At least, *I* haven't heard it."

Desiree paused, realizing she was right. "Look, whatever. All I know is you don't need to be over there all down and depressed, eating stuff you're gonna be kicking yourself about later. Just come out with us. Otherwise I'll just spend all night worrying about how you're doing."

"You don't have to worry about me, D. I'm not that fragile. Yeah, I'm a little bummed but it's not like I'm gonna try to kill myself."

"Still. We're gonna go see a movie; you love movies."

"Oh yeah, what am I supposed to do, sit in between you? Hey, maybe I can hold the bucket of popcorn that you two can take turns reaching in."

"Lovey..."

"Or would you prefer I sit on an entirely different side of the theater altogether and just meet you two at the car afterwards?"

"Will you stop? I'm trying to tell you that Roland will not mind, especially after I tell him what the deal is."

"Well, see, that's another thing; I don't want him to know all that."

"What's the big deal?"

"Look, I'm just gonna do some laundry, look over some stuff for work, and go on to bed. I have to get up early tomorrow, anyway."

"Uh, *yawn*! Look, I'm putting my foot down...you are coming out with me and Roland. That's it."

"So, what, you're gonna come over here and drag me out of my apartment?" Lovey asked amusingly.

"If I need to."

Sighing, Lovey finally relented. "Okay, fine. I'm still not thrilled with tagging along on your date, but if you're *sure* Roland won't have a problem with it..."

"I'm sure he won't have a problem with it. It'll be fine."

ROLAND HAD A PROBLEM with it.

He liked Lovey, but he couldn't say he was thrilled with Desiree informed him that she had invited her friend with them on their date that night. There were some things that he planned to talk to Desiree about, and now he wouldn't be able to. But he felt he'd look like an ass if he refused, especially when Desiree told him that Lovey was feeling a little down.

"I just don't want her to be by herself tonight," Desiree had told him. "She was really looking forward to her date with Clay and he had to cancel at the last minute."

"Hmm. I don't mean to sound insensitive or anything, but she's depressed *just* because her date got cancelled?"

"She's not *depressed*; just bummed."

"And she asked if she could go with us tonight?"

Desiree hesitated slightly. "No...I suggested it. Had to twist her arm to get her to agree, though. I just want to cheer her up."

"Well, why don't y'all just hang out tonight and we'll hook up another time?"

"Because I still want to see you. We can all have fun together. Plus, you two can spend some time, get to know each other better..."

Roland wanted to object, but didn't know how to do so without sounding incredibly selfish. "You're a good friend, huh?"

"I try to be. She's certainly an awesome friend to me."

Softening slightly, Roland acquiesced. He would just talk to Desiree another time. "Okay, fine."

CLAIMING TO HAVE AN early meeting the next morning, Desiree insisted on driving her own car to the movies instead of Roland picking her up. In truth, she didn't want to be in a confined space with Roland and give him opportunity to bring up their relationship. She thought things were going fine between them as they were, and didn't see the need to discuss anything else. She had agreed to be his woman. They were together. What more did he want?

Roland arrived at the movie theater and sighed as he parked his car. Part of him wanted to just back out of this evening and let Desiree and Lovey hang out by themselves; he didn't see the point of him being there. But because Desiree asked him to, he still showed up. He couldn't help but be a little annoyed at the thought of Lovey joining them, and when he saw Lovey, he could tell she didn't really want to be there, either. He could see the apologetic look in her eyes when she walked over to him, and he felt his attitude cool off a little. She had no doubt succumbed to Desiree's persistent persuasions just like he had.

"Hi," she greeted him, somewhat shyly.

"Hey, Lovey."

"Where's Desiree?"

"Running a little behind. She should be here in a couple minutes."

"Oh." Lovey played with the bracelet on her wrist. "Look, I'm sorry for crashing your date like this..."

"You don't have to apologize..."

"No, I do. You probably won't admit it to me, but I'm sure you don't want me here."

Roland didn't want to say she was right. "It's fine, really."

"I can make up an excuse and leave. Just tell Desiree I was coming down with a fever or something."

"Then she'll be over there trying to take care of you. You know it and I know it."

"Yeah, true," Lovey admitted with a small smile. "Well, I'll just tell her something else. I'll say my sister needs me for something."

"Lovey, for real, you don't have to do all that," Roland insisted. Seeing how sincere Lovey was being made him want her to stay. Or at least, convince her that she didn't feel like she had to leave. "You're already here. This is supposed to be a real funny movie; let's just all enjoy ourselves. I'm sure this'll cheer you up."

"Ugh," Lovey groaned disgustedly. "I hate she even told you that. She's acting like I was on suicide watch or something. I would've been perfectly fine by myself."

"She was just concerned about you, that's all."

Lovey looked at him. "You really are a good man. I hope Desiree appreciates that."

I hope she does, too. "Thank you, for saying that."

"I'm gonna go ahead and get my ticket. Which movie is it y'all are seeing? I can see something else."

Roland couldn't help but chuckle. Lovey seemed like she could be as stubborn as Desiree, but in a good way. Her stubbornness was to help or accommodate others, while Desiree's was usually just to get her way.

"We're seeing *Girl's Trip*. And I already got our tickets." He held them up.

"Oh, no," Lovey quickly shook her head. "You're not paying for mine, too. How much do I owe you?" She reached into her purse.

"You don't owe me anything."

"Roland, I can't let you do that."

"It's already done. So don't try to give me anything 'cause I'm not gonna take it."

Not being able to resist a smile, Lovey shook her head. "Okay, fine. Thank you; I appreciate it."

"No problem."

"Snacks are on me, though."

Roland lifted his hands in surrender, smiling. "If you insist."

The two of them continued to talk, falling into an effortless rapport. When Desiree finally showed up, Roland was a little surprised to realize he had temporarily forgotten about her.

"Sorry I'm late, y'all," Desiree greeted breathlessly, giving both of them a hug. She gave Roland a quick peck on the lips. "Time just got away from me."

"Glad you made it. The movie doesn't start for another ten minutes or so, so you're good." Roland glanced at his watch.

"You okay?" Lovey asked Desiree, noting her somewhat frazzled appearance.

"Yeah, girl, I'm good. Just rushing around, as usual. Did you get our tickets?" she asked Roland.

"Yep."

"Okay, then, let's go. I've gotta stop in the bathroom first."

The three of them entered the theater and after a quick stop at the concession stand, Lovey and Roland went ahead to the theater to claim some seats. Lovey automatically left the seat in between her and Roland for Desiree, who scurried in right as the movie was starting.

The movie was hilarious, and the three of them were almost brought to tears from laughing so hard. Desiree was glad to see Lovey's spirits lifted, and surprisingly, so was Roland. Without even realizing it, he had joined in Desiree's mission to cheer Lovey up. He just hated the thought of someone as sweet and nice as her feeling down.

Desiree excused herself a couple of times to go to the bathroom, and she wondered if Roland could sense that she was hiding something. She wasn't proud of it, but the reason she was late and looked so frazzled when she finally arrived was because she had been cyber-sexing with Cornell. She had totally lost track of time and when she happened to look at the clock on her laptop, she realized she was supposed to have left twenty minutes earlier. She hurriedly ended her video call with Cornell, threw some clothes on, and slapped on one of her wigs as she rushed out the door. Desiree didn't consider cyber-sexing cheating, especially since it was with someone she had no intention of meeting in person, but she also wasn't stupid enough to tell Roland the truth about what had made her late.

When the movie was over, the three of them walked outside, still talking about what a great movie it was. Lovey's mood had done a complete one-eighty from where it was when she arrived.

"I had such a good time; thank y'all," Lovey said appreciatively. "I might have to come see this again with Clay."

"I'm glad you're feeling better, girl," Desiree said, putting an arm around her. "You can hang with us anytime."

"Girl, forget it. I'm not intruding on you all's time again," Lovey immediately protested. "But I do appreciate tonight."

Roland was glad Lovey had shut Desiree's suggestion down. While he had sincerely enjoyed Lovey's company, he would still much rather be one-on-one with Desiree.

"I'm gonna head on home," Lovey informed them. "Y'all enjoy the rest of your night."

"Actually, I need to run, too," Desiree said. "I've gotta go over to Diamond's before I head home."

"Everything okay?"

"Probably. You know Diamond can be kind of a drama queen, though. She just insisted that I need to come over there tonight."

"You want me to go with you?" Roland asked her.

"No, no, I'm good." Desiree hoped she hadn't been too quick to answer that. "Like I said, it's probably nothing. I'll let you know when I make it home. Why don't you see Lovey home, though? Make sure she gets there all right?"

"There's no need for that," Lovey insisted. "I stay ten minutes from here."

"So what? That doesn't mean he can't see you home."

"I'm sure he doesn't wanna do that. I'll be perfectly fine, D."

"Girl, please. Roland doesn't mind; do you, Roland?"

Feeling put on the spot, again, Roland made himself shake his head. "No, I don't mind."

"See there?" Desiree smiled triumphantly at her friend.

"You put him on the spot, Desiree. What else was he supposed to say?"

"I did not put him on the-"

"Chill out, y'all...I don't mind," Roland insisted, though somewhat obligingly. He had hoped to be able to get some alone time with Desiree so they could talk, but evidently that wasn't going to happen that night. He could only hope that Desiree wasn't avoiding being alone with him on purpose.

Lovey still looked hesitant, but she finally relented. "Okay, fine. Thanks, Roland."

"Yeah, thanks, Roland," Desiree repeated flirtatiously, sliding her arms around his waist and giving him a kiss.

Roland leaned close to Desiree's ear so Lovey couldn't hear. "I'm not gonna front, though; I *was* hoping to get you all to myself at least for a little while tonight."

"I'll make it up to you," Desiree whispered, winking at him. Before he could respond, she backed away. "I'm gonna head on over to Diamond's and see what she wants."

"Text me when you get in," Lovey instructed.

"And call me," Roland added.

"Will do." Desiree blew kisses at them both and hurried to her car.

Roland watched her for a moment before turning to Lovey. "You ready? I'll just follow you, if you're cool with that."

"Roland, you really don't have to bother. We can just tell Desiree you saw me home."

"No need to lie when I can just do it."

"But-"

"You said yourself you only stay a few minutes away. It's really no big deal. And anyway, I wouldn't be much of a gentleman if I didn't see you home." He looked right into her hesitant eyes. "I don't mind, Lovey. For real."

"Okay. I do appreciate it."

"I know you do. That's another reason I don't mind doing it."

Blushing slightly, Lovey averted her eyes. Roland couldn't help but smile at how shy she looked all of a sudden.

"Well..." Lovey grabbed her keys out of her purse. "Let's go, then."

MEANWHILE, DESIREE was just glad that Lovey had been there to deflect some of Roland's attention.

She hadn't been lying when she said her sister wanted her to come over that night. But truth be told, Desiree could have gotten out of that if she really wanted to. She just wasn't ready to be alone with Roland and have that dreaded where-is-this-relationship-going talk.

"Not today," she muttered, choosing not to acknowledge that she wouldn't be able to avoid it forever.

Chapter 10

THANKSGIVING HAD FINALLY arrived, and Desiree was already stressing.

I love you.

Let's talk about that tonight.

That was the text Roland sent her early that morning, and Desiree was admittedly freaking out. That had been the *last* thing she was expecting, and she wasn't ready for it.

How was she even supposed to respond to that? She liked Roland a lot, but she didn't think she loved him. Would he get upset if she told him that? Would he end things with her?

"This is exactly why I don't do relationships," she muttered to herself.

She tried to push it out of her mind but it was futile. That 'I love you' kept flashing across her eyes like a neon sign. Why did he have to spring this on her?

Needing to talk to someone, she snatched up her phone and called Lovey. But the minute Lovey answered, Desiree could tell her friend had problems of her own.

"What's wrong?" she asked immediately.

"I can't find Clay," Lovey responded worriedly.

"What do you mean, you can't find him?"

"I mean I haven't heard from him since yesterday morning. He isn't answering any of my calls. He hasn't posted anything online. I'm really worried."

"Wow...girl, I'm sure there's a perfectly good reason for that."

"Like what? That he's dead?"

Taken aback, Desiree responded, "No! I just meant that maybe something came up and he hasn't had time to call you yet, that's *all*."

"How long does it take to send a text, though? I just don't have a good feeling about this. It feels like Evan all over again."

"Stop that. You know Clay and Evan are nothing alike. Hasn't Clay proven himself to you in the past few months?"

"I *thought* he had, but-"

"Then don't let yourself talk your mind into believing something your heart really doesn't," Desiree gently interjected. "Clay is a good dude. If he hasn't gotten in touch with you, I'm sure there's a good reason that he'll explain when he calls you. And I'm *sure* he'll call."

"I hope you're right." Lovey's voice was shaky.

Pushing her own issues aside for the time being, Desiree knew she just needed to be there for her friend.

"Look girl...I know it's gonna be easier said than done, but why don't you just try to think positively, get dressed, and I'll come get you so we can go have a good family dinner at Mama's."

"I don't really feel up to it, D. You know I love your family but I'm just not gonna be very good company until I know Clay is all right."

"You can't sit alone in your apartment on Thanksgiving worrying yourself to death when you can be around family that love you. I'm not gonna let you do it."

Lovey sighed. "Desiree..."

"I'm serious. I know Clay is important to you but he is *not* the only thing you have to be thankful for. Try focusing on the other great things in your life; Clay will turn up. I'm sure of it."

"It's not like I'm just being dramatic for the sake of it. I'm sincerely worried. Would you be this casual about it if Roland fell off without a word?"

Desiree wanted to say yes, but she didn't want to come off as cold. And she wasn't sure that answer was totally true, anyway. Even though she was starting to feel a little smothered by Roland, she certainly didn't want anything to happen to him. "Probably not. But I wouldn't just hole myself up in my apartment, waiting on him to call. I'd keep myself busy."

"Well, once again, you and I are two very different people."

"Yes, we are. But I still maintain that you should be around family right now, and you already told Ma you were coming. You know she'll trip if you don't show up."

Lovey paused, knowing she was right. "I guess."

"And I'm sure Clay knows how much today means to you. Just text him the address to Mama's house and he'll show up when he can. In the meantime, we can get our grub-on, watch some football, and you can hang out with my nieces and nephew. You always love that."

Lovey knew Desiree was going to make every case possible to get her over to Elyse's house. And truth be told, she *didn't* want to miss it. Thanksgiving was her favorite holiday, and she always looked forward to spending it with Desiree and her family. She told herself to take Desiree's advice and think positively; Clay would contact her soon enough.

"All right," she finally acquiesced. "I guess you're right, in that I shouldn't sit in here and stress over where Clay is. I'm still worried, but I'm sure being around family will help me feel at least a little better."

"Damn right, it will. So go ahead and get ready and I'll be over there to get you in a couple of hours."

"I can drive myself, Desiree. You don't have to baby me."

"I am not babying you. I just want to us to go together. And why drive two cars when we can just take one?"

"What about Roland? Is he still coming?"

"As far as I know."

"Is he picking you up? Because if he is, forget it; I'm driving my own car and there's nothing you can say to change my mind."

"Girl, he's coming over there a little later. He has some stuff to do first."

"Oh okay. Well, I guess I'll see you in a little while, then."

"I'll text you when I'm on the way."

"Okay. And D.?"

"Yeah?"

"Thank you for caring about me so much."

Desiree smiled. "Always."

What Desiree didn't disclose to her friend was that she and Roland actually *had* planned to ride together to her parents' house, but now she was able to use Lovey as a convenient excuse again to get out of that. She had no doubt that Roland wouldn't be happy about it; she had been deftly avoiding them being alone together, but she was especially hesitant to be in close quarters with him after that text he sent her earlier. She was simply not ready for that conversation, but she also feared his reaction when she told him so.

To avoid confrontation, she opted to text Roland about the change in plans instead of calling him, knowing she was punking out but not caring. She sent him her mother's address and made herself add that she was looking forward to seeing him later.

Lovey tried to keep herself from checking her phone every few minutes and just enjoy the family time, but it was admittedly difficult. As much as she tried to think positively, she just couldn't help but be worried about Clay. It did provide her some solace to notice a post she had missed from him on Facebook from a few days prior stating how much he was looking forward to their first Thanksgiving together.

"Do I need to take that phone from you?" Elyse jokingly asked, even though Lovey didn't put it past her to do just that.

"No ma'am; I'm sorry," Lovey apologized for the tenth time since she and Desiree had arrived. "I'm just a little preoccupied."

"Believe me, we know," Desiree's sister Dori commented. "That phone has been glued to your hand since you got here."

"I tried to tell her to chill out but you know our girl," Desiree quipped with a wink. They were all in the kitchen, helping put the finishing touches on dinner.

"Baby, I know you're worried; hell, I'd be worried sick, too, if I couldn't get in touch with Darius," Elyse sympathized as she took a huge pan of dressing out of the oven. "But you are going to make yourself sick worrying about something you can't control."

"Yeah, girl, Clay is a good dude...he wouldn't leave you hanging like that," Desiree's youngest sister, Diamond, chimed in.

"When did *you* meet Clay?" Desiree asked her.

"I was over here that day Lovey brought him to meet Mama and Daddy. My B.S radar didn't go off once."

"Yeah, I haven't met him yet, but I've heard nothing but good things," Desiree's other sister Dana added. "If you haven't heard from him, I'm sure there's a perfectly legitimate reason."

"And this is coming from the cynic," Desiree teased.

"I am not a cynic. I'm just a realist. We all know most men aren't worth doo-doo. But thankfully, we've all been blessed with some good ones. I know *I* was."

"Yes, we all know Clarence worships the ground you walk on," Elyse commented, referring to Dana's husband. "You had that man running up behind you like some kind of lost puppy for months and months."

"Well hell, he had to prove himself," Dana defended. "I wasn't gonna make it easy for him. But he eventually showed me he was for real. Now I can't get enough of him, either. With his hot self."

Lovey couldn't help but smile at this. That was the same way she felt about Clay, and she had to fight the tears she felt stinging her eyes. She missed her man. Why hadn't Clay called yet??

Desiree was trying hard to bite her tongue. It was an unspoken thing among the family that while Clarence was a good man, he was also, to put it nicely, not very attractive. Dana must have really been in love to consider him *hot*.

The women continued to talk in the kitchen, with everyone trying to assure Lovey that she had nothing to worry about. Lovey appreciated their support and loved them all for it, but she wasn't as convinced that everything was fine like they were. She didn't know what, but she knew something was wrong. Either something bad happened, or she had been extremely wrong about the kind of man he was. She almost didn't know which possibility was worse.

A little while later, it was time to eat. Roland still hadn't arrived, having texted Desiree that he was running behind. Lovey was in only slightly better spirits, having become distracted by listening to Desiree and her sisters banter back and forth, as they usually did. Her sister Liz was there but she was pretty quiet, and Lovey knew why. She was probably the one person who thought that Clay was just standing Lovey up, but didn't want to say it.

Darius, Desiree's father, blessed the food and everyone was just starting to dig in when Lovey's phone finally rang. Lovey practically knocked her chair over as she stood up, quickly excusing herself so she could take the call in another room. Desiree and Liz looked after her, then at each other with concerned but hopeful expressions.

"Clay?" Lovey exclaimed once she had retreated into the living room. "Where in the world are you?? I've been worried sick!"

"Baby, I am so, so sorry," Clay immediately apologized. His voice was thick with sincerity. "I've been wanting to call you..."

"I'm glad to hear you're all right, but I would've at least appreciated a text or something before now," Lovey gently scolded.

"I know, babe...I'm just now getting to where I can get good reception. It's been a crazy past twenty-four hours."

Lovey sighed, telling herself to calm down. She felt a lot better now that she had heard his voice. "We can talk about it later. Just as long as I get to finally see you. Are you on your way? We were all just sitting down to dinner."

Clay hesitated. "I'm afraid not, babe."

"What? Why not? Where are you?"

Hesitating again, Clay finally responded meekly, "Memphis."

"*Memphis??*" Lovey shrieked before she could stop herself. "Why are you in *Memphis*?? You said you'd be *here*!"

"Lovey, I had every intention of being there, but my boss called me late last night and told me I had to get on the first flight out to Memphis to handle an emergency at one of our plants. I couldn't very well say no."

"Why didn't you let me know that before now??"

"Everything was happening so fast, I really didn't get a chance to. I've been nonstop since I left. And like I mentioned, the reception out here has been terrible. I'm literally just now getting a chance to let you know what's up."

Lovey sank down onto the nearby couch, not believing her ears.

"I thought I might be able to wrap everything up and still get back there in time for dinner, but it's taking longer than expected," Clay continued. "I won't be back until probably sometime tomorrow. And when I do get back, you're the first person I want to see."

Lovey sniffed, not bothering to stop the tears this time.

"Lovey? Are you mad?" Clay asked after a few silent moments. "I wish I could express just how sorry I am..."

"No, I'm not mad," Lovey finally made herself say. "I get that it couldn't be helped. I'm just...disappointed. I was really looking forward to today."

"Believe me, I want to be there as much as you want me to be there," Clay assured her. "I did *not* want to come out here; I'd much rather be there with you. Please tell me you believe that."

"Yeah. I believe you."

"I'll make this up to you, babe, I promise."

Making herself speak again, Lovey simply replied, "Okay."

"I hate that I've disappointed you like this, Lovey."

Not knowing what to say to this, Lovey just sniffed.

"I'm gonna give you a call tonight," Clay promised. "By then I should know what time I'll be getting in tomorrow."

"All right."

"I'm sorry, again."

"I know, Clay. It's okay. I understand."

"That's why I love you, right there. Most women would be flipping out right now but I appreciate you being so understanding."

Lovey shrugged, her shoulder feeling like it weighed a ton. "I try."

After another minute of somewhat-strained conversation, they ended the call. Lovey wanted bury her face in the couch cushions and bawl her eyes out, but she made herself get up and head back towards the dining room. But when she heard all the happy people in there, including Desiree's sisters' husbands, she knew she needed to get out. She couldn't be around happy couples right then.

She eased out the front door, quietly closing it behind her. As soon as she stepped outside, her face crumbled. Scurrying off the front porch and around the side of the house, she let the heartbroken tears fall freely. Knowing it would be only a matter of time before someone came looking for her, she managed to send a quick text to Desiree, letting her know she needed a minute and would be right back. As much as she tried to remind herself that at least the reason for Clay's disappearance wasn't as bad as she had initially thought, that he actually *did* have a valid reason, it didn't do much to assuage her disappointment.

Roland pulled up, parking a little ways down the street due to all the cars in the driveway. He checked his watch as he got out of the car, grabbing the flowers he had brought for Desiree and her mother, Elyse. He almost didn't see Lovey leaning against the side of the house; he was about to walk right past her when he heard sniffling and soft sobs.

"Lovey?" he called out, concerned, heading over to her.

Immediately embarrassed, Lovey turned away. It was then that she hated that she let Desiree talk her into riding with her; if she had driven her own car, she'd be across town by now.

"Roland, hey," she said, her head still turned. She wiped her eyes in what she hoped was a casual-enough fashion. "Everyone is in the house; you can go on in."

Roland ignored her statement. "What's wrong?"

"Nothing."

"Clearly it is."

"I don't know what you mean."

"Lovey, I know we don't know each other that well, but I can tell already you're not the best liar," Roland informed her, stepping around so he could see her face. She tried to duck her head, but he could tell she was crying. "I'm not trying to get in your business, but I'll listen if you need to get something off your chest."

"I appreciate it, Roland, but I'll be okay. I just...needed a minute."

"I don't really feel right about leaving you out here crying by yourself," Roland persisted.

"I'm fine. I'm just gonna call an Uber and go home...I don't feel up to being around a bunch of people right now."

"Something must have *just* happened or else I imagine you wouldn't have shown up today at all. Should I go get Desiree?"

"No!" Lovey quickly responded. "No, thank you. I love my girl but she'll probably just think I'm being silly. And I just, I can't hear that right now."

"Your feelings are valid, Lovey, whatever they may be," Roland assured her. "It's not silly to have a heart, especially one of gold like I can tell you have."

Lovey couldn't help but be touched by that. She dared to look up at Roland, and felt warmed by the sincerity in his face. He looked genuinely concerned. "Thank you for that, Roland."

"Did that make you feel better? Because that was probably the corniest statement I've ever made," Roland admitted with a smile. "I meant it, though."

Not being able to help it, Lovey laughed. Some of the weight she had felt just moments before was slightly eased.

"It's good to see you smiling," Roland said, smiling himself. "I'm still willing to listen, if you wanna talk."

Lovey started to politely decline, not wanting him to think she was some kind of drama queen, but realized she wanted to vent to someone who would be somewhat impartial. She and Roland didn't know each other that well, so he wouldn't be as biased as Desiree or Liz would be.

"Okay," she relented. "Long story short, Clay got called out of town on business last night and wasn't able to let me know about it until just a few minutes ago. I had no idea where he was or if he was all right. Turns out he won't be able to get back until tomorrow."

Roland just nodded, listening.

"I don't wanna be a crybaby about it," Lovey continued. "But I admit it; I'm disappointed. I was really looking forward to our first Thanksgiving together, and us spending time with my family. And I know I can get a little emotional-"

"You don't have to justify anything to me, Lovey. I can understand you being disappointed about something like that."

"You don't think I'm just being silly?"

"No, but even if I did, it wouldn't matter. You have every right to feel however you need to feel about it."

It was the first time anyone had ever told her anything like that. Desiree or Liz would no doubt be telling her to suck it up and get over it, because at least Clay had called and explained himself, and Lovey now knew what the deal was. And Desiree was always getting on to her for being in her feelings so much.

"You have no idea how refreshing it is to hear that from somebody."

"It's just the truth. You like flowers?"

"I love flowers."

"Here." He held out the bunch of purple calla lilies he had brought for Desiree.

Lovey shook her head, even though she thought they were beautiful. "No. Thank you, but I know you didn't bring those for me. I can't take Desiree's flowers."

"I got them out of habit. Desiree doesn't even like flowers. I'm sure you know that."

"True," Lovey admitted.

"I'd rather give them to someone that will actually appreciate them. Desiree would much prefer a box of Little Debbies."

Chuckling, Lovey nodded. "Also true."

"So please, take them."

Her smile widening, Lovey hesitantly took the flowers from him. She gave them a gentle sniff, feeling surprisingly better, however slightly. "Thank you, Roland. These will look great in my kitchen. And purple is actually my favorite color."

"Yeah? Looks like it was meant to be, then."

Blushing but not knowing why, Lovey turned her eyes back to the flowers. "Right."

"Ready to go back in?"

"Sure, I guess."

"If it'll help, you can have my dressing."

Not being able to help it, Lovey burst out laughing. Some of the tension in her body lifted and she suddenly realized how hungry she was; she had been so worried about Clay that she hadn't eaten a thing all day.

"I wouldn't even deprive you of Mama Elyse's dressing, especially since you said dressing is your favorite. But I appreciate the thought. Believe me, once you have some, you won't want to share it."

"It's like *that*? Well, let's get on in there to it, then," Roland grinned, nudging her playfully as they turned to head into the house.

Everyone was still eating and talking when they reentered the dining room. When Desiree saw them come in together, her eyebrows raised slightly in surprise. She hadn't known Roland had arrived. She stood and went over to hug him, looking at Lovey in concern. She could tell she had been crying.

"Everything okay?" Elyse asked.

"Um, yeah, it is," Lovey responded, slightly embarrassed. She knew the fact that she had been crying was probably evident. "Turns out Clay got called out of town on business last night, so he won't be joining us today, unfortunately."

There was a collective chorus of 'Aww' and 'that's too bad,' and Lovey just nodded with a tight smile. Part of her still wished she had gotten that Uber home, but she figured there was no reason to mope around her apartment alone. The situation was what it was; there was nothing that could be done about it.

"It's okay, really," she made herself say. She placed the flowers on a nearby end table and went to go heat up her untouched plate of food. While she was in the kitchen, she heard Desiree introduce Roland to everyone.

A moment later, Liz came into the kitchen. "You all right, sis?"

"I'm fine."

"You're lying."

"Then why did you ask?"

"Just wanted to see what you were gonna say. Your eyes are still red, you know."

"Well, I was upset. I'm not thrilled about it but there's nothing I can do. At least I know what's going on now."

Liz hesitated before asking her next question. "Do you buy his explanation?"

Lovey looked at her sister. "Of course. Why wouldn't I?"

Holding up her hands, Liz replied, "I was just asking."

"Clay hasn't given me reason not to trust what he says. Getting called out of town on business happens with his job. The timing sucks, but it is what it is. He'll be back tomorrow."

"Well, I'm sorry he couldn't be here but I'm glad he's all right."

"Me too."

The two of them rejoined everyone in the dining room, and Lovey tried to put Clay out of her mind for the time being and enjoy this time with her family. Roland seemed to already get along with everyone, with him and Desiree's father Darius already hamming it up like old buddies.

Lovey ate and engaged in the conversation, but when she looked around the table at all the couples, she felt the somberness wash over her again. Desiree was peering at her in curious concern, and after a while, she motioned for her to join her in the living room.

As soon as they were alone, Desiree started digging for details. "Okay, what's *really* going on?"

"What do you mean?"

"Was what you said about Clay being out of town on business true or just something you made up to save face?"

"No, it's the truth."

"Aww, damn."

"It's okay."

"Really?"

"Yeah."

"Then why do you look like someone stole your last doughnut?"

"I'm really trying to snap out of it and just enjoy myself. If it wasn't for Roland, I'd have called an Uber by now. Speaking of Roland, those flowers he gave me were for you but he was trying to cheer me up and insisted I take them..."

"Good, 'cause you know I hate flowers. You'll enjoy those way more than I will. Mama sure loved the ones he gave her."

"He seems to be getting along with everybody."

"Oh yeah, girl, they love him already."

Lovey peered at her friend. "That's a good thing, right?"

"Yeah," Desiree replied unconvincingly. "But I'm more worried about *you*. Are you sure you're all right?"

"I can't say I'm walking on air right now but I'll be fine. Let's go back in there; I've already been away from the table as much as I've been at it today."

They rejoined everyone at the table. After everyone finished their dinner, the men corralled to the den to watch the game, the kids went to one of the spare bedrooms to watch a movie, and the ladies congregated in the kitchen, gossiping and cutting up the various cakes and pies for dessert. A lot of the conversation was about Roland and how awesome everyone thought he was, but to Lovey's dismay, a good chunk of the conversation was about Clay and his unfortunately-timed absence. The more she had to talk about it, the more Lovey's mood continue to sink. After a while, her desire to get out of there was more intense than it had been before Roland found her outside.

"You want some sweet potato pie, baby?" Elyse asked her. "You know it's your favorite."

"Thanks, Mama."

"Y'all better get what you're gonna get now, because you know once those men start wandering in here during timeouts and halftime, most of this stuff will be gobbled up."

"And you know they leave next to nothing," Dana added.

"I learned my lesson last year," Liz said, already wrapping a plate of pound cake in foil.

Everyone chuckled. "Yes, please fix some plates to take home; I do *not* want all this food in my refrigerator at the end of the night," Elyse implored. "After today, I'll be over it."

"But Daddy won't. You know he gets an attitude when we take everything," Desiree reminded her.

"I've already set aside plenty for him. Make sure you fix something for Roland to take with him."

Desiree balked. "If he wants something, he can come in here and fix it himself."

"I don't even know why you tried that, Ma. You know Desiree isn't gonna do anything like that," Diamond teased. "That's like catering to her man and that's *so* not her."

"Yeah, whatever," Elyse said with a wave of her hand.

Desiree sucked her teeth dismissively. She had never been one for catering to a man, unless it was her father. She saw Lovey piling food on two plates, presumably for herself and Clay. Desiree was glad that everyone liked Roland so much, but she knew that just meant that the questions and inquiries about their relationship would only increase. She was starting to feel like she needed a little break from Roland, just for a few days.

But that was something she was keeping to herself for now.

The ladies piled into the living room to watch some DVR'd episodes of *Insecure*. Usually Lovey loved this show, and she was sincerely trying to cheer up, but it just wasn't happening, not as much as she wanted to. She was putting on her game face because she didn't want to bring down the vibe with her sulking, but after a couple of hours, she just couldn't take it anymore. She just wanted to be alone.

Leaning over, she whispered to Desiree, "Hey, I think I'm gonna head on home."

Desiree looked at her knowingly. "Still not feeling any better, huh?"

"I'm sorry. I'm trying. It's not like I'm having a terrible time or anything; I'm just ready to go home."

Pursing her lips, Desiree sighed. She knew her friend was bummed but had tried her best to act like she wasn't.

"Okay. Gimme a minute." Desiree stood and padded to the den, where the men were hooping and hollering at the television. The Cowboys were playing the Seahawks and Desiree was pretty sure some money was on the line among some of the guys in the room. She got Roland's attention and motioned him over to her.

"What's up, babe?" he asked once he was close to her.

"Hey, do you think you could give Lovey a ride home? I hate to tear you away from the game, but she's ready to go and I have to stay here and help Mama clean up."

Roland hesitated. He didn't mind helping Lovey if she needed it, but he also sensed that Desiree was just trying to avoid being alone with him again. It wasn't lost on him how she had changed the plans of them coming together at practically the last minute, and did so in a text so he couldn't immediately question her or try to convince her otherwise. Something was going on with her, and he figured it had something to do with his declaration of love from that morning.

"Is there something you want to tell me, Desiree?" he asked.

She blinked. "What do you mean?"

"I told you I loved you and now you're freaking out."

"I'm not freaking out."

"Desiree, come on, let's be real. You think I don't notice how you've been avoiding being alone with me?"

Desiree looked away, feeling a little foolish for not giving him enough credit. Of course he would notice that. "Okay, we *do* need to talk. And we will. But right now, I really do need you to take Lovey home. She's trying but she just isn't having that good of a time."

Knowing the answer, Roland asked, "Did she ask you to ask me to take her?"

"No." Desiree bit her lip.

Sighing, Roland glanced back towards the television and glanced at his watch.

"I can ask her wait until the game is over," Desiree offered. She could tell he really didn't want to leave; he was getting along great with her father and brothers-in-law.

"That'll be a while. I can go ahead and take her, if she's ready to go. I'll just try to catch the rest of it when I get home, I guess."

"I really appreciate you doing this for her."

"You mean for *you*?"

Desiree started to respond, but nothing came out. So she just gave him a quick kiss on the lips and walked off.

Lovey was in the kitchen with Elyse, putting her foil-wrapped plates into plastic bags.

"Hey girl, Roland is gonna give you a ride home," Desiree informed Lovey.

Lovey frowned. "What? Why?? Isn't he watching the game?"

"Yeah, but he doesn't mind."

"Why are you leaving? We still have two more episodes of the season left," Elyse asked Lovey.

"I know, and I'm sorry, but I'm just drained and ready to get home," Lovey explained apologetically. "I've had such a good time, though."

Elyse eyed her. "Still upset about Clay?"

"No. Not really."

"Be real with me."

"Okay, a little bit," Lovey acquiesced. "I'm trying not to be, but I can't help it."

"It's okay; you're disappointed. That's understandable," Elyse replied, sliding an arm around her shoulders. "I hate that we couldn't cheer you up, though."

"Oh you did, Mama, believe me. I was a mess outside."

"And thanks to Roland, she didn't call an Uber and dip out without telling anybody," Desiree chimed in. "I want you to stay and forget about it, but I know that's easier said than done for you."

"And speaking of Roland, he is something else," Elyse commented. "Smooth, respectful, intelligent, fine as hell..."

"Ma!"

"Am I lying?"

Desiree couldn't help but grin. "Hell no, you're not lying. And believe me, you don't know the *half* of it!"

The three women giggled amongst themselves until Roland strolled into the room. Once they saw him, they tried to straighten their faces, and Roland figured he had been the topic of conversation. He chuckled and shook his head.

"Sorry to interrupt the girl talk," he winked. "You ready, Lovey?"

"Roland, you don't have to take me home. I know you were trying to watch the game. I should have just caught a ride with Liz when she left. I can call an Uber."

"I don't mind."

"Yeah, girl, no need in wasting money on an Uber when you have someone to take you," Desiree added.

"This is why I wanted to drive my own car, D."

"And if you had, you'd have left hours ago. I knew what I was doing."

"This really isn't necessary..."

"Why isn't it? You said you were ready to go."

"I was ready for *you* to take me home. You're the one that insisted on bringing me instead of me driving myself."

"Well, what's the difference? Roland said he doesn't mind taking you."

"Because you probably put him on the spot like you usually do."

"I did not."

"Ladies, come on," Roland interjected, knowing they would continue to go back and forth if he didn't intervene. He wanted to catch as much of the rest of the game as he could. "There's no need to fuss about it. Lovey, I really don't mind. If you're ready, I'm ready."

Not wanting to be any more of an inconvenience than she was already being, Lovey conceded and turned to hug Elyse. "Thanks for everything, Mama. And I'm sorry for being such a downer today."

"Don't worry about it. I understand. Call me."

"I will." She looked at Roland. "Let me go grab my purse and say goodbye to everyone and then we can go."

Several minutes later, Lovey and Roland left, and Desiree breathed an internal sigh of relief.

Chapter 11

LOVEY RODE IN THE PASSENGER seat of Roland's car, resisting the urge to apologize again for inconveniencing him. He had already made her promise not to apologize anymore, insisting he didn't mind giving her a ride. Still, Lovey felt bad. She wished she had put her foot down earlier with Desiree about driving her own car.

They rode in relative silence. Roland noticed that she was checking her phone a lot, and figured she was expecting a call or message from Clay. He figured she wasn't in the mood to talk, so he didn't try to engage her in conversation. He just asked the way to her apartment and left her to her thoughts.

When they were a few minutes away from her apartment, Lovey turned to look at Roland with a sigh. "Roland, I'm sorry."

"I thought we agreed you weren't going to apologize again."

"No, this time I'm apologizing for my behavior. You were nice enough to stop watching the game and take me home and I'm sitting over here being all antisocial."

"You're not in the mood to talk. I get it."

"But I shouldn't be like that. I've been sulking all day and I know I shouldn't. I'm going to see Clay tomorrow. And anyway, like Desiree said, he's not the only thing I have to be thankful for. I shouldn't have let his being out of town affect my whole day like I did."

"You being upset is totally understandable, Lovey. Especially with it happening the way it did, with it being last minute and not being able to let you know until today."

"You've been so kind and I appreciate it, but now I want you to be real with me," Lovey said. "What do you *really* think about all this?"

"I *have* been being real with you, Lovey. Everything I've said, I've meant; it wasn't just to appease you. And anyway, what I think is irrelevant."

"No, I mean, as a man, should I see any...*red flags* about Clay's explanation? What he said is totally probable and he's never given me any reason to doubt him..."

"But you want to know if he might be playing you?"

Lovey looked at him sheepishly, as if she didn't want to admit it out loud. "I hate myself for even asking. I've just been disappointed *so* much by men..."

"I understand that. And truth be told, you could convince yourself towards either side. This *could* be some kind of front for him creeping or he could really just be out of town on business like he said. Short of trailing or tracking him, we have no way of knowing."

Lovey nodded, looking at her hands. "True."

"If you trust him, take him at his word," Roland advised. "If he's been straight up with you so far, no need in doubting him now. Don't make the mistake of punishing him for what men in your past did to you."

Lovey surely didn't want to do that. She had seen several examples of women derailing perfectly good relationships because they couldn't let go of the pain from their past. It could be said that Desiree was doing this, because she still wasn't over the relationship she refused to talk about, and every man she dealt with paid for it, including Roland. Lovey realized that he might not be around too much longer, knowing Desiree's track record. The thought saddened her, because she really thought he was good for her friend.

"You're right," Lovey admitted. "I can't even disagree with you. Clay doesn't deserve this kind of skepticism."

"That doesn't mean be so in love that you're blind; definitely keep your eyes open and trust your gut," Roland continued. "I'm just saying don't try to create an issue if there isn't one just to justify your insecurities. And if you *do* sense something is wrong, just ask him about it. Not accuse; just ask. I've learned a while back that being straight up is the best way to go."

Lovey wanted to ask more questions because she sensed there was a story behind that mindset, but she didn't want to be nosey.

They pulled up to her apartment building and sat in the car talking for several minutes, with Roland temporarily forgetting about catching the rest of the football game. Lovey felt considerably better than she had when she left Elyse's house, appreciating Roland giving her the male perspective on things.

Suddenly remembering she was keeping Roland from getting back to the game, Lovey checked her watch.

"Let me get out so you can catch the rest of the game," she said. "Thank you again for the ride and the advice. I appreciate it."

"No problem." Roland did want to watch the remainder of the game, but he also realized he wasn't quite ready to leave Lovey's company yet; he was enjoying their conversation. She was refreshingly easy to talk to. And besides, he had a feeling he wouldn't be seeing Desiree that night, since she was so clearly avoiding him. "You wanna hang out for a while?"

Lovey looked at him, surprised. Her hand was already on the door handle. "Huh?"

"It's cool if you don't. I know you said you wanted to be alone."

Lovey *had* said that, but she could admit (to herself) that she was also enjoying Roland's company. He managed to lift her spirits more than once that day.

"Yeah, I did." She hesitated. "But I guess hanging out would be better than going in here and checking my phone every two minutes. Plus, you can just watch the rest of the game here."

"You sure? You don't have to say anything to me just to be polite or because you feel like you have to. Believe me, you won't hurt my feelings."

"No, I mean it." Lovey bit her lip. "But...let me call Desiree first."

Roland cocked a brow. "For what?"

"Just to let her know. I don't doubt your intentions or anything so please don't take it personally, it's just—"

"I get it; it's cool," Roland interjected, holding up a hand. "Go ahead."

Lovey called Desiree, who had no problem at all with Roland hanging out at Lovey's. In fact, she was all for it, sounding almost relieved. Lovey wondered what was behind that and fully planned on grilling her about it later.

"She's fine with it."

"Cool."

"Did you think that was silly?"

"I can understand it. You just wanna make sure everything is out in the open."

"Exactly."

"I can appreciate that, trust me."

Lovey wanted to ask him what he meant by that, but again refrained. She didn't want to get too deep into his business. "Good. Okay, let's go."

They went into Lovey's apartment and she told him to make himself comfortable while she took the plates she made for herself and Clay into the kitchen. She was a little nervous about her and Roland being alone in her apartment; not because she feared anything would happen between them but just because of how it might look, even though no one outside of Desiree knew about it. She would certainly tell Clay, if and when he called. She had nothing to hide.

Telling herself to chill out, she went back into the living room, where Roland was still standing with his hands in his pockets. The television was still off.

"What's wrong? How come you're not watching the game?" Lovey asked him.

"Was just waiting on you. Didn't really feel right turning on your TV and propping my feet up while you're in another room."

"I told you to make yourself comfortable. You didn't have to wait on me." Lovey grabbed the remote and turned on the television before handing it to him. "Here. I don't know what channel it's on."

Roland took the remote from her. "You're not gonna go hole up in your room and leave me out here by myself, are you?"

Laughing, Lovey shook her head. "No. I like football, though I'm sure not as much as you. I *am* gonna go change out of these jeans real quick, though. Be right back. Please, sit down. Kick your shoes off, if you want to. Get comfy."

"Aight."

Lovey went to go change into a t-shirt and some cozy pajama bottoms, and removed her earrings and bracelet. She couldn't resist checking her phone a couple of times, and tried to make herself stop obsessing over Clay. He said he would call, and she was sure he would as soon as he got a chance. Roland had been right when he said she shouldn't create an issue when there wasn't one.

She went to join Roland in the living room and they proceeded to watch the remainder of the game, which by then was in the fourth quarter. After the Seahawks wrapped up their victory over the Cowboys, Lovey asked if he wanted to watch a movie, and Roland readily agreed. He was enjoying himself and didn't really want to go back to his empty house.

"You hungry?" Lovey asked after a while. "I brought some leftovers from Mama's house."

"Man, I'm kicking myself for not getting me a to-go plate before I left," Roland stated, rubbing his stomach. He was sitting on the opposite end of the couch from Lovey, his shoes off and his legs stretched out in front of him. "But I thought those plates you brought were for you and Clay."

"You can have some of mine. I don't need to eat all that stuff, anyway."

"You sure?"

"Of course. We can just split it, 'cause I'm kinda hungry now, myself."

"That'd be cool, then, yeah."

"Be right back."

Lovey went to go heat up the food and put it on two separate plates. She headed back into the living room, handing the plate with the most food on it to Roland.

Roland eyed the disproportionate amounts and chuckled. "I had a feeling you were gonna do that."

"Do what?"

"Give me most of it."

"I've eaten plenty today. And honestly, I'm planning on having another piece of sweet potato pie, too. Did you get any of that earlier?"

"Yeah, I did. And I was about ready to propose to Ms. Elyse after one bite."

Lovey burst out laughing, almost dropping the plate in her hands. Roland jumped up to catch it, laughing himself. When Lovey realized how close they were standing and how his hands were covering hers underneath the plate, she subtly stepped back.

"You're silly," she said, hoping her cheeks weren't red. "Um, I forgot to ask you what you wanted to drink. I have bottled water, lemonade..."

"Lovey, you don't have to wait on me. Water's fine; I can get it."

"Hush; you're a guest. I'll be right back." Before he could protest again, Lovey sat her plate on the coffee table and scurried into the kitchen.

Before too long, they were heavily engrossed in a marathon of *The Office* and a comfortable conversation that at times had them forgetting about what was on the television in front of them. The more they talked, the more they realized they had quite a bit in common; aside from each having one older sibling and their parents being deceased, they also shared a lot of the same tastes, social views, and opinions about things ranging from pop culture to politics. After a while, learning about each other became something of a game:

"Favorite cereal?" Lovey asked.

"It's a tie between Frosted Flakes and Coco Puffs."

"I have two boxes of Frosted Flakes in there in the cabinet right now."

"For real?"

"Swear."

"Dig that. First job?"

"Pizza Hut."

"Domino's."

"And when is the last time you had any pizza from there?"

Lovey giggled. "Years. You?"

"I haven't had any Pizza Hut since I walked up outta there before going to college."

"Yeah, I worked at Domino's my junior and senior year of high school and quit when I left for college, too. By then I didn't even want to look at any more of that stuff. I loved it when I was working there, though."

"Oh man, I ate so much pizza back in the day, it's crazy," Roland stated. "I rarely even mess with it now."

"So what's your favorite kind of cuisine, then?"

"Oh, soul food, all day. That's one thing I miss about my mama; she could put it down with the yams, the meatloaf, the collards..."

"And of course, the dressing," Lovey chimed in with a smile.

"Hell yeah."

"That's one reason why I love going to Mama Elyse's house so much; she always sends me home with something. My mother was a great cook, too, and having Mama Elyse kind of helps remind me of her, in that way."

"I can definitely see why. I haven't had cooking that good in years. My sister-in-law usually cooks for the holidays and it's all right, but it can't touch Ms. Elyse's."

"Not much can, I imagine."

They continued to talk about their childhoods, college days, and anything else that the conversation strayed to, all the while drinking spiked apple cider and doing a whole lot of laughing. Three hours passed easily, and by the time they were practically leaning against each other on the couch, they were both too busy enjoying themselves to notice or think anything of it. Their budding rapport had blossomed, and they each felt like they'd known the other for years instead of weeks.

After a while, the long day of food and interactions caught up to both of them, and they began to doze off, with Lovey being the first to succumb. She mindlessly leaned her head on Roland's shoulder, tucking her socked feet underneath her and crossing her arms snugly across her belly. She felt more at peace than she had all day, with Roland's company and the spiked cider melting all of the anxiety and emotion she had been carrying over Clay. In fact, she hadn't even thought about Clay in hours, and had forgotten all about the fact that she was expecting his call.

She almost didn't hear her cell phone ringing from where it sat on the coffee table. It rolled to voicemail, then immediately began ringing again. Initially thinking she was dreaming, she shifted in her sleep, and it was then that she realized that there was something warm around her. Her eyes eased open and she noticed Roland's arm draped across her shoulders, and to her surprise and mild horror, she was snuggled underneath it like she belonged there.

"Oh my god!" she shrieked, jumping off the couch and waking Roland.

"What? What's wrong?" Roland asked, wiping his eyes and looking around them for anything amiss.

"I didn't mean to, um...I mean, I didn't realize that we had..." Lovey motioned towards the couch frantically with her hands, taking another small step back.

Roland looked at the couch then back at her, not getting what she was trying to say. "You didn't realize we had what?"

"Y-you know..."

"No..."

"That we had dozed off like-like *that*."

"Like what?"

"With me...laying on you."

"Oh, is that all? What's the big deal?"

"I shouldn't have done that."

"We *both* dozed off and I put my arm around you; I don't even remember doing it but it's nothing to freak out about. It's not like we kissed or slept together."

"I know, but...still. It just doesn't feel right."

Rubbing his eyes, Roland reached for his shoes. "Well, I apologize if I made you uncomfortable. It's probably time for me to go."

Lovey bit her lip as she watched him stand and put his jacket back on. "I know you think I'm overreacting..."

"Yeah, I kinda do. But it's cool. It's getting late, anyway." He headed towards the door.

"Thank you for all of your help today," Lovey blurted, following him. She realized she didn't want him to be upset with her, as it seemed he was. "I had a wonderful evening, thanks to you."

"I didn't do anything."

"Yes, you did. I feel worlds better than I did this morning. You really helped take my mind off of all my drama."

"Well, glad I could help. I enjoyed myself tonight; thank you for the hospitality."

"Anytime."

"Bye, Lovey." Roland opened the door and left.

Lovey stood in that spot for several moments, recalling the last few minutes and wondering if Roland thought she was some kind of nut now. Maybe she had overreacted, but she hadn't expected to wake up in Roland's arms like that. It was nothing, but part of Lovey still felt a little guilty about it. Roland was her best friend's man, and Lovey had a man, herself. What would Desiree or Clay have said if they had seen them hugged up like that?

Her phone ringing again in the living room jarred her out of her thoughts, and Lovey scurried to get to it, hoping it was Clay.

ROLAND WAS HOPING THAT Desiree would answer as he called her on the way home. He wanted to get rid of the awkwardness that was hovering over them. He knew when he sent that 'I love you' text that morning that she probably wasn't ready for that, but he couldn't keep it to himself. He had fallen for Desiree. But he couldn't say he really knew how she felt about him, and he just wanted to know if he was wasting his time or not.

Thankfully (and surprisingly), she answered on the third ring.

"Hello?"

"Hey, babe."

"Hey. Where are you?"

"I'm headed home, from Lovey's. We dozed off watching a movie. You at home?"

"Yeah."

"Mind if I come over?"

There was only a slight hesitation before Desiree answered. "Sure, come on."

Roland breathed a sigh of relief. He had already prepared himself for her to have some excuse as to why he couldn't come.

When he arrived at Desiree's, he got straight to the point.

"Babe, look, I know you weren't expecting to hear the L-word from me already. I'm sure that caught you off guard."

"Yeah, it really did," Desiree admitted.

"It's true, though. I sincerely do love you. But I get that you're not there yet."

"I *am* into you, Roland. For real. But..."

"Look, I don't wanna hear it from you unless you mean it. I take being in love with someone very seriously. I know it seems a little fast, but it's not something you can control."

"So I've heard."

"All I really need to know right now is if you want to keep going with me. Because if you feel this is too heavy for you, then we might as well just end things now."

Desiree looked at him in mild alarm. "It *is* heavy, but that doesn't mean I want to end our relationship."

"Desiree. I tell you how I feel about you and you fall back, avoiding me and sending me to spend time with your friend to get yourself off the hook, not to mention limiting our interactions to text messages. We're not in high school. If there's a problem or an issue, we need to be able to discuss it."

"I know. That's my bad; I could have handled things better."

"Yes, you could've."

"But, Roland, come on...you *did* kind of spring that on me out of the blue."

"So what?"

"So it threw me off."

"I hope you're not expecting me to apologize for telling you I love you."

"I didn't say that."

"If anything, *you* should be apologizing to *me*."

"For what?"

"For dodging me. That's no way to deal with things, Desiree. Then you bring Lovey into it..."

"Speaking of Lovey, how is she doing?"

"See there? Dodging again."

"I'm not!"

"Yes, you are, Desiree."

"Okay, I can admit that I have a tendency to get kind...*skittish* when I'm uncomfortable with something. I'm sorry for avoiding you; I was just a little overwhelmed. This is a lot for me."

Roland looked at her. He could see the sincerity on her face, and figured he could cut her some slack. She told him a while back that she'd only had one serious relationship and it ended badly, though she wouldn't go into detail about it.

"I get that," he said after a few moments. "As long as I know where your head is in regards to us, I can be patient. All I ask is that you just be honest with me, even if it's something you don't think I'll wanna hear. I'd rather know the real deal than think something is what it isn't."

"Understood."

"Good."

"I actually do want to know how Lovey is, though. I tried to call her but it went to voicemail."

"It might've been when we dozed off. She freaked out after that."

"Freaked out for what?"

"Because she had fallen asleep laying on my shoulder. And at some point I put my arm around her."

"Oh."

Roland eyed her. "Are you upset about that?"

"Why would I be?"

"I didn't think it was a big deal, either, but Lovey was acting like we woke up in bed together or something."

"Lovey can tend to be a little dramatic at times."

"I've noticed."

"I appreciate you taking her home and spending some time with her, though."

"It's all good. I enjoyed myself. She wasn't as pressed about Clay by the time I left, which is good."

"Between you and me, I'm a little worried about that whole situation. I mean, I like Clay and all, but I'm just afraid he's going to break her heart. Something just doesn't feel right to me."

"You think he's playing her?"

"Not really; he seems like a good guy. But for some reason, I just can't shake the feeling that their relationship isn't gonna last. I can't say why but I *really* hope I'm wrong. That would devastate Lovey."

"I hope you're wrong, too. But if something like that *does* happen, we'll be here for her."

Desiree looked at him and smiled, knowing she had a good man. She knew she should feel thankful for a man like Roland, and she hadn't lied when she said she was into him.

But what she *wasn't* saying was that she also wasn't sure her and Roland's relationship would last, either.

Chapter 12

CLAY HAD BEEN BACK in town for over a week, and while they saw each other the day after Thanksgiving as he promised, Lovey noticed that he was getting harder and harder to reach.

Before Thanksgiving, he had been easily accessible and responsive when she reached out to him. But now, more of her calls were going to voicemail, there were lengthy delayed responses to her texts, and their video chats had dwindled. Usually they spent most evenings together, with one of them spending the night at the other's apartment, but that hadn't been happening as often, either. He always said he was busy with work.

Lovey was officially worried.

Clay insisted there was nothing wrong and his increased workload was all there was to their reduced quality time, but Lovey couldn't help but be concerned. This was how it always started. She had really thought she'd hit the jackpot with Clay, but now she was beginning to wonder if she had been wrong yet again.

She voiced her concerns to Desiree, who tried to assure her that Clay was sincere.

"I really don't think you have anything to worry about, girl," she told Lovey as they waited for their food. They were having lunch at Bonefish Grill. "Clay's just busy with work, that's all. It happens."

"I know, but things just feel different, for some reason," Lovey replied. "Ever since Thanksgiving, things just haven't felt the same between us. Take today; you and I wouldn't even be having lunch right now if he hadn't cancelled on me at the last minute."

"Have you talked to him about it?"

"Yeah, we talked. He promised nothing was wrong."

"There you go, then."

"I'm not trying to be paranoid, but I just have a bad feeling."

"You always have a bad feeling."

"Can you blame me?"

"Clay is not like the men in your past, Lovey. You know that and I know it. Remember what you said Roland told you; trust him until he gives you reason not to."

"I know. You're right."

Desiree was telling Lovey all of this even though she still had doubts, herself. The feeling that Clay might not be around much longer still lingered with her. She didn't dare share that with Lovey because she knew it would only freak her out more. Lovey was already thinking Clay was starting his fade to black and Desiree wasn't about to add to that suspicion, especially since she had no real reason to.

When she talked about it with Roland, he agreed that it didn't sound very good.

"It *does* seem kind of suspect," he surmised. "To do an about-face like that..."

"That's what I'm sayin'!"

"*But* I do have to come to the brother's defense, though," Roland added. "Sometimes we want to believe something so bad that we just don't think rationally. I'm sure we all know how it is to get so busy with work that there's just not a lot of time for much else. It doesn't mean something is wrong."

"That's true."

"I think Clay should be given the benefit of the doubt, here," Roland said. "Lovey's past experiences seem to be clouding everybody's judgement. He hasn't even done anything wrong yet and we've already got the brother halfway out the door."

"Like I said, I really hope I'm wrong," Desiree replied. "But you know how you just have a gut feeling? I have that about Clay."

Roland knew what she was talking about, because he was starting to have a gut feeling about her, too. He didn't think that Desiree was as into their relationship as he was, despite her assurances that she was. He could understand her not being where he was emotionally, but he was starting to think that she didn't even *want* to be. The closer he tried to get to her, the more hesitant she got. She seemed to want to keep things fun and casual between them, and if that was the case, then they just weren't a good fit for each other.

He talked about it one day with his brother, E.J.

"She seems to want to talk more about her homegirl's relationship than ours," Roland informed him. They were sitting in the office at Barfly, going over some things for the coming week. "Whenever I try to talk to her about us, she steers the conversation to Lovey or something else."

"And what does she say when you call her on it?"

"She denies doing that, of course. Always says we're good."

"If you don't think she's all in, then it doesn't make much sense to continue the relationship, in my opinion."

"I agree but I don't want to give up on her so easily. I have the feeling there's a reason behind her reluctance; a past relationship gone bad that she won't talk about. And if that's the case, I get it. But I also have to decide how long I'm willing to wait."

"Look, bro," E.J. said, sitting forward in his chair and resting his forearms on the desk. "You want to get married one day, right?"

"Yeah."

"Is Desiree someone you can see yourself marrying? Does she seem like wife material, for you?"

Roland hesitated. "I don't know, honestly."

"If she doesn't, then you're just wasting your time, brother." E.J. sat back in his chair. "Unless you're dating her just to be dating her - which has never been your thing - I have to wonder why you're with her."

Roland looked at his big brother, pondering his words. He was deep in thought for the rest of the day, going back and forth in his mind about Desiree. He honestly did love her, but he hadn't considered if he might want to give her his last name or not. They had never even talked about marriage; he didn't know where she stood on it, if she wanted to have children, anything like that. He definitely wanted a wife and a couple of kids, and if Desiree didn't, then they really didn't have any business being together.

Lovey seemed more like wife material than Desiree, when Roland really thought about it. During their talk Thanksgiving night, she had shared with him her desire to have the kind of marriage of her parents had. She just knew she was meant to be someone's wife, and Roland knew she'd make a good one, because she sincerely wanted to. Lovey's eyes lit up when she told him about the example her mother had set for her, and how she hates that she wouldn't be around to be a grandmother.

Roland couldn't help but wonder what would have happened if he had met Lovey before Desiree.

LOVEY HAD ONLY BEEN home about a half hour when there was a knock on her door. She got a pleasant surprise when she opened it.

"Clay!" She exclaimed, breaking out into a huge grin. She threw her arms around his neck. "What are you doing here? I thought you said you were going to be busy tonight."

"I moved some things around so I could spend the evening with you; I felt it was important that we spend time together," Clay responded, hugging her waist. When he pulled back, his smile was tight.

"I'm so glad! Come in!"

Clay rubbed his hands together as he entered the apartment. He had a pensive look on his face, and Lovey looked at him curiously.

"You okay?" she asked.

"Oh...yeah. I'm okay," Clay responded. He gave her another tight smile. "Just a few things on my mind."

"Anything you wanna talk about?"

"No. I mean, not right now; we'll definitely talk about it later. Now isn't the time, though."

"You sure?"

"Yeah."

"Can I have a kiss, then? I haven't seen you in three days."

Smiling, Clay pulled her to him and kissed her, holding her tightly by her firm waist. Lovey noticed how closely he was holding her, and his kiss seemed more intense than usual. Something was going on with him, and Lovey was extremely curious as to what it was.

When the kiss ended, Lovey caressed the side of his face, giving him a lovesick smile. She was thrilled that he had made time for her, and felt that was a good sign for their relationship. She knew how important his career was to him, and the fact that he had put work aside to be with her made her budding doubts about their relationship fade into the background.

"Are you hungry? I was just about to get dinner started," she said.

"Actually, I wanted to take you out tonight," Clay informed her. "Somewhere romantic. I know we haven't had much time together lately because of me, and I wanted to make it up to you."

"Really?" Lovey beamed. "I appreciate that, sweetie. But just the fact that you're here is enough; we don't have to go out."

"No, you deserve something special, Lovey. You've been really patient and I appreciate it. And it's important that we get this time together now."

Lovey started to ask him what he meant by that, but decided to let it go. Her man was trying to do something nice for her and she wasn't about to ruin it with a bunch of questions.

"That sounds wonderful, thank you." Lovey grabbed his face and gave him another quick kiss. She looked down at the tan pencil skirt and white sleeveless top she had worn to work. "Am I dressed okay?"

"Actually, I was hoping you could wear that blue dress you had on when we met. That would be perfect for tonight."

"Oh, it's gonna be *that* kind of evening, huh?" Lovey clapped her hands together excitedly. Clay smiled, glad he could make her so happy.

"I know it's probably too cold out for that dress-"

Lovey waved off his comment. "That's what coats are for. Just give me about twenty minutes!" She hurried back to her bedroom.

Clay looked after her, his smile fading as he dropped onto the couch, running his hand wearily down his face. He had something important to talk to Lovey about, and he was still trying to figure out how and when he was going to bring it up. He just knew he couldn't wait any longer; tonight *had* to be the night.

Lovey tried to contain her excitement as she quickly changed clothes. She had missed Clay terribly, only having spoken to him a couple of times in the last three days. He'd been so busy with work, and she tried her best to just be patient and not complain. It did her heart good to know he had missed her as much as she missed him, and had changed his schedule so they could spend some much-needed time together. She started to feel silly for ever doubting him or his commitment to her.

She couldn't help but notice, though, that he seemed different. Almost nervous. Something was clearly on his mind, and her curiosity was through the roof as to what it was. As she quickly brushed her hair in front of the bathroom mirror, an idea about what the evening might be about made her gasp and drop her brush.

Could tonight be the night he was going to propose? They had only been dating a few months, but that didn't mean anything; her parents had only known each other four months before her father popped the question, and they had a wonderful marriage. And Elyse had told her several times how she and her husband Darius were talking marriage after one date.

More importantly, though, Lovey was head over heels in love with Clay, and she was confident he felt the same way about her. It would certainly explain why he looked so nervous, and this impromptu special date night. This must be what he said they needed to talk about; how sweet that he wanted to do it in some place more memorable than her living room. He wanted to make his proposal as special as when he asked her to be his woman in front of the waterfall in the mountains.

"Girl, chill out," she admonished herself, taking a deep breath. "You're jumping to some *major* conclusions. Don't get your hopes up for nothing."

Despite herself, though, Lovey could not wipe the smile off her face. As much as she tried to tell herself to be sensible, the larger part of her was already envisioning Clay asking her that special question. Her answer would surely be yes. She had daydreamed about being Clay's wife, because she just knew he was the right man for her. They were made for each other.

After freshening her light makeup and giving herself a final once-over to make sure she looked perfect, she hurried to put on the sexy silver heels that Clay had gotten for her a while back. Grabbing her off-white coat, she sauntered back to the living room, smiling at Clay's reaction. He stood upon seeing her, holding his hand out for hers.

"You're absolutely gorgeous." His eyes roamed her curvy body before resting on her face. "Just...breathtaking."

Blushing, Lovey's smile widened. "Thank you, baby." She touched the side of his face.

They gazed into each other's eyes for several moments before Clay finally cleared his throat. "You ready?"

"I'm more than ready."

Giving her yet another tight smile, Clay helped her into her coat before they walked outside. The cold December air whipped around them, but Lovey felt as warm and toasty as if it were the middle of July. She was still trying to keep her giddiness in check and remind herself that she really didn't know what it was Clay wanted to talk to her about, even though everything in her believed that he was going to ask her to be his wife. She told herself to just chill out and enjoy this evening with her man, whatever may come of it.

Lovey gasped when Clay opened the passenger door to his Lincoln and saw a small wrapped box on the seat.

"What's that?" she asked, grinning.

"Open it and see."

Lovey waited until they were both in the car before eagerly tearing at the shimmery wrapping paper. She squealed when she saw the small sapphire earrings, running her fingertips over them in awe.

"Clay, they're beautiful!" She leaned over to give him a kiss. "Thank you so much!"

"My pleasure."

"Is this an early Christmas present or something? Oh, does this mean you're going to be out of town on Christmas, too?" she asked, her smile fading.

"No, no, it's nothing like that," Clay quickly assured her. "This has nothing to do with Christmas. It's just a special gift for my special lady, that's all. And so are those." He motioned towards the backseat.

Lovey turned and gasped. She had been so excited about the gift that she hadn't noticed the backseat full of pink and white roses. Her hand flew to her chest as she looked at Clay.

"Clay..."

"There's a bouquet for every month we've been together," he informed her. He cupped her chin in his hand. "I have loved every minute of being with you, Lovey. Please always know that."

Blinking away tears, Lovey gently grabbed his wrist. "I *do* know that, babe. I love being with you, too."

Clay just looked at her for a moment before abruptly bringing her face to his and planting a deep kiss on her. It was almost as if he couldn't help himself. His hand slid through her long hair as his free hand grabbed the other side of her face, continuing the kiss fervently. Then just as abruptly, he pulled back and started the car.

"I hope you're hungry," he said, his voice thick.

Lovey looked at him curiously, then nodded. "I am, actually. Where are we going?"

"You'll see."

As they drove, Lovey noticed that Clay was unusually quiet. He was almost frowning, and didn't seem to want to look at her that much.

"Clay, are you sure you're all right? You seem awfully tense this evening."

"I'm fine, babe."

"You know you can talk to me about anything, right? If something is bothering you, maybe I can help. If not, I can at least listen."

"I know. And I appreciate it. Let's just...enjoy our evening."

"Okay." Lovey looked at him warily, then decided to drop it. If something was seriously wrong, she knew he would tell her. She wanted to do as he said and just enjoy their evening together.

Clay was truly going all out for their special night, surprising Lovey with reservations at Aria. Lovey felt like royalty as she dined on cauliflower soup, sea scallops, and passion fruit sorbet. Clay seemed to have loosened up slightly, and constantly told Lovey how beautiful she looked, appreciating how she had replaced her silver hoops with the sapphire earrings he had given her, and pulled her hair up so they could be seen. Her effortless, slightly tousled high bun still looked elegant enough to fit in with their posh surroundings, but still sexy enough to where Clay almost couldn't concentrate on his meal because he couldn't keep his eyes off of her. He couldn't wait to get her home. His lustful thoughts were almost potent enough to make him forget about the real point of the evening, which he still hadn't figured out how to broach.

Once they finished dinner, Clay suggested that they do the Art Stroll at Castleberry Hill, since he knew that Lovey liked art. She eagerly accepted. Once they found a place to park, they held hands as they enjoyed the evening together, dipping into the various galleries and marveling at the eclectic artistic pieces. Lovey felt a peace that she hadn't felt in a long time. She honestly couldn't remember the last time she had been this happy.

"This is such a beautiful evening, Clay," she commented wistfully as they left the Besharat Gallery.

"It has," Clay agreed. "You getting cold? We can head back to the car."

"It's a little nippy but I'm okay right now. Can we get some wine?"

"Of course. Come on."

After taking their time at Wine Shoe, Clay suggested they head home. During the ride, Lovey gushed about what a good time she had, and thanked him profusely for everything he had done for her. Clay was only moderately responsive, growing tenser the closer they got to Lovey's apartment. He knew the time was coming where he had to finally sit her down and talk to her.

As soon as they were through the door of Lovey's place, Clay was all over her. He released her hair and slid her dress straps down, not stopping until she was wearing nothing but sapphires and silver heels. Picking her up, he carried her to her bedroom and laid her on the bed, quickly removing his clothing before joining her. They made frantic, almost desperate love, each clinging to the other as if this was going to be their last time together. Lovey was on cloud nine, counting down the minutes until Clay popped the question. Clay was prolonging the lovemaking because he still didn't know how he was going to tell her what he needed to tell her.

When they were finally both spent, Lovey snuggled up to Clay, resting her head on his chest. She sighed contently, cementing the moment in her brain. Her skin tingled from their lovemaking as well as with the excitement of what she was sure was to come.

"I am so happy, Clay," she breathed. She lifted her head and smiled at him. "You have no idea. I just love you so much."

Not trusting himself to speak because he was becoming too overcome with emotion, Clay pulled her tighter to him, almost crushing her to his chest, burying his face in her hair. He continued to hold her and stroke her damp skin until she fell into a deep sleep, oblivious of what was coming.

Chapter 13

DESIREE WAS MUNCHING on a fried bologna sandwich as she sat at her kitchen table with her laptop, answering emails and doing some research. She was working on her calendar for the next year, glad to see that it was fuller than it was this time the year before. Business was going well, and she was extremely proud of herself for making a living doing something she loved and on her own terms.

She was getting up to get herself some more Kool-Aid when her phone rang. When she saw Lovey's name, she smiled and quickly answered. "Hey girl!"

"Desiree..." Lovey sniffed. It was obvious she was crying.

Desiree was immediately concerned. "What's wrong?"

"Clay just broke up with me."

"Oh no, Lovey." Desiree sank back into her chair. "When?"

"Th-this morning," Lovey hiccupped. "He surprised me with a romantic evening last night, and I honestly thought he was going to propose. He seemed pretty tense all night, but I thought it was because he was nervous about popping the question. We came back here and made love, then he woke me up early and said that it was over."

"Just like that? He didn't give a reason??"

"H-he said that he was going to have to move to Texas for work. I said that didn't mean we had to break up, but he didn't want to have a long-distance relationship."

"That bastard..."

"He kept saying that he didn't want to do it; that he loves me and hates breaking my heart like this, but he had no choice."

Desiree's heart hurt for her friend. Lovey sounded absolutely devastated. Desiree almost always had something to say, but this time, she was at a loss for words. She just hated that her gut feeling about Clay had been right.

"I am so sorry, girl," she finally said. "I know there's not really much I could say right now to make you feel better, but I sure wish it was."

"I'm just still in shock. I just...I can't believe it's over. Just like that. I feel so *stupid*!"

"Don't do that, Lovey."

"I actually thought he was going to *propose* to me, Desiree. As much as I tried to check myself, I was getting excited because I just felt it in my soul that the point of such a special evening was to ask me to be his wife. Look how wrong I was! Not only did he not propose, he *dumped* me!"

"Lovey, baby, doesn't it mean something that he ended things because of him moving, and not because he really wanted to? I mean, if it weren't for that, you'd still be together."

"If he *really* wanted to be with me, we could have made it work," Lovey argued, her voice strengthening. "I get that long distance relationships aren't ideal, but I thought we loved each other enough to get past that. Not to mention there's FaceTime, phone calls, instant messaging, texts, *airplanes...*"

"Lovey, calm down..."

"No, we could have made it work if he was willing to try, but he wasn't!" Lovey exclaimed. "I'm almost as angry at that as I am hurt by it. I just can't believe he was willing to throw us away so easily!"

"But maybe it *wasn't* easy, Lovey. Don't you believe Clay really loved you?"

Lovey hesitated. "Yeah. At least, I thought he did. But it's not like this would be the first time I was wrong about a man."

"Clay isn't like those other men, Lovey."

"Please don't defend him to me right now."

"I'm not trying to do that. I just don't want you to start doubting what you two had, or worse, start blaming yourself for it. This was about his job making him move to another state, that's *all*. It wasn't about you."

"Yeah, well, it's a little hard to believe that right now. Maybe I was naïve, but I thought our relationship was strong enough to withstand anything. And I obviously *was* wrong about *that*."

"Not everyone likes long-distance relationships. I know I wouldn't want to do that, either."

"Thanks a lot, Desiree."

"I'm just saying. It's not for everybody; that's all I meant."

"Whatever. I have to go."

"Why?"

"Because I don't feel like talking anymore."

"I'm sorry if I made you mad-"

"You didn't; I'm just very tired all of a sudden." Lovey's voice was weary.

Desiree hated that she couldn't cheer her friend up, and she wanted to keep trying to do so, but she didn't put it past Lovey to hang up on her. "Why don't you come out tonight? I'm hosting a party at Barfly and then Roland and I are going for a late dinner."

"Seriously? I didn't like tagging along with you two when I was happy. You think I want to do that right after being *dumped*?"

"Okay, maybe that *was* a dumb thing to ask right now. I just don't want you to be by yourself. At least call Liz to come keep you company. Or I can cancel the dinner with Roland and come by after the party."

"No, thank you. I appreciate the concern, but I just want to be alone right now."

"Lovey-"

"I'm not going to do anything stupid, Desiree. I just want to be by myself."

"Are you sure?"

"Yes, I'm sure."

"All right," Desiree hesitated. "I'll call and check on you later."

"You don't have to do that."

"Shut up. I'm calling. If you won't let me come by there and comfort you, at least let me do that."

"Fine. Enjoy your party tonight."

"I'll try. And Lovey?"

"Yes?"

"You're going to be all right. I'll be right here with you, seeing you through this. Okay?"

There was a pause. "Thanks, girl. I love you for that. And I'm sorry if I was snippy with you earlier-"

"Stop. You don't have to apologize. You know we're good."

"All right."

They ended the call, and Desiree shook her head. So her instinct about Clay had been right. At least it wasn't because he met someone else or was no longer interested in Lovey; he had an understandable reason for ending their relationship. But she knew Lovey didn't see it like that, and she certainly knew better than to say anything to Lovey that sounded like justification for Clay ending things.

She tried to resume her work, but her concentration was shot. Desiree wished there was something she could do to cheer Lovey up, but she knew her friend was going to be reeling from this one for a while.

"Damn," she whispered.

After they wrapped things up at Barfly, Desiree and Roland were seated in the back booth of Waffle House. Roland noticed how Desiree hadn't seemed like herself all evening; she was usually the life of the party, but that night at Barfly, it seemed like the last place she wanted to be.

"What's on your mind, babe?" Roland asked. He eyed her as she picked at her pecan waffle.

"I'm just pissed off."

"About?"

"Clay. The bastard dumped Lovey this morning." She dropped her fork and crossed her arms, clearly annoyed.

"Oh, damn," Roland sighed as he sat back in his seat. "Did he say why?"

"His job is moving him to Texas and he didn't want a long-distance relationship."

"Wow. It's understandable but I know Lovey is probably devastated."

"You know she is. I've never heard her sound so heartbroken. She really thought he was the one."

"That's really too bad. I hate to hear that."

"And the way he did it...surprising her, romancing her, sexing her down and then dumping her before she even had her morning smoothie. If he knew he was just gonna end things, he should have done it up front."

"Sounds like maybe he didn't really *want* to end it. I don't really know the brother but when I met him, he seemed sincerely into Lovey."

"I thought he was, too. And maybe he was. But still."

"There's no good way to end a great relationship, babe."

"There's a better way than *that*. Lovey was thinking he was going to pop the question."

Roland's eyebrows shot up. "Really? They were that serious?"

"Apparently so. Lovey was head over heels for that dude. And just because he was moving to another state, he broke her heart. I'm not personally into long distance relationships, either, but Lovey would have done whatever necessary to make things work for them."

"*Both* of them have to be willing to do that, though, Desiree. And if he isn't, then it's probably best that he ended things. At least now she knows what's up."

"I get that. But don't tell that to Lovey right now."

"I wouldn't."

"It just burns me up, you know?" Desiree picked up her fork and reached for more syrup, even though her waffle was already drowning in it. "It seemed like Lovey had finally gotten the real thing. She just doesn't deserve to keep getting hurt like this."

"True."

"It's not fair."

"No, it's not. But unfortunately-"

"Yeah, yeah, life isn't fair. I know," Desiree snapped, jamming a piece of waffle into her mouth.

Roland looked at her in mild surprise. "Hey, don't get mad at *me*."

"I'm not mad at you. I'm just mad, period. I really wish I knew where Clay lived so I could go by there and kick him in the balls with my stilettos."

Roland winced slightly at the thought. "Look, just focus on being there for Lovey. I get that it's jacked up but it's not like Clay fooled around on her; as far as reasons go, this is about as good as you can get."

"Yeah, don't tell her that, either. She's hurt that he left her but she's also angry that he didn't at least try the long-distance thing. Short of him being on death row or suddenly realizing he's gay, there isn't a reason for ending their relationship that would be good enough for Lovey."

"That's understandable."

They continued to eat in silence. Roland figured Desiree was going to be miffed all night about this. He felt bad for Lovey, too, but he more so wanted to enjoy the evening with his woman. And he knew it would be futile to tell her to forget about Lovey for the time being and just concentrate on them.

When Desiree cleaned her plate, she pushed away her plate and asked, "You ready?"

"Yeah." Roland motioned for the check as he gathered his jacket. "You wanna go back to my spot?"

"That's cool, but first I wanna go check on Lovey."

"What?"

"I just want to make sure she's all right."

"Babe, I don't claim to know Lovey better than you do, but I'm sure she probably wants to be alone right now."

"She does, but I'm worried about her."

"Why?"

"Why??"

"I mean, I know *why*, but I'm saying; you think she's gonna do something crazy or hurt herself or something?"

"No..."

"So let's just leave her alone for now."

"I don't want to leave her alone. She's probably over there stuffing her face and crying her eyes out, wearing those raggedy gray sweats and watching sad movies or listening to Sade."

"She just got dumped this morning, babe. Surely you don't expect her to be over it already."

"Of course not, but I just want to check on her, still. Just so I can see with my own eyes that she's at least stable."

Roland sighed. He knew he wasn't going to change her mind about this. "I think we should give her her space, but since you insist so much, we can stop by there."

"Thank you."

After Roland paid the bill, they headed over to Lovey's. Roland planned on just staying in the car, but Desiree insisted that he come in with her. Needless to say, Lovey wasn't exactly thrilled to see them.

"Why are y'all here?" she demanded, not even trying to hide her exasperation.

"We wanted to check on you," Desiree replied, peeking into the apartment.

"I'm fine. I told you I wanted to be alone."

"I know that..."

"I really wish you would start respecting my wishes."

Desiree reeled slightly. "I *do* respect your wishes, Lovey."

"No, you don't. You bulldoze until you get your way, regardless of how I feel about it. I told you when you offered earlier to come by that I didn't want any company. You said you would just call."

Roland tried to resist the urge to nod at Lovey's statement. Desiree *did* tend to bulldoze until she got her way. As well-intentioned as it usually was, he could certainly understand Lovey's annoyance because it annoyed him at times, too.

"Why are you getting so upset?" Desiree asked Lovey. "I was just worried about you."

"And I appreciate it but I told you I was all right. I know to call you when I need you. How many times do I have to tell you that you don't have to baby me? I'm not a freaking child!"

Desiree's jaw dropped. She was really surprised at Lovey's agitation. "Are you serious right now? I'm not doing that!"

"Yes. You *are*."

Roland didn't want to get involved but he decided to try to quell the growing ire in front of him. He cleared his throat. "Ladies, come on. Let's not let things go too far here..."

Lovey looked at Roland and folded her arms. "Roland, am I correct in guessing that you tried to tell Desiree that y'all shouldn't come by here tonight?"

Roland pursed his lips. He glanced at Desiree before answering, "Yeah, you're correct. And I know you're on ten right now, and I get it, but just know Desiree does what she does because she loves you so much, that's all."

"*Still*, though-"

"But you're right; if you want to be alone, we should respect that," Roland continued, looking pointedly at Desiree and taking her hand, preparing to leave. "We'll head out; just call if you need anything, aight?"

Lovey softened slightly. She appreciated Roland seeing where she was coming from, since Desiree didn't seem to. "Thank you, Roland."

"So I'm the bad guy here, huh?" Desiree asked, looking back and forth between them. "I'm worried about my friend when she's devastated and I'm the bad guy?"

"Nobody said that, babe," Roland assured her.

"Please don't try to make this about you, D," Lovey scoffed.

"Oh my *god*!"

"Come on!" Roland stepped between them. "Now, y'all know what this is really about. Lovey, you're pissed about Clay and need to lash out at somebody. And Desiree coming over here unannounced is just a perfect excuse for you to do it. 'Cause I imagine you wouldn't get *this* upset about it any other time. How far off am I?"

Lovey looked away. She hated to admit it, but Roland was dead-on. This certainly wasn't the first time Desiree just showed up, and while Lovey would have really preferred to be alone like she said, it was true that if she wasn't still reeling over Clay, it wouldn't have bothered her nearly as much.

"You're right," she finally acquiesced. Her arms fell. "I'm sorry for getting so riled up. I'm just...I'm just incredibly hurt right now."

"We understand that," Roland replied. Desiree just looked at her friend earnestly.

"Y'all can come in, if you want," Lovey offered.

"No, you want to be alone. We can go."

"You're already here; you might as well," Lovey said with a shrug as she turned and headed back towards her couch.

Desiree glanced at Roland before entering the apartment, following Lovey. Roland had hoped that they could leave and spend some time together, but apparently Desiree was more concerned about Lovey than about him. Again.

Lovey, with her hair covered in a pink scarf and donning the gray sweats as Desiree had predicted, curled up in the corner of the couch and mindlessly picked up a bowl of partially-melted chocolate ice cream that was topped with chopped nuts and dried cherries. There were several empty Snickers wrappers on the couch and the end table, as well as a half-empty jar of Nutella, a few empty water bottles, and a practically full jug of chocolate milk. Roland didn't have to guess what her go-to was when she was upset.

"What are you watching?" Desiree asked after several moments.

"*The Notebook*."

"I've never seen that."

"Umph." Lovey shoved a spoonful of ice cream into her mouth.

"I've seen part of it. It's all right," Roland commented. He glanced at Desiree. "You probably wouldn't like it, babe."

"Too sappy?"

"Something like that."

Desiree glanced at Lovey. "I think there's probably something good on the comedy channel."

Lovey shrugged, eating more ice cream.

"Or *Black-ish*. You know you love that show."

"You can turn it on there if you want to," Lovey droned, pushing the remote towards Desiree.

Desiree found some episodes of Lovey's favorite show on DVR and let them play, eying Lovey as she sat back on the couch. She watched her friend finish her ice cream, plunk the bowl on the cluttered end table, and fold her arms tightly around her as she curled up into a ball. She looked ready to burst into tears at any second.

Desiree glanced at Roland, who just looked sympathetically at Lovey. He wished he knew something to say that would cheer her up, but he knew there was probably nothing. Desiree, on the other hand, wasn't going to give up so easily.

"How's work been going?" she asked Lovey cheerfully.

Lovey sniffed. "It's work."

"Anything exciting or interesting happen lately?"

"No."

"Roland, who do you and E.J. have keeping your books at Barfly? Maybe you could get Lovey for that," Desiree suggested. She nudged Lovey's socked foot. "It could be your little side hustle."

Roland adjusted his jacket. "E.J. keeps the books, actually. He's a numbers guy."

"Oh. Well, you can at least come to some of the parties we have coming up, Lovey. I've got some hot things lined up!"

Lovey was silent.

"There'll be guys there that'll make you forget all about what's-his-name. If you just get dolled up and come out, I know you'll enjoy yourself."

Lovey didn't speak. Silent tears started to stream from her eyes.

Desiree looked at Roland, who just shrugged helplessly. Desiree scooted closer to her friend and slid an arm around her shoulder, figuring she might as well stop trying to engage Lovey in conversation. Lovey was waist-deep in a heartbreak hangover and nothing but time was going to fix it.

The three of them sat in relative silence, the only words spoken occurring between Roland and Desiree. Roland kept checking his watch and tried to think of a polite way to suggest they leave, but before he knew it, both Lovey and Desiree had dozed off.

"Man, we should've taken separate cars," he muttered to himself.

After mindlessly watching SportsCenter for a while, he wandered into the kitchen to get himself some water. He found the cabinet holding the glasses, noting how neatly everything was organized. Desiree's kitchen was a series of things being shoved wherever she felt like putting them at the time.

He was filling the glass with tap water when he heard shuffling behind him.

"There's bottled water in the fridge, you know."

Roland turned to Lovey see standing there, rubbing her eyes. She looked weary and tired, even a bit haggard with her ice cream-stained sweats and wild hair under her loosened scarf, but still had an adorable quality about her.

He shrugged as he turned the water off. "This is fine. I drink tap water plenty. And anyway, you've got this filter thing on it."

"Umph." Lovey shuffled to the refrigerator and opened it.

Roland watched as she just stood there, not seeming to be looking for anything in particular. After several moments, she closed it and leaned against the counter, covering her face with her hands.

"If you wanna scream, go ahead and do it," Roland suggested.

Lovey lowered her hands slightly. "What?"

"You're hurt, you're angry...you don't have to hold it in. I bet you'll feel a whole lot better if you just let out one good blood-curdling scream. The kind that makes you turn red and everything."

To his surprise, Lovey's lips twitched into a smile. Then she actually giggled.

"I don't think my neighbors would appreciate that very much," she chuckled. "It's a nice thought, though."

"Nothing like letting it all out. You just make yourself sick, otherwise."

Folding her arms across her stomach, Lovey nodded and looked at the floor. "I certainly *feel* sick."

"Too much chocolate?"

Before she could help it, Lovey laughed. Clamping a hand over her mouth, she lightly hit Roland in the arm. "So you figured out my vice, huh?"

"It wasn't hard. Snickers, chocolate ice cream, Nutella, chocolate milk ..."

"Yeah, I kind of go overboard when I'm really stressed or upset."

"So I see."

"I just can't believe all this, Roland," Lovey sighed. She gazed at her ring finger, rubbing it slowly before stopping abruptly, as if catching herself. "I was so wrong about Clay. I don't think I'll ever get the hang of men."

"Hey, most of us feel the same way about y'all," Roland quipped, putting his glass on the counter. "And why do you think you were wrong about him?"

"Obviously we were in two different places. I was thinking marriage and he was thinking break-up."

"How do you know, though, that he wasn't thinking marriage, too? Is that something you two have talked about?"

"A couple of times. We both seemed to want the same things. But, clearly, something changed."

"Yeah, something changed. His job moved him to another state. That's *all*, Lovey. It wasn't about him not wanting to be with you."

"I just don't see how he could let things go so easily."

"Who said it *was* easy? He's probably as jacked up about all this as you are."

"But he ended things when we could have made it work long-distance."

"Have you ever *had* a long-distance relationship, Lovey?"

"No..."

"It's not for everybody. I've done it and it takes a *lot* of effort, from both sides. And a lot of people just can't handle not being able to physically be around their partner for such long stretches of time. And you have to *really* trust each other."

"I trust Clay. And I would have been willing to at least try it."

"Look, I know you probably don't want to hear this, but I really think it's better that he ended things now rather than getting to Texas and things fizzling out because he's either too busy with work or decided he just couldn't handle the distance."

"Or that he met someone else," Lovey muttered.

"Yeah, that's possible. But that could've happened here, too. I really think Clay was as into you as much as you're into him, Lovey, for real. This is just an unfortunate situation. Maybe if he was able to stay here, he *would* be proposing soon. Who knows? But there's no need in beating yourself up over something that's absolutely not your fault."

"Or Clay's fault," Lovey added in a low voice.

"Yeah, true. If it'll make you feel better to blame somebody, blame his bosses. But Clay could have very well just moved to Texas without a word and left you here worried sick and torturing yourself over what happened. What is it y'all call it? Fading to black?"

"Yeah."

"He was straight up with you about what was going on. It hurts, I know, but be thankful for that. Because a lot of dudes would have taken the punk route just to avoid the difficult conversation."

Lovey looked at him in realization. "That's true. That's happened to me more times than I can count."

"When you think about it, then, can't you at least take some solace in the fact that Clay told you to your face, instead of leaving you flat *on* your face? I know it hurts like hell, and it should; you love him. And I know it probably seems unfair, too. But just know he loves you too, and only left you because he had to, not because he wanted to."

Pondering his words for several moments, Lovey slowly nodded. She looked at Roland with an appreciative smile.

"I didn't really think about it like that," she admitted. "That actually does make me feel better about all this. I'm still hurt but...what you said helped ease the pain a little bit."

Roland smiled. "Glad I could help."

"You help me a lot. I sincerely appreciate it."

"Just trying to be a good friend."

Looking at him, Lovey felt like she really did have a friend in him. Without thinking about it, she stepped over to him, opening her arms for a hug. Roland didn't hesitate to return the gesture, wrapping her up in his strong arms.

Lovey closed her eyes, enjoying the comfort that being around Roland brought; he always seemed to know what to say or do to make her feel better, or take her mind off of her issues. She appreciated that immensely, especially now. To her surprise, she was already feeling a little better about her breakup with Clay; it was still painful, but Roland's words made that pain slightly less intense.

Several moments passed as the two of them just stood there, seemingly in no hurry to break apart. Lovey took a deep breath before sighing in temporary contentment, and it was then that she noticed how good Roland smelled. Then she began to notice how firm his body was; the hard back muscles under her hands, the defined pecs her cheek was resting on, even the strong yet gentle way his hand was gripping her shoulder. His other hand was lightly clamped to her waist and Lovey felt her skin there begin to tingle slightly. The more she stood there in Roland's arms, the better she felt. She hadn't felt this safe and warm since...

"Hey, where are y'all?"

Upon hearing Desiree's voice, Lovey jumped away from Roland, blushing. She touched her warm cheeks, actually feeling embarrassed. What had gotten into her?

"We're in here," she called out.

"What's wrong?" Roland asked her.

"Nothing," Lovey quickly replied, not wanting to overreact like she had on Thanksgiving when they dozed off on the couch together. "I guess I'm still just a little out of it, that's all."

"You sure?"

"Yeah."

Roland chuckled. "It was just a hug, Lovey."

Lovey's eyes snapped to him right as Desiree entered the kitchen. How did he always seem to know what she was thinking?

"What are y'all doing?" Desiree asked, running her fingers through her slightly disheveled long black wig.

"Just talking," Roland shrugged, picking up his water glass.

"Yeah, Roland really gave me another perspective on this thing with Clay," Lovey added. "There's something to be said for a guy's take on things."

"So you're feeling better?" Desiree asked her.

"I actually am."

"I'm so glad to hear that!"

"Yeah. I'm not gonna front like I'm over it or anything, but I'm looking at the whole situation a little differently now, thanks to Roland."

"You just have the magic touch, huh?" Desiree joked, sliding her arms around Roland's waist.

"I don't know about all that," Roland replied, actually looking a little embarrassed. "I just gave her some more stuff to consider, that's all."

"Like what?"

"Why don't I tell you about it on the way home; I'm tired and I'm sure Lovey is, too," Roland suggested, taking Desiree's hand. "It's damn near four o'clock in the morning."

"Is it??" Lovey glanced at her watch. "Oh, wow."

"You gonna be all right?" Desiree asked.

"I'll be fine. I'm just gonna take a hot shower and then hibernate in bed until nature calls."

"Well, call me if you need anything," Desiree instructed, moving over to give her a hug. "I'm glad you're feeling better, though I wish it was me that made you do it instead of being the one to piss you off earlier."

"I wasn't pissed off. I was just annoyed. And taking some of my anger at Clay out on you. I'm sorry for that."

"No sweat," Desiree waved off the apology. Roland noticed that she didn't apologize for defying Lovey's wishes and coming by in the first place.

"See you later, Lovey," he said, taking Desiree's hand and leading her out of the kitchen. He was ready to get home and into his own bed.

"Bye, y'all."

Lovey just stood in the same spot after they left, touching her shoulder where Roland's hand had been.

LOVEY SLEPT UNTIL WELL after noon, having no desire to get up and do anything. Her eyes eased open and she stretched languidly, then reached for her phone on the nightstand. She had gotten used to expecting a morning message from Clay, and her shoulders slumped slightly when she realized that wouldn't be happening anymore. But to her surprise, she didn't feel any tears or overwhelming sadness at the realization. Part of her appreciated that she and Clay had made a clean break, and that he hadn't laid the classic 'I hope we can be friends' line on her. And she knew she wasn't yet at the point where she could hear his voice and not wish they were still together.

The talk with Roland really shed a new light on things. Her breakup with Clay was painful and probably would be for a while, but Lovey at least could acknowledge that it wasn't about her choosing the wrong man again or Clay's feelings not being on the same level as hers. It was just an unfortunate situation. Roland had made it all seem so simple and clear.

Speaking of Roland, she hadn't forgotten about the hug they shared. It might have seemed harmless, but Lovey felt she enjoyed it more than she should have. Her relationship with Clay had barely ended a full day ago, and Roland was her best friend's man. She didn't need to be savoring his embrace like she did.

But she couldn't deny, though, that the hug was much needed. And she *had* enjoyed it, as much as she told herself she shouldn't have. Being in Roland's company had become a welcome thing for her, and Lovey started to wonder if she was getting a little too comfortable with him. She usually got along fine with Desiree's men, but most of them were never really around long enough for her to form any kind of bond with them. Roland was different, though; she felt like they were friends. She cared about him, and it was apparent he cared about her. Was that a bad thing?

"Ugh, get a grip," she chided herself. "This whole thing with Clay has my mind all over the place, obviously."

She made herself get out of bed. Shuffling to the kitchen, she thought about making pancakes but opted for a green smoothie, especially after her chocolate binge the night before. She was pulling the spinach out of the refrigerator when her cell phone rang. She rushed for it, automatically thinking it might be Clay, then caught herself.

"Yeah, getting past this is gonna take a while," she muttered.

When she saw it was Liz calling, she smiled and picked up the phone. "Hey, sis."

"How you holding up?"

"I'm doing okay."

"Really?"

"Yep."

"You *do* sound better than you did this time yesterday," Liz acknowledged. "Did you talk to Clay or something?"

"No. Roland actually gave me another perspective that made me feel better about everything."

"Roland?"

"Yeah, he and Desiree came by late last night and we talked. He made me realize that it's not about anything I did or Clay not wanting to be with me. And I can't expect him to want a long-distance relationship just because I would. Or at least I think I would. They're not for everybody, apparently."

"They're really not. You remember when I was dating that guy that moved to Minnesota? We tried to make it work but it just didn't, especially since our living situations weren't going to change. I damn sure wasn't moving to Minnesota."

Lovey chuckled. "Yeah, I remember that. Roland said it takes a lot of effort from both sides."

"Very true."

"Roland really has a way of making me feel better about things," Lovey continued. "It's almost effortless; he just has such a chill vibe about himself and it almost always calms me down."

"Yeah, he's a cool guy. We only talked for a few minutes at Thanksgiving but I liked him. I'm kinda surprised Desiree hasn't found an excuse to kick him to the curb yet."

"I think she realizes she has a good one. Roland challenges her in a way most men don't. She likes that, whether she'll admit it or not."

"She won't."

"But there is something about Roland I've been thinking about today," Lovey admitted.

"What's that?"

"After we talked last night, we shared a hug. It was harmless, but I found myself feeling...sort of attracted to him."

"Did he make a move on you?"

"No! Not at all. He didn't do anything inappropriate. To him it was just a friendly hug. This was all in my own jumbled-up head."

"And what, you're feeling guilty?"

"Well, a little bit. I shouldn't be feeling attracted to my best friend's man."

"Why not? Hell, *I* was attracted to him. Roland is a very attractive man. And anyway, it's not like you're going to act on it."

"Yeah..."

"And you're still messed up about Clay. Your emotions are all over the place and you're feeling stuff you wouldn't normally feel. Had you felt any attraction to Roland before last night?"

"No, I haven't," Lovey realized.

"There you go, then. I'm sure it's nothing. Don't obsess over it, like you do so many other things."

"I'm not obsessing, but it just...doesn't feel right, you know?"

"Well, the next time you're around him, see how you feel then. If that same attraction is there, then yeah, maybe you have something to be concerned about. But if not, then it was just a fleeting moment that's over with."

"Good point."

"But since I know you well enough to know you're not gonna let it go that easily, I suggest you either try to meet someone else, or stay away from Roland altogether. Or both."

Lovey didn't like either of those options. For one, she knew she wasn't ready to meet anyone new. And two, she could admit that she wasn't ready to stay away from Roland, either. For whatever reason that was.

Chapter 14

ROLAND DIDN'T WANT to think about Lovey, but for some reason, he couldn't take his mind off her.

Ever since he and Desiree left her apartment that night, he hadn't been able to shake the feeling that something had changed between them. He'd always liked Lovey, but he never looked at her as anything other than this girlfriend's BFF. But after they shared that hug, he started noticing *her*, as a woman. Sure, he had known she was attractive, but he never took note of how beautiful she really was. And despite himself, he couldn't forget how her body felt in his arms. She was soft, warm, and curvy, different from Desiree. And she had smelled like lavender and chocolate.

He wanted to call her. But how would he even explain that? He never called her before. The only reason he even had her number was because Desiree had given it to him; he didn't even know if Lovey was aware of that or not. He was still wondering why Desiree had given him the number in the first place.

That had to be what all this was about; Desiree was still keeping him at arms-length, giving more attention to Lovey and her issues then theirs, and he was starting to pay more attention to Lovey, too. He and Desiree still hadn't talked about where their relationship was headed, if anywhere. To him, they were just going through the motions. Desiree might have been spending more time with him since he called her out on Thanksgiving, but she was still avoiding talking about their relationship. And really, Roland's patience was running thin.

After they left Lovey's that night, Desiree claimed to be too tired to do anything but sleep, so he just dropped her off without suggesting they spend the night together. He'd expected her to make some kind of excuse not to be alone with him, and he wanted to be alone, anyway. He knew he had some decisions to make in regards to their relationship. How long was he willing to stay with a woman who clearly had a problem with them getting closer?

For the next couple of days, Roland stayed to himself as much as he could. As he usually did when he had a lot on his mind, he did countless push-ups, trying to work out the jumbling thoughts in his head. He really did love Desiree, but he was starting to see they weren't right for each other. It was like E.J. said; if they weren't on the same page, they were just wasting their time.

Pushing himself off the floor, he wiped his face with a towel and reached for his cell phone. He actually felt better knowing what he needed to do.

"Hey," he greeted once Desiree answered the phone. "You have some time tonight? I was hoping we could meet up for a while." He paused, listening, and rolled his eyes at her excuse that she had some work she needed to do. "Don't worry, I'm not gonna take up too much time. You'll have plenty of time to do whatever you need to do."

AROUND SEVEN O'CLOCK that evening, Roland knocked on Desiree's door. He was anxious about his decision to end things with her, but he knew it was the right thing to do. They simply wanted different things; he was thinking about the future, while she just wanted to have fun.

Desiree opened the door, wearing a tank top and some leggings. She wasn't wearing one of her wigs, and her natural hair was fluffed out around her head. Roland smiled at how cute she looked, and hated that things were going to end between them like they were about to.

"Hey there," she greeted him with a grin. "Come on in."

Roland stepped inside the apartment, and she gave him a quick hug and peck on the lips before trotting back to the living room.

"Lemme just finish up what I'm doing and then I'm all yours," she promised, picking up her laptop from the couch.

"Do your thing."

Roland took a seat in the armchair, his hands in his coat pockets. He eyed Desiree as she typed away at her laptop, knee bouncing, occasionally munching on potato chips from the bag next to her. She seemed to be in a good mood; almost excited. He figured she had secured some kind of work deal or something.

After about thirty minutes, she closed her laptop. Roland was perusing Barfly's social media accounts on his phone, answering questions and responding to comments. He almost didn't notice when she finally finished her work and turned her attention to him.

"So what's up? I haven't heard from you in the last couple of days," she said.

"Yeah, I had some things going on I had to deal with."

"Like what?"

"Some decisions I had to make that I had been putting off."

"Oh, I know all about *that*," Desiree agreed, tucking a leg underneath her. "I'm the queen of procrastinating. That's what I've been doing all day, stuff I was supposed to do last week."

"Hmm. Well, I'm sure you probably have more to do, so-"

"Actually, I'm pretty much done," Desiree interjected. She patted the spot on the couch next to her. "Why you sitting over there? Come sit here."

Roland got up and sat next to her, leaving a little space between them. He didn't want to send mixed messages, but apparently his standoffishness wasn't sending her any signals that something might be wrong.

"Desiree-"

"Before you say anything, I have something I want to talk to you about," she cut him off again, her voice excited.

Roland tried to keep his frustration in check. He hated when people interrupted him as he spoke and she had done it twice in a minute. "What?"

"I want to make a suggestion about our relationship."

Roland cocked an intrigued brow. "Yes?"

"I think you need to start spending more time with Lovey."

"Excuse me?"

"I've noticed that you always manage to make her feel better about whatever she's dealing with. Even *I'm* not able to do that at times. I think it would be good for her."

Roland frowned, sitting back in his seat. He was totally thrown for a loop. "Umm, I can't say that I see how me hanging out with Lovey has anything to do with our relationship."

"Well, I don't think I have to tell you that things have been kind of...*strained* between us lately," Desiree replied. "And I know a lot of that is my fault. Maybe I'm just not ready for things to get so deep between us, but at the same time, I don't want to lose you altogether."

"Still confused. So you want me to date Lovey? And still date you?"

"Date? I just said spend some time with her."

"You are making absolutely no sense, Desiree."

"Maybe I'm not explaining this right..."

"It sounds like you're trying to put me off on your friend, again, and still be able to come around to me whenever you feel like it."

"I wouldn't put it like that, Roland. Don't make this into a negative thing."

"What? Be straight up, Desiree. Are you interested in someone else or something?"

"No! This isn't about anybody else. I'm just finally telling you what I've been thinking about, in regards to that 'I love you' text you sent. It was really sweet, but I can honestly say I'm just not there yet. I'm not good at relationships, and that just showed me that I'm not ready for a super-serious thing. But I like you too much to just let you go completely."

"So...you still want to date me, just not exclusively?"

Desiree bit her lip. "Again, this isn't about me wanting to get with someone else. We can still be exclusive. I just need to cool things down, at least for now. My head has been all over the place since you sent that text."

"I'm glad that you're at least being straight up with me, even though I can't say I'm thrilled about what you're saying."

"I know. But you said you'd rather know the real deal than think we're something that we're not."

"And that's true. But I still don't see how Lovey fits in to all of this."

"I just figured that you two could keep each other company; you seem to have a good time together," Desiree explained. "I know she's not over Clay and probably won't be for a while. And since you and I probably won't be seeing each other as often..."

"Wow, you think a whole lot of yourself, huh? You think I'm gonna be so broken up about you essentially dumping me that I need you to get me some kind of stand-in to ease my pain? And of course it has to be someone you approve of..."

"I didn't even say all that."

"You didn't have to say it. That's what you're doing."

"You're taking this way too personally. I just think you and Lovey would be good for each other right now, that's all. I'm not trying to hook you two up. *Or* dump you, for that matter."

"Uh-huh."

"So you'll at least think about it?"

Roland eyed her. He would never admit it out loud, but he was mildly intrigued by Desiree's suggestion. It was true that he did enjoy Lovey's company. And after they hugged in her apartment, she had been on his mind as much as Desiree, if not more.

"Lovey doesn't know anything about this, does she?" he verified.

"Not yet. I haven't been able to talk to her today. But I'm certainly going to mention it to her."

"And you really think she's going to go for this?"

"She'll come around."

"You mean you'll bug her about it until she agrees just to get you off her back. I'm good on that."

"Roland, come on. I'm worried about Lovey still; she might be feeling better about Clay dumping her, but I *know* she's still in pain over that. There's no way she's not; she thought he was going to ask her to marry him, for pete's sake. I wouldn't be surprised if she still had moments when she breaks down over it. You have a way of calming her down. Don't take this the wrong way, but she needs you right now more than I do."

"I see." Roland thoughtfully tapped his thumb against his thigh.

Desiree looked at him cautiously, trying to gauge his reaction. "What are you thinking?"

"Don't know yet."

"Can you at least say you'll think about it?"

Roland looked at her for a moment before standing. "Yeah, Desiree. I'll think about it. I just hope you really know what you're asking for."

Without another word, he walked out. Before he even got to his car, his decision was made.

DESIREE FIGURED HER talk with Roland had gone as well as it could have. She knew he would scoff at her suggestion to put the brakes on their relationship and for him to spend more time with Lovey instead, but at least he didn't flat-out tell her no. She figured emphasizing how much Lovey needed the attention would soften the blow of her essentially saying she just wanted a more casual relationship with him and not a serious one.

It was true that she hadn't met anyone else, and even more true that she liked Roland too much to stop seeing him altogether. But him telling her he loved her only showed her what she pretty much knew all along: that she was not ready for a deep, serious relationship. What if Roland ended up proposing to her? Not only would she have to devastate him by turning him down, Lovey would surely reel from that. She was the one that wanted to get married, not Desiree. Desiree wasn't sure marriage would *ever* be in her future. So this solution of hers was good for everyone; she got a break from an intense relationship with Roland but still would be able to see him when she wanted, and he and Lovey could be there for each other, helping each other heal from their respective broken hearts.

Now she just had to get Lovey to agree to it.

She quickly picked up her phone and called Lovey, hoping she answered. To her relief, Lovey answered on the second ring.

"Hey, D."

"Hey, girl." Desiree was glad to hear Lovey didn't sound like she had been crying or sulking. "How you doin'?"

"I'm good. Just got home a little while ago."

"You went to work today?"

"Yeah. Why wouldn't I?"

"I just thought maybe you took the day off."

"No, I'm not still over here crying and gorging on chocolate, if that's what you mean."

"Hey, I'm glad to hear it. I know it's one thing to be good around other people or for the moment but when you're alone, you start reminiscing and fall back into the funk."

"I'm not gonna lie and say I don't have my moments, but I'm doing okay, considering," Lovey admitted. "I do miss Clay but that's not gonna make him come back, so I just have to move on best I can."

"Exactly. I'm so glad to hear you say that, girl. I have way to help you do just that."

Lovey paused. "I almost don't want to ask. What is it?"

"You spend more time with Roland."

"Excuse me?"

"See there? Y'all are good for each other. You both responded the exact same way."

"You've already talked to him about this??"

"Yeah, he just left here a little while ago."

"Just out of curiosity, what did he say?"

"He said he'd think about it."

"I'm lost, D. *Why* are you suggesting this?"

"Because he seems to have the magic touch with you; when you fell apart on Thanksgiving after Clay bailed, no one could cheer you up but him. When Clay broke up with you, you only felt better after talking to Roland. Clearly, that means something. And I bet you two have more in common than he and I do."

"So this is all about helping me, huh? Nothing to do with you trying to wiggle out of a relationship with him because he told you he loves you?"

"I can admit it; that's part of it. I still want a relationship with him, though. Just not so serious of one. I'm not ready for all that and this will give me some space."

"So you're using me."

"No! Why would you even say that?"

"Because that's what you're doing."

"I'm not! I honestly think it would be good for both of you. I know he likes hanging out with you, too."

"Well, whatever. No, thank you."

"Why not??"

"Desiree, I'm not interested in keeping your man entertained until you're ready to deal with him like I'm some kind of opening act."

"Oh my god..."

"Who did you meet that you're trying to get with?"

"I haven't met anybody. This isn't about that. I just think this will benefit all of us. I'll get the space I need, he can help you keep your mind off Clay, and you can help keep his mind off me."

"What makes you think he'll be pining over you like that?"

"Well, he *did* say he loves me..."

"Desiree, have you *really* thought about what you're asking, here? You're passing your man off on another woman."

"It's not just any woman. It's you."

"Even so. What if he and I hit it off so well that he doesn't *want* to hang with you when you decide you're in the mood for him? Could you handle that? Could you handle him choosing me over you if we were to realize that we're better suited for each other, since you think he and I have so much in common? What if he totally ends things with you and focuses on me? That would kill our friendship. No, thank you."

"That wouldn't happen."

"And why not?"

"I hear the attitude. I don't mean that the way you're probably taking it. I'm just saying our friendship is strong enough not to let some man come between us. And like I told Roland, I'm not trying to hook the two of you up."

"You might not be, but you never know what could happen. That's what *I'm* saying."

"What, are you interested in Roland?"

"No," Lovey answered quickly. "I'm not. Despite everything that's happened and as pointless as it may be, I still miss Clay and part of me still hopes he'll come back. That maybe he'll realize he can't live without me and turn down that promotion in Texas. I know it's a long shot but the heart wants what it wants. And my heart still wants Clay."

"Right. I'm not even surprised to hear you say that, girl, and it's totally understandable. And because you still miss him so much, you're going to have times when you get down and depressed about him being gone again. Roland would be good to go to during those times, don't you think?"

Lovey couldn't disagree, although she didn't want to admit it to Desiree. Roland had been instrumental in making her see the light in some of her dark times lately. And as much as she tried not to, she still thought about him since the night they hugged in her kitchen. She hadn't been lying when she said she still wanted Clay and wished he'd come back. But she didn't totally hate the idea of spending some of her newfound free time with Roland.

"I still don't know about this," she finally said. "It just seems to be asking for trouble."

"Girl, this is not one of those Lifetime movies you're always watching. You should know me well enough to know I'm not gonna trip over no man like that. I honestly don't see this as anything but good for all of us."

What Desiree wasn't saying was that she didn't believe there was any way Roland would ever choose Lovey when he could still have her. Lovey was an amazing catch by anyone's standards, but Desiree didn't think *any* woman could hold a candle to her, not even her best friend. Desiree still wanted Roland; she just didn't want *so much* of

Roland. And she truly believed that he would choose having part of her than having all of any other woman.

She *had* made him fall in love with her, after all. If his feelings were real—and Desiree believed they were—there was no way he could just move on to another woman. Them seeing each other occasionally would be enough to keep him pacified. Desiree was confident of that.

"You certainly seem like you've given this a lot of thought," Lovey commented.

"Of course I have."

"And Roland actually said he'd consider this?"

"Yep."

Despite herself, Lovey was a little glad to hear that. "Well, I'll think about it, too, then. Only because you feel so strongly about it. But I'm not promising anything, D."

"Understood. But watch, you'll see what I'm talking about and be right on board with it. Both you and Roland are gonna be thanking me."

A COUPLE OF DAYS LATER, Desiree was hosting a football brunch party at a private club downtown. Just about everyone was decked out in red, black and white to represent the home team Atlanta Falcons. The vibe was classy-casual; slightly more upscale than a regular football party but not so much that people couldn't have fun enjoying the game.

She was still waiting to hear back from Roland and Lovey about her suggestion. Both of them might have initially scoffed at her, but she thought she had been able to make them see her side of things after a while. Desiree felt smothered in her relationship with Roland, and she needed some air. And while she hadn't met anyone else yet, that didn't mean she wouldn't.

That would happen sooner rather than later. A couple of hours into the party, she met Aaron, a chocolate stack of muscles with wavy hair and two strong arms full of tattoos. He looked like he played football himself, and Desiree was increasingly intrigued by him the more they made eyes at each other. Desiree kept her distance, but when he finally approached her, she couldn't resist smiling like a child about to get something off their Christmas list.

"What's up?" he asked, his strong voice piercing through the voices around them. "I'm Aaron."

"Desiree."

"Oh, I know. I checked you out already."

"Is that right? Should I be flattered?"

"That's up to you. But just know I had the best of intentions."

"Yeah? And what would those be?"

"Wanted to know the name of the woman I'd be spoiling soon."

Desiree didn't want to smile at that, but she couldn't help it. In fact, more than one part of her was reacting to his statement. She had to cross her legs to try to quell her *reaction*.

"You're smooth," she finally replied.

"I can be."

"What else can you be?"

"Yours."

I'm gonna have to change my panties.

"I guess we'll have to see about that," she held her hand out to him. "Mr...?"

"Calloway." Aaron took her hand in his, bringing it to his lips. "And we *will* see about that, Ms. Mashburn."

Desiree cocked a brow. "You *are* thorough."

"In everything I do." He eyed her seductively.

Biting her lip, Desiree boldly looked back into his eyes. In that moment, she hated that there was a room full of people around them. She wanted very much to be able to concentrate on Aaron and get to know him better. A *lot* better.

"You busy after this?" Aaron asked her.

"I am now."

They smiled at each other.

This is why I can't do monogamous relationships, she reminded herself. *Look what being tied to Roland would make me miss out on!*

Desiree and Aaron continued to flirt heavily for the rest of the party. When things started to wind down, he stayed to help her oversee the cleanup and tie up all the loose ends, then suggested they go somewhere they could get better acquainted. They ended up back at his townhouse where he served her multiple servings each of fried chicken, fruit salad...and orgasms. Desiree couldn't get enough of Aaron's thick, muscular body; every time she looked at all of his tattoos, it just turned her on more.

"You tryin' to wear me out?" Aaron joked when she climbed on top of him yet again.

"You can handle it," Desiree winked at him. Her hips began a slow grind on him. "Can't you?"

Groaning, Aaron gripped her hips with his hands and began to move with her. "Damn right."

After they went another round, they both sat up in Aaron's bed, on their phones. Desiree could tell he was texting someone, but she didn't ask who because she didn't care. And he didn't seem concerned about what she was doing, either, which Desiree liked.

What Desiree was doing was texting Roland. Meeting Aaron only cemented what she was sure needed to happen with her and Roland's relationship, and what she could admit she didn't quite have the nerve to say to his face:

I like you, Roland, but a 1-on-1 relationship is just too much for me. I still wanna see you, but I don't think we should be exclusive anymore. Ok?

Chapter 15

"IS SHE FUCKIN' SERIOUS??"

Roland was still staring at his phone, waiting on Desiree to send another message saying she was just kidding. When none came, he dropped it onto the couch next to him and sat back in disbelief.

He really couldn't believe her nerve. First, she comes at him with the suggestion that he spend more time with her friend instead of her, and then she sends a text saying they don't need to be exclusive. That all of a sudden, it was "too much" for her. Roland started to call her, but changed his mind. She probably wouldn't have the nerve to answer, just like she didn't have the nerve to tell him this to his face. He had long since observed that she resorted to texting when she had news or information that she knew he wouldn't like.

Roland immediately surmised that Desiree had met someone else. To him, it was the only way to explain this sudden turnaround. True enough, she'd been pulling away from him for weeks, then suggested he spend more of his time cheering up Lovey than being with her. His frown slowly deepened as his mind began to churn.

Maybe this *wasn't* so sudden. Maybe Desiree had been seeing someone else this whole time. And maybe Lovey knew about it and they were both trying to make a fool out of him. He hadn't been this angry since he found out about Anna's indiscretions.

He snatched up his phone and called his brother, his leg bouncing aggressively.

"What up?" E.J. greeted him.

"You're not gonna believe this shit."

"Must be something big if it's got you cussin'. What's going on?"

"Desiree just told me she doesn't want to be exclusive anymore. And in a fucking text."

"Just out of the blue like that?"

"Yeah!"

"She met somebody else."

"Yeah, that's what I thought, too. But she made sure to emphasize she still wanted to see me, as if that would make me feel better."

"How did you respond?"

"I haven't yet."

"You gonna end it?"

"As far as I'm concerned, *she* just ended it. Ever since I told her I loved her, she's been pulling away from me. I didn't even tell you how she suggested a couple days ago that I start spending more time with her friend Lovey."

"For what?"

"Some bullshit about me being the only one to know what to say to her and make her feel better. Lovey had been going through some relationship stuff and I just gave her a male perspective, is all. But really, I feel like they're both just trying to play me."

"If you feel like that, call 'em on it. Even if they don't admit anything, they'll know you're not some gullible sucker."

"I don't trust myself enough to talk to Desiree right now, man. Mama taught us to never call a woman out her name and I might not be able to honor that if I heard her voice."

"So talk to Lovey. You told me she's super nice, right?"

"Hmph. I *thought* she was but I don't even know what to believe right now."

"Couldn't hurt to try. She might not even have anything to do with Desiree's about-face, but I imagine if anybody can give you more insight or answers, besides Desiree, it would be her."

Roland figured E.J. had a point. If he was going to have any luck finding out anything, it would most likely be through Lovey. He knew Desiree would probably avoid him like the plague, at least until she knew how he felt about her suggestion.

Doing his best to keep the anger out of his voice, he called Lovey and asked if he could meet up with her. Sounding like her usual sweet self, she agreed with no hesitation. Roland didn't detect anything suspicious in her voice, but maybe she was just a really good actress.

Lovey said she was out running some errands and offered to meet him at Barfly later, since he had mentioned going there to look over some things. Roland agreed, figuring that would give him enough time to cool off some. And Desiree wouldn't be there that night, so they didn't have to worry about running into her.

Reading Desiree's text again, Roland shook his head and got up off the couch. He dropped to the floor and pushed out fifty push-ups before heading upstairs to take a shower. He was looking forward to seeing Lovey so he could hopefully get some answers about this woman he had chosen to be with.

Thankfully, it was a Sunday night, so Barfly was closed. Roland liked to go on some Sundays when no one was there to look over things for the upcoming week, or to brainstorm ideas. But the last thing he could concentrate on was work, though, try as he might. He just couldn't get Desiree's text out of his head. And as much as he'd like to just write her off, his feelings for her didn't allow him to do that so easily. At least, not without getting some kind of answers. And if he couldn't get them from Desiree, he hopefully could get some from Lovey.

He was sitting at the bar sipping from a bottle of water when Lovey walked in. She looked around briefly before spotting him, then smiled and headed his way.

"Hey, Roland," she greeted him. She leaned in for a light hug, then looked around as she adjusted her purse strap on her shoulder. "Wow, this place looks so big when it's empty."

"Yeah, it can, I guess," Roland grunted.

Lovey looked at him, immediately able to tell that something was wrong. "You okay?"

"Honestly, no, I'm not. Come on, let's go to the office."

After Roland locked the front doors to the building, he led Lovey back to the office, trying to block out the memory of him and Desiree fooling around in there. He took a seat behind the desk and motioned for Lovey to sit in the chair in front of it.

"What's going on, Roland?" Lovey asked, placing her purse in her lap. "You seem a little grumpy."

"I'm not grumpy. I'm pissed, Lovey."

Her eyebrows shooting up, Lovey asked, "Why??"

He glared at her. "I'm going to ask you something and I want you to be totally honest with me. Straight up."

"Of course."

"Did you know anything about what Desiree texted me earlier?"

Lovey frowned. "What are you talking about?"

"About her saying she wanted to see other people."

"What?? She said that?"

"Well, she said she didn't think we should be exclusive anymore. Which pretty much means the same thing. Who did she meet?"

Lovey held up her hands. "Roland, I *swear* I don't know anything about that. She didn't tell me she was going to send you that and if she's met someone else, I have no idea who."

"Please don't lie to me, Lovey. I know Desiree is your girl and all..."

"I'm not lying. Desiree is like a sister to me, but she knows I'm not gonna lie for her, and she wouldn't ask me to. But it's not necessary in this case because I sincerely don't know anything."

Roland eyed her for several moments before leaning back in his seat, exhaling a long breath. Something told him she was telling the truth. That didn't make him feel much better, unfortunately.

"The last time I talked to Desiree, she was telling me about her bright idea about you and I hanging out more."

He looked at her. "Oh, so she *did* tell you about that?"

"Yeah. Apparently right after she talked to you about it."

"And what did you say? About her suggestion?"

"When she said that you told her you'd think about it, I said I would too, though it was mainly to appease her. I knew she would stay on me until I at least said that."

"You think it's a bad idea?"

Lovey shrugged. "I don't see the logic in her asking her man to spend more time with me than he does with her."

Roland grunted. "It's just another excuse for her to keep me at arm's length. She's been doing that ever since I foolishly told her I love her."

"Don't say that. It's never foolish to tell someone how you feel about them. Desiree is just...well, she's not very good with relationships. Really, I was surprised when she agreed to be with you in the first place; it meant she *really* liked you."

"Hmph. Well, I guess the novelty has worn off because you see what she's doing now."

"She's just freaking out in her own Desiree way. She's not big on emotions."

"I've noticed."

"I know she's still into you, though. Otherwise, she would have ended it altogether."

"Am I supposed to be flattered? I'm not trying to be on standby while she goes and does whatever with whoever. I'm a one-woman man and always have been."

"I get that. And I totally understand you wanting it to be all or nothing. How did she respond when you told her that?"

"I haven't said anything to her yet."

Lovey looked surprised. "Why not?"

"Because I had to clear my head first and get some answers."

Realization washed over Lovey's face. "You thought *I* had something to do with all this?"

"I thought you both were playing me. Like a let's-see-how-big-a-fool-we-can-make-out-of-Roland thing."

"Not at all! I don't have time for that kind of nonsense, Roland. What would even be the point, anyway?"

"What's the point when anybody plays anybody? People have their own stupid, selfish reasons."

"Well, I assure you, that's not the case here. Not with me and I'm willing to bet not with Desiree, either. She might not know how to handle her feelings at times and doesn't always make the best decisions because of it, but she's not purposely trying to make a fool out of you. I'd bet anything I have on that."

Roland really wanted to believe everything Lovey was saying. He could say he believed her when she said she didn't know anything about Desiree meeting someone else, or about her having no hand in trying to make a fool out of him, but he didn't quite buy that Desiree wasn't being dishonest. She wasn't telling him everything, and he figured there might be a way to get some truth out of her.

"You know Desiree better than I do, but something in my gut tells me she's not being straight up," Roland said. "And usually, I have no patience for that at all. I had enough of being lied to and led on in my last relationship."

"Oh, no. She cheated on you?"

"Yeah. But that's another story for another day. How 'bout if we see if she's really about it like she thinks she is?"

Looking at him skeptically, Lovey asked, "What do you mean?"

"You and I start hanging out more, like she wants us to. When she calls or wants to hang out with one of us, we say we have plans with each other and can't. We'll see if she can *really* handle that."

Lovey immediately shook her head. "I'm not into playing games, Roland. Especially not with my best friend."

"It's not a game. We'd just be doing what she said he wanted."

"But the whole thing about acting like we already have plans whenever she calls..."

"That doesn't have to be a lie."

Lovey blushed slightly. "Still, though, Roland. I don't like the idea of doing it just to get a rise out of her."

"We're just seeing if it would, but that doesn't have to be the point of it. I actually *do* like hanging with you so it's not like it's some chore, at least on my part. And since it doesn't look like I'll be seeing much of Desiree soon..."

"What, now *I'm* the fallback plan?"

Roland's eyebrows shot up. "I didn't mean it like that-"

"I know, I know. I'm just messing with you." Lovey giggled. "I get what you mean."

"Good." Roland realized he didn't want Lovey upset with him.

"Look, I totally see where you're coming from with all this, and I even get why you're suggesting it. But I'd just rather not be a part of anything malicious."

Roland scoffed. "It's not *malicious*."

"It has ulterior motives, though. You're trying to use Desiree's suggestion against her."

"Is that such a bad thing? You didn't seem like you were all that gung-ho about her saying we should hang out more, either."

"I just thought her logic was off. Plus, it's not like I'm in the right frame of mind for this, anyway; I'm still hung up on Clay."

"Aww, damn. Have you heard from him?"

A hint of sadness clouded Lovey's eyes. "No. Unfortunately not."

"So this could be good for both of us, then; it would help take your mind off Clay and help me feel better about this jacked-up excuse for a relationship I'm in."

"I can't, Roland," Lovey said, standing. "If you and I decide to spend time together, I don't want it to be solely because we're trying to get back at Desiree or make her jealous. It just wouldn't feel right. I hope you can understand that."

Roland sighed. He couldn't say he was totally surprised by Lovey's response; it was just the kind of person she was. She wasn't going to knowingly do anything that would be detrimental to anyone, namely her best friend. He at least felt better that she had no part in Desiree's antics.

"Yeah," he finally said, rearing back in his seat. "I understand. It's all good."

"Good." Lovey smiled. "I better get going. I'll talk to you soon, okay?"

"Okay. Here, let me walk you out."

After he walked Lovey to her car and saw her off, Roland went back to his office and plopped down into the chair. At least he had the answers he wanted, as far as Lovey's part. He was glad to confirm that she didn't know anything about Desiree's actions and had no hand in them, and realized he actually felt relieved. It would have disappointed him if she had been involved.

Roland pulled out his phone and looked at Desiree's text again. He didn't get angry as he did when he initially read it, but it still bugged him. He wished Desiree would just be honest with him about having met someone else, which he was still sure was the case. If all she wanted was a causal relationship, she should have said that from the beginning. Roland suspected it was more about Desiree just wanting her cake and eating it too more than her just wanting to keep things light.

Rubbing his chin thoughtfully, Roland finally began typing a response to Desiree's message:

If you say so. I'll see Lovey and whoever else I want. Just remember, you asked for this.

THE NEXT DAY, LOVEY was at work, trying to concentrate. She was still thinking about her conversation with Roland the night before. She still couldn't believe he thought she had a part in Desiree cooling off their relationship, but when she thought about it, she could understand why he did. What she told him about Desiree not being good with emotions was true, and Desiree was proving exactly that. She liked Roland more than she wanted to and was rebelling against it. And instead of just being honest and telling Roland that to his face, she did what she usually did and took the easy way out, this time by sending a text. No wonder Roland was upset.

Ever since Desiree made the suggestion about her and Roland spending more time together, Lovey had been going back and forth about it. She didn't admit it out loud, but she wasn't totally opposed to the idea. She liked hanging out with Roland, and it was true that he had a way of making her feel better.

But she just didn't think it was right to spend time with him for the sole purpose of making Desiree jealous, or seeing if she would be. Lovey just wasn't interested in the games.

And Lovey could admit (to herself, at least) that she was a little apprehensive about significant alone time with Roland. She was *still* thinking about that hug they shared in her kitchen, and it was jumbling her thoughts as to why that was. It was just a hug, but Lovey didn't see it that way. If it was *just* a hug, she wouldn't still be reminiscing about it like it meant something. So she felt like she needed to work that out within herself before spending time with Roland and possibly confusing herself more.

She was getting ready to head to lunch when her cell phone rang. When she saw it was Clay, she gasped, almost convinced her eyes were playing tricks on her. Answering it right before it went to voicemail, she lowered herself into her chair and answered with a shaky breath, "Clay?"

"Hey, Lovey." His voice sent her insides racing. "How are you?"

"I'm okay," Lovey replied, placing a hand over her racing heart. "How are *you*? How's Texas?"

"It's all right. It would be better if you were here."

Lovey's heart felt like it would jump out of her chest. "Oh?"

"Yeah. I *really* miss you, Lovey. You have no idea."

"Oh, Clay...I miss you, too!"

"I'm sorry again for how things went down that morning at your apartment," Clay said. "Please know, telling you it was over was the *last* thing I wanted to do..."

"I believe you."

"I've been miserable ever since, to be honest with you. Sure, the promotion is great, but what good is it if I can't enjoy it with the woman I love?"

Lovey's jaw dropped. What was he saying? Did he want her to move to Texas to be with him? Her hand gripped the arm of her chair as her excitement bubbled like soup in a pot.

"I-I don't know what to say," she replied in a small voice.

"I know I'm probably catching you off guard with this," Clay admitted. "Really, I can't even say it was the smartest thing to do, calling you. I hadn't planned to. But I just couldn't help it. I *had* to hear your voice, Lovey. I just...I had to."

"I'm *glad* you called me." Lovey was grinning so hard her cheeks were getting numb. Tears of happiness were already ticking her eyes. To know that Clay was missing her as much as she was missing him made her feel on top of the world. Maybe their relationship wasn't over, after all. "You've made my day. I was thinking maybe you forgot about me or something..."

"What? I could *never* forget you, Lovey. When I say you're the love of my life, I mean that."

Lovey grinned harder. Her mind began making a list of what she would need to do in order to move to Texas. "I feel the same way. And for the record, I've been pretty miserable, too."

"I really hate this," Clay sighed. "We need to do something about it, baby."

Almost squealing out loud, Lovey wiggled excitedly in her seat. Clay was going to ask her to come be with him! She wondered when she would give notice to her job, and how long it would take for her to get everything in order. The thought of being with Clay again was making her want to get up and run around the building. Whatever it was she needed to do to get her behind to Texas with her man, she was going to do it with lightning speed.

"I agree," she finally managed to say. "I'm willing to do whatever."

"Good; I'm glad we're on the same page."

"We usually are."

"So you'll agree that we shouldn't talk or communicate anymore after this."

"Absolut-" Lovey stopped, not initially registering what he had said. "Wait, what??"

"I don't think we should talk anymore after this," Clay said again. "It's just too hard. Hearing your voice, communicating with you knowing we can't be together...I can't handle that."

"Wait a minute..." Lovey's head was spinning. "You're the one that called *me*, remember?"

"I know. Like I said, it might not have been the smartest thing to do, but I had to hear your voice. But now that I have, it just confirms what I already thought. I can't be this far apart from you and stay in touch. If we can't physically be together, then I'd rather just not be in contact at all."

Lovey couldn't believe what she was hearing. She had gone from being elated to enraged in the span of a minute. "Why do you like playing with me like this, Clay? What did I ever do to deserve being kicked around so much?"

"What? What are you talking about?? I'm not-"

"Save it! You take me out for a romantic evening only to sleep with me and dump me the next morning. Then you move darn near across the country, and I *finally* begin to start healing from that, only for you to call me out of the blue talking about how much you love and miss me and all this *crap*!"

"I *do*!"

"Well, then you should've kept it to yourself, because if all you were gonna do was pull the rug out from under me *again*, I didn't need to hear it."

"Lovey, I'm sorry if you feel like I was leading you on. That was never my intent. Come on, you have to know me better than that, baby!"

"Stop calling me that! I am obviously not your baby or anything else! Clearly, I don't mean that much to you!"

"For real, Lovey? How can you even say that??"

"Because you ended our relationship when you didn't have to, that's why! You decided it was over and I didn't have any say in it whatsoever. Then you throw me off yet again with all this sweet talk, just to tell me we can't talk at all anymore because it's too hard for you. I'm so sick of being treated like I'm nothing!"

Lovey knew she was practically yelling, but she didn't care. She was officially fed up.

"Lovey!"

"Erase my number. Delete me on Facebook. Forget you ever knew me. Do whatever you want, as long as you never, *ever* contact me again! Bastard!!"

With what were now angry tears running down her face, Lovey hung up the phone and threw it on the ground, before burying her face in her hands and crying her eyes out.

KNOWING SHE WOULDN'T get any more work done that day, Lovey cancelled the rest of her appointments and went home, dodging any questions from the receptionist Tara or any of her other coworkers asking if she was all right. She wasn't. She felt like she had been kicked in the gut, spat at in the face, and yanked by the hair into a scalding pool of skin-melting mud. Clay had just burned her, even worse than he had when he dumped her that morning after their surprise romantic evening. That had been bad enough, but to leave her, call her out of the blue, sweet talk her and lead her to believe that he was going to suggest some kind of way for them to be together, only for him to tell her that they shouldn't talk again. The more she thought about it, the angrier she became. By the time she got close to home, she was absolutely fuming.

Resisting the urge to stop by the store and load up on chocolate, Lovey pulled up in front of her apartment building, killed the engine, and just sat there. Her heart was still racing, and her nostrils were flared in anger.

If we can't physically be together, then I'd rather just not be in contact at all.

Gritting her teeth, Lovey screamed and hit the steering wheel so hard that it hurt her hands. But she was too pissed to feel anything. In that moment, she felt like she hated Clay. And she had never felt hate towards anyone in her life. That's how angry and fed up she was; the more she thought about Clay and what he did, the more she remembered all the men before him who had led her on only to leave her high and dry. She felt something inside her shift; a person could only take so much. And Lovey felt like she had finally reached her breaking point.

Knowing she needed to calm down (or at least try to), she fished her phone out of her purse and called her sister, Liz. She wasn't quite ready to talk to Desiree because she knew she would just ask what her response was to the suggestion of her hanging out more with Roland, and

Lovey wasn't ready to talk about that with her yet. And right now, that wasn't first and foremost on her mind, anyway.

Liz didn't answer, but she called back a minute later. Lovey was still sitting in her car, staring at nothing ahead of her.

"Hey, sorry I missed you," Liz greeted her. "My phone was in the other room."

"Okay."

"What's up?"

"You know how you hear those stories about someone getting bullied and kicked around so much that they eventually snap?"

Liz paused. "Yeah..."

"Like in that movie *Carrie*?"

"Lovey," Liz said cautiously, "What's going on?"

"Clay called."

"He did? I thought you'd be happy about that."

"Oh, I was. I was thrilled, especially when he told me how much he misses me and how miserable he is in Texas without me and how can he enjoy life there without the woman he loves..."

"Wait a minute. Don't tell me you're moving to Texas."

"I'm not moving anywhere. Because in the next *freaking* breath, he tells me that we shouldn't talk anymore because hearing my voice and not being able to physically be with me is just too painful."

"So...why did he call you?"

"Said he just *had* to hear my voice. Whatever. As far as I'm concerned, he's jerking me around. Playing with me.

Like a let's-see-how-I-can-make-Lovey-jump-this-time kind of thing."

"You really think he would do that? Clay seemed like a stand-up guy."

"Whether or not he mindfully intended that, that's what it felt like. We were in love; what did he expect to happen when we talked? Did he think that would make him miss me *less*? He had to know that us talking would re-ignite some feelings. If he knew he didn't want a long-distance relationship, and that he couldn't handle speaking to me if we weren't together, he shouldn't have called me at all unless he was going to ask me to move there with him or that he was going to move back here. As far as I'm concerned, that was just cruel."

"I can understand you feeling that way. Especially if he was talking like he wanted to make some kind of move to bring you two closer."

"Exactly."

"You have every right to be hurt by that."

"I think I skipped right over hurt and went right into anger. I honestly can't remember the last time I've been *this* angry, Liz."

"Is that why you're bringing up movies about bullied folks who killed a bunch of people after being doused in pig's blood?"

"Yeah. I feel like I'm drenched in emotional pig's blood."

"Well, I hope you're not thinking of hurting anyone or yourself. Matter of fact, where are you?"

"I'm at home, in my car. I'm not thinking about doing anything to anyone, though I wish I *could* hurt Clay as much as he's hurt me. I'm so tired of being men's throwaway."

"I know you are, sis. It's totally understandable. Maybe you should do something to get your mind off Clay. Didn't you used to be into scrapbooking?"

"Years ago. But I lost interest in that. Desiree *did* suggest something the other day to get my mind off Clay, though."

"Oh, lord. What?"

"That I spend more time with Roland."

"What? She actually suggested that you spend more time with her man?"

"She sure did."

"Dare I ask why?"

"She thinks Roland would be good for me right now. Since he seems to always manage to cheer me up or make me see things differently, she figures that he and I hanging out will help ease the pain of my breakup with Clay."

"That's too selfless of a reason. There's more to it than that."

"Well, she did admit that her and Roland's relationship was getting too deep for her and she needed a reprieve from it. Ever since he told her he loves her, she's fallen back. So it's also about me keeping him company when he's not with her, since she insists she still wants to see him."

"So...she's trying to push you and Roland together."

"Not in a hook-up kind of way."

"Still, though. She must have met somebody else."

"That's what Roland thinks, too. I don't know if she has or not."

"I'm willing to bet anything she has."

"You know you've never thought terribly highly of Desiree, overall. It doesn't have to have anything to do with another man. It *could* just be about her needing to cool things off with Roland."

"It could be. But I'm willing to bet my car that it's not."

"Well, I don't know, either way."

"What did you say when she suggested this? What did Roland say?"

"We both told her we'd think about it, but I know *I* only told her that to get her off my case at the time."

"Roland wants to do it?"

"He was so angry about Desiree telling him in a text that she didn't want to be exclusive anymore that he said we should hang out and decline any invitations from her just to call her bluff. He doesn't think she'll be able to handle it as well as she says she will."

"Hell, he's right. I don't think so, either."

"Really?"

"Of course not. If you and Roland hit it off so well that y'all no longer have time for her, she'll throw a fit. You know it as well as I do."

"Yeah, well, I told him I didn't want to play that game. Doing it just to get a rise out of her doesn't interest me."

"So do it for the reason she suggested; to get your mind off Clay. You said yourself Roland always makes you feel better. It wouldn't be the worst thing in the world to spend time with someone like that, especially after this latest episode with Clay."

"True. I'm just worried about what it could do to me and Desiree's friendship. It's easy to say that it won't affect it *now*..."

"True, it *could* get messy. But it might not. Desiree probably thinks no other woman can have his nose open other than her, anyway."

"She's not *that* conceited."

"Yes, she is."

"Stop, Liz."

"Whatever. All I'm saying is, think about yourself first for once, instead of putting Desiree's feelings ahead of yours like you always do. I'm not saying she's a bad person or a bad friend to you. But she's clearly doing her thing. You need to start doing yours."

Lovey thought about her sister's words. It was true that if she decided to start spending more time with Roland, it didn't have to be for any other reason than she wanted to. She never hated the idea, she was just more worried about how it would affect her and Desiree's friendship. But she hadn't even spoken to Desiree in a few days, which usually meant she was sheets-deep in a new conquest. She didn't want to believe that was the reasoning behind Desiree's sudden text to Roland to stop being exclusive, but she couldn't deny it made sense. And it's not like it would be the first time, either.

A smile began to form on her lips. Maybe it *wouldn't* be so bad to think about what was best for her for a change.

SEVERAL HOURS LATER, Lovey was feeling considerably better. There was still a burn in her belly about Clay, but she wasn't seething like she had been right after talking to him.

After making herself work out, do some laundry, and make herself some dinner, Lovey took a long shower before curling up in bed with a book of crossword puzzles. She was halfway through her first one when her phone rang. It was Desiree.

"Hey, girl," she greeted her friend.

"Hey!" Desiree sounded absolutely giddy.

"Why do you sound like you just hit the lottery?"

"I don't know about the lottery, but I *do* kinda feel like I hit the jackpot," Desiree gushed.

"What does that mean?"

"I met somebody."

Lovey set her book aside. So Roland was right. "Who? And when?"

"His name is Aaron. We met a few days ago at that day party I threw for the Falcons game. Girl, he is fine with a capital F. Used to play semi-pro himself before he blew out his knee. But he stays in that gym, though. Muscles for days."

"I'm pretty sure I know the answer to this, but you haven't slept with this man already, have you?"

"Do birds have beaks? Is the almond a nut? Do the-"

"Okay, okay, I get it." Lovey rubbed her eyes. She didn't know how to feel about what Desiree was telling her.

Usually she didn't think too much of it when her friend bedded someone so quickly, because Desiree had long since established she was going to do whatever she wanted to do. But this time, it involved someone she had grown to care about. How would Roland react if he heard about this?

"So, this is why I need you to be spending time with Roland," Desiree continued. "So he won't be so worried about what I'm doing."

"You've talked to him?"

"We haven't communicated since he sent me that text saying he'd see you and anyone else he wanted."

Lovey's jaw dropped. "He what?"

"You didn't know about that? Yeah, after I texted him saying I didn't think we should be exclusive, he said he'll see you and whoever else. Oh, and to remember that I asked for this."

"*Have* you seriously considered that yet, Desiree? What exactly it is you're asking for?"

"Girl, are you still worried about that? Look, both you and Roland insist you aren't interested in each other romantically. Unless that's changed, then nothing can go wrong. If anything, you'll grow to love each other like brothers and sisters. That's a good thing. And it's not like I won't be seeing Roland occasionally, myself."

"As you're seeing Aaron."

"Damn right. That man is delicious. And he's not all clingy like Tobias was. He gives me my space, I give him his."

"Then why not just see him and forget about Roland?"

"I don't *want* to forget about Roland. Believe it or not, I *do* have feelings for him. I just can't do the whole serious relationship thing."

"But that's what he wants, it seems like."

"He wants *me*. And he'll take me any way he can get me."

"Well, aren't we confident."

"It's just facts. He did say he loves me, after all."

"So what? That doesn't mean he'll just put up with whatever. Clay said he loved me and look where we are. I didn't even tell you the crap he pulled on me today."

"What? You talked to him?"

"Yeah, he called me at work." Lovey recounted the earlier conversation with Clay, trying her best to keep her anger from reigniting.

"What the hell??!" Desiree exclaimed after Lovey finished. "What an asshole! Girl, I have half a mind to fly to Texas right now and knock him across the head with a cinderblock. How could he be so insensitive??"

"He wasn't thinking, clearly."

"Girl, forget his ass. Block him and he won't be able to pull that kind of okie-doke on you anymore."

"Yeah. He's already texted me several times, trying to apologize. I just ignored them."

"See, this is why you need to be spending time with Roland. I bet he'd know just what to say right now. Have you talked to him?"

"Not since this happened, no."

"Well, get off the phone with me and call him. I need to go, anyway. Aaron is coming over."

"This late?" Lovey looked at her watch.

"Prime booty call hours."

Lovey rolled her eyes. "Bye, Desiree."

"Bye. Oh, and Lovey?"

"Yeah?"

"Don't tell Roland about Aaron."

Lovey started to ask the reason for that, but decided she didn't have the energy. Plus, she suspected Roland wouldn't like hearing that and Desiree knew it too, hence her request.

"I'm not getting in the middle of all that," she replied tiredly.

They ended the call and Lovey slid down under the covers, deep in thought.

THE NEXT DAY, LOVEY got through most of the day just fine. She went to work, ran some errands, and went home, intending to look through some information for the upcoming tax season. After she changed out of her work clothes, she was putting her shoes away in the closet when she spotted one of Clay's t-shirts behind one of her shoeboxes. It was one that he had given her a while back and she usually just wore it to bed or around the house. She didn't know how it ended up on the floor of her closet, but she found herself picking it up and bringing it to her face, inhaling the faint scent of him. Her eyes slid closed, and she felt herself becoming overcome with sadness. As furious as she still was with Clay, her love for him was still there. And realizing that they really were over, with most likely no possibility of reconciliation, was quite disheartening.

The shirt still pressed to her face, Lovey wandered over to her bed. She sat crossed-legged, bringing the shirt to her lap and mindlessly playing with it. Clay had really seemed like the one for her. Everything in her believed they were going to be together forever, even with all of her consistent internal warnings to be sensible and not let her heart get ahead of itself. It wasn't infatuation or some crush she had on Clay, like it had been with Evan and most of the men before him. She was sincerely in love with him. And to realize that she was really alone, again, made her wonder if she would ever have the happily ever after that she dreamed of.

Tears came to her eyes, but Lovey hastily wiped them away, refusing to cry. Crying wasn't going to bring Clay back, or make any other man appear at her door. Lovey began to wonder if the problem was with her; maybe she was too sensitive or her expectations were too high. Maybe happily ever after was just too much to ask of anyone nowadays. Forever was a long time, and most people seemed to only be worried about the here and now.

Shoving the t-shirt to the floor, Lovey turned away from it, bringing her knees to her chest and wrapping her arms around them. She had always thought she was a good person who treated others with respect, and she didn't understand why she wasn't getting that in return from the men she dealt with. Obviously, she had been choosing the wrong men, but she thought Clay had been different. She didn't have Desiree's discernment when it came to the opposite sex; Desiree almost never had these kinds of issues.

But then again, Desiree didn't want a real relationship the way Lovey did. Desiree only wanted to have her fun with a man and then move on, which was apparently more desirable than trying to build a foundation towards marriage and a family. Even if it would guarantee her constant companionship, Lovey couldn't make herself change her values. It just wasn't her. But clearly *something* had to change. She was simply tired of getting kicked in the teeth when it came to love.

After several more moments, Lovey slid off the bed, kicking Clay's t-shirt underneath it as she walked out of the room. She grabbed her laptop and sat on the couch, intending to get some work done, but her mind couldn't stay on the task at hand. Giving up after a while, she moved her laptop to the side and grabbed the remote, but there was nothing she really wanted to watch. And it seemed like every channel she landed on showed something that reminded her of Clay.

"This is crazy," she muttered with a deep sigh, running a hand through her hair. "If only I could forget about them as easily as they seem to forget about me."

She grabbed her phone and called Desiree, but the call went to voicemail. She tried to call Liz, but she was in the middle of something and said she'd have to call her back. Her two main go-to's occupied, Lovey hesitantly texted Roland, asking him if he was busy. She had almost forgotten that she had his number; Desiree gave it to her a while back, though Lovey hadn't known why.

Roland quickly replied that he wasn't busy at the moment and could call her shortly, if she wanted. She did. Five minutes later, her phone rang.

"Hey, what's going on, Lovey?" he greeted her.

"Hey, Roland. Y'all don't have anything going on at Barfly tonight? I don't want to take you away from anything."

"You're not. There's people here, but it's not a full house. My employees are holding things down while I'm back here in the office. I can see everything from the security cameras."

"Oh okay."

"So, how's everything going?"

"Ugh...you know what? We don't need to talk about me. I *do* have some stuff on my mind, but I don't want to be always whining and complaining to you about my issues."

"When did you ever do that?"

"Come on. Me crying outside about Clay on Thanksgiving, sulking and drowning in chocolate after he broke up with me..."

"Both totally understandable situations where anybody would be upset..."

"Not to mention tagging along on you and Desiree's date the night Clay had to cancel our plans."

"I know Desiree nagged you into that. And you clearly didn't want to be there."

"You probably think I'm the most fragile thing walking."

"I think you're a woman who loves hard and isn't afraid to feel things. Doesn't make you fragile."

"I just don't want to be one of those people where something is wrong *every* time you talk to them. That's draining."

"I'm too deep to get drained so easily. Let *me* worry about that. If you've got something on your mind, I'm more than willing to listen."

Lovey couldn't help but smile. "I definitely appreciate it."

"I know you do."

"How's everything with you, though?"

"Everything's everything. Business is good here, I'm in good health and well, you already know what's going on with your girl. So, not much to tell this way. Now quit stalling and tell me what's going on with you."

Chuckling, Lovey went ahead and told Roland about Clay's last phone call, and how she had been feeling since. She confided in him about her anger, her contemplation about herself, and the sadness she felt about possibly remaining alone for the rest of her life.

"I'm just starting to think it's not in the cards for me, the whole happy marriage thing," she admitted. "I'm in my thirties and keep hitting brick walls. No one seems to want forever anymore."

"A lot of people don't," Roland replied honestly. "Or they're not willing to do what it takes to get it, as far as being steadfast, toughing it out through the hard times, being honest with each other no matter what. People give up so easily nowadays. That old school 'for better or for worse' mentality is a thing of the past, generally speaking."

"So I've learned."

"If you ask me, it's too easy to get married and divorced now," Roland continued. "That's why a lot of people don't take it as seriously as they should, in my opinion, because they know at any given time they can just get out of it. It's not the sacred union it's supposed to be."

"I totally agree. For my parents, divorce just wasn't an option. They vowed to just work through whatever came up, together. Desiree's parents are the same way. Short of something major going on like abuse, I think that's the way it should be."

"What about infidelity? Are you one-strike-and-you're-out on that?"

"Honestly, if it happened once, I think I could get past it, eventually. But if it was a constant thing, then no. I couldn't trust you, and I need to be able to trust my husband. It would break my heart, but I can't be with someone who doesn't have enough respect for me to be faithful."

"And what trips me out is that people act like they have no control over that. Like sleeping with someone else is something that 'just happens.' No, you make the choice to do it."

Lovey paused, wondering if she should ask what was on her mind. "Was that the excuse your ex gave you?"

"Among others, yeah." Roland cleared his throat. "I forgave her and took her back after the first time, but after she did it again, I was done."

"Oh wow."

"That's why I have so little tolerance for nonsense now," Roland continued. "If you can't be straight up with me, I don't need to deal with you."

"I'm the same way, especially after everything I've dealt with. This latest thing with Clay has really messed my head up, Roland. I've never felt anything close to hatred in my heart for any human being, ever, but I'm sure feeling it now. I don't like that. I don't like that anyone can take me there. But it's just how I feel."

"That's exactly how I felt when I found out about Anna creeping around behind my back. You don't want to let anyone have that kind of power over you, but the hurt from being betrayed and disrespected is so raw, you almost can't help it."

"Exactly!"

"I certainly don't think it's healthy to carry that around for too long, but everyone has to be allowed time to heal. And you're gonna heal from this thing with Clay, in your own time."

"I hope so. I'm just feeling very fed up right now."

"That's a good thing. When you're fed up, you make changes. And maybe it's time for that."

Lovey had never looked at it that way. She had always considered getting to the point of being fed up as some kind of end point, not a starting one.

"Wow," she marveled aloud. "How in the world did you get to be so wise?"

"A mixture of good home training, learning from my mistakes, and paying attention. I guess. I've never thought of myself as *wise*, though."

"I think you are."

"Well, I'll take the compliment, then."

They continued to talk until Roland had to take care of some things at the club, but he called her back when he was on his way home. They talked well into the night, both of them totally losing track of time.

"So I have a question for you," Roland said. He had gotten home and was lounging on his bed, as Lovey was simultaneously lounging on hers. "I hope you don't take offense to it."

"Okay..." Lovey replied with a cautious smile. "Lay it on me."

"Is that all your real hair?"

Lovey laughed. "Yeah, it is."

"It's just so rare to see women rocking their real hair nowadays."

"True. And it's hard to tell what's real and what's not sometimes. Desiree wears wigs all the time, even though she has plenty of hair. Sometimes it's just about needing a break from it."

"I'm sorry..."

"Please, no need to be sorry. I get asked that a lot."

"Do people also ask if you're all Black?"

"Oh absolutely! I get the 'what are you mixed with' question at least once a week."

Roland chuckled.

"And in case you're wondering and just don't want to ask, I'm not mixed. Both of my parents were Black. I'm just on the lighter end of the color spectrum, that's all."

"I feel you. I just couldn't help being curious, but it wouldn't have made any difference whatsoever. You do know that, right?"

"Oh, I know. I don't take any offense to it."

"Good," Roland said, relieved. "Here's another question for you: is Lovey your real name?"

"It's a lifelong nickname, but the name on my birth certificate is Estelle."

"Estelle? Really?"

Lovey chuckled. "Yep. Very few people know that, though."

"Does Desiree know that?"

"Of course. She knows I don't prefer that name, though, and thankfully never uses it."

"How did you get the name Lovey?"

"According to my parents, I was *very* affectionate practically out of the womb; I was always hugged up on someone. I even tried to hug people I didn't know, apparently."

"For real?" Roland laughed.

"And I was always telling folks I loved them. Would actually cry if they didn't say it back. Thankfully I grew out of that part."

They both laughed. Their conversation continued until their yawns began to outnumber their words, and by then the sun was starting to come up. Lovey knew she would be stopping by Starbucks on the way to work in a few hours, but as she curled up beneath her light blue comforter, she had a satisfied smile on her face.

Maybe Desiree had been right; getting closer to Roland was looking to be just what she needed.

Chapter 16

IT WAS CHRISTMAS DAY, and Desiree was at her parent's house with her sisters, exchanging gifts and stuffing their faces as they did every year. It wasn't quite as big a gathering as on Thanksgiving, but practically the entire family was there again, enjoying their traditional brunch and tearing into their gifts. Once all the gifts were opened, the men and children convened in the den to watch the NBA basketball games, while the women made themselves comfortable in the living room. It didn't take long for the topic of conversation to turn to Desiree's relationship saga.

"So you really told your man and your best friend to hook up?" her mother Elyse asked. "You crazy for that, girl."

"I did not tell them to *hook up*; just to hang out together," Desiree corrected.

"One might lead to the other, though."

"I doubt it."

"Is that why Lovey isn't here?" her sister Diamond asked. "Because she's hanging out with Roland?"

"No, Liz has the flu, so she's over there taking care of her."

"Oh."

"Where's Roland today, then?" Dana asked.

Desiree shrugged. "No idea."

"Y'all haven't talked?"

"Not much, really, since I told him I didn't want to be exclusive anymore. He seems to still be a little miffed about that."

"I bet he is," Dori chimed in. "Especially since you didn't *tell* him that but texted it to him. You know you punked out with that, right?"

"Whatever. Shut up."

"I still can't believe you just *gave* Roland to Lovey like that," Diamond marveled, shaking her head.

"Hell, I can't believe he agreed to it," Dana added. "Or Lovey either, for that matter. I'd be wondering if they were harboring some kind of feelings for each other while you and Roland were still together."

Desiree rolled her eyes. "We're still together now, just not exclusively, and of course they don't have feelings for each other like that. They're friends, buddies. That's all."

"Uh-huh. You hope."

"Look, y'all know Lovey just like I do; she's not down for anything shady. Her and Clay haven't even been broken up a month yet. She's still trying to come back from that, and Roland is keeping her company as she does it. And she's helping to keep his mind off me when he and I aren't together. This is a good thing for everybody."

"Girl, what did you hit your head on?" Elyse asked, garnering a laugh from her daughters. "First, I love you but you aren't so potent that a man is just gonna be blind to another beautiful woman while he knows you're out doing whatever with whoever. And Lovey is beyond beautiful, inside and out."

"Yes she is. But she's not me."

Her sisters laughed again. "Somebody's smelling themselves hard," Dori muttered.

Elyse shook her head. "And two, you put two attractive people together like that, something is bound to go down after a while. Especially if they're really friends like you say. The best relationships start out that way, you know."

Desiree hadn't actually thought about it like that, but she still waved off her mother's comment. "Nah."

"Don't be so quick to dismiss that, Desiree. Roland might console Lovey right into realizing that she's better suited for him than you are," Dana warned.

"Yeah, girl, this could really backfire on you," Dori added.

"I'm willing to bet fifty bucks that you're going to regret this," Elyse said. "You probably won't admit it if you do, but you will."

"Hell, I want in on that, too," Dana chimed in.

"Me, too!" Diamond and Dori exclaimed.

Desiree gaped at them. "Really, y'all??"

"Yep!" they all chorused.

Everyone but Desiree burst out laughing. She sucked her teeth, cutting her eyes at them.

"That's all right; laugh all you want to. I'll just be proving all y'all wrong and getting $200 on top of it."

As her mother and sisters continued to talk about how dumb she was, Desiree got a text from Aaron.

U wanna come over later tonight?

Grinning, Desiree excitedly typed her response:

Hell yeah. I'll be there with bells on.

And nothing else, right?

You'll see. It's gonna be a merry Christmas for you either way.

I like that. And I'll definitely be making those jingle bells rock.

Yeah, I don't have anything to worry about, Desiree thought to herself. *I'm already getting everything I want.*

THE DAY AFTER CHRISTMAS, Roland called Lovey and invited her out to lunch.

"Sure!" Lovey eagerly replied, her smile evident through the phone. "I'd love to."

"Good. How's Liz doing? She feeling better?"

"Yeah, thankfully. She's well enough to kick me out. Got tired of me mothering her."

Roland chuckled. "Glad to hear it. That she's feeling better, I mean. Not that she kicked you to the curb."

"I'm not complaining. Liz is not the most pleasant patient." She giggled. "As long as I knew she was okay, I was glad to get out of there. Thankfully I didn't end up sick, myself."

"I would've had your back, if you did," Roland assured automatically.

There was a somewhat awkward pause and Roland wished he hadn't said what he said out loud. He meant it, but he didn't want to freak Lovey out, which he had already seen she was prone to doing.

Finally after several moments, Lovey spoke. "That's nice of you to say, Roland."

They continued to talk for several more minutes, each of them looking forward to seeing the other. Roland had a smile on his face that he didn't even realize as he continued on about his work. He'd been kicking around the idea of inviting Lovey to lunch all morning, and he finally just bit the bullet and did it. Ever since their all-night phone call, Roland really felt closer to Lovey. She shared with him things about her childhood, her family, and her fantasies, even the ones that she thought were a little silly but still maintained because they brought her joy to think about, like running across a mountain singing like Julie Andrews in *A Sound of Music*. Roland had laughed at that and caught himself, immediately apologizing, but Lovey insisted the apology wasn't necessary because she was fully aware of how corny that fantasy was. Roland loved that. He loved that she didn't take herself so seriously.

He also loved that she was such an open book; she willingly shared things about herself. Nothing was off limits. And not only was she open about herself, she was just as interested in learning more about Roland, too. It wasn't one-sided like it usually was with Desiree. Conversations with her usually consisted of him asking her a bunch of questions like an interview or something, and her not really trying to learn as much about him in return. It didn't flow into a conversation like it did with Lovey.

And Desiree was still tight-lipped about several areas in her life, and Roland couldn't help but wonder what it was she was hiding. Things had gotten slightly better with their communication since he had pointed the unevenness out to her, but only marginally. That only led Roland to believe she just wasn't interested in learning about him and getting to know him. That wasn't the case with Lovey.

Lovey was certainly interested. She was enjoying getting to know Roland better, and talking to him usually provided a boost to her day. Ever since their all-night conversation, he was on her mind steadily. Talking to him was so easy, so soothing. He didn't make fun of her for her admittedly corny childhood dreams and fantasies, or for being a sap who believed in and wanted happily ever after. He hadn't scoffed when she said she wanted to be a more traditional wife like her mother had been. A lot of men before him had, which is why Lovey had stopped sharing such things until she was sure something has heavy as marriage could even be discussed without freaking them out. But Roland had taken everything in stride, wanting to know more. And it made Lovey want to tell him more. Desiree probably would have said she was telling too much and should be more elusive, but Lovey wasn't interested in pretense. They were adults. To not share things because she just weren't ready to do so was one thing; to not share them because she was strategizing was a game. And Lovey simply wasn't interested in games.

They talked almost daily, and a good chunk of their conversations still consisted of things about Desiree. It was like an unspoken reminder for both of them that she was the main reason they were hanging out and getting closer, and it wasn't about anything else. Mentions of Desiree were peppered throughout their conversations sparingly, just enough, as if to fill a silent quota so they could feel comfortable steering the conversations to things they'd rather talk about without feeling guilty.

That feeling of guilt remained mostly with Lovey. Part of her still didn't feel totally right about getting so close to Roland, even if he and Desiree weren't exclusive anymore. When Desiree called her an hour or so after Roland extended his lunch invitation, Lovey was sure to mention it.

"Is that okay?" she asked her friend. "I just want to make *sure* you're still cool with it."

"Girl, will you chill out? Of course I'm still cool with it," Desiree insisted. "I'm glad y'all are spending time together. Where are y'all going for lunch?"

"I don't know yet."

"Well, you don't have to worry about me. I'm not backtracking about anything."

"If you say so."

"I'm gonna be seeing Aaron for lunch, myself," Desiree informed her. "Though it remains to be seen if any actual eating will be done, though. Well, on my part, at least."

"Girl," Lovey shook her head as she clicked through some emails on her computer. "Do y'all actually date or just get it in all the time?"

"I guess today's lunch is supposed to be a date. That's what he called it."

"That's a good thing, right?"

"I guess. I just know I'm looking forward to seeing him."

"Sounds like you really like him."

"I certainly like sleeping with him. And he's a cool guy, too."

"You've been getting to know each other?"

"Some. Whenever we see each other, we're more focused on tearing each other's clothes off to think about anything else. But we talk about some stuff here and there."

"Hmm."

"I don't mind that, though. I don't need to know the man's entire history. We're keeping it light and easy right now and I like that."

"Well, hey, if you're happy with it, I'm happy for you."

"Really?"

"Why wouldn't I be?"

"I thought you'd be salty about how I cooled things off with Roland."

"Honestly, D., you *could've* handled that whole situation better than you did, but it was your decision. If you're not willing to be all in, Roland deserved to know that."

"Yeah. I guess. I can acknowledge that texting him something like that wasn't the coolest thing to do. But I knew he'd be pissed and I, well, I don't like him being upset with me like that."

"I'm surprised you care."

"Damn, Lovey, I'm not heartless. I still like the man. Of course I care."

"I guess I just figured since you don't want to be with him, anyway..."

"For the hundredth time, I *do* still want to be with Roland. Just not exclusively."

"But y'all aren't even talking, D."

"I'm just giving him time to cool off. I'll ease back in there once he's not so heated at me."

"All right, I guess you have this all worked out," Lovey said. "I still hope you know what you're doing."

"I know exactly what I'm doing."

"If you say so. Well, I need to get some stuff done before I get ready to go meet Roland. I still have to find out where we're going."

"Okay. Enjoy. I'm over here oiling up for Aaron."

Lovey chuckled. "Bye, D."

Lovey worked for another hour or so before she headed out for her lunch with Roland. After a few exchanged texts, they agreed to meet at a local wing spot that wasn't too far from either of them. Lovey noted the anticipation she felt about seeing Roland, but brushed it off as just being glad to see her friend again. That didn't stop her from scrutinizing herself in the bathroom mirror of her office to make sure she looked perfect before leaving, though.

Roland arrived a couple of minutes before her, and was just getting out of his car when she pulled into the parking lot. When he noticed her, he smiled and waited, his hands casually in his pockets. Lovey couldn't help but note how handsome he looked, standing there in his long black coat, white Polo shirt and black jeans, the sun beating down on him as if it was his own personal spotlight. She had to make herself tear her eyes away, and then immediately wondered if he had noticed her staring.

Roland was appreciating Lovey's appearance, too. When she stepped out of the car, he actually grunted in approval, then quickly looked away, wondering if she had possibly heard him. She was wearing a coat, but that didn't stop him from seeing how the emerald green sweater dress she wore underneath hugged her body. Her long hair was slicked back into a ponytail, and she was sporting a pair of tan knee-high boots that Roland suspected wouldn't look as good on anyone else. He could admit that he never *really* noticed just how much Lovey had it going on until then.

"Hey, Roland," she greeted him with a smile.

"What's up, Lovey. Glad you could make it," Roland replied as he gave her a hug.

"Of course! Plus it's just nice to get out of the office for a while."

"I feel you. Come on, let's get inside. This wind is really starting to pick up out here."

After they placed their orders, they claimed one of the side booths. When Lovey slid out of her coat, Roland had to look away again. He hadn't seen a figure like hers since the last time he watched a rap video. But he would bet that Lovey's body was all natural, unlike a lot of those video dancers.

Their conversation picked up easily, sharing how their mornings went and a couple of things that were going on in the news. Lovey did mention that she had spoken to Desiree earlier, and Roland just kind of shrugged, not having much to say about that. He still hadn't spoken to Desiree, and realized he wasn't in a big hurry to. Like

Desiree claimed she wanted, Lovey was keeping his attention occupied.

When their order was ready, they each tore into their baskets of wings and fries, the conversation halting as they did so. Roland never thought he would enjoy watching a woman eat chicken wings, but seeing Lovey sitting there in her office attire and manicured nails devouring her honey barbecue wings like they were the best things she ever tasted sent a warm feeling coursing through him. He liked how she could be ladylike but not so much so that she wouldn't suck the sauce from her fingertips or rest her forearms on the table. The only reason they were even there was because Lovey had insisted; she remembered him saying how much he loved wings and hadn't had any in a while, so she suggested they go get some. He was going to take her someplace a little nicer, but she wouldn't hear of it.

"It's not all about what I want," she had said. "And I love some good wings, too."

Roland had marveled at that. Lovey was selfless in a way he just wasn't used to. Especially since Desiree didn't make those kinds of concessions for him; they usually went wherever she wanted to go. She usually didn't even ask him what he wanted because she had gotten used to him being cool with whatever she chose. Roland knew he played a part in that because he never spoke up or made a big deal about it, because most of the time it wasn't. He wasn't terribly particular when it came to things like restaurants. But the fact that Lovey considered his wants like she had certainly didn't go unnoticed, or unappreciated.

Meanwhile, Desiree was out with Aaron and unfortunately, wasn't having as good a time as Lovey and Roland were. She had really hoped that his lunch invitation was just a pretense to him getting her into bed again, but it turned out he actually wanted to go out somewhere.

"We don't have to go anywhere," she said flirtatiously when he arrived at her apartment. She slid her arms around his neck and laid a tongue-filled kiss on him. "You can fill up on me all you want."

"And you know I love that, but I wasn't frontin' when I said I wanted us to have lunch today," Aaron responded, his hand gripping her backside. "I'm in the mood for some Subway."

"Subway?"

"Yeah, girl, I love those meatball subs. Come on, change clothes real quick so we can go."

Desiree was a little jarred. She'd been sure that when he saw her in her cute yellow teddy that he would forget about any lunch plans he may have had. But he really wanted a meatball sub more than he wanted her right then.

"Umm, okay," she finally muttered. "I'll be back in a minute." She started to walk off, then looked back at him. "I wouldn't be mad if you followed me back here."

"I know you wouldn't. But we can get to all that later; my stomach is growling like a mug."

With a slight frown, Desiree stomped off to her bedroom.

When they got to Subway, Aaron ordered his precious meatball sub and then tried to order for Desiree, but she stopped that in its tracks. She could place her own orders, and the fact that he even tried that irritated her. After they got their food, Aaron sat at the nearest table without even caring that it needed to be cleaned off, and tore into his sandwich before Desiree had wiped off her seat and sat down.

"So what's going on with you?" he asked her with his mouth full.

Rolling her eyes, Desiree started unwrapping her sandwich. "Nothing much."

"Cool," Aaron nodded as if she had just told him she had adopted a litter of puppies. He took another huge bite of his sub before calling out to the employees behind the counter, "Hey, bruh, can you make me another one of these? This so *good*!"

"You couldn't just walk up there and order that instead of hollering from the table?" Desiree hissed, slightly embarrassed.

"It's not like there's anybody in line. And the counter is like five feet away."

"Still, though. Have some class."

"You don't worry about how much class I got when I'm bangin' that back out, do you?" Aaron winked at her as he licked some sauce from his mouth.

Desiree just stared at him. As irresistible as she always found him before, she was utterly turned off by him now. She started to wonder how Lovey and Roland's lunch was going.

It was going great. Lovey and Roland almost lost track of time as they talked and laughed while they ate, with the owner of the wing spot coming to introduce himself and strike up a conversation. He even let them sample some new sauce flavors he was working on, and gave them each a piece of pound cake, on the house. Lovey knew she was going to be drinking nothing but green smoothies for the next few days to account for all of these calories, but she was having too good a time to care.

"Y'all make such a nice looking young couple," the owner, who everybody called Big Saul, commented as he brought them refills on their drinks.

"Thank you, Big Saul, but we're just friends," Lovey quickly corrected, glancing at Roland with a smile. "And you're so sweet to bring our drinks but we could've gotten those."

"Yeah, you're gonna have everybody wanting you to bring them their stuff," Roland joked. "Everybody else has to go to the drink machine."

"They'll be all right. I bring 'em for who I wanna bring 'em for," Big Saul replied with a wave of the hand. "Y'all enjoyed everything?"

"Oh, yes, it was awesome. And thank you again for the cake," Lovey said, still smiling.

"You don't have to keep thanking me, sweetheart. I like treating nice people."

"I'll have to make sure I tell everybody about your place, here. These were the best wings I've had in years, seriously."

"Hell, you send a bunch of customers in here and I'll feed you 'til kingdom come."

He and Lovey laughed heartily, making Roland smile. He just listened to them go on and on like they had known each other for years instead of just the last half hour. Lovey seemed to have a way of drawing people to her. She had a warmth that people wanted to be around and bask in. Roland knew an hour had probably come and gone but he hadn't even looked at his watch; even though he knew he had things to do at work, he was in no hurry to leave Lovey's company.

Desiree was about to make up an excuse to get away from Aaron. He was getting on her nerves and she no longer wanted to be around him. When he finished scarfing down two meatball subs, he proceeded to talk about his football playing days, claiming he could have been the next Bo Jackson if he hadn't blown out his knee. Desiree just nodded occasionally as she half-listened to his stories of grandeur, wondering if and when he was going to notice that she was hardly saying anything at all.

Damn, has he always been this stuck on himself?

Roland didn't do that. He asked her things about herself, tried to get to know her. While it was true that Desiree hadn't been super-eager to divulge too much information to Roland, she appreciated that he even cared to ask about it.

"Yeah, looka here," she finally droned, not being able to take it anymore. "Thanks for the sandwich and all, but I need to get some things done. Can we go now?"

"Oh, I see; you ready to work off these calories, huh?" Aaron surmised, leaning back in his seat with a smirk.

Desiree couldn't deny he was still sexy to look at, but at the moment she wasn't interested in anything but him getting her back to her apartment and then leaving her alone. "No, baby, I really do have some things I need to do. If you wanna stay here and eat another sub, I can just call an Uber."

Aaron looked at her for a moment, then chuckled. "Girl, stop. Let's go."

They didn't say much during their ride back to Desiree's apartment, which was fine with her. When they got back to her place, she started to just get out of the car with nothing more than a 'thank you,' but Aaron grabbed her arm and pulled her into a kiss that made her temporarily forget about his lunchtime behavior. Before she knew it, they were fooling around behind the tinted windows of his car.

"You still mad?" Aaron asked when they were done, his voice breathless.

Adjusting her bra, Desiree looked over at him with a smirk. "*Was* I mad?" She lifted her hips so she could pull her jeans back up.

"You seemed like you were, since you were claiming to have something to do all of a sudden."

"That wasn't a lie. I *do* have stuff to do."

"But I see I made you forget all about that, huh?"

Desiree looked at him, then lightly sucked her teeth. "Whatever."

"Girl, you know you can't resist me. I don't even know why you're acting like that."

Rolling her eyes, Desiree grabbed her purse that she had thrown on the backseat. "Yeah, okay. You enjoy the rest of your day. And thanks for the sandwich. I guess."

"Where you goin'?" Aaron grabbed her arm. "I can come in so we can finish what we started."

"Oh baby, I'm finished right now," Desiree insisted, pulling her arm free. "And don't be grabbing on me like that."

"I thought you liked it when I got rough."

"Bye, Aaron."

Desiree got out of the car and stomped to her apartment, thoroughly annoyed. She was annoyed that Aaron had preferred a sandwich more than her, that he had acted like he had no home training while they were out, and then like he was god's gift to the vagina afterwards. Desiree *had* actually hoped that they could spend the rest of the afternoon working off those subs, but after the way he was acting, she just wanted to get away from him. So she was annoyed about that, too.

Not to mention that their car tryst hadn't been nearly enough to satisfy her immense sexual appetite, so she felt like she had been left hanging. And she was *absolutely* annoyed about that.

Pouting, she made herself be productive and get some work done. After a while, her mind began to wander towards how Lovey and Roland's lunch outing was going. She glanced at her watch; she figured it was probably over with by then; it had been almost three hours since Lovey was getting ready to meet Roland. Surely they were both back at work by then. Desiree figured she'd call Lovey later, after she got off work, to get the likely mundane details of how things went.

When Desiree called Lovey a few hours later, though, she was shocked to hear that Lovey wasn't exactly available to talk.

"What did you say?" she asked, sure she hadn't heard her friend right.

"I said I'm still with Roland," Lovey repeated matter-of-factly.

Momentarily speechless, Desiree cleared her throat. "Still? Lunchtime was hours ago."

"Yeah, but we were having such a good time that we decided to hang out some more."

Desiree frowned slightly, then made herself stop. "Oh...okay. Well, that's nice, I guess."

"It is. This is the best day I've had in a while."

"Oh, really?" Desiree started to ask what exactly they were doing to make this day so special, but before she could, Lovey jumped in.

"Yep. In fact, let me get off this phone; I don't want to be rude. I'll talk to you later, D., okay?"

Slightly put off, Desiree made herself respond. "Um, yeah. Okay."

Lovey hung up.

Desiree just sat looking at the phone, the frown back and in full force. Did Lovey really just blow her off? Why was she in such a hurry to get off the phone? And since when did Lovey ditch work for a man, much less a man she claimed she wasn't interested in?

"Okay, I'm trippin'," she told herself, shaking her head to clear it of such thoughts. There was nothing but friendship going on between Lovey and Roland; she was sure of it. So they had a good time together; so what? That was the whole point of them hanging out together, wasn't it? If anything, Desiree felt she should be proud of herself for the part she played in it; Lovey hadn't sounded so relaxed and content in a while. This was all thanks to her.

Pushing away from her kitchen table, Desiree went to get a frozen pizza out of the freezer. After she popped it into the oven, she leaned on the counter, mindlessly tapping her fingers on the edge.

Yeah, this was a good thing, she told herself. Lovey and Roland still being together hours after their lunch was a good thing. *They're just keeping each other company. That's all.* For all Lovey knew, Desiree was still with Aaron. And Desiree hadn't talked to Roland lately, but she knew that he was still not over her. He couldn't be.

As she waited on her pizza, she tried to text Aaron, but got no response. She checked to see if her cyber-sex buddy Cornell was online, but he wasn't. She thought about hitting up Tobias, but didn't want to open that can of worms again, especially after threatening to have him beaten up if he didn't leave her alone.

She considered calling one of her sisters or her mother, but that wasn't the kind of *company* she wanted.

There were a couple of guys that she kept far on the backburner just in case, but when she called the first guy, his phone was disconnected. And with the other, a nice but boring teacher named Christian, the female that answered the phone announced (very strongly) that she was his fiancée and that there was no need for Desiree to call there again. It was clear she knew about Desiree, which only made Desiree wonder what Christian had been saying about her.

Scrolling through her phone contacts, there wasn't anyone else that she felt like tolerating enough to call. So she just grabbed her laptop, logged on to her favorite porn site, and wished she could trade places with the women getting banged onscreen. As she munched on her supreme pizza, she tried not to wonder if Lovey and Roland might be doing anything close to what she was watching.

Chapter 17

OVER THE NEXT COUPLE of weeks, Lovey and Roland's time together increased. It happened naturally, without either of them planning or overthinking it. They enjoyed each other's company; it was as simple as that.

A small part of Lovey still felt guilty about the time she was spending with Roland (and that she was enjoying it so much), but both Liz and Roland assured her that there was nothing to feel guilty about. Desiree had insisted over and over that this was what she wanted, so Roland didn't even feel the need in bringing her up when he and Lovey were together. And over time, Lovey was starting to feel the same way.

The day they went to lunch, neither Lovey nor Roland wanted to go back to work, but after sitting in the wing spot for close to two hours, they knew they had to get back to their days. Roland walked Lovey to her car and looked at her thoughtfully as he opened her door for her.

"What's wrong?" Lovey asked, wondering if some stray barbecue sauce or something was on her face.

"I don't want you to leave," Roland said frankly.

Gasping slightly, Lovey knew her cheeks were probably bright red already. She touched her fingers to her lips as she bit them nervously, not wanting to let on how happy his statement made her.

"Honestly, I can't say I'm in a huge hurry to get back to work, either," she shyly admitted.

"Do you have to?"

Lovey made herself look at her boots because the way his eyes were boring into her was making her squirm a little bit, and not in the bad way.

"Um, not really. I don't have any appointments this afternoon; I was just going to get caught up on some paperwork."

"Well, I *do* have to get back to the club for some stuff, but if you want, you can come hang," Roland offered, actually looking a little nervous. "Maybe you can even do your work in the office."

"Yeah?"

"Yeah. And then afterwards, you can stick around, if you want. We're doing our first open mic night tonight."

"That sounds like fun."

"It should be. You know there's always folks that think they're the next superstar but couldn't carry a tune if you glued it to 'em. We can laugh at them together."

Lovey giggled. "You're so awful."

Roland smiled. "Is that a yes?"

Not even bothering to act like there was anything to think about, Lovey nodded. "It's a yes."

Roland's smile widened. "Good. And I'll feed you, of course; we can get something from the kitchen at the club or order in. Or go for a late dinner after we leave."

"You sure know how to entice a lady."

"I like to think my parents raised me right." Roland winked.

"I would agree. So..." *Why am I so nervous??* "I'll just run by my office, grab my laptop and files and meet you over at Barfly. Sound good?"

"Sounds great."

That was the best evening Lovey had enjoyed since the night before Clay dumped her. She and Roland had a blast that night after they each finished their work, laughing at the wannabe singers and comedians. Lovey felt a little bad about laughing because she certainly wouldn't have the nerve to get up there herself, but some of them were so abominably bad that she just couldn't help it. More than a few times, she buried her face in Roland's shoulder, not wanting the performers to see her laughing at them, especially when being funny wasn't their goal. After a while, though, she stopped worrying about it and just enjoyed herself.

Ever since that night, not a day went by that Lovey and Roland didn't communicate in some form. They would send occasional texts throughout the work day and call or video chat in the evenings. They would meet for lunch or Lovey would go by the club after she got off work, or Roland would come by and watch movies with her at her place. One night, Roland even cooked for her, which is something he never did for Desiree. She thanked him over and over, and insisted on helping to clean up, despite his telling her she didn't have to. Her appreciation was evident, and it only made Roland want to do more things for her. It was nice to be with a woman that didn't expect everything to be done for her but appreciated everything that was.

And even though nothing more than hugs happened between them, that didn't mean the attraction wasn't there. The appreciative perusals when they thought the other one wasn't looking, the subtly bitten bottom lips, the heart-racing nervousness...all of that increased the more they were around each other. Their platonic hugs were starting to become tighter and more lingering. Hands lightly roamed each other's backs instead of staying firmly in one spot. When they sat together on a couch, they each automatically sat closer instead of at opposite ends. Still not touching, but close enough.

There were a couple of times when Lovey had her hair pulled up that Roland wanted to bury his face in her neck; she always smelled so good, it was almost intoxicating. And Lovey caught herself staring at Roland's lips several times, wondering what they felt like. She tried to attribute it to just being on affection withdrawal since her breakup with Clay, but if she was honest with herself, she knew that wasn't it. Truth be told, she rarely even thought about Clay much anymore. There were the occasional moments that he would ease into her mind, but even when that happened, she didn't feel sad or even angry like before. She just pushed the thoughts away. There was no need in wasting emotion on a man she wasn't going to have or probably even talk to again. Roland was occupying the head space Clay had vacated, and while there were a couple of times where Lovey had to admonish herself for wanting to freak out about it, mostly she enjoyed it.

Roland was enjoying it, too, and not feeling guilty in the least. He loved being around Lovey and wasn't interested in pretending he wasn't. Desiree was barely even a factor for him; she finally called him for the first time since sending them that brush-off text, and when she did, Roland realized he just didn't have a lot to say to her. There were a few times where she tried to slyly dig for information about what he and Lovey did during their time together, but Roland told her nothing. It wasn't any of her business. The couple of times they talked, Roland kept the calls to just a few minutes. He could sense that she was slowly trying to start integrating herself back into his mix, and he wasn't going to make it easy on her.

Desiree could admit that she didn't expect for things to go this way. When she suggested that Roland and Lovey spend more time together, they were never supposed to enjoy it so much that they forgot about *her*. But she was noticing that they were both becoming harder to reach; a lot of the time when she would call Lovey, Lovey was either on the phone with Roland or hanging out with him. And Desiree noticed that Lovey never offered to tell Roland they could hang out later so that she could spend some time with Desiree. It's almost like it never even crossed her mind. Desiree was a little offended by that.

And Roland acted like she was some telemarketer when she called; he indulged her for a few minutes before making up some excuse and ending the call. That's if he answered the phone at all. He never sounded happy to hear from her, and getting any substantial conversation from him was almost impossible. This was not what Desiree wanted to happen at all. This wasn't the plan.

In fact, if she was honest with herself, Desiree was jealous.

Buy why, though? It wasn't like Lovey and Roland were a couple; they were just hanging out. And they hanging out because Desiree felt she needed some space from Roland (and also to help Lovey deal with her breakup from Clay), but Desiree could admit that she didn't really expect them to enjoy each other *this* much. They weren't supposed to leave her out. Lovey was her best friend and she still considered Roland her man, but it seemed like she was second fiddle to both of them.

It didn't help that she was officially losing interest in Aaron. Ever since their raggedy Subway date, she wasn't as enamored with him as she once was. Now whenever they saw each other, she spent more time silently nitpicking and tallying new flaws than she did enjoying his muscular body, which at one point had been irresistible to her. She just didn't want to be bothered with him much at all.

One thing Desiree had never worried about was being able to find a man. They flocked to her like ants to sugar. And in her line of work, she had occasion to meet plenty. But no matter how many parties she did and men she flirted with, her mind still drifted back to Roland. She didn't expect that. Was it because she had practically let go of Aaron and needed someone to fill the void, or because she sincerely missed him? Or maybe it was because he seemed to be distancing himself from her. That wasn't what she wanted to happen when she suggested they cool off.

But New Years Eve was coming and she had a party planned at Barfly to bring in the new year. And when the clock struck midnight, she fully intended on the heat between her and Roland to be reignited.

ROLAND WAS DOING A masterful job avoiding Desiree.

The New Years Eve party at Barfly was in full swing, and the place was packed. Both Roland and Desiree had their hands full with business and making sure everything ran smoothly, but Desiree was putting just as much effort into getting Roland's attention. So far, he was ignoring her. But she wasn't going to give up.

"Hey, mister," she greeted somewhat breathlessly when she finally cornered him near the bar. He was talking to a couple of patrons and she snuck up behind him, seeing her opportunity. When he turned to her, she tried to remain unfazed by how unhappy he looked to see her. The opposite of how it used to be.

"What's up?" he greeted indifferently.

"I'm still waiting on my dance."

His brow lifted slightly. "I beg your pardon?"

"Come on, don't play. We always dance together."

"I'm good. I've got some things I need to check on. I'm sure you can find someone else to dance with, though."

He walked off, not giving her a chance to respond.

Desiree looked after him, slightly dumbfounded and honestly, a little embarrassed. It was one thing for him to avoid her, but it was quite another for him to brush her off when she was right in his face. Especially when she was wearing her low-cut yellow mini dress that pushed her boobs up to Athens. It was the dress she wore on their first date and she specifically wore it for his benefit. But he didn't even notice. And if he did, he didn't seem to care.

Shake that off, girl, she told herself. *He might be acting all tough right now but keep wearing on him; he won't be able to resist you forever. He's still a man, after all.*

Her determination renewed, Desiree ducked into the dancing crowd, keeping an eye on where Roland was at all times. She saw several women flirt with him, and he smoothly kept it moving with a charming smile, not even letting them get their hopes up. Desiree started to wonder if he was doing that because he wasn't interested in them, or because of Lovey, but she shook that thought out of her mind. Roland and Lovey were just friends, that was it. That was the deal.

When Roland had his back turned, Desiree quickly weaved her way over to him and began seductively dancing against him, her hands lightly resting on his hips. He turned and saw it was her, and she tried her best to remain undeterred by the unwelcoming look in his eyes.

"I told you I wanted a dance," she reminded him, trying to run her hands up his chest. "I see I'm just gonna have to take it."

Roland gently removed her hands. "What are you doing?"

"I told you. I just want a dance."

"Uh-huh. And that's all, huh?"

"For now."

Roland glared at her, shaking his head slightly. "I don't know what kind of game you're playing, Desiree, but I don't have time for it."

"Games? I'm not trying to play any games. If anything, I should be asking *you* that, since you're playing all hard to get and stuff."

"Why would I need to do that? You didn't want me, remember?"

Desiree moved closer to him, wondering if the people around them could hear their conversation. This wasn't a discussion she wanted to have in the middle of the dance floor. "Let's go to your office."

"We don't need to go to my office. There's nothing to talk about."

"Come on, baby," Desiree cooed, rubbing her leg against his. "Don't be like that. I just want to talk to you."

"Yeah. I bet. Like I said, I'm good."

He turned to walk off again, but the floor was so packed, he couldn't get away as quickly as he wanted. Forgetting about the people around them, Desiree stepped closer and grabbed his butt with both hands before sliding them around teasingly close to his crotch. He firmly grabbed her hands and whirled around, clearly not pleased.

"Now see, if I did some shit like that, I'd be brought up on charges," he hissed. He moved away from her, practically pushing people aside as he did so.

Slightly taken aback, Desiree told herself to keep her head in the game. He was clearly still salty about her changing things up in their relationship, and she was simply going to have to wear him down. She was just glad that Lovey wasn't there; she hated being out and about on New Years Eve. Desiree had Roland all to herself, and she was going to take full advantage of it, no matter how hard Roland tried to make it for her.

The party continued, but Desiree had eyes only for Roland. She didn't even want to be bothered with her party patrons, and kind of hated that she was in charge of this little shindig and was technically working. She had to tend to a couple of things, and lost sight of Roland a few times. Any time she tried to ease closer to him, he moved farther away, clearly trying to keep as much distance from her as possible.

It was getting closer to midnight and Desiree was no closer to being back in Roland's good graces than she had been when the night started. The more she watched him, the more she got turned on at how incredibly sexy he looked. His goatee was like a frame to the artwork of his lips, and Desiree wanted nothing more than to kiss them again. The top few buttons on his black shirt were unbuttoned, and she bit her lip as she imagined ripping it open the rest of the way and sliding her tongue across his chest like a brush on a fresh piece of canvas.

She started to question her decision to back away from this man. She'd had him all to herself, and because of her forcibly-suppressed issues, she left the door open for someone else to come in and take her spot.

It was time to get her man back.

Scurrying to the bathroom, Desiree locked herself in a stall and quickly shimmied out of her dress. Unhooking her bra, she hung it on the hook behind the door. Wearing nothing but a gold chain necklace with a pendant that rested right between her breasts and heels (she hadn't worn any panties), she snapped several pictures of herself, varying her pose and sexy expression with each one. For extra assurance, she recorded a brief video complete with breasts fondling and masturbation, trying not to moan too loud but wanting to make sure she could be heard over the music. Other people had come into the bathroom, but they were talking so loudly that Desiree was sure they hadn't heard her.

Sending the video and all of the pictures to Roland, she quickly got dressed and stepped out of the stall. Two ladies were standing near the sinks giving her an amused look.

Hmm. I guess they did hear me, she mused. She quickly washed her hands and with her chin raised, strode out of the bathroom and headed back to the dance floor, her eyes peeled for Roland.

He was standing up on the DJ platform, having just reminded everyone that midnight was fast approaching and telling them to get ready to bring the new year in. She watched as he took his phone out of his pocket slid his thumb across the screen. A few moments later, his jaw dropped slightly, and he immediately glanced at the DJ and stepped away, holding the phone out of his view. He stood off to the side and looked down at his phone again, seemingly transfixed for a several moments. Desiree smirked triumphantly. She knew he was looking at what she sent him.

After a couple of minutes, Roland looked up and scanned the crowd. Desiree stood in the middle of the dance floor, waiting on him to find her. Most everybody was wearing black or some other dark color and she stood out in yellow. She wouldn't be hard to find. When his eyes rested on her, they narrowed slightly, and Desiree wasn't quite able to determine if that look was annoyance or arousal. Choosing to believe it was the latter, she slowly slid her index finger into her mouth, looking right into his eyes. His jaw clenched.

Like I said, he's still a man, she thought to herself.

While he was still watching her, Desiree turned and headed towards the offices, confident that Roland would be following her. She leaned against the wall in the hallway, twirling the hair of her long brown wig around her finger. She had every confidence that it would only be a matter of time before Roland made his way to her.

And she was right. Several minutes later, Roland quickly strode towards her, his expression serious.

"So this is what you're doing now, huh?" he demanded, holding up his phone before stuffing it into his pocket.

"You liked it," she stated confidently. "I *know* you did. I saw the look on your face out there."

"Even if I did, so what? Why are you playing games?"

"Oh, I'm not playing games at all." Desiree pushed herself off the wall and moved towards him seductively. "I had to do something to let you know how much I wanted you."

"Why? Ol' boy dump you or something?"

Desiree shook her head. "This doesn't have anything to do with anybody else. I miss you, Roland." She placed her hands on his chest and used her body to back him into the wall. He didn't resist; he just looked at her. "Don't you miss me?"

Despite himself, Roland swallowed.

Her hand brushed his crotch. "How many times did you watch that video I sent you?"

Grunting, Roland licked his lips. Try as he might to resist it, Desiree was getting to him. When he saw those pictures and that provocative video, it took sheer mind strength to keep his manhood from popping up like a diving board. His mind knew that Desiree probably just couldn't handle not having all of his attention like she thought she could. She was like a child who wanted her parents' attention back after there was a new baby in the house. Roland knew the smart thing would be to walk away from her right then. But his feet didn't seem to want to move.

When Desiree took his hands and placed them on her body, silently encouraging him to touch wherever he liked, he didn't stop her. He reacquainted himself with her smooth, tight dancer's figure, wishing he didn't enjoy how good she felt.

"I want you so much, baby," she whispered, her lips grazing his ear. She ground against his quickly-growing erection. "I've got to have you. *Tonight.*"

Groaning, Roland felt his resistance disappearing like water down a drain. "Why are you doing this?"

"What do you mean? It's not like we ever broke up; my feelings for you never stopped." She eased back slightly and looked into his eyes. "And I know yours for me didn't, either."

Before Roland could respond, she grabbed his face and kissed him, sliding her tongue deep into his mouth. He didn't resist her, returning the kiss with equal intensity. Their hands were all over each other, forgetting about the party they were hosting. Much like the first night they kissed in that same hallway.

By the night's end, Roland was in Desiree's bed.

They ravaged each other as if their relationship had never changed. Desiree screamed her pleasure, loving how Roland pounded into her, slinging her around the bed to give her new angles of ecstasy. As she moaned and panted how glad she was that they were back together, Roland responded only with concentrated grunts, intent on focusing his attention on the task at hand.

The next morning found them in a tangled pile of sheets and limbs. Roland woke up first and slowly untangled himself before gathering his clothes and moving towards the bathroom. By the time Desiree's eyes eased open, Roland was fully dressed and looking for his keys.

"Where are you going?" she asked, sitting up.

He looked at her. "Home."

"Why?"

"Why wouldn't I?"

"I wanted us to spend the day together. Or at least for you to stay long enough for me to brush my teeth."

"I have some stuff I need to do today." He checked his phone.

"Okay..." Desiree wondered what was up with the aloof attitude. "What about later, then? You wanna come back over tonight?"

He shook his head, his eyes still on his phone. "Can't."

"May I ask why not?"

"Got plans with Lovey."

Jarred, Desiree shook her head, convinced she was still partially asleep. "Umm, what?"

"Not sure what the shock is about. You know full well we hang out. Or did you forget hounding both of us to *keep each other company* while you do your own thing?"

Not even bothering to keep herself covered with the bed sheet, Desiree stood and placed her hands on her hips. She looked at him incredulously. "Are you kidding me right now, Roland?"

"What exactly is the problem, Desiree?"

"I just...I guess I figured when you came over here-"

"What, you thought us having sex was going to make everything go back to the way it was? I thought you knew better than that."

"So you just used me?"

Roland actually chuckled. "You stepped to *me*, remember? Pulled out all the stops, too. I would think you'd be happy right now, since you clearly got what you wanted."

"I didn't want just sex, Roland, I want *you*!"

"Oh yeah? Until you start feeling smothered again and decide you can't handle it. You said it yourself, Desiree; you're not good at serious relationships. And I'm not good at being with women who aren't good at serious relationships. So..." He headed for the door.

"Roland!" Desiree grabbed his arm. "Are you seriously leaving right now?"

Roland looked right into her wide eyes. "Yes, Desiree. I'm seriously leaving right now. This is what you wanted and now, it's what I want, too. I rather like everything not being all about you."

He left Desiree standing there, naked and humiliated.

Chapter 18

ROLAND TOLD HIMSELF that he was going to keep the little tryst with Desiree to himself.

But as the next few days passed, he felt more and more compelled to tell Lovey. He was actually feeling a little guilty, even though he wasn't entirely sure why. He and Lovey were just friends; they weren't a couple. They were each free to do as they pleased. Even knowing that, he still felt a little funny about giving in to Desiree like he had. He couldn't help but wonder how Lovey would react if she found out.

After going back and forth about it until his head hurt, he decided to go ahead and tell her. Bite the bullet. His only hope was that Desiree hadn't spilled the beans about it first.

He sent Lovey a text asking if it was okay to come by her office, and she quickly responded that it was. Actually nervous, Roland took a deep breath as he walked towards the building, trying to decide how he was even going to tell her this.

"Hey!" Lovey greeted him, giving him a brief hug after Tara showed him into her office and closed the door.

Roland couldn't help smiling as he returned her warm hug. He figured she still had no idea about what he was there to tell her, given how happy she was.

"I don't wanna take up too much of your time; I know it's the middle of the day," Roland said when they separated.

"It's totally fine; my next appointment isn't for another hour or so." Lovey patted the chair in front of her desk. "Have a seat. You want something to drink?"

"Nah, I'm good." Roland sat down, nervously rubbing his hands together.

"You okay? You look like you have something on your mind," Lovey observed, perching herself on the edge of her desk in front of him. Her face looked concerned. "Talk to me."

"Lovey...I'm actually a little embarrassed to even tell you this..."

"What is it?"

"I..." He looked at the floor and took a deep breath. "I slept with Desiree."

He could hear the tiny gasp above his head. After several moments, he dared to look up at her. Lovey was clearly surprised, her hand on her chest. She didn't look angry, just shocked.

"Oh..." Her fingers started playing with the thin gold necklace around her neck. She averted her eyes. "Okay..."

"I really don't even know why I'm telling you, really," Roland forged ahead. "I mean, it's not like...you and I..."

"No, no, of course," Lovey quickly concurred. Her fingers were still fumbling with her necklace as her eyes darted everywhere but at him. She cleared her throat. "You don't have to explain anything to me. What you and Desiree do is your business."

"No. I mean, yeah but, I still want to be straight up with you," Roland replied. "You and I have gotten closer these last few weeks, and Desiree is your girl..."

"It's fine, Roland."

"For real, Lovey. I don't want things to get weird between us. Nothing has changed between me and Desiree; it was just one impulsive night."

"When was it?" Lovey found herself asking.

"The other night. After the New Years Eve party."

"Oh..." Lovey shook her head, waving her hands in front of her. "I don't even know why I asked that. It's none of my business."

"No no, feel free to ask whatever you want."

"Roland, please..." Lovey eased away from him. Her face was slightly red from embarrassment but she made herself look at him, straightening her spine. "I appreciate you wanting to be up front with me but, like I said, you and Desiree can do whatever you want. It's not like you two fully broke up, right?"

Roland stood, turning to her. "That's what *she* said. But we didn't have any kind of relationship left, Lovey, you know that. I was barely even talking to her."

"Yet you still slept with her." Lovey placed a hand over her mouth briefly as if she regretted her statement, but she didn't try to retract it.

"Lovey-"

"I, um, I have a few things to go over before my next client comes in," Lovey fumbled, walking around her desk. She busied herself straightening some papers. "Thank you, for coming by."

"Can I call you later on?"

"Of course, sure."

Roland eyed her. "Lovey. Lovey, look at me."

Stopping her movements, Lovey turned her eyes to his concerned face.

"Be straight up. Are we good?"

Lovey could tell he was really worried about upsetting her. She told herself to get a grip; Roland wasn't her man. She didn't have any right to get upset about him sleeping with someone else, namely Desiree, who he had been in a relationship with (and according to Desiree, was *still* in a relationship with). This was no big deal.

So why did it feel like someone just punched her in the gut?

Forcing a smile, she kept her voice even when she replied, "Yes, Roland, we're good. You don't have to worry about that. We'll talk later, I promise."

Giving her a relieved smile, Roland nodded. "I'm glad to hear that. I'll let you get back to your work."

"Okay."

"I'll call you later."

"Great."

Roland wanted to give her a hug but she had put the desk between them, so he just quit while he was ahead and left.

"WHY DID YOU TELL HER anything?"

Roland and E.J. were in the office at Barfly and E.J. was looking at his little brother in surprise after Roland mentioned sleeping with Desiree and then telling Lovey about it.

Roland stopped trying to pretend he was concentrating on the inventory reports in his hand and dropped them to the floor next to his chair. "You don't think I should've, huh?"

"Not really. It's not like you owe her any explanations. And pick those damn papers up off the floor."

Shaking his head, Roland retrieved the papers and put them on the desk. "I know Lovey and I are just friends. But part of me just didn't feel right keeping it from her. And really, I'm kinda surprised that she didn't hear it already from Desiree."

"So, what...you feel guilty or something?"

"Yeah but I don't know why."

E.J. leaned back in his chair. "Is your guilt about Desiree or about Lovey?"

Roland looked at him. "What do you mean?"

"Why did you get with Desiree, bro? You said you weren't even really feeling her like that anymore."

"It was just sex, man. I know that's not really my thing, sleeping with someone just for the hell of it, but I admit, she got to me. I'm not proud of it but it is what it is."

"So you feel bad for leading her on?"

"I don't feel like I *led her on* at all. She was the one chasing me around the club all night and sending videos of her touching herself."

"And it worked, apparently."

"Yeah. But the next morning, she was acting like things were back to how they used to be, and actually got upset when I said I couldn't see her later 'cause I was meeting up with Lovey. For me it was just sex but it was apparently more than that for her."

"So that's what you feel guilty about?"

Roland thought about it briefly. "As bad as it may sound, not really. Desiree and I are in the place we're in now because of her. She's the one that wanted to keep things casual. If she suddenly changed her mind on that, she sure didn't hip me to it. And I'm not even sure that's what I want, anyway."

"Because of Lovey."

"In part..."

"You're feeling her?"

"I can't deny it, man, I am. It's just hard not to."

"So *that's* why you feel guilty. That's why you told her about you and Desiree."

Roland nodded thoughtfully. "Yeah. I know I technically didn't have to but I just didn't want her to be blind-sighted again. She's had enough of that from dudes."

"Yeah, you really *do* care about her."

"Absolutely."

"Do you know how Lovey feels about you?"

"I think she's kinda feeling me, too, but probably feels like she shouldn't because of Desiree. And she doesn't talk about her ex much but I can't imagine she's over him completely already. She's been in way better spirits lately, though."

"I'm sure that's because of you, at least in part. Which was the point of y'all hanging out in the first place, right?"

"Yeah, that was Desiree's justification for getting me out of her hair so she could date other dudes. And I'll admit, I mostly only agreed to it to show her up. But after a while, it stopped being about that and started just being around Lovey. My day just doesn't feel right until I talk to her."

E.J. peered at his brother. "Yeah, bro. You're hooked."

"I don't know about *hooked*..."

"Get off it. No man tells a woman about stuff he has no obligation to tell her about unless he's heavy into her. You should see the look on your face when you talk about her, man. Just admit it."

"Okay, fine," Roland acquiesced, holding up his hands. "I like her. A lot. I just hope she doesn't think differently of me after this."

"There's no telling with women."

"And I'll admit something else, too. When I hooked up with Desiree the other night, yeah it was mostly just about sex for me, but..."

"Aw, hell. But what?"

"I'd be lying if I said I didn't feel *anything*."

E.J. shook his head.

"I *was* in love with her, after all," Roland justified. "Regardless of what she did, that doesn't just stop. True enough, I haven't wanted to be bothered with her ever since she changed things up but when I got close to her that night...I don't know." He sighed.

"So you're saying you like both of them," E.J. concluded.

"One more than the other, but I guess, yeah. There has to be a reason I didn't just go ahead and end the relationship with Desiree myself instead of agreeing to this casual stuff. Maybe part of me just didn't *want* to."

"So her not wanting to be with just you means nothing now, huh? You were all pissed off about that before. You mean to tell me her opening her legs to you made you forget about all that?"

"No, I didn't forget about it. I'm just being real about where my head is at right now."

"You do realize you're kinda contradicting yourself from what you said a minute ago, right?"

"I meant everything I said. But yeah, I guess."

Shaking his head again, E.J. sat forward in his chair. "Well, honestly, I think you're crazy for even messing with Desiree at all. She seems to be all about just getting what she wants at the moment, regardless of how it affects anyone else. You said she already admitted that she's not good at relationships; why the hell are you even wasting your time?"

"Look, man, I know it doesn't make sense. And it's not like I'm about to run out and propose to her. I just didn't realize how much she was still under my skin. It was easy to forget about all that when I was pissed off and keeping her at arm's length but it's different now. It just is."

"Do what you want, but I'd be careful dealing with two friends like that. This is almost guaranteed to get messy. You could end up hurting both of them and jacking up their friendship, to boot. You need to think about that while you're doing all this going back and forth."

Roland knew his brother was right. The last thing he wanted to do was come between Lovey and Desiree; they'd been best friends for years. And he certainly didn't want to hurt either of them, especially Lovey; she didn't deserve any more heartbreak.

But he couldn't deny his feelings. He didn't want to feel anything for Desiree, but he simply did, even if it wasn't on the level as it was before. And he definitely felt something for Lovey. He just had to decide what he wanted to do about it.

AS ROLAND TALKED TO his older brother about the situation, Lovey talked to her older sister.

"Are you upset?" Liz asked her.

"Part of me is," Lovey admitted. "Though I know I have no right to be. Roland and I aren't dating. He didn't do anything wrong."

"But you like him. So the thought of him banging Desiree can't sit well with you."

Lovey sucked her teeth. "Do you have to be so crass about it?"

"Oh, that was nothing. I *could've* said-"

"Never mind," Lovey interjected, not wanting to hear her sister go into 'potty mouth' mode. "And I never said I liked him like that."

"Oh please, girl, I don't know who you think you're fooling. This is me you're talking to, here."

Lovey sighed, tucking her feet underneath her on the couch. She had Liz on speakerphone and was glad that her sister wasn't there to see her conflicted emotions, which she had never been very good at hiding.

"Okay...maybe I do. But I shouldn't!"

"Who says?"

"Liz, come on. He's still technically with Desiree."

"Please. Desiree just wants to have her cake and eat it, too. You know that as well as I know it, whether you'll admit it or not. And if you and Roland want to make a serious go of things, you shouldn't let Desiree stop you."

"I don't want a man to come between me and my best friend, I don't care how good of a man he is."

"Okay, well then talk to Desiree about it. Maybe if she knew you were sincerely into Roland, she might step aside if for no other reason because she loves you and wants to see you happy."

Lovey paused, not having considered that. "You really think she'd do that?"

"Honestly, it would shock me into oblivion if she did. But I wouldn't put it all the way past her."

"Maybe."

"Have you talked to her?"

"Not really. We talked for a few minutes yesterday but didn't really get into anything. She seemed to rush off the phone. Ever since then I haven't been able to get in touch with her."

"Maybe she's avoiding you."

"Why would she need to do that? I'm not mad at her."

"Easy. She seduced Roland because she didn't like how much attention he was giving you."

Lovey scoffed. "That's crazy!"

"No, it's not. Think about it, Lovey. Any other time, you know she would've called you immediately to give you all the dirty details. But you still wouldn't know anything about them hooking up if Roland hadn't told you. And by the way, that can only mean he's into you, too, because dudes don't voluntarily divulge that kind of stuff for no reason."

Lovey considered her sister's words, then shook her head. "No. I just can't believe that."

"You don't know drama like I know drama. Forget about Desiree being your bestie for a minute and think objectively. Desiree likes having all the attention. You said yourself that y'all haven't been talking as much since you started hanging out with Roland."

"Well, that's my fault. I've let that come before-"

"Girl, if I was there right now I'd slap you clear across the face. Shut up with that. It is *not* your fault for thinking about yourself, not to mention doing exactly what Desiree said she wanted. I just think that Desiree didn't expect for you and Roland to hit it off so well and wanted to remind him that she's supposed to still be number one. You're just essentially the stand-in for when she gets bored with him. Y'all aren't supposed to actually *like* each other like that."

"Liz, come on..."

"And you not being at that New Year's Eve party was the perfect opportunity to get her hooks back into Roland. And sadly, he fell for it, so that's another thing you need to consider."

Lovey chewed her lip.

"If Roland is at all still into Desiree like that, it might be best to just leave him alone," Liz continued frankly. "I'm not saying he's not a good dude and I know you like him.

But I can just see this whole situation being nothing but a big mess down the line."

Lovey didn't like the thought of that at all. "I totally see your point; this could very well be more trouble than it's worth. But honestly, Liz, I don't really want to lose Roland. As funny as I feel admitting it, I *do* have feelings for him. He's just been such a help to me since Clay left...I don't want to let go of that."

"Are you sure this *isn't* just about still being hurt about Clay? Is Roland just an emotional rebound or do you really want to see where things can go with him?"

"At first it was just about getting over Clay. But now, I can honestly say it's about my feelings for Roland. I might not *want* to feel them, but I do."

"Okay, well here's where I'm about to contradict myself. If Roland is who you want, then you need to fight for him."

Shaking her head immediately, Lovey protested, "I'm not gonna battle Desiree for Roland's affections. Either he wants me and only me or he doesn't."

"I'm willing to bet that man doesn't really know *what* he wants. I'm just saying, if the feeling turns out to be mutual, then you shouldn't feel guilty about going for it. Especially if you two are on the same page about marriage and other meaningful stuff like that instead of it just being a physical thing. If Desiree *really* loves you, and I can at least say that about her, she'll accept that."

Lovey knew she had a lot of thinking to do.

OVER THE NEXT COUPLE of days, Lovey did just that. She went back and forth about what she really wanted so much it almost sent her face-diving into a pan of fudge brownies. She just wasn't used to this kind of thing.

Desiree was Lovey's best friend and there wasn't a doubt in Lovey's mind that she didn't want to lose her, especially over a man. But at the same time, the thought of Roland being out of the picture made her chest hurt. As wrong as it was or wasn't, she had feelings for Roland that went deeper than just friendship. Being around him, or even just thinking about him, brought a happiness that she couldn't describe. Most nights when she laid in bed, she fantasized about the two of them until her eyes would tear up from wanting them to come true so badly.

Ever since he told her about him and Desiree hooking up, Roland left Lovey several messages, asking for them to talk. Lovey only responded that she would get back to him when she got her head together. She wanted to talk to Desiree about all of this first, but her friend still wasn't answering the phone. Lovey didn't know what was going on with her, but with every call that went ignored and every message unanswered, Lovey's irritation grew. Desiree would only be avoiding Lovey like she was if she felt she'd done something wrong, which meant there must have been something to Liz's theory about Desiree seducing Roland only to get his attention off Lovey. And if that was the case...well, Lovey just didn't know what to think about that.

When another day went by with no response from Desiree, Lovey decided enough was enough. She wasn't going to chase her. This was one thing about Desiree that always annoyed Lovey; she could be extremely childish and stubborn when she wanted to be. And right now, Lovey just didn't have the patience for it. Since Desiree was apparently only thinking about herself, Lovey decided she would do the same.

Roland was who her heart wanted. And Lovey was done trying to deny that she deserved that out of deference to a friend who wouldn't even respect her enough to talk to her.

Before she lost her nerve, she called Roland and asked if she could come over.

ROLAND LOOKED OUT THE window for the tenth time, watching for Lovey's car. He felt like a kid waiting on Santa Claus.

He was relieved that Lovey finally wanted to talk, but he couldn't deny being nervous about what it was she wanted to say. He had no idea where her head was, or what she now thought of him after his little romp with Desiree. The last thing he wanted to hear was Lovey telling him that she no longer wanted to see him. The thought alone made him want to punch something.

When he saw Lovey's car come down his street, he eagerly went outside, way too anxious to wait. By the time she parked, he was standing there ready to open her door.

"Hey," she greeted him, allowing him to help her out of the car.

"Hey. I'm glad you came."

"Yeah. I figured it was about time we talked."

Stuffing his hands into his pockets, Roland leaned against Lovey's car, looking at the ground. "Am I going to like hearing whatever it is you want to say?"

"I don't know," Lovey admitted, standing next to him. They were close but not touching. "I guess that depends on what you want."

"I've certainly been doing a lot of thinking about that these past few days."

"So have I. I've gone back and forth about everything, the pros and cons, the what-ifs...over-analyzing every little detail and possibility to death until I realized I'd never get anywhere like that. I don't like all this tension."

"Me, either."

"So be honest with me, Roland," Lovey looked over at him. "Are you and Desiree back together? Like you were before, I mean?"

"No," Roland quickly responded with a vehement shake of his head. "Nothing has changed, as far as that. I haven't even talked to Desiree since then."

"Hmm. Okay."

"Why, what did she tell you?"

"She hasn't told me anything. I've talked to her a total of two minutes since the new year started. It feels like she's avoiding me, though I don't know why."

"I bet *I* know why."

Lovey's eyebrows shot up. "You do?"

"She's probably pouting because I wouldn't stay with her after we slept together. She didn't like that I couldn't come back later that night because I had plans with you."

"Are you serious??"

"Yeah."

Lovey didn't want to believe that Desiree could be so childish as to hold a grudge about something that she asked for actually happening. She wanted to believe that there was another legitimate reason behind Desiree's recent scarcity that she just didn't know about yet.

Putting Desiree out of her mind for the moment, Lovey turned her focus back to Roland.

"I'm going to be up front about this," she hedged, nervously rubbing her fingers. "When you told me about you and Desiree hooking up, it got to me a little bit. While I know I have no right to be jealous, I honestly was."

Roland bit his bottom lip, trying not to smile. He knew Lovey was probably embarrassed to admit that so he kept his eyes on the ground, not wanting to make her any more nervous than she clearly already was. "Because you don't want me with Desiree?"

Working up her nerve, she closed her eyes momentarily. "Because...I don't really want you with anyone...but me."

The smile came before Roland could catch it. He released a pent-up breath. "For real?"

"Yeah. This is not at all easy for me to say, but I do have feelings for you. And I'm certain that it has nothing to do with trying to get over Clay or anything else. It's just *you*."

That was music to Roland's ears.

Lovey continued. "I was going to tell you that I'd just try to get over it-"

"I don't want you to get over it," Roland interjected, too anxious to wait for her to finish.

Lovey looked at him, mildly surprised. Her heart quickened. "You don't?"

"That's the last thing I want." He took one of her fidgeting hands in his.

"Roland..."

"I don't want to lose you, Lovey," he stated, moving closer to her. Their hips touched. "That's what I was worried about; that you were going to tell me that you were done with me. I most definitely have feelings for you, too."

Now Lovey was smiling. Still she said, "But you must still have feelings for Desiree, also. I can't imagine you sleeping with her if you didn't."

"I'm not gonna lie; part of me does, yeah." Roland felt her hand stiffen slightly in his. "I didn't expect to, after how everything went down. It was just a reminder that me being angry at her doesn't mean my feelings turn off just like that."

"I see." Lovey looked away, already starting to feel like an idiot.

"But..." Roland stepped directly in front of her, bracing his hands next to her shoulders against the car. He gently grabbed her chin and turned her face back to his before continuing, "That doesn't mean that she's the woman I should be with."

"Oh," Lovey breathed, relief washing over her. She looked into his warm brown eyes, feeling like a teenager with a major crush. When he licked his lips, everything in her body lit up. Being so close to him like this was intoxicating in ten different ways.

"I meant what I said, Lovey," he assured her, his voice low. He eyed her lips, then looked back into her eyes. "I don't know how I would handle it if I don't have you."

"Roland...this whole thing...everything can just get *so* messy. What about Desiree?"

"Don't think about Desiree; think about yourself first, for once." Roland moved closer to her, hearing her small intake of breath when he did. His body was aching to get as close as he could to Lovey, but he didn't want to freak her out. Even though everything in him was sure she shared the same feelings he had. "What is it *you* want?"

Lovey opened her mouth, but nothing came out. Not because she didn't know the answer, but because she was too shy to give it.

Sensing this, Roland leaned in even closer. "Let me make it easy for you, then. Do you want me, Lovey? 'Cause I most definitely want you. And I don't mean as just friends, either." He tenderly moved an errant lock of her hair as his face almost touched hers. "All you have to do is nod..."

Barely hesitating, Lovey bit her lip and nodded.

Without another word, Roland grabbed the sides of Lovey's face and kissed her. He went in gentle at first, but within moments, the kiss deepened, and he wrapped her up in his arms. With that kiss Roland wanted to protect Lovey, revere her, make her forget about every bastard that had broken her heart before him. Kissing her was like a whole new experience, unlike any first kiss he'd had.

Lovey felt like home to him. He held her tighter, not being able to get close enough to her.

Neither of them noticed Desiree's car several feet down the street, where she sat behind the wheel with her eyes bugging in disbelief. She had come to surprise Roland, and finally see what was really going on with them. The last thing she ever thought she'd see was her man and her best friend making out.

"What the hell??" she exclaimed. "What...they're like a couple of horny teenagers!"

But as Desiree kept watching, she noticed that Roland and Lovey weren't groping all over each other. There was no grinding or fondling. Their touches were tender. They were taking their time, like they were savoring each other. If Desiree didn't know better, she'd think they were deeply in love or something. They were at the other end of the spectrum how Roland and Desiree would probably look, and she knew it. If that was her, she'd probably be trying to get Roland to take her against the car, right out in the open. It would be more about passion, not feelings. The realization made her face harden.

Feeling betrayed, Desiree sped off down the street, passing right by them. Neither of them even noticed.

Chapter 19

"I TOLD YOUR DUMB ASS this was gonna happen."

"Feeling pretty stupid right now, huh? You're lying if you say you don't."

"How many eggs is that you got on your face?"

"All I gotta say is gimme my money!"

Desiree sucked her teeth. "Really, Mama?"

"Hey, a bets a bet."

Desiree knew she was going to regret telling her family anything. Ever since she griped to them about catching Lovey and Roland sucking face, they'd been clowning her. They thought it was the funniest thing ever but Desiree didn't see the humor in it at all. She felt like she had been stabbed in the back.

"I'm glad y'all think my being betrayed is so funny," she huffed, folding her arms defiantly.

"Betrayed? *You* pushed them together!" Diamond reminded her. "All of this was your idea, remember?"

"No, *my* idea was for them to hang out and keep each other company. *Not* to start making out like two teenagers under the bleachers."

"And we tried to tell you that this might happen," Dana chimed in. "They became attracted to each other."

"Despite all of your confidence that Roland would *never* find another woman attractive as long as you grace the earth."

"Shut up, Diamond." Desiree rolled her eyes.

"I still can't believe that you really thought you had that man's nose open so much that he wouldn't become attracted to Lovey," Elyse shook her head. "He wants a relationship and you know Lovey does. Maybe they just realized they were better suited for each other than you and Roland are."

"Damn, aren't y'all supposed to be on *my* side? My man and my best friend are messing around behind my back and y'all are blaming *me*? How come y'all aren't mad at *them*??"

"Girl, stop," Diamond scoffed. "We have your back and everything but you know we're gonna keep it real with you. And we told you that this little plan was gonna blow up in your face but you weren't trying to hear it."

"And you were messing around with that dude Aaron," Dana added. "So why is it okay for you to see other people but not Roland?"

Desiree frowned. She wanted her sisters and mother to be mad with her but they were just reminding her of her part in all of this, and she didn't like that. Regardless of the truth to it. "Just...because. That wasn't the plan."

"That wasn't *your* plan. And anyway, when it comes to love, plans tend to go out the window. It just happens when it happens."

"Love? Who said they were in love?"

"Who says they aren't?"

"Well hell, if that's the case then maybe the kiss I saw wasn't the first one. Maybe they've been messing around for weeks. I mean, have they had sex yet? He got with me on New Year's so, what, he's sexing both of us?"

"Girl, we don't know!" Elyse exclaimed. "That's stuff only Lovey and Roland can answer. Have you talked to either one of them? What does Lovey say about all this?"

Desiree didn't want to admit that she had been dodging Lovey's calls. She'd never hear the end of it.

"I haven't really talked to her," she mumbled, scraping at her slightly-chipped nail polish.

Her mother and sisters exchanged looks. Desiree and Lovey had been tight since they were budding teenagers. Lovey was like another sister to Desiree, and Desiree often reached out to her before anyone else. If they weren't talking, things must really be getting deep.

Dori cleared her throat. "Why not?"

Desiree shrugged, feigning indifference. "Haven't really had time. I mean, she's called a few times but I've been busy with some stuff."

Elyse went to sit next to her daughter on the couch, motioning for Dana to move over. They were in Elyse's living room, their favorite spot to kick back together. So many deep conversations had taken place in that room and Elyse could sense they were about to have another one.

"Baby girl...are you sure you know what you're doing?" Her voice was gentle, not judgmental.

"What do you mean?"

"Don't start pushing away your best friend because of some man. Especially if you don't give her the chance to explain herself."

"What's to explain? Regardless of what I said or did, there's some stuff you just don't do. Messing with anybody your homegirl ever messed with is one of 'em. She broke the girl code."

"Oh, boo," Diamond waved off the comment. "Truth is, you were just proven wrong about Roland being interested in anybody but you and now you're in your feelings about it. Let's call it what it is."

"And if this had happened while you and Roland were exclusive, I'd be the first one wanting to go key his car and bust his windows," Elyse added. "But you didn't want exclusivity; you wanted to be able to do what you wanted to do. And whether you like it or not, baby, that means Roland can, too."

"And as far as the girl code, girl...life is just too short," Dana commented. "If Lovey and Roland realized they were right for each other—and honestly, it makes sense, from what I know of them—then the fact that he used to date you shouldn't keep them apart."

"And if you stop pouting and make yourself think logically for a minute, you'll remember who we're talking about, here," Dori stated. "This is *Lovey*. She wouldn't purposely hurt or stab anybody in the back, especially you. And you know that. If she allowed anything to happen between her and Roland, it had to be something real."

Desiree looked at her sister, knowing she had a point but not quite ready to admit it out loud.

"And if Roland is gonna be with anybody else, wouldn't you want it to be with Lovey? Doesn't she deserve that?"

Desiree chewed her lip.

"You need to quit being stubborn and talk to your girl," Elyse instructed, sliding an arm around her daughter's shoulders. "'Cause I know you're not trying to say Roland means more to you than she does."

"No," Desiree grudgingly admitted. "Of course not."

"Why don't you just do your own thing and let them be together?" Dana asked. "You wanted to see other people, anyway. And you don't even like serious relationships like they do. Just let it go."

Desiree didn't want to let it go. As much sense as her mother and sisters made, Desiree wasn't ready to totally let go of Roland yet. She didn't know why (or didn't want to admit why) but she wasn't ready to just step back and let Lovey have him just like that.

But she knew she needed to talk to Lovey. As stubborn as she was acting, she knew that she didn't want Lovey out of her life any more than she wanted Roland out of it. She felt slighted when Roland rejected another night with her in favor of hanging with Lovey, and she built a wall around herself, deliberately keeping Lovey out while she tried to mend her bruised ego. It was the first time she had ever straight ignored her best friend's calls, and it didn't even feel right as she was doing it, but at the time, Desiree felt totally justified. But she knew things couldn't keep going like this.

It was time for them to come up with a new plan.

AFTER A COUPLE OF DAYS of kicking things around in her head, Desiree felt she was ready to talk to Roland and Lovey.

The truth was, she missed her bestie. They were friends before Roland was in the picture, and she wanted them to still be friends if and when he was out of it. And her sister Dori was right when she said Lovey would never purposely stab Desiree in the back; that just wasn't the kind of person she was. Desiree had let the shock of catching her and Roland kissing send her mind in all sorts of crazy directions.

She texted them both, saying she wanted to meet up and get everything out on the table. Enough was enough. She just hoped they hadn't run off and eloped by then.

They agreed to meet at Lovey's apartment, since she lived closest to Barfly and Roland had some things to wrap up there first (and Desiree's place was a mess). Desiree was a little nervous, but she was more anxious than anything. There were a lot of questions that she needed answers to.

When they were all convened in Lovey's living room, Desiree cleared her throat before kicking things off.

"I appreciate y'all agreeing to meet up," she began. "I know things are kinda weird right now."

"Are they?" Roland asked with a raised brow. He was sitting between her and Lovey on the couch.

Desiree looked at him in surprise. "You don't think so?"

He shrugged. "Not really. Not for me, at least." He looked over at Lovey. "What about you?"

Lovey looked thoughtfully at them both before her eyes dropped to her hands in her lap. "A little, I guess."

"Well, I don't see why anything would be weird," Roland stated. "*I'm* cool."

It was then that Desiree remembered that they didn't know she had caught them kissing outside of his townhouse. She crossed her arms and turned her body to face them both.

"Well, when I catch my man and my best friend making out against a car like they don't have a care in the world, it doesn't exactly leave me with the warm and fuzzies, you know?"

Lovey's head snapped towards her, her face reddening. "You saw that?"

"I surely did."

"What were you even doing there? You spying on me or something?" Roland asked, his voice bent with accusation.

"I wasn't *spying* on anybody. I wanted to surprise you. Turns out I'm the one that got the surprise."

"And what do you mean, you *caught* us?" Roland continued, folding his own arms. "'Caught' implies we were doing something we weren't supposed to be doing. You and I aren't exclusive anymore, remember? Lovey is single. So we didn't do anything wrong."

Desiree pursed her lips, silently reminding herself to stay calm. "Was that the first time? Has anything else happened between y'all?"

"Why do you think that's any of your business, Desiree?"

Before Desiree could respond, Lovey sat forward and placed a hand on Roland's arm, a move Desiree immediately noticed.

"Let's not let things get heated," Lovey suggested. "Yes, that was our first kiss, Desiree. We have not slept together. Our feelings...they're new. I wanted to talk to you about all of this before anything happened, D., but you weren't returning my calls. And I admit, I got a little fed up."

That took a little of the air out of Desiree's attitude. It was true that she had dodged Lovey's calls, all because she was smarting over Roland seeming to favor Lovey over her. Desiree felt that if she could get him back into her bed, Roland attention would return to her and he wouldn't want to hang with Lovey anymore. But that wasn't the case.

"Okay, look," she finally said. "I admit that I wasn't expecting this to happen..."

Roland eyed her knowingly. "You weren't expecting *what* to happen?"

He's not gonna make this easy on me, I see. "I wasn't expecting for you two to hit it off this well. Or for it to affect me so much. Especially after you came home with me after the New Year's party..." Her eyes snapped to Lovey, but she didn't look surprised in the least.

"I told her about that already," Roland informed Desiree.

"Oh really?" Desiree cleared her throat, trying to hide her surprise. She didn't think that Roland would voluntarily tell Lovey about the two of them sleeping together. Did that mean he felt guilty about it? That he felt he owed it to Lovey to tell her? Just how deep did this friendship of theirs go?

"Yep."

"And...you're cool with it?" Desiree asked Lovey.

"I can admit that I was a little jealous when I heard it, even though I had no real right to be. It just made me really own up to the feelings I was developing for Roland."

She and Roland shared a small smile, and Desiree felt her face flame. Her jaw tightened.

"Well, um, we clearly have a situation here, then," she said loudly, trying to break their little lovestruck gazing. "Because I want to go back to the way things were."

They both looked at her. Neither looked all that surprised by her declaration; it was as if they were prepared for it.

"So you see me starting to have feelings for somebody else and all of a sudden you want me back all to yourself, huh?" Roland almost sounded amused. "This little plan of yours backfired and you can't handle it."

He was right. But Desiree wasn't about to admit it. "I didn't say all that. We tried it for a while but now it's over, that's all."

"Oh, so I'm just supposed to run when you snap your damn fingers, huh? I don't know what you think this is or what kind of dude I am, but it doesn't work like that."

"I never said that was supposed to last forever, Roland. I just needed a little space."

"And who was helping you take up that *space*? 'Cause I know you've been seeing somebody. Be straight up."

Desiree took mild comfort in that Lovey hadn't told Roland about Aaron. But she knew she might as well come clean if she wanted any shot at getting Roland back.

"Okay, yeah, I was seeing somebody. But that's over with."

"Yeah, that's over with and now it's my turn again, huh?"

Desiree sighed, putting her face in her hands. This wasn't going at all like she'd hoped. "Roland..."

"Desiree, believe me, I didn't *want* to have these feelings," Lovey assured her. "I really didn't. I tried to suppress them, ignore them, everything. My main concern has always been our friendship and I didn't want a man to get in the way of that."

"And what, you changed your mind about that now?" Desiree snapped. She hadn't meant to sound so snide, but she couldn't help it.

Lovey's face hardened. "It was more like I was tired of always thinking of you and your feelings before my own. I was tired of ignoring what *I* felt because I was so worried about how *you* felt. Especially when you didn't have the courtesy to return any of my messages."

Desiree swallowed.

"Roland and I have been getting closer these past couple of months," Lovey continued. "And we realized how much we have in common and just how compatible we are, overall. And I decided I wasn't going to keep fighting my feelings. Roland makes me happy and I deserve to be happy. Don't you think so?"

Hesitating only slightly, Desiree replied, "Of course you do. But...Roland makes me happy, too."

"Come on, Desiree," Roland scoffed. "I'm like a toy you didn't appreciate until you saw someone else with it, then you want it back."

"That's not it!"

"Yes, it is. I warned you something like this might happen, you know."

Yes, yes, everybody told me this was a stupid idea and I didn't listen. I get it. "Be that as it may, this is where we are now. Just to be blunt, I want you back."

This time, Lovey crossed her arms. "And what about me, D.?"

"Look, I'm sorry, girl, but it is what it is."

"It is what it is? Just forget about me and my feelings, huh?" Lovey shook her head. "Well, if this was a couple of weeks ago, I might have just stepped aside. If you hadn't ignored me for days on end, we could have discussed all of this like the best friends we're supposed to be. But that's not what happened. And since we're being blunt, I'm tired of putting myself last. So I'm not stepping *anywhere*."

The two women glared at each other, temporarily forgetting about Roland sitting between them. It was the first time they had ever faced off like this and Lovey didn't like it, but she wasn't giving in this time. She always let Desiree get her way in the name of being a good friend or just keeping the peace, but it was her turn to get something *she* wanted now.

Roland looked back and forth between them, a little surprised at this whole scenario. He was impressed that Lovey was standing up for herself like she was, and he was equally annoyed at Desiree's nerve to think that he would just take her back because she didn't want to see him with anyone else.

But if he was honest with himself, there was a part of him that was a little flattered that two beautiful women were digging in their heels about him like this. He knew he needed to put Desiree all the way in her place and tell her where she could go, but he found himself enthralled with this whole scene.

"So you're trying to tell me you're *totally* over Clay?" Desiree asked Lovey. "You were so head-over-heels for him. That's all forgotten now, huh?"

"Clay is gone. He's not coming back. And besides, you know what he did to me; I wouldn't want to have anything to do with him, anyway."

"What if he *does* come back?"

Lovey shrugged. "I wouldn't know about it. I blocked his number and on all of my social media. That was actually Roland's suggestion; it really helped me heal from that faster since I couldn't sit and pine over him while I kept track of what he was doing every day." She smiled at Roland. "I appreciate that."

Roland winked at her, and Desiree felt her face tighten so much she thought it was going to snap.

"Well, since neither of us clearly wants to fall back here...how 'bout we *both* date him?"

She hadn't meant to say that but now that it was out, Desiree waited to see what they would say.

Lovey frowned. She couldn't believe her ears. "What??"

"I mean, why not? It can be one of those polyamorous relationship-things."

"Are you crazy? You've said a million times how you don't do serious relationships. You didn't want to be tied down which is why you backed off Roland in the first place. But when you see he has an interest in me, you all of a sudden want him back. What kind of game are you playing?"

"I'm not playing any games. But it's like they say, I guess; you don't know what you have until you lose it."

"You didn't lose it. You *dumped* it."

Desiree's eyes narrowed.

It was then that they realized Roland hadn't spoken yet. He was just sitting there, looking thoughtful.

"Uh, Roland?" Desiree nudged him. "You want to chime in, here?"

He looked back and forth between them before finally speaking. "Look, I'm not proud of this but I'm not *totally* opposed to Desiree's idea."

Lovey's eyes snapped to him and Desiree grinned triumphantly. "I beg your pardon?"

"Like I said, I'm not proud of it...but I've told you about what I was feeling, Lovey. Real feelings don't just disappear."

"I see." Lovey looked away.

"But I don't want to lose you," he quickly assured her, taking her hand.

"And I'm not going anywhere," Desiree asserted, hurriedly taking Roland's other hand and breaking up their little moment.

Lovey knew she should just get up and leave, walk away from all of this and let them have each other. As much as she adored Roland, if he still wanted Desiree in any way then they obviously weren't meant to be together.

But as she looked at Desiree, she could tell by the look in her eyes that she was fully expecting Lovey to back down, and Lovey felt a stubborn flame ignite. It wasn't her nature to be spiteful, but frankly, she was tired of Desiree getting her way all the time while she just stepped aside like the good girl she always tried to be.

Maybe she should take Liz's advice and fight for Roland. Lovey always just backed away quietly; she'd done it with Evan, she did it with Clay (pretty much), and plenty others.

Well, those days were over. It was time to do something different.

And besides, maybe Roland would see that she was the woman he needed to be with and this foolishness wouldn't go on that long.

"Fine," she finally agreed, looking right into Desiree's daring eyes. "I'm in."

Both Desiree and Roland were visibly surprised. Desiree certainly hadn't expected Lovey to go for something like that. She had always been all about monogamy. The fact that she was willing to essentially share Roland was either a sign of how deeply she felt for him or how desperate she had become.

Either way, she had agreed, so they were in it now. Desiree wasn't about to back down, especially since she had been the one to put the idea out there.

And anyway, it would only be a matter of time before Roland chose her over Lovey. Desiree was sure of that.

Rather thrown for a loop, Roland felt he needed to speak up. "Look...if we're gonna do this, we need to set some ground rules."

"Such as?" Lovey asked, still glaring at Desiree.

"Respect is mandatory. If I'm out with one of you, the other one steps off. No random pop-ups, no 'sudden' emergencies, no blowing up anybody's phone...none of that."

"Fine. What else?" Desiree's eyes were still on Lovey.

"Don't try to dog each other to me. I don't want to spend my time with either of you hearing all the bad things you can think of about the other."

"Mmm-hmm," the women panned.

"And no grilling me about what I do with the other, either. Let's respect each other's privacy."

"Mmm-hmm."

Roland looked back and forth between them. "Are you two sure you wanna do this? I mean, you're best friends and all..."

"Oh, I absolutely wanna do it," Desiree assured him.

"So do I," Lovey concurred.

Roland eyed her. This didn't sound like something Lovey would go for at all and he was still reeling from her agreeing to it. He wanted her to look at him but she was too busy giving Desiree the evil eye. "Are you *sure*, Lovey?"

"Yes, Roland. Now what other things do we need to discuss before we make it official?"

They all established a few more parameters, and it was on. Lovey still couldn't believe she was going along with this but she was in it now.

"I'm gonna head out," Desiree announced after a while, gathering her purse. "I'm glad we got everything out on the table like this. I'll be calling you, Roland."

"Yep. All right."

She turned Roland's face to hers and gave him a quick kiss on the lips, resisting the urge to look at Lovey's reaction.

As she strode out of Lovey's apartment, she was rather proud of herself. This wasn't exactly the result she originally wanted from this meeting, but it certainly could've gone a lot worse.

She got in her car and started the engine before she realized what she was doing; she was leaving Roland and Lovey alone together. Lovey was going to get a jump on this new arrangement. They could start talking, kissing, which could lead to other things...like Roland deciding that Lovey was who he really wanted to be with before Desiree even had a chance to have a turn at all.

This thought sent her scrambling out of her car and back to Lovey's door, glad that she had forgotten to lock it behind her. When she burst back into the living room, Roland and Lovey were sitting in the exact same spots they were sitting in when she left, talking amongst themselves. They both looked surprised to see her.

"What are you doing, D.?" Lovey asked, curious. "Did you forget something?"

"No. It's just that as long as Roland's here, *I* need to be here."

"What?"

"You're not about to get any time alone with him right off the rip," Desiree declared, stomping over to the couch and retaking her seat. Part of her wanted to insert herself between Roland and Lovey, but she decided against it. "It's not going down like that."

"Oh, come on, Desiree," Roland shook his head. "I don't want it to be like that."

"Like what?"

"Like it's some kind of competition."

"Isn't it?"

"No. It's not."

"Maybe not for you but that's clearly not the case for Lovey," Desiree persisted, actually pointing at her. "This isn't even her kind of thing so it's obvious she's just doing this to spite me."

"How would you know why I'm doing anything, Desiree?" Lovey challenged. "You haven't been talking to me, remember?"

"Come on, chill out, y'all..." Roland tried to quell the growing tension.

Desiree sucked her teeth and looked away. Lovey just shook her head, already sensing that this was going to be more trouble than it was worth.

After several silent moments, Desiree couldn't stop herself from speaking again. "Be for real, Lovey. You know good and well that this is all about you wanting what I have. Just admit it!"

Lovey frowned. "What are you talking about?"

"You know damn well what I'm talking about. Look at your track record. You've never been able to keep a man and if anything, I've never been able to keep men off me. And you just want somebody that you know won't dog you, for once, regardless of the fact that he's not over me. If you're that desperate, fine, but at least be woman enough to admit it."

Lovey gasped.

"Desiree!" Roland almost shouted, clearly angry.

Her face crumbling, Lovey quickly got up and hurried out of the room, not wanting to cry in front of Desiree and let on just how much her words hurt her. It was like Desiree tried to find the most hateful thing to say, and she knew Lovey's track record with men was her sore spot. The only way she could have hurt her more would be to slander her dead parents.

Roland stood to go after her, but not before glaring at Desiree with a shake of his head.

"You proud of yourself?"

He walked off.

Desiree knew she crossed a line. She hadn't meant to come at Lovey like that. Regardless of their shared desire for the same man, Lovey was a good person and she didn't deserve that. It hurt Desiree to see that hurt look on Lovey's face, even more so knowing she caused it.

But instead of going to make it right, Desiree stayed in her seat. Lovey would probably just kick her out if she tried to go back there now. And anyway, Lovey knew what kind of person she was; she might say stupid things at times but she didn't really mean them. They'd been friends long enough to where Lovey should know when Desiree was serious and when she was just lashing out.

So Desiree remained on the couch, still refusing to leave as long as Roland was there.

Chapter 20

OVER THE NEXT FEW DAYS, the tension between Lovey and Desiree only grew.

Since the showdown over Roland in Lovey's apartment, neither of the friends did anything to try to mend fences. Lovey was hoping Desiree would at least apologize for the hurtful comment about her past with men, and Desiree concluded Lovey should already know how sorry she was without it being said. So nothing got better; things just got worse.

Lovey didn't want things to be like this. If they were both going to be seeing Roland, she didn't think that had to mean her and Desiree had to be at odds. But Desiree seemed determined to make this some kind of grudge match. There were a few times she started to call Desiree and try to bury the hatchet, but when she remembered Desiree's words, she decided she wasn't going to be the one to give in this time. And when it became evident that Desiree wasn't going to apologize for what she said, Lovey knew she had to put her game face on, since it was evidently a war. It was a war she didn't want but one she wasn't going to back down from.

The women competed for Roland's time, never interested in the three of them hanging out together. They each wanted him all to themselves. Desiree knew she had an advantage because she was still putting on events in Roland's club, but oftentimes Roland would leave there to go see Lovey. Everything in Desiree wanted to find an excuse to text or call him when she knew he was with her friend, but that was against their rules. So she just tried not to imagine what they might be doing while she waited her turn.

Aaron called a couple of times, but she wasted no time telling him she was no longer available.

"I got a man," she bluntly informed him.

"What? Since when??"

"Don't worry about all that. Just know you don't need to call me anymore."

"Hold up, so just like that, we're not kickin' it no more? Damn, Desiree, you could give a brotha a heads-up."

"*This* is your heads-up. And after the way you acted when we went to Subway, I was about done with you, anyway."

"Oh, it's like that? You just decide shit and I don't have any say whatsoever, huh?"

"When it comes to who I do and do not want to be with, no you *don't* have any say. Look, it was fun while it lasted. But I'm with the real thing now."

"And what the hell was I?"

"You and I were fuck buddies, Aaron. It's not like we were really dating. I don't know what you're trying to act all hurt for."

"You know what? To hell with you, Desiree!" He hung up.

"Whatever," Desiree muttered, tossing the phone aside with a shrug. She had a date with Roland to get ready for.

Speaking of Roland, he couldn't help but love all of this attention. As crazy as it was, he enjoyed the fact that both Lovey and Desiree were vying for his affections. The only thing he hated about it was what it was doing to their friendship. Neither of them ever wanted to talk about the other, and Roland knew that wasn't just due to the rules he laid out. They wouldn't even mention each other's name. Roland feared that when it was all said and done, their years-long friendship would be a thing of the past.

The little devil on his shoulder told him to enjoy this little arrangement for a while, though.

"I'll stop it before things go too far," he kept telling himself, hoping he actually could.

When Lovey was at work, she tried to put the drama with Desiree and Roland out of her mind. Her friendship with Desiree was rocky, at best; her relationship with Roland was straight off some kind of reality show...at least she could keep a handle on things at work.

She was getting ready to meet with a new client, Taylor Cartright. After sending out a couple of emails and responding to Liz's eighth text of the day asking how she was doing, Lovey went out to the waiting area to ask Tara a question. She noticed the tall, cinnamon-skinned man at Tara's desk, and apparently everyone else did, too. He was causing quite a stir, as waiting female clients couldn't take their eyes off of him and a couple of the other accountants kept passing through the waiting room, hoping to catch his attention.

"I'm here to see Lovey Tate," she heard the man announce, his smooth voice sending the women into a deeper tizzy. He even had a slight English accent. "I'm Taylor Cartright; we have an appointment this afternoon."

Tara was blushing as she checked the calendar on her computer. "Um, yes, Mr. Cartright, we have you down for three o'clock."

"I know I'm a little early; with all of the stories I've heard about the Atlanta traffic, I wanted to be sure I was on time. I don't mind waiting if she's not quite ready for me."

Lovey headed over to him, a smile on her face. "It's all right, Tara. Hi, Mr. Cartright, I'm Lovey Tate. If you're ready, you can come on into my office."

"Are you sure?" he confirmed, taking her extended hand in his. His green eyes swept over her. "I can wait a bit, if needed."

"No, you're fine." She gently eased her hand from his. "Please follow me."

"Umph, he sure *is* fine," Lovey heard a woman mutter as they passed by. She was sure Taylor probably heard it, too.

"Have a seat," Lovey pleasantly instructed once they were behind the door of her office. "Can I get you some water or coffee or anything?"

"Oh, no thank you."

"Okay, well, we'll just jump right in, then."

Over the next hour, they went over what needed to be done for the inheritance Taylor had just received from a deceased uncle, as well as some preliminary information for a new business venture he was considering. During the course of their time, Taylor would smoothly interject a personal question or two, seeming to try to get to know Lovey on more than just a business level. Lovey would answer his questions, though succinctly, and steer the conversation back to business. She didn't seem to notice how Taylor would gaze at her as she perused some paperwork or typed information into the computer.

"Do you mind if I ask a question?" he hedged, sitting forward in his seat.

"Of course not."

"Would you like to..." His voice trailed off when she looked up at him, adjusting her glasses. The sunlight coming in from the window behind her illuminated her to the point of looking angelic. And he had a feeling she probably had no idea how beautiful she was.

"Yes?"

"Would you...like to hear some of the other things I was thinking of, regarding the inheritance?" He internally kicked himself for losing his nerve.

"Sure, absolutely."

A little while later, their initial business was done and Lovey looked at him with a smile.

"That about does it for now," she said. "I'll be in touch to discuss next steps. And please feel free to call if you have any questions."

Following her lead, Taylor stood. "I appreciate it, Ms. Tate. It's such a relief having someone knowledgeable helping me keep track of everything."

"It's my pleasure. And I told you, please call me Lovey."

"Lovey." Taylor was gazing at her again, his green eyes roaming her face.

Feeling slightly uncomfortable, Lovey cleared her throat and moved around her desk towards the door. Opening it, she swept out her hand graciously. "After you."

"Nonsense. Ladies first." He swept out his own hand.

With a tight smile, Lovey led him back towards the waiting room. A couple of her co-workers were gathered at Tara's desk, and they all looked up as Lovey and Taylor approached. Lovey subtly shook her head at them.

"Thank you again, Lovey." Taylor took her outstretched hand into both of his. Those eyes of his subtly rolled over her frame, liking everything they saw.

"Not a problem. Enjoy the rest of your day, Taylor. We'll be in touch."

"Yes, we will." Taylor looked at the women at Tara's desk and gently bowed his head in acknowledgement. "Ladies."

"Bye," they chorused. Lovey had to resist the urge to roll her eyes.

With another glance at Lovey and a bite of his bottom lip, Taylor walked out.

"Oooh," Tara swooned, wasting no time. She playfully fanned herself. "Be still my heart."

"Can you say *gorgeous*?" Giana, one of the accountants, gushed with a hand on her chest. Lovey's eyes fell to the silver rings she had on every finger. After several times of them getting caught in her wild, curly red hair, she started wearing her tresses pinned back at work. "And he smelled so good I wanted to melt. I will *gladly* take him as a client if you don't have time for him, Lovey."

"Girl, I don't want him as a client, I want him in my *bed*," Cherell, another accountant, proclaimed. She rested her thick curves against Tara's desk. "Those eyes of his would have me late to work every*day*. And he has an accent, too??"

"You're late to work everyday, anyway," Lovey teased, playfully nudging her.

"Whatever!"

"It doesn't matter. Those green eyes couldn't seem to stay off Lovey," Tara stated.

Lovey waved a dismissive hand. "Please."

"Oh, don't tell me you couldn't see how he was looking at you. The man is absolutely smitten."

"He was not."

"Yes, he was."

"I hate to admit it, but I noticed that, too," Giana added.

"Well, it doesn't matter...I didn't notice and I'm not interested, anyway." Lovey shrugged a nonchalant shoulder.

"Not interested? I don't know what kind of standards you have, girl, 'cause if you're not interested in *that*, they must be sky high," Cherell mused, her strong voice making everything she said seem twice as loud. Thankfully, there were no clients in the office at the moment. "And I know good and well it's not 'cause you don't like men."

"I bet it has something to do with that chocolate cutie that comes by here sometimes," Tara offered. "Roland, I think his name is."

Lovey tried to keep her face even at the mention of Roland's name. "Yeah, that's his name. But we're...not in a relationship or anything." *That's not what I would call this three-way mess we're in.*

"Could've fooled me."

"Well damn, Lovey, you just have all the men after you, huh?" Cherell chuckled.

"I wouldn't say that at all," Lovey muttered bitterly before she could catch herself. Realizing how she sounded, she chuckled nervously. "I'm just saying...y'all know how men are. You never now *what* they really want."

"You're sure right about that, Lovey, 'cause this guy Andy that I dated for a while sure threw me for a loop," Giana quickly concurred, her words speeding up as they tended to do when she got excited. When she got really riled up, she'd talk a mile a minute. "Things were going along just fine and then all of a sudden, he started acting all funny like he wasn't all that interested. Yet he was plenty interested when he would come over at damn near midnight trying to get some-"

"I've gotta go make a phone call," Lovey lied, inching towards her office. They all just waved, still enthralled by Giana's latest tale. Lovey just wanted to take a minute, because the mention of Roland had her a little jumbled. And besides, Giana's story sounded all too familiar.

Lovey hadn't seen Roland in a couple of days, though he had called her a couple of times and they'd video chatted that morning. She wanted to spend some time with him, but she already knew he was going to be with Desiree that night. Everything in her tried to keep her mind from wandering to what they would most likely be doing by the night's end.

"What the heck am I doing?" she mumbled, sighing deeply. "Is this even worth it?"

Before she descended into a pit of questioning her decisions yet again, Lovey turned her attention back to her work. She grabbed some files from the end of her desk and looked for the most complex issue she had, trying to put everything else out of her mind.

About an hour later, there was a knock on her door.

"Yes?" she called out, frowning slightly. She took a quick glance at her calendar to make sure she didn't have an appointment she'd forgotten about.

When she saw Desiree's head peek around her door, Lovey wondered if she was daydreaming again. Actually removing her glasses, she leaned forward slightly. "Desiree?"

"Don't tell me you're gonna start acting like you don't know me now," Desiree quipped lightly, smiling.

Lovey just looked at her.

"Can I come in?"

"Uh, yeah. Sure."

Desiree fully entered the office, dressed casually in a v-neck t-shirt and skinny jeans. Her bushy sandy brown wig and large hoop earrings completed her carefree vibe. There was a canvas bag in her hand.

"I thought it was time we finally talked," she announced, taking a seat in the chair in front of Lovey's desk. "I figured, you know what? *I* should be the bigger person for once."

Clearly surprised, Lovey marveled, "Really?"

"Of course. I'd like to bury the hatchet. We've been friends too long to be acting like this. Just because we both want Roland doesn't mean we have to behave like two kids fighting over the Ken doll."

Lovey played with her pencil thoughtfully. "True."

"I want us to be friends again."

Not able to resist a smile, Lovey looked at her bestie gratefully. "Just because we butt heads doesn't mean we're not friends, D."

"I'm glad to hear you say that," Desiree replied, clearly relieved. "I know this whole situation is a trip. And I'm not gonna ask you to give Roland up or anything; that's not even what I'm here for. My concern is our friendship. I just need to know we're still good."

"Well, you *did* say some really hurtful things to me, Desiree..."

"I know..."

"But it does mean a lot that you came by here," Lovey continued. "I do appreciate that."

"Well, hey; I have to grow up sometime, right?" Desiree chuckled.

Lovey giggled, feeling better than she had in a while. "Your words, not mine."

Desiree looked at her friend, sitting there in her emerald green blouse with her glasses and her long hair in a top knot, looking like she belonged on a Sexiest Librarians of the South calendar, and Desiree knew she had done the right thing in coming there. Something had to change and she knew it was up to her to change it. Things certainly couldn't keep going the way they were.

After a few moments, she slapped her hands against her thighs. "Look, girl, I know you're busy so I'll get out of your way now. We should hang out soon, just the two of us. It's been forever since we've had a girls' night."

"Yeah, we're long overdue for that," Lovey agreed.

"We'll make that happen, then. In the meantime..." Desiree stood, lifting the bag she was holding and placing it on Lovey's desk. She reached inside, looking at Lovey mischievously. "I brought a little peace offering."

"That's so sweet, D. But we're okay now; you don't have to give me anything."

"No, I want you to have it, regardless," Desiree insisted. She pulled out a large plastic container and placed it in front of Lovey.

"What is this?"

"Open it and see."

When Lovey pried open the lid, she gasped. Her office was almost immediately filled with the decadent aromas of what she knew was one of Elyse's homemade treats.

"Is this what I think it is?" she asked excitedly.

"Yep. Mama's hot fudge chocolate pudding cake. Made fresh today. I had to hurry up and get some because once Daddy got to it, that would've been all she wrote."

Lovey lifted the container closer to her face and inhaled, closing her eyes and moaning as if someone was licking her toes under the desk. "This smells so *good*..."

"Dig in, girl. I just came from Mama's so it's probably still warm. I put a fork in there, too."

Noticing something else in the bag, Lovey nodded her heads towards it. "What's that?"

"Oh, it's some ice cold milk." Desiree set the large insulated cup on the desk. "And it's full-fat, *real* milk, not that almond crap you buy."

"Why are you doing this to me?" Lovey whined playfully.

"I know you usually try to stay away from a lot of dairy, but you know real milk is the only thing to have after Mama's hot fudge chocolate pudding cake. You've gotta do it justice, girl!"

"I suppose one indulgence won't kill me. You want some? Looks like you gave me a ton of it."

"Oh trust, I had some already." Desiree patted her flat stomach. "That's all you."

"Thank you, D.!"

"Oh, please, it's nothing. Well, come on and give me a hug so I can get out of here and let you have at it."

Lovey grinned as she rounded the desk and opened her arms to her friend, gladly embracing her. It felt like they hadn't hugged in forever, and it felt good. She was so glad that Desiree put away her pride and made the first move.

After Desiree left, Lovey eagerly dove in to her dessert, only intending to eat a few (big) bites and save the rest for later. But it was so incredibly good that she kept dipping back into it. Before she knew it, the container was empty.

"Can't believe I just ate all that," she muttered to herself, a hand on her full stomach. "Gotta be more careful."

Promising herself she'd show more restraint next time, Lovey leaned back in her chair and drained the entire container of milk.

LOVEY THREW THE EMPTY container in the trash, kicking herself yet again. Six cupcakes, gone in one sitting.

Ever since Desiree showed up at her office a couple of weeks before to smooth things over between them, she'd been sending Lovey decadent treats, each time with a note saying how much she wanted Lovey to have it. Lovey thought it was really sweet how Desiree was spoiling her like she was, but she wished she'd do it with things like flowers or a cute pair of shoes. She tried to tell Desiree to stop sending her desserts, because it wasn't necessary and also because Lovey obviously didn't have the willpower to resist them while they were in front of her.

It didn't help that she hadn't been seeing that much of Roland lately. He was either busy at the club or hanging out with Desiree, who seemed like she was booking his time days in advance. Lovey felt like they should have made a ground rule about things being a little more even when it came to sharing Roland's time.

The last time she saw him, they went to a movie, where he held her hand the entire time and occasionally whispered things in her ear that had her blushing and giggling like a schoolgirl. Then they went back to his place and just held each other while they talked well into the night, taking plenty of long kissing intermissions between topics. They still hadn't slept together, and that was something Lovey was in no rush to do. And thankfully, Roland wasn't pressuring her, either. She tried to believe that it was because he respected her and not because he was getting all the sex he needed from Desiree, because she'd bet her apartment that they were still getting it in.

Lovey was taking advantage of the time alone by re-reading the changes for the upcoming tax season. This wasn't exactly the time of year she looked forward to, and filling her head with all the new tax laws tended to make her want to pull her hair out from the root. So when she got a timely delivery of Krispy Kreme doughnuts, she tore into them, licking the glaze from her lips as she prepared her mind for more tax jargon. She mindlessly kept reaching into the box as she continued to read, the sugar making the mind-numbing words more tolerable. By the end of the evening, she had finished the documents, finished the doughnuts, and collapsed on her bed with a full head and a stomachache.

The phone ringing woke her up. She groaned as she blindly felt around for her phone in the dark, releasing a substantial belch that she was glad no one was there to hear.

"Hello?"

"Lovey? What are you doing?"

"Sleeping..."

"Why are you still in the bed?"

"Why wouldn't I be? It's the middle of the night."

"It's ten o'clock in the morning."

"What??" Lovey shot up, which is when she realized that she had been buried under her covers, explaining why it was so dark. She ran a hand through her disheveled hair and flopped onto her back. "Oh gosh..."

"What's wrong with you? You sick or something?"

"Stomach kinda hurts. But I'm fine."

"You still want me to come over and bring you those papers today?"

"What papers?"

"Damn, you *are* really out of it. You asked me to bring some documents so you could finish my taxes, remember?"

"Oh, right, yeah. Sure, you can bring them. Just come by whenever. I don't have anywhere to go today. Wait, what day is it?"

"It's Saturday, girl." Liz chuckled. "Did you get drunk last night or something?"

"No. Just OD'd on doughnuts while I was doing some reading for work."

"Yeah, I know how you get this time of year. You sure you're not doing anything tonight? No plans with Roland?"

"No, no plans with Roland."

Liz paused, as if she was deciding whether to say something or not. She finally said, "All right, then. I'll text you when I'm on the way."

"'Kay."

After plugging her nearly-dead phone into the charger, Lovey started to get up and try to get her day started. But she only ended up swigging some Pepto Bismol and diving right back under her covers.

A COUPLE OF HOURS LATER, Lovey was meandering around her apartment, doing some light cleaning and sorting her laundry. Liz texted that she was on her way over, and Lovey was looking forward to seeing her.

"Hey!" she enthusiastically greeted her sister when she arrived, giving her a big hug. Liz had been out of town on a solo vacation, so she hadn't seen or talked to her much in the last couple of weeks.

"Hey, girl," Liz smiled, returning the hug. She gave her a curious look before plucking the arm of Lovey's gray sweats. "I am gonna burn these things."

"My sweats haven't done anything to you."

"I'm sick of seeing 'em. How's your stomach feeling?"

"Oh, it's fine. Some good ol' Pepto Bismol did the trick for that."

"Good. What are you doing?"

"Just cleaning up and stuff. You never told me how your vacation went."

"Oh, it was awesome. Bali agrees with me."

"I still don't know how you can travel all that way by yourself like that."

"I love traveling solo. Don't have to worry about what anyone else wants to do; I can just find my own peace, be on my own agenda...do my own thing. There's nothing like it. I'm thinking Tokyo for next year."

"Maybe that's what I need; a good vacation. Where are your papers?"

"Right here." Liz held up the file in her hand before handing it over. "It is such a blessing to have a sister that's a wiz with numbers."

"I don't know about *wiz*, but I'm pretty good with 'em," Lovey chuckled, flipping through the file contents before placing it on the coffee table. "I'll get started on yours in the next couple of days."

"That's cool. So is this all you're gonna do today?"

"Pretty much."

"We should go out later."

"I suppose it would be nice to get out of the house. Haven't done much of that lately."

"You mean since this wonderful *arrangement* you agreed to with Desiree and Roland?" Liz's voice was ripe with sarcasm.

Lovey shook her head. "Don't start."

"What, is Desiree hogging all of Roland's time or something?"

"You just think you know Desiree *so* well..."

"And I'm usually not wrong..."

"Whatever. I don't want to get into all of that. It's not like this is my proudest moment, as far as decisions go."

"At least you know that much. Why *did* you agree to this nonsense, anyway?"

Sighing, Lovey dropped down onto her couch. "As childish as it sounds, I didn't want to let Desiree get her way again. She was just being impossible, acting like Roland and I betrayed her or something. She saw him taking an interest in me and decided she wanted him back like some kind of spoiled child. It just ticked me off."

"So is this about Desiree or is it about Roland? And I should point out that the fact that he agreed to this crap drastically reduces my opinion of him."

"Honestly, I'm not even sure," Lovey replied thoughtfully. "I can say it's *mostly* about Roland, but I'd be lying if I said it wasn't about Desiree at all. But there have been plenty of times when I asked myself why I'm even bothering with all of this. I mean, if Roland doesn't know he wants to be with just me..."

"Exactly."

"But at the same time, if I back off, then Desiree will just think she wore me down or something and I don't want that. I know it's childish. And I know I shouldn't let my pride drive me like this. But after the things Desiree said to me..."

"I get it, sis," Liz said, gently squeezing her arm. "Believe it or not, I see where you're coming from with all this. After you told me what she said to you about your past with men, I actually went to pay her a visit."

Lovey sat forward, surprised. This was the first she was hearing of this. "You did? Why?"

"Why do you think? I was going to snatch her by the roots. That was below the belt, even for her, Lovey, and I wasn't havin' it. Her ass better be glad she wasn't at home."

Lovey couldn't help but grin. Liz always had her back; when they were kids and Lovey would get teased for being so sensitive, or for apparently thinking she was better than the other girls because she was 'high yellow with long hair' (which she didn't), Liz would always make them pay. She either got the offenders right there or she made Lovey point them out to her later.

And after their parents died, Liz stepped up even more when it came to being there for Lovey. When Desiree entered the picture years earlier, Liz never let their friendship threaten her and Lovey's bond. She generally stayed out of her and Desiree's business, saving her opinions for when Lovey asked for them (or when Liz just felt it was absolutely necessary to give them). Lovey knew she couldn't always be totally objective when it came to Desiree, and she appreciated Liz being the voice of reason when she needed it.

And it made her feel good to know that Liz was still as ready to bust some heads for her as she was when they were kids. Having someone in her corner unconditionally like that was invaluable, especially now.

"Thank you so much, Liz," Lovey gushed appreciatively, briefly grabbing her hand. "Part of me is glad she wasn't there but it means so much to me that you had my back like that, especially since all I did at the time was run off crying."

"Has she even apologized for that?"

"Not in so many words..."

"Why am I not surprised?"

"But she *did* come to my office a couple of weeks ago saying she wanted to bury the hatchet," Lovey urged. Even after everything that's happened, part of her still felt compelled to defend Desiree, at least a little bit. "So that's something."

"Hmph. I guess."

"She even topped off her gesture with some of Mama Elyse's hot fudge chocolate pudding cake. It is *so* sinfully good. Desiree knows how much I love that so I thought it was really sweet of her."

"Not as sweet as that cake sounds. Hot fudge chocolate pudding? I'm surprised you have any teeth left."

Lovey laughed. "Hey, if I didn't, it'd be worth it. Especially since she brought me a lot of it."

"And you ate all of it right then, didn't you?"

"I couldn't help it! That cake is addictive. It's damn near better than sex."

"Ooh, girl. I need you to get you some dick, ASAP."

"Me? When's the last time *you* had any?"

"Hey, what happens in Bali *stays* in Bali."

They both laughed heartily. Lovey certainly wouldn't have minded some between-the-sheets action, but she was keeping Roland at bay when it came to that because she didn't want to be sleeping with him during the same time her best friend was. Outside of him, she had no prospects. And it wasn't like she was just going to hook up with some random man. So for the time being, she just relied on the battery-operated toys in her nightstand.

The sisters talked about Liz's Bali trip while they half-watched an episode of *Say Yes to the Dress*. Lovey would sometimes watch that show and imagine herself there, trying on dresses in front of Liz and Desiree, narrowing them down to the perfect one. She'd always envisioned herself in a body-hugging mermaid gown that would send her future husband's jaw to the floor as soon as he saw her in it. Just the thought alone made her smile, and ache for that day to come.

It can still happen, she silently assured herself, as she did often. *Your man is out there.*

Before she could start musing whether that man could possibly be Roland or not, Liz thankfully spoke up.

"Let's go get some mani/pedis," she suggested. "And you know what I haven't had in a while? A good massage. I'm overdue for some pampering."

"Oh my gosh, that sounds amazing right now," Lovey exhaled, grateful for the distraction. "I could use some sprucing up, too."

"Girl, yes. If I thought we could possibly get an appointment this late on a Saturday, I'd suggest going to get your hair done, too. 'Cause it needs it." Liz playfully swatted at Lovey's frizzy hair.

Lovey batted her hand away with a smile. "I'll admit I haven't felt like dealing with this stuff. But that's what cute hats are for."

"Well I hope you have one, 'cause you're not going anywhere with me looking like that."

"Shut up, Liz!" Lovey threw a sofa pillow at her sister before standing up and stretching. "Let me go take a quick shower and get dressed and then we'll go."

Humming to herself, Lovey stepped into the shower, using too much of her favorite lavender body gel like she usually did, enjoying the enveloping feeling of the warm water. She was thankful that Liz had come and saved her from another Saturday night home alone. Desiree and Roland were at Barfly, and probably would be spending the evening together afterwards. Lovey didn't want to just sit around feeling like a kid waiting their turn on the merry-go-round.

Wrapped in a large fluffy green towel, Lovey padded to her closet to find something to wear. She grabbed her favorite pair of jeans, but had to do more wiggling than usual to get them on, and she had an even harder time buttoning them. She frowned, but shrugged it off, figuring she was just bloated or something. Shimmying out of the jeans, she kicked them aside and chose something else.

But everything she put on was more snug than usual, even her designated 'fat pants' that she kept in the back of the drawer. She didn't weigh herself much at all, but something told her to check her number then. When she pulled her scale from under her bed and stepped on it, her eyes almost popped out of their sockets. When had she gained twelve pounds??

"Lovey, you all right? What's taking you so long?" Liz appeared in the bedroom doorway.

Hopping off the scale, Lovey kicked it back under the bed. She felt exposed in the bra and panties she wore. "Huh?"

"What are you doing?" Liz entered the room, looking at her curiously.

"I...don't have anything to wear," Lovey muttered, looking away. She hastily wrapped her bath towel back around her and sank onto the bed.

"What do you mean? You have plenty of clothes, Lovey."

Actually embarrassed, Lovey held her towel closed with one hand as she covered her face with the other. "They don't fit right."

Realization washing over Liz's face, she went to sit by her red-faced sister on the bed. Telling herself to choose her words carefully, she hedged, "It *did* seem like you were a little thicker around the middle when we hugged earlier, but I figured you were just PMS'ing or something. It's not a big deal, Lovey. There's not a woman alive whose weight doesn't fluctuate some."

"It's not PMS. I already had my period this month."

"Maybe you've just been overdoing it with the sweets, then. You had all that cake Desiree brought you and then you said something about doughnuts last night. But even so, it's still not a big deal. So you binged for a while, so what? Just get back on track now, that's all."

"I just don't know how I didn't notice this," Lovey marveled. "I know I didn't gain it overnight, but this is honestly the first time I've seen it. I actually feel a little ridiculous right now."

"Aww, girl," Liz put a comforting arm around her sister. "You don't have any reason to feel ridiculous. So you gained a few pounds..."

"*Twelve* pounds."

"Okay, fine. It doesn't mean anything."

"*You* would've noticed it, if you'd been here."

"Probably. But now that you see it, you can fix it. Come on, let's not let this ruin our day. And anyway, twelve extra pounds doesn't mean you're not still hot. Don't let it get you down."

Grateful for the encouragement, Lovey smiled at her sister and patted the hand gripping her shoulder. "I appreciate that, sis. You have no idea how much I needed to hear that right now." She sighed and stood up, scanning her closet for something loose-fitting. "I guess the next time Desiree sends me something, I should have more willpower."

Liz looked up at her, frowning slightly. "What?"

"You're right; I should just refuse it altogether. Don't even tempt myself."

"No, I mean what are you talking about? Desiree's been sending you sweets?"

"Yeah. Ever since she came to my office a couple of weeks ago, I've gotten some kind of delivery with a different dessert almost every other day. She knows how much I love chocolate."

Liz shook her head, not believing what she was hearing. Desiree really was a piece of work.

"Yeah, she knows how much you can't resist it, either," she muttered, trying to keep her frustration in check.

Lovey turned to her. "What are you saying?"

"So...since she showed up at your office with a big hunk of calories, how many times have you seen her? Have you been hanging out?"

"I actually haven't seen her since then. But we've talked a few times, which is more than before that. It's really sweet how she always checks to make sure I got her surprises. I think this is her way of apologizing for how she acted over this Roland situation."

"And speaking of Roland, you probably haven't seen much of him either, have you?"

"No..."

"Uh-huh," Liz's leg bounced rapidly, feeling like she was going to explode. "That *bitch*!"

"Liz!"

"Lovey! Don't you think it's a little curious how she's all of a sudden sending all this crap to you *now*? When has she ever done that?"

"We've never been in a situation like this before, Liz."

"But she knows that you try to stay away from that stuff. Why not send an Edible Arrangement or something? At least that's fruit, even if some of it might be covered in chocolate. She knows you love flowers; how come she couldn't send those? There's plenty of things she could send if she was trying to just make amends for acting like an asshole, but she chose to send the most fattening desserts she could find."

Lovey folded her arms. "Just say what you're getting at, Liz."

"You know damn well what I'm getting at. She's fattening you up on purpose."

Even though she sensed that's where Liz was going, Lovey still shook her head emphatically. "No way. There's no way that's true."

"Think about it, Lovey," Liz persisted, standing. "Desiree knows how this whole situation with Roland is probably affecting you. And she knows you binge-eat when you get really stressed or upset."

"So?"

"*So* she's probably laid up under Roland while she sends you comfort food, 'cause she knows you'll stuff your face with it trying to feel better. And by the time Roland *does* get around to you, you'll be so freaked out by any weight you've gained that you probably won't want to see him. And she'll be right there to go in your place. *Tell* me that doesn't make sense!"

It *did* make sense. But Lovey still refused to believe it. "Regardless, Desiree wouldn't stoop that low. She wouldn't do that to me."

"Wouldn't she?" Liz cocked a brow. "You didn't think she'd ever throw your hurtful past with men in your face, either, but she did that."

"That's different, though, Liz. I'm not trying to defend what she said, but who *hasn't* said something they shouldn't in the heat of the moment? Hurting my feelings and intentionally trying to sabotage me are two different things."

"Neither of which I'd put past her."

"That would mean she actually *plotted* this," Lovey emphasized. "That she actually carried out a plan to try to hurt me. Regardless of what's going on with this situation with Roland, she's wouldn't do something so diabolical. Not to me."

Liz sighed. She knew Lovey wouldn't want to believe such a thing about Desiree, regardless of what's been going on between them lately. Liz totally believed it, but she knew that it would be a hard sell on Lovey. She loved Desiree too much and truly believed their friendship meant as much to Desiree as it did to her.

Unfortunately, it seemed to Liz that Desiree cared more about winning Roland back than she did about her friendship with Lovey, even if temporarily.

"Well, for your sake, I hope you're right," Liz finally said. "Believe me, I'd love to be wrong on this. And if I am, I'll apologize to Desiree's face for it. But you and I both know I'm usually right about this kind of stuff. So..." She shrugged helplessly. "Just keep it in mind. That's all I ask."

Lovey nodded, her mind all over the place.

After a few quiet moments, Liz clapped her hands loudly. "Well, enough of that. Come on, let's find you something to wear so we can go."

WHILE SHE WAS OUT WITH Liz, Lovey forced herself to put her sister's speculations out of her mind. Lovey was the first to acknowledge that Liz had a knack for figuring things out before she did and possessed what seemed like a sixth sense when it came to drama, but she was wrong about Desiree this time. She had to be.

Because if she was even partially right, what did that say about her and Desiree's friendship?

After Liz dropped her off a few hours later, Lovey turned on one of her favorite episodes of *Black-ish* and proceeded to finish her laundry. Her mind would occasionally stray to her earlier conversation with Liz, but she pushed those thoughts away. If she let it, her imagination would run all over the place, and before she knew it, she'd be breaking down every little thing from her and Desiree's friendship, looking at it under a new microscope. She refused to do that.

She was a little surprised when her phone rang and Roland's name flashed on the screen. Mindlessly tugging on her shirt, she picked up the phone.

"Hey, stranger."

"What's up, Lovey?" His voice still sent her insides spinning.

"Nothing much. Just folding this laundry."

"Now I know you can do something better on a Saturday night than that."

"I hung out with Liz earlier. We got some massages, got our nails done..."

"Oh okay, so y'all had one of those kinds of days, huh? Dig that."

"Yeah, it was much-needed."

"So you're probably feeling real good about yourself right now, huh?"

"Uh, yeah, I guess..."

"Can I see?"

"What?"

"I want to see you tonight. It's been a minute. I miss you."

"Oh..." Lovey's hand roamed over her thighs, which felt twice as big to her now. "I thought you had to work tonight."

"That's what employees are for. I'd rather spend the evening with you."

"That's so sweet, Roland. And I miss you, too, but...I can't tonight."

There was a pause. "Everything okay?"

"Yeah, everything's fine. I'm just not in the mood for company, that's all."

"Lovey, look, I know I haven't been giving you much time lately, and I'm sorry about that. Let me make it up to you, though. Come out with me tonight."

"It's not that."

"If you're mad at me, just tell me."

"No, Roland, it's not...I'm sorry, I have to go."

She ended the call then buried her face in a pillow, feeling stupid.

DISAPPOINTED, ROLAND put the phone down, deciding against calling Lovey back.

She had to be upset with him. Why else would she turn him down flat then essentially hang up in his face? He knew he'd been letting Desiree take most of his attention lately, but he wanted to rectify that now. When he said he missed Lovey, he meant it.

Part of him wanted to go straight to her apartment and see what was going on with her, but he wanted to respect her wishes. She said she wasn't in the mood for company, and he wasn't going to barge in on her. He could only hope that she wasn't starting to lose interest in him.

Sighing, he picked up his phone and returned Desiree's text, letting her know he'd be able to come by later, after all.

Chapter 21

NOW THAT LOVEY WAS falling back, Desiree was putting extra effort to get all of Roland's attention and keep it.

It became her mission. She called or texted him first thing in the morning and before she went to bed at night, wanting to be the first and last thing on his mind every day.

She filled his phone with pictures and videos, wanting to dominate his fantasies.

She catered to him, making sure he ate, even cooking for him a few times, giving him massages, straightening up his townhouse when she was there, doing a bunch of things for him that she barely did for herself.

She believed that the more she met Roland's needs, the faster he would fall in love with her again and they could quit this stupid three-way mess.

Desiree was over it. She had fully expected Lovey to have dropped out by now, but she hadn't. Desiree just wanted Roland all to herself, which is why she always declined his suggestions that the three of them hang out together. She wasn't interested in group dates. And she wasn't thrilled about how concerned Roland seemed to be about making sure Lovey felt included, though she learned she had to be mindful of how she let him know that.

"I thought our time was *our* time," she noted after he made such a suggestion. They were reclining on her couch with her feet in his lap. "I'd really appreciate you not always trying to bring Lovey in our mix."

"It's not like I'm talking about inviting her over here now. I was talking about us just planning something together."

"I'm good."

Roland looked at her. "Why are you acting like that?"

She blinked innocently. "Like what?"

"Like you don't even like your best friend anymore. And I hope you don't think that puppy-dog look is gonna work on me."

Desiree sighed. "Can I help that I want you all to myself?"

"I don't know, but you *can* help always trying to make everything about you."

"How am I doing that now?"

Roland rubbed his eyes, looking tired, and shook his head. "This isn't how it was supposed to be," he mumbled, almost as if he was talking to himself as much as he was to Desiree.

"What are you talking about?"

Sighing, Roland practically pushed her legs off his lap and stood up. "Nothing. Look, I'm gonna roll."

Scrambling to her feet, Desiree grabbed his arm before he could walk off. "Why??"

"I'm tired and honestly, I'm just not in the mood for this tonight."

"Not in the mood for what? Me? Does that mean you're about to go see Lovey right now?"

Roland looked at her, and the look in his eyes made Desiree start to feel a little uneasy. She hoped she wasn't pushing too hard. It was just that the thought of losing Roland made her sick.

"And if I did? What are you gonna do, come over there and say some more foul stuff to her? Send her to her room crying again?"

Desiree averted her eyes. "I already apologized for that."

"To me. But did you do the same to Lovey?"

Desiree knew she couldn't just flat-out lie, because he could simply ask Lovey for the truth. It had taken a lot of effort to get back on his good side after she made that remark to Lovey about her failures with men, Desiree didn't want to get back in Roland's doghouse when she had to swallow her pride so hard to get out of it.

"Lovey...Lovey knows I talk crazy sometimes," she finally averted. "She knows I don't really mean it."

"So in other words, no. You *didn't* apologize to her."

Knowing there was probably nothing she could say to explain herself, Desiree sighed. "Roland, look..."

"You know what? I'm not really trying to hear you right now," Roland interrupted, holding his hands up and stepping back. "Good night."

Desiree was hurt by that. Not only by the fact that he left like he did, but also because he seemed to be punishing her for not apologizing to Lovey. Desiree didn't feel like that was entirely fair, since that was more between her and Lovey than the three of them, but she knew he wouldn't see it that way. He was apparently too worried about Lovey's ego to see her side of things.

After that night is when Desiree kicked her efforts into high gear. During her time knowing Roland, she learned that he didn't hold grudges that long; he would get over things after a day or two, especially if he thought you were really sorry. It wasn't until you really screwed him over, like his ex-girlfriend Anna did, that he just cut you off altogether. Of if you kept making the same mistakes without really learning anything from it. Desiree wasn't trying to be the next person on his dismissed list, not knowing how many more silent strikes she had before she was out.

One afternoon when Desiree was moping around her apartment, mindlessly scrolling through Facebook, she came across a post from Lovey, checking in at Maggiano's. Desiree sat up. Lovey didn't really like going to restaurants alone, so she was probably there with someone. And if Desiree remembered correctly, Liz hated Italian food. And since Lovey never really hung with any of her coworkers outside of the office, Desiree was almost sure that she was probably out with Roland.

Even though this was part of their arrangement, Desiree still felt as if Roland wasn't supposed to go out with Lovey. Or rather, he wasn't supposed to *want* to go out with Lovey. Desiree should've been enough. What else did she have to do to make him see that?

"IS THAT WHO I THINK it is?"

Desiree peered at the reddish-brown hair of the man a few feet away from her at Walmart. She was there picking up a few things for the week and happened to look up and see him, and she immediately wondered if that was Evan, the man who left Lovey high and dry by starting a relationship with some personal trainer before he even gave Lovey so much as a 'see ya.' He just faded to black, like so many other men had. Desiree winced when she remembered how she had callously thrown that in Lovey's face.

When the man turned around, Desiree smiled. That *was* Evan. She'd only met him once but those freckles stamped him in her memory.

"Evan?"

He turned towards her, frowning slightly as if trying to place who she was. "Yeah?"

"I'm Desiree," she reminded him. "Lovey's friend."

His expression immediately melted into one of regretful realization. "Oh..."

"Don't worry, I'm not about to go off on you or anything," Desiree assured him as she walked closer to him. "How have you been?"

"I'm all right." Evan was still eying Desiree rather warily, as if he expected her to snap at any second. "How about you? And Lovey, how's she doing?"

"Honestly?" Desiree hedged dramatically. "She misses you."

Evan's eyebrows shot up, surprised. "Really? I thought she'd hate me or something after what happened."

"Oh, she *was* mad, believe me. And incredibly hurt. But despite that, she still has some lingering feelings; she was really into you, you know."

"Wow," Evan rubbed his chin thoughtfully. "Can't say I'm not surprised to hear that."

"Matter of fact, I don't think she'd mind hearing from you."

"Really?"

"Absolutely. Lovey's a sweetheart; she doesn't hold grudges forever. If nothing else, I bet she'd like to hear your voice."

"I might just give her a call, then. Truth be told, I really did feel bad about how things went down. She didn't deserve that."

"I'm glad you recognize that."

"Of course. Lovey is a good woman."

"You should definitely hit her up, then. I'm sure she'd appreciate hearing an official apology from you."

"I might just do that."

"While you're at it, you might even think about asking her out," Desiree suggested with a conspiratorial smile. "I don't know what your relationship status is right now, but Lovey isn't seeing anyone seriously. I'm sure she'd appreciate something to do in the evenings besides work. Not to mention, she's looking *really* good lately."

"Lovey always looked good," Even replied somewhat wistfully, as if he was imagining her right then. "I doubt she'd want to see me, though. And anyway, I'm still seeing Alexis."

Desiree figured Alexis was the woman he cheated on Lovey with. "Evan, I'm telling you...if you come at her correct, she would. It doesn't have to be anything romantic.

And think about it; who else would know better than me? I *am* her best friend and all."

Nodding as if agreeing with her point, Evan shrugged a shoulder. "What the hell. If nothing else, I can at least apologize for what I did to her."

"Exactly. Don't mention me when you talk to her, though; she'd kill me if she knew I told you any of this."

"I got you. Well, I'm gonna get going; nice seeing you again."

"It was surely good seeing you, too, Evan." Desiree grinned as he walked off. "Definitely."

DESIREE COULD TELL that Roland was still a little miffed with her, and she wanted to try to get back on his good side. There were certain spots on his body that tended to make him forget about everything, and Desiree knew if she could just get a chance to work her magic, this latest disagreement of theirs would be just a memory.

But when she called to ask if she could meet him at his place later, he turned her down, saying he had a date with Lovey. Desiree almost threw her phone in frustration. She was surprised that Lovey was *still* hanging with this arrangement, especially after consuming all of the treats Desiree had been sending her. She knew how Lovey got when she thought she put on a couple of pounds; she would freak out and stay to herself until she thought she was back to normal. But apparently, Desiree's little gifts weren't doing what they were supposed to do, at least not enough.

She was going to have to kick things up a little bit.

Early in the evening of Lovey's date with Roland, Desiree paid her friend a visit, arms laden with a couple of surprises. When Lovey opened the door, Desiree grinned at her.

"Hey, girl!" she greeted.

"Hey..." Lovey looked at her curiously.

"Can I come in?"

Hesitating slightly, Lovey finally stepped aside. "Sure. Come in."

Strutting into the apartment, Desiree placed the gifts on the couch and turned to her friend, the smile still on her face. Lovey was wearing a sweater and leggings, and she was noticeably thicker than she was the last time Desiree saw her. Desiree was glad to see for herself how her efforts were paying off.

Lovey looked at the things Desiree brought over. "What's all this?"

"Oh, we'll get to that in a minute," Desiree said with a wave of her hand. She pulled Lovey in for a hug, mostly to further confirm the weight gain. "I haven't seen you in a little while; what's been going on?"

Shrugging, Lovey stepped back and replied casually, "Nothing much, really."

"No? How are things at work?"

"Busy. You know how it is this time of year."

"Yeah, true. My calendar is jumping, too. Business has really picked up."

"I'm glad to hear that, D. I know how hard you've been working."

"I have. How's Liz? I haven't seen her in a while, either."

"Oh, Liz is..." Lovey paused, as if trying to find the right words. "You know Liz."

Desiree was a little curious as to what she meant by that, but decided not to comment on it. "Yeah."

"I *did* get a surprising call yesterday, though," Lovey informed her.

Desiree's ears perked up. "Really? From who?"

"Evan, of all people."

Feigning shock, Desiree gasped. "Whaaat? What in the world did *he* want?"

Lovey went to sit on the empty end of the sofa, tucking a leg under her. "Said he wanted to apologize for what he did. Even asked if we could meet up. Can you believe that?"

"Girl, shut up!" Desiree frowned but inside, she was ecstatic. She nudged her gifts aside and sat next to Lovey. "Are you serious?"

"Yeah. I appreciate the apology but he has a lot of nerve, asking to see me."

"Wow. So you turned him down, huh?"

"Of course I turned him down. We don't have anything to talk about."

"Are you still mad at him?"

"No; I don't really feel anything towards Evan."

"So why not see him? Even if it's just for the entertainment of hearing what he could possibly say to explain himself."

"I'm not interested. It's ancient history."

"I feel you." Desiree's mind raced for what to say. "I'm just saying, though...how many times has a dude come back and showed any kind of remorse for doing you wrong? Usually you never hear from them again. It has to mean something that he had enough nerve to call you after all this time, right?"

"It could just mean that he wanted to clear his conscience, for some reason."

"Maybe he still has feelings for you. Is he still seeing that other woman?"

"I don't know. I didn't ask."

"Hmm. Well, just my opinion, but I think you should see him. I mean, what could it hurt?"

Lovey didn't respond; she just looked at Desiree skeptically.

Reading the look, Desiree quickly added, "I don't have any ulterior motives, Lovey, come on. This has nothing to do with our situation with Roland. In fact, that's why I'm here."

"What do you mean, that's why you're here?"

"I know you and Roland have a date tonight, so I brought you something." She grabbed the boxes next to her and handed them to Lovey. "White chocolate truffles...white hot dress."

Lovey glanced at the boxes, then back at Desiree. The skeptical glint was still in her eye. "You bought me a dress?"

"I couldn't resist. When I saw it, I immediately thought of you. Really, I wanted to keep it for myself, but knew I don't have the hips and booty you do; I wouldn't do it any justice. You should wear it tonight."

Lovey eyed Desiree for a few moments before setting the boxes down. "Desiree, what's going on?"

"What?"

"Sending me all this food lately, and now you're buying me clothes..."

"I told you, I just wanted to do something to show you that there are no hard feelings. You know I hate when we're not speaking or when we fight. Call it bribery, if you want; I wouldn't totally deny it. It's just my way of trying to make up for my part in things getting so heated between us, that's all."

"And that's all it is, huh?"

Desiree tried to keep a straight face. "Of course that's all it is. What else would it be?"

Lovey looked as if she was still on the fence as to whether she bought Desiree's explanation or not. But she eventually said, "Well, I appreciate that. I certainly don't like how things have been between us lately, either."

"That's all I'm saying. I know we both want the same thing, but we should be able to handle it like mature adults. I mean, he's gonna choose who he's gonna choose, right?"

"You can say what the 'thing' is, D. We both want Roland. Let's just call it what it is."

Holding her hands up, Desiree shrugged. "Just trying to avoid any tension."

"Uh-huh." Lovey glanced at her watch. "Speaking of Roland, I need to start getting ready."

"Where are y'all going?" Desiree asked as Lovey stood up.

"To a jazz lounge he heard about somewhere."

"Oh, you should *definitely* wear this baby tonight, then," Desiree suggested as she picked up the dress box, inwardly trying to keep her jealousy in check. A jazz lounge sounded romantic and intimate; she could just picture Roland and Lovey all cuddled up while enjoying some smooth music. The image fueled her determination. "I know it'll turn heads wherever you end up going."

Lovey hesitated. "I don't know..."

"What's not to know? You already have something picked out?"

"No..."

"Well, I just saved you some time. Here, at least try it on. I bet you're gonna look amazing in it."

Finally taking the box, Lovey gave her a small smile. "Okay. Thanks."

"Let me know when you have it on so I can see."

"Okay."

Lovey disappeared down the hall and Desiree smiled to herself. Plopping back onto the couch, she turned on the TV and waited, feeling deliciously anxious.

After about twenty minutes, there was still no sign of Lovey. Desiree checked her watch then headed back to Lovey's bedroom, knocking on the closed door.

"Lovey?" she called out, trying to suppress her smile. "What's taking so long? You okay?"

A few moments passed before there was a sniff. "Um, I guess."

"Do you have the dress on? Can I see it?"

Lovey wordlessly opened the door, watching Desiree's face for a reaction. Desiree kept her expression even as she entered the room, perusing the look.

"I think it looks great," she finally said. She noticed Lovey's deflated expression. "What's wrong? You don't think so?"

It was a clingy, one-shoulder dress that stopped just above the knee. Normally, it would've looked amazing on Lovey. But after weeks of stress-eating decadent desserts, it seemed to only highlight areas Lovey wanted to hide. She stood barefoot in front of her full-length mirror, tugging and pulling at the dress as she twisted and tried to see every angle she could.

"I-I don't know about this," she stammered, holding both hands over her stomach. "It seems a little tight..."

It should be. I bought it two sizes too small. "Come on, Lovey, stop pulling on it. It looks good."

Truth was, it actually did, despite Lovey's extra weight. But Desiree knew Lovey wouldn't agree.

"I'm not comfortable in this, D..."

"I don't know why. Hell, I *wish* I could fill out a dress like that."

"I look fat."

"What? Why would you even say some foolishness like that?"

"*Look* at me!"

"Lovey, come on. Roland is gonna love you in that."

As if she had temporarily forgotten that Roland was the entire reason she was getting dressed in the first place, Lovey placed both hands over her mouth. "Oh gosh! No, there's no way I'm letting Roland see me in this!"

Sighing, Desiree threw up her hands. "Okay, fine, put on something else, then."

"What's the point? I'll look just as fat in anything else." Lovey ripped the dress off and tossed it to the floor, flopping onto the bed in her nude-colored bra and panties.

"So, what, you're not going?" Desiree asked after several moments.

"I want to, but..."

"Lovey, look..." Desiree joined her on the bed. "I might as well go ahead and tell you this, since you're suddenly so self-conscious about your weight and stuff."

Lovey looked at her. "Tell me what?"

"A while back, I heard Roland telling someone that he...he doesn't really care for...for *thick* women," Desiree gently revealed.

Looking at her thighs in horror, Lovey gasped.

"And you know how men are, girl; if you start acting all insecure and stuff about your weight, that's all they'll start to notice. They start analyzing every little thing. And then things just get awkward-"

"That's it, I'm not going!" Lovey exclaimed. She stormed into the bathroom, emerging a few seconds later in her bathrobe. "I'll just cancel the date. I'm not trying to make a fool out of myself."

"I wasn't saying that so you would cancel, Lovey," Desiree lied. "I was just trying to prepare you, is all."

"Yeah, well, thanks. You prepared me, all right. I'll just spend the evening by myself and catch up on some work or something."

"Are you sure?" Desiree asked. "I hate to think I'm the reason your evening is messed up."

"*I'm* the fat pig. So I did this to myself. Now if you'll excuse me, I'd prefer to be alone right now."

Pursing her lips as her insides did a dance, Desiree followed Lovey to the front door. "Call me if you change your mind and decide you want some company, okay?"

Her head turned away, clearly embarrassed, Lovey just nodded slightly.

Desiree walked out, giving Lovey's arm a sympathetic squeeze as she passed. As soon as the door was closed behind her, Desiree couldn't resist the grin that was spreading across her face like syrup on a short stack.

She practically skipped to her car, figuring that Lovey was breaking into the box of truffles right about then.

Chapter 22

"SERIOUSLY??"

Lovey just cancelled yet another date via text. She'd been doing a lot of that lately, and Roland was totally in the dark about what was going on. She wouldn't let him come over, she wouldn't go out with him, they didn't even talk on the phone as much as they used to. It was like she was avoiding him.

Desiree gladly filled his free time, and Roland usually enjoyed her company, but he missed Lovey. He just wished he knew why she was pulling away from him like she was.

Needing some answers, he decided to stop by her office. He hated to surprise her at work, but he figured that would be the one place she would see him if for no other reason than to be polite. And since he'd been there several times, it wasn't like he was a stranger. He'd grown to be pretty cool with the receptionist, Tara, so he wasn't worried about getting her to squeeze him in to Lovey's day.

But when he got there, he learned Lovey had apparently thought ahead.

"I'm sorry, Roland, she's busy all day," Tara informed him regretfully.

"For real? She doesn't have five minutes?" Roland hated how desperate he sounded, but he couldn't help it.

"I'm sorry," Tara said again. "She specifically instructed that she was not to be disturbed. But I can definitely let her know you came by."

"Okay. Thanks." Frustrated, Roland stormed out of the office.

Something was going on. Roland began to wonder if maybe Lovey was losing interest in him. Their dinner at Maggiano's was a couple of weeks ago, and he'd had to practically beg to get her to go out with him then. But ever since that date, she'd gone scarce on him, canceling their date at the jazz lounge at practically the last minute and then declining all invitations since. He didn't know what could have happened to make her change course so suddenly.

He hated to do it, but he asked Desiree if she knew what was going on with Lovey. Ever since the three of them started their little arrangement, he tried not to talk to them about each other. He didn't even know if Lovey and Desiree were back on speaking terms like they had been before. But he felt he didn't have any other choice.

"Hey, I hate to ask you this but...do you know what's going on with Lovey?"

They were on the phone as he headed back to Barfly. Desiree paused a second before answering. "Why do you ask?"

"I just haven't seen very much of her lately, is all." He was trying to sound aloof, even though he felt anything but. "Just wanted to know if anything was wrong."

"Nothing wrong that I know of. She did mention being back in touch with one of her ex-boyfriends, though...maybe she's been seeing him."

Roland jammed on his breaks a little too hard and lurched forward. Running a hand down his face, he cleared his throat. "Yeah?"

"Yeah. I figured she hadn't told you yet; she was worried about how to break it to you."

"Break it to me? What, they got back together or something?"

"Not that I know of. She just didn't want to keep anything from you, that's all."

"I see." Roland's fingers felt like they could rip the steering wheel right off. "And when did she tell you all this?"

"Look, Roland, I'm not trying to get in the middle of that. You know Lovey isn't shady. If it was something serious, I'm sure she would have told you herself by now."

Roland was only mildly relieved by that. He didn't like the thought of Lovey dealing with another man at all, no matter how casual. "Is this the cat that moved to Texas?"

"Nah, not him. Somebody else."

"Hmm."

"While I have you on here, you know I'm gonna be throwing a grown and sexy bash for Valentine's Day. It's gonna be *hot*, especially afterwards. You wanna be my date, handsome?"

Roland was actually planning on asking Lovey out for Valentine's Day. But she probably already had other plans.

"Sure."

SCRUTINIZING HER BODY in front of the full-length mirror had become Lovey's subconscious hobby. Just about every day, she stripped out of her clothes and tried to see what new bumps and bulges she could find. Whenever she found or noticed something else, she got more depressed about how she looked. This was the lowest her self-esteem had ever been, and she didn't know how to handle it. Her automatic thing was diving into some sweet or decadent treat while crying about how sad her life had become.

She missed Roland terribly. But after learning about his distaste for bigger women from Desiree, she just didn't want to see him. Lovey was never thin, but before her recent weight gain, she was curvy and voluptuous and firm. Now, in her mind, she was just fat.

And she didn't want to see that look in his eye that asked *what the hell happened?* Then he'd try to figure out a way to let her down easy, canceling dates, ignoring messages, fading to black like so many other men before, until he disappeared altogether. So Lovey figured she'd just beat all that to the punch this time and save herself the embarrassment.

Liz was out of town again, this time on business, and Lovey seemed to forget all of her sister's earlier speculations about Desiree's motives. There'd been a couple more dessert deliveries, and Lovey always ended up eating them all, despite telling herself she wouldn't. She chose to go for the temporary high of the delicious treats because it made her feel better, even if only for a short time, and even if she was almost sure to regret it afterwards.

She was about to get a slice of triple chocolate cheesecake from the kitchen when her phone rang. Seeing that it was Roland, she started not to answer it but changed her mind at the last second.

"Hello?"

"Lovey, what's up? You busy?"

"Not at the moment. Why?"

"I wanted to see you tonight."

"I can't," she immediately replied.

She nervously bit her lip when she heard his exasperated sigh. "May I ask why not?"

"I just have some things I need to do that I can't get out of."

"Lovey." Roland's voice was strong. "What is going on?"

"Nothing is going on, Roland."

"Every time I ask to see you, you give me some excuse. Or you agree then cancel at the last minute. You know how I am about people being straight up. If there's something I need to know, I wish you would just tell me."

Lovey didn't want to mislead Roland, but what was she supposed to say? *I've been stuffing my face with junk for weeks and now I'm too embarrassed to hang out with you because I know you don't like thick women*?

When Lovey thought about it, she concluded that Roland wasn't being totally straight with her, either. The last time they went out, he *had* to notice that she gained weight. And if what Desiree said about his body preference was true, then why was he acting like he was still interested? She was only thicker now than she was then.

"Is there something you need to tell *me*?" she countered, crossing her arms under her lush breasts. "I don't think I'm the only one that's not being totally forthcoming, here."

"Oh, so you're gonna try to turn it around on me?"

"I'm not trying to do that at all. But it occurred to me that we both might be keeping some things to ourselves."

"When can I even keep anything to myself, Lovey? You've barely been talking to me."

"And why is that? You've been spending most of your time with Desiree since we started this whole shared relationship thing. And now when you want to get around to me, you act surprised when I'm not over the moon about it."

"Lovey, I apologized for that," Roland reminded her, much of the edge leaving his voice. "I've never done anything like this before; I absolutely acknowledge that I haven't been the best at balancing things. But I've been trying to rectify that."

"I know you have. But I'm just not feeling it now."

There was a considerable pause. Roland's voice sounded a little different when he finally asked, "So what are you saying?"

"I'm saying..." Lovey blinked back tears. How had it come to this? "I'm saying that I just need some time to myself for a while."

"I see." Roland cleared his throat. "Well, if that's what you want...you got it. I won't keep bothering you." He hung up.

Holding the phone for several moments, Lovey just let the tears stream down her face. Everything in her wanted to call Roland back and tell him everything. She wanted to just be honest about her physical insecurities and how she was past tired of this stupid arrangement they were in the middle of. She stayed in it because she hadn't wanted to give Desiree the satisfaction of outlasting her, but it was getting to be pointless. She and Roland had only drifted apart since the whole thing started.

She tried to call Liz, but was unable to reach her. The only other person she briefly thought about calling was Mama Elyse, but even though she loved and treated Lovey like a daughter, Desiree was still her *actual* daughter. Lovey couldn't make herself believe that Elyse would be totally impartial. But more than that, Lovey was just too embarrassed to admit to anyone else that she had agreed to such an arrangement in the first place.

There was a knock on her door, and she threw on her bathrobe and rushed to answer it, screaming in pain when she accidentally banged her foot on the coffee table as she passed it. Limping to the door, she looked through the peephole. It looked like a delivery guy.

"Great," she muttered. She started not to answer it, but curiosity got the better of her so she hastily wiped her tears and opened the door. The food aromas hit her immediately. "Yes?"

"I have a delivery for Lovey Tate?" the young man announced, adjusting his baseball cap.

"Um, that's me."

"Sign here and it's all yours."

Lovey hesitated before signing the form and accepting the large tin. She thanked the deliveryman before kicking the door closed with her good foot and limping over to the couch. Sniffling, she pried open the tin and groaned. It was full of thick, gooey, freshly baked chocolate chip walnut cookies.

"*Gosh*, these smell good," she whispered, almost burying her face in the tin. Catching herself, she quickly slapped the lid back on and pushed it away from her, trying to resist the instant temptation. She didn't put it past herself to polish off the majority of those cookies in one sitting, and she was determined not to do that.

Getting up to take the tin to the kitchen, she went back to the living room and examined her hurt toes. Her foot was hurting, her heart was hurting...she tried not to think about her earlier conversation with Roland and if it would be the last one they had for a while. Or ever. The thought alone brought fresh tears.

She grabbed her laptop and logged into Facebook, hoping for a distraction. She didn't use social media as much as she used to; after Clay dumped her, she started to wean herself off of it to resist the temptation to un-block him and stalk his page. Now, she just did the occasional check-in or sharing of a funny meme.

But laughter certainly wasn't an option when she ran across a picture of Desiree and Roland. Bolting upright, Lovey leaned closer to her laptop screen, as if wanting to see every detail of the photo. The picture had been posted a few days prior; in it, Desiree had her arm around Roland's shoulders, her cheek pressed against his, her other arm extended to take the picture. It looked like they were in a movie theater. Desiree was grinning proudly while Roland's smile was tight. Lovey could imagine him only agreeing to take the picture to appease Desiree; he told Lovey during one of their many marathon conversations that he wasn't too big on pictures and never had been. He just took them when he felt like it. There were more pictures of Roland on Barfly's social media pages than his own.

Lovey wondered if Desiree had posted that picture just to goad her, then immediately admonished herself for the thought. Why would Desiree need to do that? It wasn't like Lovey didn't already know the two of them were seeing each other. And Desiree *loved* taking pictures; her social media pages were packed with them. A lot of them had to do with business and her party promotions, but most of them were personal. So her posing and profiling in the movie theater certainly wasn't anything new.

What *wasn't* usual, though, was Desiree posting pictures of whoever she was dating. Since she never really got serious about anyone, she never broadcasted who she was seeing at any given time. In fact, Lovey recalled several times over the years when Desiree called couples pictures on social media corny. So the fact that Desiree was posting a picture of her and Roland, complete with a heart and a kissing emoji, made Lovey wonder again just whose benefit the picture was for.

She couldn't resist scrolling through Desiree's page some more, and while there weren't any more pictures of Roland, there were certainly some allusions to him:

That party was lit tonight; thanks to everyone who came out! And a special thanks to you-know-who for helping me de-stress afterwards. ;)

Mixing business with pleasure isn't always a bad thing, as long as everyone knows what the deal is. #wegrown

Isn't it crazy how quick some folks catch feelings?

I might act a certain way but...well let's just say some people aren't as good at expressing themselves as others. Who feels me?

I bet y'all didn't bring in the new year better than I did. ;)

I'm thinking about things a whole lot differently now. Might not want to, but I can't seem to help it...

But it was Desiree's latest post that really got Lovey's attention:

Your girl has been on a mission, y'all. And y'all know I don't lose. #justsayin

THAT COULD HAVE VERY well been about work. Maybe Desiree had a new promotor or venue she wanted to work with, or had set some kind of other professional goal that Lovey just wasn't privy to. But Lovey suspected that it didn't have anything to do with work; it was about Roland. Desiree was staking her claim and she apparently wanted everyone to know it.

Lovey went back to the picture of Desiree and Roland, her eyes perusing every detail. Roland might not have been grinning the way Desiree was, but he didn't look unhappy.

And Lovey knew that if Roland had been *that* against taking that picture, and *that* against Desiree posting it (because Lovey was sure he knew about it), it wouldn't exist. He apparently didn't mind the public inference that they were a happy couple. Maybe that's what they were.

But if that was the case, Lovey wondered, why was he acting like he was still interested in her?

Roland wasn't the kind of man to knowingly lead a woman on. He had too much compassion for that, too much decency. And before that nighttime against-the-car kiss happened, Lovey and Roland were friends. He wouldn't do anything to hurt her, especially knowing how much she had been through with men already.

Lovey frowned. What if that was what all this had been about? What if Roland had just been feeling sorry for her this whole time?

It made sense. She had cried on his shoulder about Clay more than once. She spilled her guts about all the times she had been duped and dumped by men in the past. Maybe all their time together had just been about lifting her spirits. Wasn't that why Desiree suggested Lovey and Roland hang out to begin with? Because Lovey was apparently so pathetic that her friend felt she needed to 'loan' her man to her to get her self-esteem out of the gutter?

The thought was embarrassing. Lovey couldn't believe she had misread Roland like that. She was sure his feelings for her were as sincere as hers were for him, but clearly, she was wrong again. He had spent the majority of his time with Desiree since they began this shared dating thing; he wouldn't have done that if he didn't want to. What other signs did she need?

Even with everything Desiree put him through, he still went back to her. It wasn't fair. Lovey would never have dropped Roland like Desiree had, but apparently it didn't matter. Maybe he was one of those men that liked a challenge. Maybe the sex was so good between them that he was willing to put up with her antics.

Or maybe...Roland just wanted Desiree and he *didn't* want Lovey.

The thought made the tears well in her eyes and overflow like a salty waterfall.

Waterfalls. Like the one they were next to when Clay asked her to be his woman.

And where was *that* relationship?

"Dammit!" she screamed, pushing her laptop to the floor. She only worried that she had damaged it for one brief second; in the next, she didn't care. She buried her face in her hands and cried, embarrassed, angered, and convinced that she was going to spend the rest of her life alone.

She let herself cry. She didn't try to stop it. There was no more energy to try to conjure up another self-pep talk. No desire to try to think positively or find the bright side. No little voice in her ear saying that she was overreacting or just in her feelings at the moment. All of the men who disappointed her flashed through her mind like a slideshow on repeat. Her imagination was running away from her, and she could do nothing but sit there and watch.

"Why am I not good enough?" she whimpered.

Without trying to, Lovey mentally analyzed herself, scrolling through every fault she could think of. There had to be a reason she kept getting dropped by men. After so many times of the same thing happening, it was hard to just keep blaming them; there had to be something wrong with *her*. There *had* to be. She considered any and everything she might have done to push them away, or send them running for the hills.

Was it her light skin? Was she too nice? Maybe they took that to mean she was weak. Was she boring? Too affectionate? Needy?

After a while, Lovey was exhausted, physically and emotionally. She wiped her eyes, not even wanting to imagine how her face looked at that moment. Her face half-buried in a sofa pillow, her eyes drifted to her laptop on the floor. The thought that she might have damaged it with her tantrum only brought a new kind of anxiety. She squeezed her eyes shut, wishing she could just disappear.

Lovey didn't know when she had gotten up and retrieved the tin of cookies from the kitchen, but there they were right next to her on the couch. Knowing it was probably the only thing that would bring her any kind of pleasure right then, Lovey indulged, helping herself to a cookie. It practically melted in her mouth. She had another. Then another, closing her eyes and turning her mind off to what she was doing. She just mindlessly kept reaching for more.

Her phone rang, and Lovey didn't bother answering it. Seconds later, it rang again. Sighing, Lovey picked it up as she licked the chocolate from her fingertips, not bothering to see who it was.

"Hello?"

There was a slight pause before a familiar voice spoke. "How you doin', Lovey?"

Frowning, Lovey sat up a little straighter. "Evan?"

"Yeah." Another pause. "What's up?"

"What do you mean, what's up?"

"I mean...how are you?"

"Why do you care? What are you calling me for?"

"Whoa," Evan sounded genuinely shocked; he had never heard Lovey speak so harshly. "What's up with you? What's wrong?"

"I don't know why you're asking. You proved I'm of no concern to you when you cheated on me. So if you'll excuse me..."

"Lovey, wait a second!"

Sighing, Lovey held the phone to her ear. Hearing Evan's voice had immediately agitated her, and was only a reminder of what he'd done. "What?"

"Are you seriously still that upset with me?"

"I just don't think we have anything to talk about. You already apologized. And honestly, I'm not in the mood for any small talk that I'm sure you'll just forget about two seconds after we hang up. So why waste each other's time?"

"I'm not trying to waste your time, Lovey. I just want to talk to you."

"And I want people to keep it real with me, but we all can't get what we want, can we?"

Evan wasn't sure if her comment was about him or someone else, but there was something clearly going on with Lovey.

"Okay..." he began. "Look. I know what I did was jacked up. I should have just been up front about getting with Alexis. You absolutely did not deserve that. So I know I've already said it, but I have no problem saying it again; I'm sorry, Lovey. I truly am."

He sounded sincere. Lovey started to soften a bit, before she remembered how many times she'd been wrong about men's declarations before. How many times had she been lied to? Men were good actors. Evan certainly was when they were dating.

"Thanks," she eventually panned. "I'm overflowing with gratitude. Now that your conscience is clear, are we done?"

Without waiting for a response, she hung up on him.

Lovey started to reach back into the cookie tin when her phone rang again. She ignored it and stuffed another cookie in her mouth as she retrieved her laptop from the floor.

"Please don't be broken..." she muttered with her mouth full.

She breathed a huge sigh of relief when her screen opened right back to the page she was looking at before her dramatic display. Everything seemed to be working properly.

"Thank God," she breathed.

Her phone chimed with a text. It was from Evan.

Ok, I'm officially worried. U don't even sound like yourself.

Lovey rolled her eyes as another text came in.

I know you think I'm full of shit but I honestly care about you. Please answer your phone.

In the next couple of seconds, her phone rang again. Lovey sucked her teeth and turned her eyes back to her computer screen. It was still on her Facebook feed, and as she mindlessly scrolled through it, the picture of Desiree and Roland appeared again.

The happy couple.

Telling herself not to cry again, she moved her laptop to the coffee table and leaned back against the sofa cushions. Her eyes were still on the picture.

Her phone rang again. This time she answered it.

"Lovey?" Evan immediately called out.

"Yes?" Her voice sounded tired. Because she was.

"Can we please talk?"

Turning her eyes away from the image of the man she had foolishly fallen for hugged up with her best friend, Lovey finally said, "Okay."

Chapter 23

"MA...I'M NOT REALLY sure I want to look at your sex toys."

Elyse rolled her eyes. "Nobody asked you to look. You're the one that came in here being nosey."

"Well, when I saw this big pretty basket in here, I figured it was for a picnic or something. Like sandwiches, fruit..."

"The fruit and the caramel are in the refrigerator."

Desiree was sure that those things would be used more in her parents' bedroom than anywhere else. She shook her head.

Desiree had come by to visit, only to find her mother Elyse knee-deep in preparing a sexy surprise for her husband, Darius. The dining room table was already decked out with the good plates and candles, and Elyse was in the kitchen preparing her man's favorite surf and turf meal. Desiree chose not to think about what was going to go down after they ate it, if they even got that far.

"I don't even know what to say about y'all," she chuckled, replacing the large silk scarf that had been covering the basket's contents.

"Uh-huh. What are you gonna be getting into tonight?"

"Hanging out with Roland."

Elyse gave her a surprised glance as she got some seasonings out of the cabinet. "Wow."

"Wow, what?"

"I'm surprised Roland is still around. Usually you would have found something wrong with him by now. Or just got tired of him."

"Damn, Ma, you don't have to say it like that."

"Am I telling the truth or not? You know that's what you do."

"Well, not this time. I might have needed a break for a minute but I realized I wasn't ready to let him go yet."

"After he started showing interest in Lovey, right?"

Desiree looked at her. "What?"

"Don't try me like that."

"I'm sayin'...I don't know what you're talking about, Ma."

"The hell you don't. You were right over there in the other room talking about your brilliant plan to pawn Roland off on Lovey, acting like you were doing it for them even though we all knew what the real deal was. And we tried to tell you that it could blow up in your face, but you swore up and down that Roland had eyes only for you."

Desiree sighed. "Yeah, I know what I said, Mama..."

"Then when the two of them started feeling each other, *like we all said they might*, you decided you wanted him back."

"You're making that sound like it's a bad thing. Sometimes we don't realize what we have until we let it go. Isn't that what folks always say?"

"Yeah. But I'm wondering if you really want Roland, or if you just don't want Lovey to have him?"

The question pricked Desiree, but she shook it off. "If I was worried about that, then why would I agree to both of us dating him?"

Elyse stopped her action of seasoning the steaks. "Excuse me?"

"Lovey and I are both dating Roland. She didn't want to let him go, and I didn't, either. So..."

"So, what, you're sharing him?"

"I guess you can look at it like that..."

"I can't even believe Lovey would actually agree to something like that. You sure you didn't talk her into it?"

"No! I mean, I presented the idea to them and they were both down, so...I don't really see what the problem is."

"Girl, I didn't raise you to be this stupid."

Desiree's jaw dropped. "Why I gotta be stupid, Ma? We're all grown, we all agreed..."

"As if that means anything. Maybe *some* best friends can handle something like this but you and Lovey can't."

"And why not?"

"Because Lovey is too sensitive and you're too selfish. When you think you're being challenged, you pull out all the stops to win it, no matter who ends up hurt in the process. And I'm just worried where that's gonna leave you and Lovey's friendship whenever all this is over."

Desiree wasn't about to admit her mother had a point. "I think you're exaggerating a little bit, Ma. It's not gonna last much longer, anyway."

"Why isn't it?"

"Because I've been wearing Lovey down. I can't imagine she'll put up with it much longer. Then Roland will be all mine."

Elyse turned towards her daughter, crossing her arms. Her eyes showed clear disapproval. "Do you even hear yourself, Desiree?"

Hunching her shoulders, Desiree innocently held up her hands, her eyes wide. "What?"

"That look didn't work when you were twelve and it doesn't work now. What the hell do you mean, you've been wearing Lovey down? What did you do to her?"

"Come on, Ma, please. I haven't done anything *to* her. I wouldn't do that. All I mean is that I'm tipping the scales in my favor, that's all. Showing Roland I'm the woman he should want."

"He *did* want you, remember? You're the one who didn't want *him*."

That reminder left Desiree speechless for a second. She didn't like the way her mother was looking at her, in that judgmental, accusatory way. But Desiree could see something else, too: disappointment. If there was one person who could make her feel two feet tall with a single look, it was Elyse.

"And think about what you just said," Elyse continued. "You didn't say anything about showing Roland how much you want him. You just want him to want *you*. At least be woman enough to admit this is all about your ego."

Shooting out of her chair, Desiree slid her feet back into the fuzzy booties she had kicked off, avoiding her mother's piercing glare by pretending to look for her keys.

"Suddenly remembered somewhere you need to be, huh?" Elyse asked knowingly.

"No, it's not that. I just, umm..."

Elyse crossed the room and gently grabbed her daughter by the shoulders. "Look at me."

Desiree did as she was told.

"You need to really think about what you're doing," Elyse instructed pointedly, looking square into Desiree's eyes. "Lovey has been there for you since day one. Not to mention, she was the main one holding your hand through that *incident* you don't like to talk about."

Wincing slightly, Desiree swallowed.

"Lovey wants marriage. You've told me Roland wants marriage. *You* don't; you've said it a million times. Has that changed? And don't try to lie to me."

Shame averted Desiree's eyes.

"Exactly. Now why would you go so hard for a man that doesn't want what you want if this wasn't just about winning?"

"I...umm..."

"If Lovey has sincere feelings for Roland, and Roland has them for her, what does it say about you that you would want to do *anything* to interfere with that? Don't lose your day one over a man that could be gone tomorrow." Elyse dropped her hands and stepped back. "I hope you keep that in mind while you're *wearing her down*."

Desiree stood there awkwardly as Elyse went back to resume her meal preparation. Needing to get out of there, she quickly left her mother's house.

TRY AS SHE MIGHT, DESIREE couldn't erase Elyse's words from her mind. For the rest of the day, they replayed in her head like a broken record.

Don't lose your day one over a man that could be gone tomorrow.

Desiree didn't want to lose Lovey as a friend. She was certain of that. This whole thing with Roland had gotten out of control, and Desiree knew it.

Was all this just about winning, like Elyse said? Of course she had taken it personally when Roland and Lovey started paying more attention to each other than to her. And when she saw them kiss, it set something off in her that she hadn't felt in a while: jealousy. Not to mention embarrassment. So maybe part of her determination to win Roland's affections back was to save face. It wasn't exactly fun sitting there listening to her mother and sisters reminding her how wrong she had been.

At least be woman enough to admit this is all about your ego.

But her feelings for Roland were real. Maybe not to the level of wanting to have his last name and bear his child, but as real as they could be for her. She could admit that she didn't really think beyond getting Roland back; if he *did* choose her, eventually he would start talking about their future. And they would be right back to the point that had made Desiree step back in the first place, because Desiree wasn't ready for that and probably never would be. At least, that's what she told herself.

What was she so afraid of? Why was she so adamantly dead-set against the idea of marriage or anything remotely permanent?

She knew why. And her mama and Lovey were the only other people that knew, too. Desiree had been running from it for years, so much so that she'd convinced herself that being tied down was something she'd never, ever do.

Sighing, Desiree flopped back onto her bed. She missed Lovey. They hardly talked much anymore, and Desiree knew that was on her. She began to wonder if their friendship would ever be the same after all this. The catty comments, the pseudo-truce, the deliberate attempts to nudge Lovey out of the picture by playing on her self-esteem issues...how had she let things get this far? Lovey would never, ever do anything like that to her, and Desiree knew it.

But she didn't want to lose Roland, either. He affected her; had somehow wedged his way into parts of her that she thought were closed for business. It freaked Desiree out, because she hadn't felt like this since *then*. Which is why she backed away from it, and also why she tried so hard to get it back when she thought she lost it.

This had become a mess that Desiree had no idea how to clean up. Either way, something was going to be permanently smudged.

"COME IN, DESIREE."

Desiree entered the office, trying to appear cool and collected even though she was anything but. She hadn't been looking forward to this meeting at all.

"Should I close the door?" Her hand rested on the door handle.

"Please."

After pushing the door closed, Desiree took a seat in front of the desk, forcing herself to look right at. E.J. His eyes pierced into her for several moments before turning his attention to some papers on his desk. More than a few minutes passed before he even looked at her again. There was none of their usual banter or friendly small talk. No questions about how her family was doing. No accolades on how well her last couple of parties had gone. He just made her wait. Just like he'd been doing ever since she ended her exclusive relationship with Roland. E.J. never commented on it, but Desiree wasn't delusional enough to think his attitude was about anything else, especially since they always got along fine before.

Finally, E.J. spoke. "So you wanted to discuss something for Valentine's Day?" He still wasn't looking at her.

"Um, yeah," Desiree cleared her throat, surprised at how nervous she was. "I just wanted to run things down with you and make sure we were on the same page."

"You could've done that with Roland." His voice was sharp.

"But I usually handle this portion of things with you."

"Doesn't have to be like that."

"Okay, E.J.," Desiree sighed. "Let's just go ahead and get everything out on the table, okay?"

He finally looked at her, cocking a brow. "Meaning?"

"Meaning this thing between me and Roland."

"Whatever is between you and Roland is your business."

"But you clearly have a problem with me. I've felt nothing but animosity from you since I walked up in here. And since you and I have never had an issue before, I can only assume it's because of me and Roland's situation."

He glared at her.

"If you have a problem with me, just say it," Desiree declared. "No need in pretending or insulting my intelligence."

"No, I'll leave that kind of stuff to you."

Reeling slightly, Desiree sat back in her chair. "Excuse me?"

"You know exactly what I'm talking about." E.J. slapped down the papers and looked right at her. "I wasn't ever going to comment on this to you because like I said, it's not my business. And as much as I'd like to think I'm mature enough to keep my personal feelings out of things regarding business, obviously I'm not. I don't take kindly to people jerking my brother around."

"That's not what I'm doing!"

"The hell you're not. He catches feelings for you and you can't handle it, so you back up. He starts feeling someone else, and all of a sudden you're interested again. What is that?"

"Haven't you ever heard of someone not appreciating someone until they think they're gone?"

"I sure have, but I don't think it had anything to do with appreciation. You didn't count on him actually falling for Lovey. And when he did, you started acting like a kid who wanted their bike back after seeing how much somebody else was enjoying it."

Crossing her arms, Desiree frowned. "Oh really?"

"Yes, really."

"Well, I'm glad you think you have this all figured out, but you are way off. Despite what you think of me, I really do have feelings for Roland."

"Maybe you do. But I still doubt your intentions. I'm sure it's only a matter of time before some other dude catches your eye and Roland won't look as good to you, and you'll be high school-texting him again that you need *space*."

Desiree's jaw dropped. "How dare you, E.J.!"

"What? You're the one that wanted to talk about this; I was gonna keep my mouth shut. And since I'm on a roll, I'll go ahead and say this, too: I think Lovey is way better for Roland than you are. And if he'd quit thinking with the wrong head, he'd see that, too."

Anger surged through her. "I really don't appreciate you sitting here judging me like that. You don't know a damn thing about me!"

"I know that if one of your sisters was constantly confiding in you about the roller coaster some man was always taking them on, you wouldn't be singing their praises any more than I'm singing yours." E.J. folded his own arms, leaning back in his chair. "Before anything, Roland is my little brother. I'm always gonna have his back, *period*. And I simply don't think you're good for him."

Desiree swallowed, unexpected emotion swirling in her chest. Narrowing her eyes slightly, she asked, "Have you told him that?"

"No, I have not. When he confides in me, I mostly just listen. I *did* tell him that he doesn't need to waste time with a woman he doesn't see a future with. But he's a grown-ass man and is gonna do what he wants."

"Right. And what he wants is *me*. Regardless of what you think about it."

"If it makes you feel better about yourself to think that, go right ahead."

"You know what, E.J.? I don't have time for this." Desiree shot up from her chair, grabbing her briefcase. "I don't really give a damn what you think. If Roland wants to be with me, and he *does*, then that's what's gonna happen. And you and anyone else that has a problem with it can just kiss my ass!"

Storming out of the office, Desiree stalked through the near-empty club to the front door, ignoring the curious looks of any employees she passed by. She kept her feet moving until she got to her car, blinking back angry tears as she exited the Barfly parking lot as fast as she could.

She was still reeling from E.J.'s words. She really hadn't expected him to say all those things to her. It certainly wasn't the first time that someone didn't like her or disagreed with something she'd done, but E.J. saying that he thought Lovey was better for Roland than she was hit a major nerve. What did Lovey have that she didn't?

E.J.'s rantings also made Desiree wonder what exactly Roland had told him about her. She knew she shouldn't be surprised that Roland was confiding in his brother; she certainly spilled her guts to her loved ones. But what exactly had Roland said? Was he unhappy? Did he really want to just be with Lovey but didn't know how to break it to her? Was he just keeping Desiree around for the sex?

She tried to call Roland but it went straight to voicemail. With her mind racing a thousand miles a minute, she made another call.

"What's up, Desiree?"

"Hey, Lovey." Desiree tried to keep her voice chipper. "You sound tired."

"I am."

"Well I won't keep you long, then. I just wanted to know what you were planning on doing for Valentine's Day."

A couple of moments passed. "Why?"

"Just wanted to know. I'm going to be with Roland, of course, and I was hoping you weren't going to be just holed up in your apartment by yourself, eating your weight in chocolate or something."

"Oh...you have plans with Roland already?"

"Sure do."

"I see." Desiree had no idea that Lovey had been working up the nerve to invite Roland out for Valentine's Day, so they could try to work some things out. She was disappointed, and it clearly reflected in her voice.

"What's the matter?" Desiree asked, grinning victoriously. She could absolutely hear the dejection in her friend's voice and it automatically lifted her spirits.

"Nothing." Lovey sniffed. "Um, I don't really have any plans for that right now. Haven't even thought about it much, really...I'm sure I'll come up with something to do."

"Maybe you can hang out with Liz. Go to a movie or something."

"Maybe, yeah. Well, look, I have some stuff I need to finish. I'll talk to you later, Desiree." She hung up.

Actually squealing, Desiree clapped her hands as she stopped her car at a red light. Lovey clearly didn't like hearing that she had already locked Roland down for what they both knew was one of Lovey's favorite holidays. E.J.'s words were forgotten as Desiree basked in what she considered another victory.

Then she caught a glimpse of herself in the rearview mirror, and her smile faded slightly. Was she actually cheering for disappointing her best friend? She had only called Lovey to rub her plans with Roland in her face; she didn't even think to ask how she was doing, what she had been up to or even why she sounded so tired. Her only goal was to gloat. And hearing Lovey sound so sad actually made Desiree feel better.

She didn't even notice when the light turned green. The car behind her honked their horn loudly, and Desiree jumped, quickly stepping on the gas. She pulled into a nearby shopping center parking lot and just looked out the window, realizing that she was quickly becoming someone she didn't recognize.

Chapter 24

"LOVEY, YOU HAVE A VISITOR."

Sighing, Lovey pressed the button on the speakerphone. "Thank you, Tara. Please tell them I'm busy and to set an appointment." She didn't even care who it was.

A moment later, she heard Tara's voice again. "I'm sorry, Lovey, but he's pretty insistent to see you now. He promises it'll only be for a few minutes."

He? Immediately wondering if it was Roland, she smoothed a hand over her ponytail and straightened her sweater. "Okay, fine. Send him in." She quickly checked her appearance in the small mirror she kept in her desk and smoothed a fresh coat of lip gloss across her lips with lightning speed.

Her door eased open, and Lovey was considerably disappointed to see it was Taylor.

"Oh, Mr. Cartright." She closed her desk drawer.

"I'm sorry to disturb you," Taylor stepped into the office and gently closed the door behind him. "I needed to see you regarding something rather urgent and I didn't want to wait any longer."

"What's going on? And please, have a seat."

Taking a seat in front of her desk, Taylor anxiously rubbed his hands together before blurting out, "I wanted to ask you to accompany me this evening."

It took a second for Lovey to register exactly what he said. She blinked rapidly, clearly surprised. "You...came here just to ask me out?"

"Yes."

"Oh..."

"I realize this is abrupt, but I haven't been able to get you off of my mind since our first meeting. I would be honored if you would join me for dinner."

Briefly touching her flushed cheeks, Lovey tried to unscramble her tangled thoughts. This was certainly the last thing she was expecting. It took her several moments to remember how to speak.

"Mr. Cartright, umm..."

"Taylor, please."

"Okay, Taylor. Umm, I am very, very flattered, but...I'm not sure that would be the best idea."

"Why not?"

"Well, because you're a client. And..."

Taylor looked at her expectantly. "And?"

How could Lovey tell him that she didn't feel worthy of dating anyone new because of her recent weight gain? She was feeling anything but attractive. Part of her was wondering why he was asking her out anyway, because surely he should have noticed it.

"It just wouldn't be a good idea," she finally answered.

"Are you involved with someone?"

"No..."

"Is there some kind of spiritual reason that prevents you from dating?"

"No, it's nothing like that..."

"I don't mean to pressure you. I'm just so drawn to everything about you that I don't want it to be said that I did not put forth adequate effort towards being in your company beyond business."

Lovey couldn't help but be flattered by that. It was a nice little boost to her self-esteem. She stayed to herself even more since she started putting on more weight. And with this shared relationship mess she was in, with Roland seeming to prefer Desiree over him, it was nice to feel desired.

"Okay, sure," she blurted out before losing her nerve. "Why not?"

"Why not, indeed." Taylor smiled, and Lovey couldn't resist smiling back. He really *was* rather handsome.

"I do have a lot of work I'll need to get done this evening, though, so would you mind if we make it lunch instead of dinner?"

"No problem at all. Shall we go now?"

"Now?" Lovey glanced at her watch. "Umm, okay."

"Excellent."

"If you wouldn't mind meeting me outside so I can wrap something up, I'll be right there."

"Of course." Taylor sensed that Lovey just didn't want her coworkers to see her leaving with him. He stood and flashed her another smile before stepping out of her office.

Lovey's hands were actually shaking a little as she locked her computer and grabbed her purse. She kept telling herself that it would be a good thing to shake things up; too much of her time had been spent agonizing over Roland that she never gave possibility to meeting anyone else. Not that she thought anyone would be interested in her now, anyway, with the extra pounds she was carrying.

But Taylor didn't seem to mind that. She smiled at the thought as she headed outside to meet him.

To her surprise, she really enjoyed their time together. He told her about moving to America from England when he was ten years old, and how he used to hate his accent.

"It seems to be rather endearing now, though," he chuckled, sipping on his coffee. "Faint as it is."

"I must admit, most of us ladies are suckers for a nice accent," Lovey admitted.

"I've noticed," he grinned. Lovey actually blushed. "But I can hide it when I want to."

"Really?"

"Most definitely," he replied, sounding like he was straight from Atlanta. "It's a cool thing to be able to do. Trips people out, really."

Lovey laughed.

"A Black man with an English accent can draw a lot of questions, at times. Sometimes I just want to be like everyone else."

"I can understand that."

"So what about you?" Taylor leaned forward in his seat, gazing at her intently.

"Me? I was born here. Original Georgia peach."

"Nice. Besides that, though."

Lovey played with her napkin. "What is it you wanna know?"

"How in the world such an intelligent, kind, beautiful, and might I say, incredibly sexy woman is possibly still single. Is it by choice?"

Scoffing slightly before she could stop herself, Lovey cleared her throat and answered, "No, I wouldn't say that. I just...haven't met the right man, apparently."

"I see." He continued to gaze at her. "And what do you think of me so far? Is there any chance I might be the right man?"

"Umm..." Lovey's cheeks were on fire. "It's a little soon to tell."

"Well," he gently took her fumbling fingers in his, "I hope you'll let me be around long enough to find out."

Biting her lip, Lovey couldn't help but smile. "We'll see."

"Can I see you again?"

"I'd like that, Taylor."

"I'm glad." His thumb tenderly stroked her hand.

"In fact..." Lovey took a deep breath, "What are you doing the night before Valentine's Day?"

LOVEY HAD ENJOYED HER afternoon with Taylor. But as she prepared for bed later that night, she couldn't help but think about Roland. She missed him.

She missed how they used to be before this ridiculous shared relationship started. The friendship they were building was something that Lovey cherished, and when it became apparent that their feelings were deepening, it was a delicious journey of emotions. Lovey hated that things had changed between them so drastically, and all because neither she nor Desiree were willing to back down. Or because Roland didn't really know what he wanted.

Well, Lovey knew what *she* wanted. She wanted to be in a real, one-on-one relationship with someone she adored, and who adored her. She wanted someone who had no questions about who it was they wanted to be with. A few weeks ago, she thought that might have been Roland. But, apparently, she had been wrong about a man yet again.

She tried not to think about what Roland and Desiree might be doing together, but her mind kept drifting there. It only made her wonder if anything Roland had told her about his feelings for her had been true. How could they have been, when he was so quick to entertain Desiree?

But then again, he had been in love with Desiree first; maybe Lovey was just a vengeful rebound after Desiree put the brakes on their relationship.

Her mind was still analyzing all of this when she heard a knock at her door. Frowning and glancing at her watch, she slid off of her bed and shuffled to the front door, tying her bathrobe around her.

"Who is it?" she called out.

"It's Evan."

"Evan?" Lovey checked the peephole before easing the door open slightly. Her frown was still in place as she peered at him curiously. "What in the world are you doing here?"

"I came on an impulse, I'm sorry." Evan stood there with his hands in his pockets, his shoulders hunched. "I was thinking about you and next thing I knew, my car was heading in this direction."

"It's late."

"Yeah, I know. Again, I'm sorry. I guess I just really wanted to see you tonight."

She just looked at him.

"I'll go if you want me to but I'd love to come in, if I can."

After several silent moments, Lovey pursed her lips and stepped aside, wordlessly granting him access.

As soon as Evan was inside and Lovey had closed the door behind him, his lips were on hers as soon as she turned around. She squealed in surprise, initially pushing against his shoulders, but she eventually began returning the kiss, allowing him to pull her closer. He backed her against the door as she gripped his arms, the kisses trailing down to her soft neck.

"You smell so good," he murmured, inhaling the scent of her lavender body wash.

"Thanks," she whispered, biting her lip.

His lips returning to hers, he kissed her harder, deeper, remembering with each second what had drawn him to her in the first place. Her soft moans only made him want to get closer to her, and his hands began slowly untying her thick robe. He reacquainted himself with her body. They never got to the point of sleeping together when they dated, but there had been plenty of petting. Lovey's body fascinated him then, and it fascinated him now. It wasn't lost on him that she had gained some weight, but in the moment, he didn't care.

Lovey couldn't help but wonder what was going through Evan's mind as his hands roamed all over her body. There was no way he wouldn't notice that she was heavier than she was when they dated. But it felt so good to be kissed and touched that those self-conscious thoughts eventually melted away. She hadn't been underneath a man since the night before Clay dumped her, and she was realizing just how much she missed that.

Evan was easing her robe down her shoulders, kissing along her collarbone before moving lower. Lovey shivered.

"Oh god..."

When his hands eased underneath her nightshirt and gripped her panties, easing them down, Lovey didn't stop him. When he pressed his hardened groin into her, she pressed back. She boldly gripped his backside as he grinded against her, becoming lost in the mindless passion. She had squelched the little voice in her ear asking her what the heck she was doing. Lovey didn't want to think; she'd done more than enough of that lately. This was all about feeling.

"I've got to taste you," he whispered against her ear. "Can I?"

Lovey had been rendered speechless by Evan's fingers making music between her legs. "Mmm-hmm."

In the next few seconds, time seemed to stop. The tip of Evan's tongue caused Lovey to shudder, call out words she usually didn't say, and open her legs wider to get more. Thoughts of anything outside of that moment were nonexistent. She just enjoyed Evan pleasuring her, because he wanted to. This might've been the whole reason behind his impulsive visit, and where Lovey normally would've been insulted or put off, right then she was thankful for it.

They ended up in her bed. Lovey was aggressive, her long hair falling over her face as she moved her voluptuous body against Evan's. Her bedside lamp was the only light shining over their increasingly sweaty bodies. Evan gripped her breast as he continually thrust into her, loving how she grunted every time their bodies met. She was so into it, to his complete surprise; he hadn't expected her to be such an animal. Whenever he had fantasized about getting Lovey into bed, he always imagined it would be good, but he had no idea it would be like *this*.

"You feel so good, baby," he growled, after he flipped her over and was enjoying her from behind. He lowered his chest against her back, pinning her to the bed, his hips varying the rhythm and speed. He grabbed a handful of her hair and yanked her head so she could at least partially see him. "You feel so *fucking* good it's ridiculous..."

"Don't stop." Lovey's voice was breathless. Her hands gripped the damp sheets. "Keep going..."

Evan did. They enjoyed each other until their bodies went limp. Lovey rolled over to one side of the bed before easing out and going to the bathroom without a word, not bothering to cover her body. Evan propped himself on his elbow, waiting for her.

When she emerged a few minutes later, still naked, Evan noted the slight paunch in her belly and the faint cellulite in her thighs. He briefly wondered if that was there when they were together, and then if he was the reason she had packed on the extra pounds. It *had* been a shock how she found out about him and Alexis, after all.

He waited until she rejoined him in bed before asking, "How do you feel about me, Lovey?"

She glanced at him, the question clearly catching her off guard. But her expression quickly went from surprised to aloof as she shrugged a smooth shoulder, resting her back against the headboard.

"I can't say I really have *any* feelings towards you, honestly."

His eyebrows shot up. "Really?"

"Yes."

"Then what was this?" He waved a hand back and forth between their nude bodies.

"It was sex, Evan. That's all. I'm not delusional enough to think it means anything."

"Wow." Evan didn't expect such a cavalier attitude out of Lovey after what they just did. "What if I said it did?"

"I don't think I would believe you."

Evan sat up, a concerned frown marring his slightly freckled brow. "What's up with you, Lovey?"

She shrugged again. "Nothing at all. Should I be confessing an all-consuming love for you or something? I'm not sure why you're looking so thrown."

"Well, because I *am*. I was hoping you wouldn't be all jaded now."

Lovey actually laughed. "I'm not jaded, Evan. I'm just not the same googly-eyed girl you dated months ago, that's all. I would think that you would be happy that I'm not reading more into this than it is or asking to resume our relationship."

"But what if that's what I want? What if I wanted us to get back together?"

She looked at him. "What?"

"I told you I've been thinking about you a lot lately. And I've never felt right about how I handled things between us. It's been knawing at me, you know? We never really got to see where this could go."

"That was *your* choice, Evan."

"I know, and what I'm saying is that I'm not all that sure I made the *right* choice." He took her hand and kissed it before looking up at her. "I think I want us to get back together; try it again."

Eying him warily, Lovey used her free hand to cover her upper body with the bed sheet.

"So...just like that, we're supposed to get back together? What if we hadn't slept together just now, would you still be saying all this?"

"Lovey, this isn't because we had sex."

"Well, whether it is or it isn't, us trying to go back in time isn't something I'm interested in doing. There's a reason you chose to be with another woman instead of me. And I've changed since then; my feelings and interests lie elsewhere."

"I thought you weren't seeing anybody."

"I'm not. Not exclusively. It's not about that; it's just about this not being a move I want to make, that's all. I hold no grudges towards you; the past is the past. And whatever happened to Alexis, anyway?"

Evan looked away, sheepish. "Honestly...she's not totally out of the picture."

Lovey pursed her lips.

"Things between me and Alexis haven't been all that great lately and I realized I started distancing myself from her without even realizing it."

"Like you distanced yourself from me?"

"I guess."

"Evan, I'm in no position to judge, but I suggest you learn to start closing one door before trying to open another. Why not take the time to figure out what it is you want in a woman before making commitments you're not ready to keep?"

He sighed. "I feel you. I'm sorry."

"Sure."

He scooted over and laid his head on her thigh, drifting off to sleep within minutes. Lovey leaned her head against the headboard, her eyes mindlessly gazing at the ceiling.

Her evening had surely taken a different turn. Evan had unknowingly saved her from another night of torturing herself about Roland and Desiree and what a joke her love life was. She just threw caution to the wind and indulged. Surprisingly, she didn't even feel guilty about enjoying casual sex with Evan, even after it was revealed he wasn't really single. The news hadn't even surprised her. She wasn't flattered by his desire to resume their relationship, wasn't hurt to discover he was still a backstabbing cheat. In truth, she just didn't care.

After Evan started snoring slightly, she gently eased his head off of her lap and slipped her nightshirt back over her head. Grabbing her phone, she padded into the living room and turned the television on, curling up in the corner of the couch.

Sexing Evan had done more than just please her body; it also fueled her with a jolt of confidence. Enough to throw caution to the wind again and have a discussion that was long overdue. It was late, but she knew Roland was usually up late.

What she didn't expect was to hear Desiree's voice. But she figured she probably should have, given how things had been going up until that point.

"What's up, girl?" Desiree greeted her in a hushed voice.

"Desiree." Lovey shook her head wryly. "I wasn't expecting you..."

"Oh, I know. But Roland's all tuckered out, *if you know what I mean*." Her voice was so sly it made Lovey's skin itch. She was clearly getting a kick out of this. "And I figured if you were calling so late it had to be about something important."

"Yeah...yeah, it was. But never mind."

"You sure? I'd be happy to give him a message when he wakes up."

"Don't bother, Desiree. You don't even have to bother telling him I called. Sorry I disturbed you." She hung up and sat her phone to the side, looking at the floor.

Chapter 25

THE LAST THING ROLAND felt like doing was partying.

He didn't even realize how he let things get to this point, going back and forth between two women. And that had morphed into him spending most of his free time with one woman for a reason he still hadn't figured out yet, when the one who stayed etched on his mind was barely in his life at all.

"I hope you're not going to be looking pitiful like that all night," E.J. said as they handled things at Barfly the day of the pre-Valentine's Day party. "You look like this is the last place you wanna be right now."

"It kinda is," Roland admitted, plopping his clipboard on top of the bar with a sigh. "I'm just not in the mood for this tonight."

"What's the matter with you?"

"I've just got some things on my mind."

"Would any of these *things* include either of the women you're seeing?"

"Don't even get me started on that."

E.J. eyed him before heading towards the office, tapping Roland's shoulder as he passed. "Come on. Let's talk, brother."

Roland wordlessly followed E.J. to the office, closing the door and plopping into the chair in front of the desk. E.J. leaned against the wall, his arms folded.

"Talk to me," he ordered.

"I've been such a dumb-ass."

"Yeah."

Roland's head whipped towards him. "What do you mean, *yeah*?"

"Never mind. Go ahead."

Eyeing his big brother skeptically, Roland continued. "This whole shared relationship with Lovey and Desiree was stupid. I don't know what I was thinking, agreeing to this mess. This isn't even me, man...I've never been one to date more than one woman at a time."

"True. So why did you do it this time?"

"I don't even know. Maybe I was flattered that both of them were battling over me like they were. I got to remembering how good things between me and Desiree were before things got crazy...it helped me convince myself that it was some kind of sign that Desiree and I still had unfinished business or whatever."

"Or maybe you let yourself believe that so you'd have an excuse to run from what you were starting to feel for Lovey."

Roland thought about it, then shook his head. "I wouldn't need to run from that. When have I ever been one to run from my feelings for a woman? If I'm into her, I'm into her."

"Yeah, and when you're into somebody, you go hard," E.J. reminded him, going to sit behind the desk. "You fell hard for Desiree and wanted to get back at her for changing up your relationship like she did. Hanging out with Lovey was just supposed to make Desiree jealous."

"Not *just*. I sincerely liked spending time with Lovey."

"You didn't plan on falling for her, though. And when you did, you got confused. And then when you got with Desiree on New Years, it scrambled your brain even more. So to avoid facing the hard decision and figuring out who and what you really wanted, you just took the easy way out and agreed to date both of them, regardless of the damage it could do to their friendship or your ultimate relationship with either one of them."

Roland rubbed his chin thoughtfully.

"You chose the wrong woman with Anna. You probably felt you chose the wrong woman with Desiree, since she was so resistant to things getting too close. And despite how right Lovey seemed for you, you didn't want choose wrong again. So..." E.J. held up his hands, "You didn't."

He hadn't thought about it like that, but Roland could see E.J.'s point. Had it just been a matter of him questioning his own judgment when it came to women? This whole shared relationship thing was just a way for him to delay taking a risk at love again.

And allowing Desiree to dominate his free time was like turning his mind off. They didn't talk about the future or their dreams or anything of any real substance. They were all passion and not much else. But it was deeper than that with Lovey and Roland hadn't been ready to let himself totally fall again.

"Wow," he finally muttered. "Now that you put it to me like that, it makes sense. I don't know how I didn't realize that before myself."

"It's hard to see stuff when you're in it."

"I guess."

"So when are you gonna stop wasting time with this shared relationship bullshit and get with who it is you want? And for the record, I really hope it's *not* Desiree."

Roland looked at him, intrigued. "Why do you say that?"

"Come on, man. You and I both know which woman is more your speed. Desiree isn't trying to have anything long-term like you are. I bet if you told her you loved her right now she'd go running for the hills again."

"Maybe. Now that I think about it, Desiree and I have never really gotten into why she is the way she is. I think it's deeper than just preference. There's a reason she only lets me get so close."

"And...what? You're sticking around until you find out what that is?"

"I'm not saying that. I'm just saying that maybe that's at least part of the reason why I haven't wanted to totally dismiss her, you know?"

E.J. shook his head. "You've got issues, brother. Sounds to me like just another excuse."

"It's true, though."

"Is Lovey coming tonight?"

"Desiree said she might."

"If she does, I hope you take some time to talk to her. You don't want to run the risk of her meeting somebody else." He cocked a knowledgeable brow. "They might be ready to snatch her up right now while you're still making up your mind."

MEANWHILE, DESIREE was practically skipping around her apartment, she was so giddy. She couldn't wait for the party that night. Her pre-Valentine's Day party was always one of her biggest, but her excitement was more for personal reasons than professional ones.

Right or wrong, Desiree couldn't help but look forward to Lovey seeing her and Roland together. Yes, it was petty and childish. But Desiree was just sure that this evening would be the final push she needed to get Roland all the way back to her side. Then eventually, they could go back to how things were before all of this started.

"Lovey will find somebody else," she told herself as she held a hot pink mini dress against her body in front of the mirror. "Then she'll forget all about Roland."

After deciding on her outfit and hair for the evening, Desiree picked up her phone and checked on the order she had placed earlier that morning. In about an hour or so, a box of éclairs and a small party dress would be arriving at Lovey's apartment. There was no way Lovey would fit into the dress, which would most likely drive Lovey straight into the box of eclairs. Desiree briefly worried that her plans would go off *too* well, to the point that Lovey would get so down that she would skip the party altogether, so she sent her a quick text:

Looking forward to hanging with my girl tonight! Make sure you come find me, ok? #missyou

It wasn't a lie. She really did miss Lovey. But without even realizing it, Desiree had let her pursuit of Roland consume her again, to the detriment of their friendship. Anytime she started to feel any worry about passing the point of no return, she quickly convinced herself that she would be able to earn Lovey's forgiveness, even if it took some time.

Lovey would forgive her. She always did.

A FEW HOURS LATER, Barfly was swirling with dancing and drinking party-goers. Just about everybody was decked out in some shade of red. Roland stayed holed in the office as long as he could before grudgingly making an appearance. The only thing he was even remotely looking forward to this evening was seeing Lovey, even though he was still figuring out exactly what he would say to her when he did.

Desiree was strutting around in her hot pink dress, and Roland figured she was looking around for him, the way she kept scanning the crowd. He wasn't in the mood to deal with her, and tried to stay as far away from her as possible. The last time he tried this, she used some impromptu sexting to get his attention and get him back to her bed. He was determined that nothing like that would happen tonight, even if she walked onto the dance floor in nothing but her silver stilettos.

"Wanna dance, handsome?"

Roland barely glanced at the random woman before answering, "Maybe later. I need to go handle some things."

"All right. But I'm gonna find you later."

"Great," he muttered, subtly rolling his eyes as he walked away. Now he had two people to stay away from.

Someone alerted Roland to an issue at the front door, and he rushed over just in time to see two women about to come to blows thanks to discovering that their party invitations had come from the same man. One of the bouncers quickly stepped in and separated them, and Roland tried to diffuse the situation best he could, before the people in line behind them started easing back to their cars.

"Y'all are about to tear each other's hair out over some dude that's literally over there laughing at both of y'all," he informed them, pointing. The stocky man who had been identified as Don and had instigated the whole scene was outwardly amused by it. He seemed perfectly willing to watch them go at it, seeing as how he made no move to stop either one of them. "See how he hasn't done a damn thing but watch y'all make a fool of yourselves? He's clowning y'all on purpose."

The ladies, decked out in the exact same dress (no doubt thanks to their shared suitor), glared at each other, then at Don. Their chests were still heaving with anger, but Roland could tell his words struck a chord.

"Two beautiful sistas like yourselves don't need to be fighting over some bum who would play y'all on purpose like that," Roland continued. "Forget him, come in, and enjoy the party. But only if you can leave the drama outside, 'cause I'm not having it in here."

One of the women looked over at Don before sucking her teeth. She slung her long brown ponytail over her shoulder and adjusted her strapless dress.

"You're right; forget him," she declared. "He's not worth it, anyway."

"Exactly."

The other woman apparently wasn't willing to let it go so easily, because she stomped out of the club in a huff, shouting at Don that she was gonna get him back for this. Roland just shook his head and instructed his bouncers that Don was not welcome, and to escort him from the premises.

After that whole scene, Roland wanted nothing more than to be left alone. It drained him of the little energy he had for this party. Just when everything was settled at the door, Desiree came rushing over to him.

"I heard somebody was about to start fighting; what happened?" she asked, clearly concerned.

"It's handled already; don't worry about it." Roland started to walk past her.

She grabbed his arm. "Hey, not so fast. Where are you going? I've barely seen you all night."

Roland gently pried his arm free of her grasp. "We'll talk later, Desiree. Right now I have other things to do."

"Like what?"

He shot her a look. "Later."

Leaving her standing there, he went back to his office and closed the door, locking it in case Desiree decided to follow him. Plopping into the desk chair, he leaned his head back and rubbed his eyes. He wasn't even sure why he was feeling so glum. It was the night before Valentine's Day, and while that was never necessarily his favorite holiday, he usually enjoyed it when he was in a relationship. Now, it could be said he was in a relationship with two women but he was more unhappy than he would be if wasn't in one at all. It just reaffirmed what he already knew: he was a one-woman man only.

He kept an eye on the security monitors as he mindlessly checked messages on his phone. There still hadn't been any sign of Lovey, and he started to wonder if she changed her mind about coming. They hadn't talked since she told him she needed some time to herself, and Roland wondered if she would want to talk to him if she did show up. There was just so much he felt they needed to get out on the table.

Finally, he saw her. Shooting upright in his chair, he watched her as she happily greeted a couple of people with warm hugs, then leaned closer as they engaged in animated conversation. There were three women surrounding her, all genuinely happy to see her and wait their turn to get some of her positive energy. As cliché as it sounded, she really was like a ray of sunshine. Roland smiled, not being able to take his eyes off of her.

He saw Desiree approach Lovey, and the whole aura changed. Lovey's smile became tight, and the hug they shared was nothing like the one's Roland had seen between them when he first entered the picture. Desiree seemed to be talking rapidly, waving her hands around and occasionally touching Lovey's arm. Lovey was nodding, but not responding much, looking like she was waiting for the right moment to ease away. When she finally did, Roland got up and hurried out of the office, intent on talking to her.

By the time he made it to the dance floor, though, Lovey's attention was again occupied. A man was standing close to her, holding both of her hands in his. She was grinning up at him in a way that made Roland think he was more than just a friend. Was he her date? Or had they met just then? Roland had been so focused on her when he saw her on the monitor that he hadn't noticed if she had come alone or not.

Now, he wasn't sure if he should approach her. He didn't want to make her uncomfortable or be greeted with one of those tight smiles that she gave Desiree. Roland actually felt a little awkward, even embarrassed, though he wasn't quite sure why. It never occurred to him that she might bring a date, if that's in fact who the man was. E.J.'s words about someone else snatching Lovey up rang in his head. Was this why she needed space from him, because she had met someone else? If that was the case, why didn't she just say so?

Moving away from them, Roland's disappointment slowly morphed into anger. He never took Lovey for a tease. But if she was seeing someone else while luring Roland into her web, he didn't know what else to call her. Roland thought that Lovey's disappointing past with men would cause her to be considerate when it came to another person's feelings, but evidently not. Maybe she was doing what a lot of women did and making her current man pay for past men's mistakes. Roland wasn't perfect and he knew it, but he thought he at least deserved honesty.

He didn't want to keep looking at them, but he couldn't help it. It felt like it had been so long since he'd seen her. He couldn't deny now amazing she looked. Her long hair, curled and swept to the right side of her face. Her flowing red dress that stopped at her knees. Matte red lipstick that automatically made him think of the kiss they shared outside of his house. He ached to kiss her again. And the fact that he couldn't only sent a different surge of anger shooting through him.

With all of the attention he was paying to Lovey, he didn't notice that Desiree was approaching him. Just as she did, Lovey happened to look their way. The smile that was on her face faded slightly, as she watched Desiree slide her arms around Roland's waist.

"I know you said we would talk later, but can we at least dance now?" Desiree asked him, pressing her body close to his.

After briefly glancing at Lovey and seeing that she was still eyeing them, Roland grabbed Desiree's waist tightly. He felt like he needed to save face, as if Lovey bringing a date was a personal affront to him.

"Yeah, we can dance," he answered Desiree, his eyes still on Lovey, who was dancing with her date.

Grinning, Desiree danced seductively, glad to have Roland's attention finally. Her back was to Lovey so she didn't notice who Roland seemed mildly preoccupied with; she just figured he was keeping an eye on things in general. She caressed his face, gently pulling it closer to her.

"I'm glad we're here together like this," she crooned into his ear. Her arms slid around his neck. "I've been missing you, you know."

"Is that right?" Roland glanced over at Lovey again, who was laughing at something her date said to her. He frowned slightly.

"You know it is."

"Mmm-hmm."

"Do you like my dress? I thought of you when I bought it."

"Yeah."

"Are you okay?" Desiree leaned back and, seeing Roland's eyes fixated somewhere else, turned to see what was so fascinating. Lovey was a little ways away with a man Desiree had never seen before, and with the way they were dancing and talking, Desiree figured they hadn't just met that night. From what she could see, the man was super cute, and pretty smooth with the dance moves. She automatically wondered where Lovey had met him, and from the way Roland was mean-mugging them, he probably was, too.

"Who is that?" Roland couldn't resist asking about Lovey's date. The curiosity was about to drive him crazy.

"I don't know. I've never seen him before."

"What?" Roland frowned. "You mean that's not her ex?"

"No...guess she met somebody new."

His jaw clenched.

Lovey was looking at them again. Sensing what an opportunity this was, Desiree turned and pressed her backside into Roland, pulling his arms around her from behind. He allowed it. She was rather glad to see Lovey there with someone else, but clearly Roland wasn't. Whether she was trying to or not, Lovey was drawing too much of Roland's attention, and Desiree saw she needed to remind both of them who the queen bee was. Reaching up and grabbing the back of Roland's neck, Desiree was ready to give the performance of a lifetime.

With Jodeci's "Come and Talk to Me" blaring through the speakers, Desiree grabbed Roland's hand and placed it high on her thigh before bending at the waist and smoothly winding her hips to the beat. Then she swiftly turned towards him, dropping into a low squat despite her short dress and then slowly rising to full height, snaking and rolling her body as she did so. She boldly moved Roland's hands to her butt, circling her hips and leaning back to let her groin press further into his. Her moves were deliberate, the whole scene a complete turn-on for her. She could feel Roland's body respond, even if his eyes did keep straying somewhere else.

Grabbing the front of his red silk shirt, Desiree leaned up and placed a lingering wet kiss on Roland's neck. His body stiffened. Almost forgetting they were still on a dance floor surrounded by people, Desiree proceeded to openly suck Roland's neck, her body still winding against his, her other hand wandering teasingly close to his crotch.

"You like that?" she whispered in his ear.

Roland just looked at her, knowing she was putting on a show just like he was. Her eyes had a mischievous glint to them as she ran her long nail around his lips. Not being able to resist, he glanced up at Lovey again, and her expression caused a yank in his stomach. The hurt in her eyes was glaring. Swallowing hard, Roland told himself not to feel bad about it. She was the one who wanted space. She brought some other man to his club, knowing he'd be there. He wasn't going to let her make him feel guilty for doing his own thing when she was clearly doing hers.

Desiree grabbed Roland's face and brought it to hers, giving him a long, deep, intense kiss. She could see his attention straying again. Holding him by the back of the neck, Desiree prayed Lovey was still watching as she continued the kiss, moaning her pleasure for both the act and the situation. This night was turning out better than she'd hoped.

When she eventually tapered the kiss off, Desiree boldly looked over her shoulder towards Lovey. The expression on her face was one of disappointment as well as disgust. Shaking her head slightly, Lovey whispered something in her date's ear before turning and heading towards the door. Her date followed, with a slight scowl in Desiree and Roland's direction.

Grinning triumphantly, Desiree turned back to Roland, but he wasn't anywhere near as happy as she was. He was watching Lovey leave with a pained frown on his face, his jaws clenched and his chest heaving slightly. He even made a move as if he was going to follow her, then stopped himself.

"Wanna celebrate?" she asked him over the music. Her body was moving all on its own.

Not being able to stand it anymore, Roland turned and bolted away from her, heading back to his office where he planned to remain until the party was over.

Desiree wanted to go after him, but figured she'd give him a little time to get himself together. Once he calmed down, he'd realize that all of this was for the best. Lovey needed to see with her own eyes the blazing chemistry that Roland had with Desiree. Now she could go be with whoever the guy was she brought with her tonight and Desiree could have Roland back all to herself.

Feeling as light as air, Desiree made the rounds to check on things. Everything was going so smoothly, it was almost unreal. Outside of that small spat at the door that Roland took care of, there had been virtually no issues, which almost never happened. Desiree took it as a sign that this was an extra special night. Fluffing her shoulder-length wig, she stepped up onto the DJ booth and after whispering something to him, motioned for the microphone.

"We're 'bout to take it back to those house party days, y'all, so grab somebody sexy and let's make it hot!"

The DJ put on "Knockin' Da Boots" by H-Town, and the crowd erupted in cheers, approving of the old school classic. Practically everybody migrated to the dance floor. Desiree stopped by the bar and asked for a ginger martini, taking a long sip as she watched her success play out in front of her. This Pre-Valentine's Day party was way bigger than last year's, and Desiree was so proud of herself she wanted to shout.

Finishing her drink, she joined everyone else enjoying the music, squeezing her way back towards the middle of the floor. She wished Roland was out there dancing with her, but at least he wasn't dancing with anyone else.

When the song changed to Boyz II Men's "Uhh Ahh", Desiree felt a tap on her shoulder. She turned and found herself eye-level with a Burberry-scented chest. Stepping back a little, she looked up into a face that she felt like she'd seen before, but she didn't know where. He had to be at least 6'6.

"Somebody as sexy as you shouldn't be dancing alone," he stated, leaning down so she could hear him.

His voice was toffee-smooth. Desiree couldn't resist smiling flirtatiously.

"I like a man that can follow directions."

With a sly smile, the man stepped closer to her and grabbed her waist, firmly enough to make his intentions known but not enough to seem too aggressive. Not that Desiree minded, anyway. She gladly went into his arms, swaying smoothly to the music. She gazed up at him, trying to recall where she knew him from.

"I'm Desiree," she informed him.

"Miles."

"Have we met before?"

"I don't think so."

"You look really familiar."

"I get that a lot."

Deciding to leave it at that for now, she just slid her hands up his defined arms and enjoyed the dance.

After a while, Desiree and Miles made their way over to one of the couches so they could chat a little. Desiree was still trying to place where she knew him from.

"Did you go to FAMU?" she asked, referring to her alma mater.

"Nah." He looked amused.

"Then where do-"

"Hey Miles, when are we gonna see you back out on the floor, man?" some guy asked, seemingly appearing out of nowhere.

"As soon as I get this knee back together," Miles replied. "It's getting there."

"Hope it's soon, man. That defense hasn't been the same since you went down."

"I appreciate that, brother, thanks."

The man walked off and Desiree looked at him curiously, her eyes slightly narrowed. He just smirked, waiting for her to put two and two together.

"Wait a minute..." she finally hedged. "Miles Yoates? Don't you play for San Antonio?"

"I did, before I got traded to Charlotte."

"Isn't it the middle of the season?"

"All-Star break. But I'm on IR, anyway, since I tore my ACL last year. And my folks live down here, so..." He shrugged.

Desiree's intrigue shot up. She knew several professional athletes, had even dated a couple, but they were mostly local. She didn't watch a lot of professional basketball so it made sense that she couldn't quite place who he was.

"I guess I should be flattered that you wound up at my little ol' party, then," she teased, resting her elbow on the back of the couch. "Though I *am* curious as to how you heard about it."

"Good stuff gets around." Miles winked at her. Desiree grinned.

They continued their flirtatious banter, eventually exchanging numbers. Desiree had temporarily forgotten about Roland, only remembering that he was still holed up in the office after Miles left. She just went on about her business, looking forward to when she could get home and talk to Miles more intimately, without a bunch of nosey ears around them. And she was already imagining what those big hands of his could do to her.

Desiree felt she was justified. She wasn't in an exclusive relationship with anybody, thanks to Roland dragging his feet. And until he got his head together, Desiree was free to do as she pleased.

Chapter 26

IT WAS VALENTINE'S Day, and Lovey usually took this day off of work. But this time, she broke that tradition. She was feeling okay, despite the events of the previous night.

After witnessing Roland and Desiree's little show on the dance floor, Lovey asked Taylor to take her home, not wanting to be in the same space with them anymore. Taylor repeatedly asked who they were and what was going on, but Lovey didn't have the energy to get into it. She just said they were two former friends of hers who had made it clear she was no longer welcome.

Seeing those two carrying on like they were, practically putting on a sex show for her benefit...it hurt. It wasn't seeing them together; she already knew they were together. It was the fact that they were rubbing it in her face. It was such a mean thing to do, and Lovey didn't understand what she had done to deserve such treatment.

The tears hadn't come yet but she knew it was only a matter of time. For now, she just wanted to keep herself occupied by burying herself in work.

Both Taylor and Evan had called to ask her out for the evening, but she declined both invitations. If she couldn't spend Valentine's Day with someone special, then she'd rather just spend the evening alone. Surprisingly, she didn't feel as bad about it as she thought she would. Maybe she'd been spending too much time focusing on men, or her lack of the right one. There were so many other important things to think about; people with far more serious problems than hers. Remembering that helped when she felt herself starting to slide back towards the abyss of self-pity.

Towards the end of the day, Liz called.

"Hey, what are you doing tonight?"

"Nothing at all," Lovey replied, her voice light.

"You sound almost chipper about that," Liz observed. "What's going on?"

"Nothing's going on. I just realized that there is way more good in my life than bad, and I don't have to be down on myself because I'm not in a relationship, that's all."

"Wow." Liz sounded genuinely shocked. "That's awesome. May I ask what brought on this epiphany?"

"Why don't you come over tonight? Do you have something to do?"

"Yeah, but he'll be gone around seven or so. I can come by afterwards."

Chuckling, Lovey shook her head as she finished putting some papers into her briefcase. "You are too much. I'll be there whenever you roll from on top of whoever it is."

Lovey went home, changed into some shorts and a sweater, and pulled her hair into a messy bun. She started to look at some stuff from work, but decided she wasn't in the mood and put it aside. She grabbed a Lolita Files novel that she hadn't made the time to read and curled up on the couch. Before she knew it, Liz was knocking on her door.

"Wow, is it seven o'clock already?" Lovey swung open the door after quickly checking the peephole. She waited for Liz to step inside and close the door before heading back to the couch.

"Almost eight. He took his little blue pill."

"Ah, yes. I almost forgot about your penchant for older men."

"Hey, you don't have to be older to take those things." Liz kicked off her boots and removed her jacket, tossing it onto the armchair before flopping onto the couch. "He doesn't really need it; just took it to kick things into overdrive, ya know?"

"Sounds like fun."

"So what's up with you? Usually when you don't have a date on Valentine's Day, you're moping around in those gray sweats watching movies that make you yearn."

"Yeah, well, not this year." Lovey put her book on the coffee table.

"Not that I'm not glad about it but what changed?"

"I just realized that I'm a good woman. A good person. And I'm so blessed in so many other ways. Why not just focus on those things instead of what I *don't* have?"

Liz looked at her, knowing there was more to it. "That's wonderful. And you're absolutely right. But I want you to keep it real with me. Did something happen?"

It was times like this that Lovey hated her sister's sixth sense when it came to drama. Lovey still wasn't in a hurry to discuss last night, but she knew Liz would drag it out of her eventually.

"The whole shared relationship thing? I think it's over. Desiree won."

"What do you mean, she won?"

"Roland made his choice."

"He told you that?"

"Actions speak louder than words."

"What in the world...will you just tell me what happened, please? Did something go down at the party last night? I still can't believe you went to that, by the way."

"Yeah, well, I almost didn't." Lovey thoughtfully raked her nails up the back of her hair. "But it's kind of a good thing I did."

"I'm gonna tickle you..."

"Okay, fine. Taylor and I went to the party. Everything started out fine; I saw a few people I hadn't seen in a while, the music was jumpin', and Taylor was great company. He really helped me feel more at ease."

"That's good..."

"Desiree came over to me and was saying all this stuff about how we should go shopping and have a spa day and do all this stuff together soon, and it just seemed so disingenuous. Like she was putting on some kind of act."

"Sounds about right."

"Oh believe me, that wasn't the worst of it. A little later, while Taylor and I were dancing, I saw Roland not too far away from me. I was going to go speak, you know, since we haven't talked in a while, but then Desiree came and started hugging up on him. Pretty soon they were practically simulating sex on the dance floor."

"*What*? Roland actually did that??"

"He had this strange look his eyes; like he was...on some kind of mission or something." Lovey shook her head slightly, trying to find the right words. "Like he was punishing me."

"Girl...he didn't like that you were there with Taylor."

"Why should he care? He was there with Desiree. Heck, he's been spending most of his time with Desiree since this whole mess started."

"Maybe he really wanted to be with *you* last night."

"Then why didn't he just say so?"

"Oh sweetie," Liz rubbed her arm. "Sometimes all it really comes down to is...men are stupid."

Lovey started to laugh, but it didn't take long at all for her laughs to turn into sobs.

"What's wrong??" Liz scooted closer to her. "Is it Roland?"

"It's all of this," Lovey admitted. "I'm mad at myself for letting my pride drive me to agree to this ridiculous shared relationship. I'm mad at Roland for not being able to choose. I'm mad at Desiree for being too stubborn to step aside when she learned I was developing feelings for Roland. I'm mad at Clay and Evan and every other man that's made me look and feel like a fool..."

"You *don't* look like a fool, Lovey."

"I sure feel like one," Lovey sniffed. "Roland...Roland seemed so different. And I fell for him. I always thought he was so sincere, so genuine. But as soon as Desiree decides she's not done with him, I practically get tossed to the side. That really hurts."

"Of course it does! That's totally understandable."

"Desiree doesn't even seem like the same person I've been friends with for years. I think that's what hurts the most; that our friendship is damaged. And I don't know how it can be the same after this." Sighing, Lovey wiped her eyes and stood. "I need some water. You want some?"

"I'm good. You want me to get it for you?"

"No, no, I can get it. I'll be right back."

Liz looked after her baby sister worriedly as she shuffled into the kitchen.

Lovey grabbed a bottle of water out of the refrigerator and leaned against the counter, swallowing several large gulps. She remembered her and Roland standing right in this room, sharing their first hug. That was when she started looking at Roland as more than just a friend. That was when everything changed.

She eyed the box of éclairs that had arrived yesterday. Thankfully, she managed to resist at the time, immediately stashing them in the kitchen and then forcibly forgetting about them. It was the first time she hadn't immediately torn into something Desiree sent her. But now, the urge for that temporary sugar high was inching its way back.

With little effort to resist, Lovey reached for the box. She was getting ready to take her first bite when Liz walked in.

"Lovey!" She rushed over and snatched the eclair with a frown. "What the hell are you doing?"

"What's the big deal? I was just having a snack."

"You said you were coming in here for *water*!"

"I forgot these were in here. Why in the world are you getting so upset?"

Liz put a hand on her hip. "Where did you get these?"

"They were delivered yesterday."

"Delivered?" Liz's frown deepened. "Let me guess; from Desiree?"

"Yeah."

"Damn, are you still falling for this? What, you just mindlessly scarf down whatever she sends you? At some point, Lovey, you have got to wake up!"

"I don't think I'm *falling* for anything, Liz. I acknowledge that I should have more self-control-"

"It's not even just about self-control, Lovey. You have to start taking some of the responsibility, here. Desiree has done this kind of backstabbing, self-serving stuff before. But because it involves you, you refuse to believe she's capable of it. I know you love to find the good in people but at some point you have to take off the rainbow-colored glasses and wake the hell up. Desiree planned all of this and you're feeding right into it!"

"I asked Desiree flat-out what she was doing when she brought over a dress and truffles the day I was supposed to have a date with Roland. She said she was just trying to make up for how things have been between us. Why is that so hard to believe?"

"Wait a minute. She brings you clothes, too?"

"Just a couple of dresses..."

"Where are they?" Liz demanded. "Show them to me."

Lovey led Liz to her bedroom and retrieved the two dresses Desiree had sent her from the closet. Liz snatched them and immediately looked at the tags. Chuckling sarcastically, she shook her head in disbelief.

"Just like I damn thought," she sneered. She held the tags close to Lovey's face. "Since *when* do you wear a size *eight*??"

Lovey's jaw dropped. She was embarrassed to realize that she never even thought to check the size on the dresses; she just assumed they didn't fit right because of her weight gain. She was a curvy size ten and Desiree knew it.

"As long as you two have been friends and as many times as you've gone shopping together, do you *really* think this is an honest mistake?" Liz asked, throwing the dresses to the ground. "Now how are you gonna try to pretty *this* up, huh? How are you gonna try to justify and let Desiree off the hook for *this*?"

"Maybe I don't *want* to believe it, okay?" Lovey yelled, finally losing it. "Do you think this is easy for me? If I let myself believe that Desiree would do such things to me then what do I have left? I'd never be able to look at her the same after this!"

"You *can't*, Lovey! If you even try, you're fooling yourself!" Liz took her tearful sister into her arms. "I *know* this isn't easy for you, sis. But if you don't finally accept the truth, you're not hurting anyone but yourself."

Lovey sobbed on her sister's shoulder, the pain of hard truths finally setting in. As much as she hated to, she had to come to some realizations about Desiree. She knew that short of a lie detector test, Desiree would never admit to any wrongdoing, and even then she'd probably deny the results. Lovey would need some kind of evidence that Desiree couldn't possibly deny, and she didn't have any.

Which meant she had to trust her gut, as much as she might not want to.

"You really need to think about disassociating yourself from both Desiree and Roland," Liz advised, rubbing Lovey's back. "If not forever, at least for a while. I think you need that for yourself. Roland might be a good man overall but he simply isn't worth all this trouble that's been caused."

Lovey realized she didn't disagree. If she'd had any idea that all of this would have transpired after agreeing to the shared relationship, she would've just let Desiree have him.

"You're right," she agreed, sniffling.

"If there's *any* good that has come from all of this, it's that you get to find out what kind of person Desiree really is." Liz stepped back and smoothed some of Lovey's hair from her face. "I'm not saying she doesn't love you, sis. But she clearly doesn't love you enough. For this kind of stuff to even enter her mind, let alone her actually carrying it out, proves that."

It hurt Lovey to agree to that one. But she knew not doing so would just be delusional.

"Yeah," was all she could manage to say.

"I'm right here with you, okay? Whatever you decide to do."

Lovey knew the first thing she would do. With a wipe of her eyes, she stalked straight to the kitchen and stuffed the entire box of uneaten eclairs in the garbage. And she disposed of any other sweets she had in the kitchen. Liz stood in the doorway, giving her an encouraging smile.

"I'm sending those dresses back to Desiree," Lovey told her.

"I would've burned them and sent her the ashes, but yours is probably the more mature option."

"And before I talk myself out of it, there's something else I need to do, too. Something I should've done a while ago."

"What's that?"

"Where's my phone?"

"You left it on the couch, I think."

Going to retrieve it, Lovey sent a text to Desiree and Roland:

Thank you both for last night. Mission accomplished. I'm officially done. This shared relationship was a mistake I never should have agreed to. I wish you nothing but the best together.

As soon as she hit SEND, Lovey felt a huge weight lift from her.

"Well," she tossed the phone back to the couch and sighed. "That's that."

Liz eyed her. "You okay?"

"No." Lovey smiled through the tears that were still flowing. "But I will be."

MEANWHILE, DESIREE was getting ready for a date with Roland.

She really felt like this was one of the best times of her life. Business was booming. Her family was the best. She practically had Roland back and she had a professional basketball player sweating her. And, she could eat all the honeybuns she wanted without having to worry about it ruining her figure, unlike Lovey.

Speaking of Lovey, Desiree wasn't delusional enough to think that things were well with their friendship. But she had every confidence that Lovey would forgive and forget in due time. Desiree was her best friend; if she would forgive anyone, it would be her.

She was blasting Jay-Z's *Blueprint* album and dancing around her bedroom when her phone rang. Seeing it was her sister Dori, she quickly turned down the music and answered the phone.

"What up, sis?"

"Hey, can I borrow that silver and turquoise necklace? Brad and I are finally having a date night."

"Yeah. But you better come get it in the next hour or so, because I have a date with Roland, myself."

"Yeah? So that's still going on, huh?"

"Why wouldn't it be?"

"After everything we all talked about, I just can't believe you're still doing it, that's all."

"I'm not gonna say y'all didn't make any good points. But that's just how important it is to me to get Roland back."

"You admit that you love him?"

Temporarily jarred, Desiree cleared her throat. "I never said that."

"Why haven't you? Can you say that you don't?"

"I thought you called about a necklace."

"I really don't know what your aversion to being in love or anything resembling monogamy is. It's a beautiful thing with the right person."

"Marriage isn't for everybody, Dori."

"Who said anything about marriage? You can't even admit your feelings for the man. If not to anyone else, at least admit it to yourself. 'Cause otherwise, you're just being cruel by wasting his time, especially since he's already admitted he loves you."

"Look...Roland knows how I am. He gets me. I'm sure if he had that big of a problem with it he wouldn't still be here."

"Right. 'Cause most men deny practically unlimited sex when it's being offered to them on a silver platter."

"It's not just about sex with us. Of course I have feelings for him."

"Uh-huh."

"Oh, I didn't tell you...I met Miles Yoates last night."

"The basketball player? Don't tell Brad; he'll be bugging you to get autographs. Where'd you meet him?"

"At my party last night. We danced and talked for a while. Girl, he's so smooth and sexy. He didn't waste any time calling me after he left the club, either."

"Wait...you gave him your number?"

"Hell yeah!"

"Why would you do that?"

"Because it's *Miles Yoates*. Defensive Player of the Year, two-time All-Star Miles Yoates?"

"So what? Weren't you *just* saying stuff about your feelings for Roland and it being so important to you to get him back? And what about all this stuff you're doing to get with him?"

"Damn, I knew Ma was gonna tell y'all."

"Tell us what?"

Desiree cursed under her breath. "Oh...I thought Ma might've said something..."

"About what? What did you do, Desiree?"

"It's not a big deal. I've just been...kind of ensuring my place with Roland, you know. Nudging Lovey out a little bit."

Dori paused. "Exactly what did you do? And do not lie."

Desiree hadn't planned on ever giving anyone the details of what she'd done, but she told her sister everything, from the initial cake-and-milk truce at Lovey's office to the show she and Roland put on for Lovey's benefit the previous night at Barfly. When she listed everything like that, it sounded bad even to her, but she still tried to put a playful spin on it.

"I know one day Lovey and I are just gonna laugh about all of this," Desiree finally said, trying to keep her voice light. She forced a chuckle. "I mean, when you think about the stuff they do in movies-"

"Have you lost your damn mind?!" Dori exclaimed angrily. "You're actually trying to act like that's no big deal??"

"It's *not*!" Desiree tried to insist. "I'm not trying to say I'm proud of it, but-"

"What kind of person *are* you? You would do such things to your best friend over some man?"

"He's not just *some* man!"

"You can't even admit you love him, Desiree, not that it would excuse your behavior any more if you did. I-I can't even believe this..."

"Look, Dori, this is between me and Lovey, all right?" Desiree stated defensively. She didn't appreciate the judgmental tone her sister was taking with her. "It's not like you're some angel, either. Don't act like you've never done anything wrong. Remember that time you took some of your Girl Scout cookie money to buy a bracelet and told Mama somebody stole it?"

"Yeah. I do remember doing that *over twenty-five years ago*. I also remember admitting I did it and apologizing, not to mention getting my ass whipped. But I'm willing to bet you have no plans on owning up to any of this. And we all know you hate apologizing."

"I do not...look. Regardless, you're in no position to judge, is all I'm saying."

Dori was quiet for a few moments. "I am so disappointed in you, Desiree," she finally said, her voice soft and pained. "You've done some foul stuff, but I never, ever thought you would stoop *this* low. And to Lovey, of all people."

"Dori..."

"No, Desiree. Please don't make it worse by trying to justify it or defend yourself or deflect or any of your other tricks, okay? Just shut up."

Sighing, Desiree did.

"It hurts me to say this, but I'm actually ashamed to call you my sister right now," Dori admitted.

Desiree swallowed. It hurt to hear that. She and her sisters had always been close, and with all the fights they've had over the years, none of them had ever said anything like that to her. It was like a punch in the stomach.

"Umm..." She blinked rapidly, shaking her head to fend off the threatening tears. She hated to cry. "Are you...are you gonna tell Mama or Dana or Diamond about this?"

"Wow," Dori scoffed. "*That's* what you're worried about, huh? You know what? Keep the necklace. I don't think I wanna have anything to do with you for a while." She hung up.

It took a few moments for Desiree to move. She picked up the phone to call Dori back, but decided against it. She just hoped her sister didn't go straight to their mother and sisters with what she'd learned. Desiree didn't need four people judging and condemning her; five, if they told their father.

Trying her best to shake it off and force that conversation out of her mind, Desiree turned the music back up and proceeded to get ready for her date with Roland, her moves not having the same energy as before.

A COUPLE OF HOURS LATER, Desiree and Roland were at Bhojanic, the Indian restaurant Roland had taken her to on their first date. Desiree suggested they go there for their first Valentine's Day together, and Roland didn't care enough to disagree. He hadn't said much ever since he picked her up, and Desiree's attempts to get him to talk were futile. Desiree was still trying to get her sister Dori's words out of her head, so she wasn't as talkative as she usually was, either.

It wasn't until she got a text from Miles that she perked up. She tried to be discreet about looking at it, but when she saw Roland mindlessly picking at his tikka masala, his mind clearly somewhere else, she went ahead and read it. Her smile was automatic when she read how he was looking forward to seeing her again. After typing a quick 'Me too', she put her phone to the side, but it was only a matter of seconds before it buzzed again.

"How come you're being so quiet?" she asked, trying to resist looking at her phone.

Roland shrugged. "Don't have a lot to say."

"Why not? What's wrong with you?"

"I just have some stuff on my mind, that's all." Roland dropped his fork.

"Well, this is supposed to be a romantic evening. Can't you put whatever it is out of your mind for a while?"

"Apparently not," he replied with a piercing glance before looking away again.

Desiree eyed him. "What, are you mad at *me* or something?"

"Let's drop it, Desiree."

"Fine." Desiree wasn't in the mood to pull Roland out of this funk he was in. She grabbed her phone with one hand and dug back into her byriani with the other, ignoring him like he was ignoring her. She had enough on her mind without whatever Roland was pouting about. For the rest of their dinner, she texted back and forth with

Miles while Roland repeatedly looked at his watch, not caring either way.

When they finally left, Desiree managed to convince him to go back to her place with her. She was sure she would be able to cheer him up once they were out of a public place. As soon as they were inside, she pulled him to her and laid a deep kiss on him, wasting no time pulling his shirt from his pants. He returned the kiss, though not as passionately as usual, but Desiree wasn't fazed. She just kicked her shoes off and pushed him onto the couch before straddling him. They made out for a few moments, Desiree gently grinding on him.

"Take your shirt off," she panted, lowering the straps of her dress and unhooking her bra.

Roland moved like he was about to do as she asked, but suddenly stopped.

"What?" she asked.

"I think we need to chill out."

"Why??"

"I'm not really feeling this right now."

"Maybe if you just loosen up and take your mind off of whatever is bothering you-"

"You don't think I've been trying to do that?" He moved her off of his lap and rubbed his hands down his face.

Sighing, Desiree told herself to be patient. Maybe Roland's mood had something to do with an issue at the club or something personal he just hadn't told her about yet.

"Okay," she hedged, pulling her dress straps back up. "What's wrong?"

Roland shook his head, looking away from her. Right then, Desiree's apartment was the last place he wanted to be. And Desiree was just about the last person he wanted to be with. He started to call her a couple of times earlier in the day to cancel the date, and now he wished he had. Ever since the night before, seeing Lovey with that guy at the club and then the look in her eyes after he and Desiree put on their little show on the dance floor. That look haunted him for the rest of the night, and he was no less affected by it today. He knew he and Desiree had taken things too far, and he wanted to call Lovey and apologize. There was a lot he wanted to say to Lovey, but he hadn't been able to work up the nerve.

Glancing up, he looked across the room and frowned slightly.

"Where'd you get the flowers?" he asked, pointing to the tied bouquet of roses on a small table near the television.

Desiree kicked herself for not putting those away. Miles had sent those earlier that day, and she just laid them down and forgot about them after calling to thank him.

"Just from someone who doesn't know I'm not really into those," she shrugged, hoping she sounded casual enough.

"Must be somebody new, then." He eyed her over his shoulder.

"Why does it matter? They're just some tired, played out roses. You see they're not even in a vase."

"Uh-huh."

"Come on, let's not spend our evening talking about nonsense," she purred, leaning over to nuzzle his neck. Her arms slid around him. "Let's go back to the room so I can get your mind back on me."

She grabbed his face and began slowly kissing his cheek, occasionally giving it small nips with her teeth, something he usually liked. But now, it only irritated him. When she started to slide her hand underneath his shirt collar, then tried to push him back so she could straddle him again, he stopped her.

"I'm gonna go," he announced.

"You sure about that?" Desiree asked, lowering her dress again to reveal her breasts. She seductively massaged and caressed them with her hands, looking right into his eyes. "I don't think you really wanna leave right now, do you?"

Roland found himself temporarily transfixed by Desiree's self-manipulations. He swallowed, hating that he couldn't deny how sexy she looked. And when she slid one hand between her legs and began masturbating, he groaned. Smirking triumphantly, Desiree pulled him on top of her, and he offered no resistance. Their kissing was hot and heavy, with Roland grinding frustratingly hard against her, suddenly willing to just get lost in Desiree for the time being.

"Oh *yes*..." Desiree panted, clawing at his clothes.

She was trying to push his pants down when his phone chimed in his pocket. To her surprise, he actually sat up immediately to check it.

"Are you serious right now?" she exclaimed.

Ignoring her, Roland pulled the phone out of his pocket. The temporary heat he had just built up with Desiree was instantly squelched when he saw it was a text from Lovey, telling them she was done.

"Shit!" He pounded his fist into the sofa cushion.

"What? What is it?"

Roland wordlessly handed Desiree his phone as he stood and began straightening his clothes.

Desiree read the text from Lovey that had been sent to both of them. She grinned and looked up at Roland, but she could see that he didn't see this as the good news she did.

"Why are you leaving?" she asked, standing. "This is a good thing! Now we can be together like we were before without having to worry about anybody else. Wasn't that the point of all this?"

Roland looked at her, and in that moment he wondered what he ever saw in this woman.

"No, there *was* no point to all this," he informed her, taking his phone back. "This was a complete waste of time, Desiree. And I just don't have any more time to waste."

"Wait a minute!" Desiree exclaimed, scrambling off the couch when he started towards the door. "What are you saying?"

"I'm saying I'm done too, Desiree," he replied strongly, looking right into her eyes.

"Done with what? Lovey already quit the shared relationship."

"Well then that only leaves you, then, doesn't it?"

"Hold up." Desiree held up her hand. She realized her heart was racing way faster now. "Are you trying to break up with me?"

"No. I'm not *trying* to do a damn thing. It's done."

She grabbed his arm, not believing her ears. "Roland!"

He shot her a look that could melt ice. "Let me go, Desiree."

Desiree looked at him, her eyes pleading for him to stay. He just stared back at her, unaffected. Finally, she reluctantly let him go, and he walked out without another word.

Chapter 27

ROLAND FELT LIKE THE stupidest man on the planet.

He was too old to make dumb mistakes like this. The whole shared relationship thing was stupid and juvenile. He let the physical attraction he shared with Desiree cloud his judgement, because now that he was thinking clearly, he was fully aware that she was the wrong woman for him.

There were a bunch of times he wanted to end the shared relationship, but he was too caught up in the idea of two beautiful women doing a standoff over him. And he convinced himself that Desiree going so hard for his attention meant that her feelings suddenly matched the ones he had for her before, but the more he thought about it, the more he realized that it was more about her pride than anything else. She didn't even want him back until she saw him kiss Lovey.

Desiree didn't want him; she just didn't want to lose.

"It's about damn time you came to your senses," E.J. told him a couple days later. "I was wondering just how much longer you were gonna let this nonsense go on."

"It's almost embarrassing to think about now, man," Roland admitted. "The fact that I agreed to date both of them at the same time when I really just wanted Lovey...I don't know what I was thinking."

"You and me both."

"When Desiree and I were out to dinner the other night, she kept texting somebody else. Judging from how she kept smiling, I bet it was another dude. But I didn't even care. Yet when I saw Lovey with another man at the club, it drove me crazy."

"Of course it did. You're feeling her."

"I'm more than feeling her, man. I love her."

"You sure? I thought you were in love with Desiree."

"I thought I was, too. And maybe I was, at the time. But now, I don't even see Desiree when I think of my life down the line. But picturing me and Lovey growing old together makes me happier than anything else. There's not a doubt in my mind she's the one I want to be with."

"Glad you finally realized that, brother, now what are you gonna do about it? Have you talked to Lovey?"

"I've called and sent a bunch of texts, but she hasn't answered."

"I'm not surprised."

"Part of me wants to give her some time and the other part wants to camp outside her door until she agrees to hear me out."

"You can't push her, man. After what you said you and Desiree did on the dance floor right in her face..."

"Ugh, I know. Don't remind me." Roland rubbed his eyes. He hated thinking about that.

"Maybe you should just make a clean break; move on from both Desiree and Lovey and start fresh."

"Man, forget that. I'm not trying to give up on Lovey that easily. I'll eventually get her to talk to me and hopefully, she'll forgive me for being such a dumb ass. I wouldn't care if I never saw Desiree again, though."

"Well, our agreement with her is still going, though we did reserve the right to terminate it whenever we saw fit. How are you planning on handling that?"

Roland sighed, wishing he had listened to E.J.'s initial warnings about getting involved with Desiree.

"You want to handle the events for a while?" Roland asked him. "At least for the next few events she has here?"

"No," E.J. replied bluntly. "But I will if you need me to."

Breathing a sigh of relief, Roland smiled gratefully. "I appreciate it."

"We'll just play things by ear," E.J. said. "At the end of the day, we're all professionals. Desiree brings a lot of people in the door, but I have no doubt we'll be just fine if our business relationship terminates. Atlanta is full of good party promoters, but we've built up enough of a following that we'd be good whether we work with one or not. You and I would just have to ramp up the promotion ourselves."

"True."

"As long as Desiree doesn't come in here showing her ass, we're good. We just still have to be mindful of how we deal with her so she doesn't start some kind of smear campaign."

"I'd like to think she wouldn't do that."

"You never know. But like I said, we'll just play it by ear. In the meantime, though, what are you gonna do about this Lovey situation?"

"I think she'll eventually hear me out," Roland replied, trying to make himself believe it. "And when she does, I just hope it does some good."

AFTER A LONG NIGHT at the club, Roland trudged through his front door, physically and mentally exhausted. He hadn't been able to resist going by Lovey's first, but she wasn't home. Of course, she still wasn't answering his calls or responding to his messages.

He just wanted to take a long shower and put this whole day out of his mind. Before he could even kick his shoes off, though, there was a knock at his door.

When he peeked out the side window and saw Desiree standing there, he groaned. He didn't have the energy for this.

"What do you want, Desiree?" he called out through the door.

"I think we need to talk about all this, Roland."

"We really don't."

"Come on. Let's just get everything out on the table. And I don't want to keep yelling through the door like some Neanderthals."

Roland was silent.

"Please?"

Sighing, Roland opened the door slightly. She stood there in jeans and a sweater, her natural hair fluffed around her makeup-free face. Roland almost didn't recognize her.

"If you're not gonna be straight up about everything, you might as well leave now," he warned her.

"I will."

He stepped aside, opening the door fully. She followed him to the couch and sat down, looking at him pensively.

"Why did you do me like that, Roland?" she asked.

Roland frowned, incredulous. "Excuse me?"

"You just walked out on me and I didn't have any say in it whatsoever."

"So this is how you're gonna try to play it, huh?"

"I'm not playing at all. I thought we wanted to be together but as soon as you saw that text from Lovey, you were done."

"Yeah, I was done, Desiree. And I'm still done. Let's be real; our entire relationship was a waste of time."

It was Desiree's turn to frown. "How are you even gonna say some mess like that to me?"

"Because it was. My feelings for you were real and you couldn't handle it, for whatever reason, so you backed up. On some level I can respect that; if you're not feeling it, you're just not feeling it. But as soon as I start feeling somebody *else*, then all of a sudden you want me back. Then you suggest that stupid shared relationship mess, and acted like it was some kind of competition. Just admit it, this was all a big game to you."

Desiree automatically started to refute this, but he shot her a look, silently reminding her to be honest. She sighed and played with the small hole in her jeans.

"All right, I admit when you started spending so much time with Lovey, I got jealous. It felt like y'all were shutting me out or something."

"You're the one that bugged us about spending time together, Desiree."

"I know that. And I admit that I didn't expect for you to enjoy each other's company *that* much. Then when I saw y'all kissing...I just, I didn't like it. You told me you loved *me* but you were kissing *her*."

"I did love you, Desiree. But you weren't ready for that. And the more time I spent with Lovey just showed me that she and I are a lot more compatible than you and I could ever be. You don't want the same things I want; there's no way something like that can work."

Desiree looked at him. "I could change."

"I doubt it. That's something you have to want to do, and I don't think you do. You like doing your own thing too much. Even if you managed to convince yourself for a while, it wouldn't last."

"How do you know that, Roland?"

"Maybe I don't for sure. But I do know I have no interest in trying to find out."

"Why are you being so cold to me?"

"I'm not trying to be cold. I'm just not beating around the bush."

"If your feelings for me were real, they shouldn't have just vanished that quick, Roland. You can't tell me that whatever you think you feel for Lovey is on the same level of what you feel for me. Our chemistry, our passion-"

"Yeah, we had passion. And that's what I let cloud my brain for too long. Passion by itself can only keep things going for so long. Eventually it fades out. Then what?"

"So you're trying to say all we had between us was sex?"

"That's exactly what I'm saying. At least recently."

"So you've never slept with Lovey?"

"That's totally none of your business, but no, I haven't. I fell for her without having to do that."

Desiree pursed her lips. "You can try to downtalk what we had all you want to. I *know* it was deeper than that."

Roland eyed her. This woman really was stubborn. "When we were out at dinner on Valentine's Day, who were you texting?"

A little of the color drained from Desiree's face. "Umm..."

"Miles Yoates, perhaps?"

"Wha-what? How do you-"

"Did you forget that the club has security cameras? When I was in the office, I saw y'all dancing like lovers and hugged up on the couch. You gave him your number, Desiree."

Knowing there was nothing she could say to that, Desiree just looked away.

"He's the one that sent the roses I saw, too, right?"

"Yeah." Her voice was low.

"So tell me again about what we had being real and deep?"

"Okay, Roland," Desiree threw up her hands. "I've always been honest about monogamy never being my thing. But you're the first man in years that made me even consider it."

"I'm flattered."

"For real. That's saying a lot, for me. Maybe I didn't go about some things the right way, but I absolutely have real feelings for you. And that's the most I can say about any man in years."

Roland shook his head wearily. "You might be telling the truth about that, Desiree. It's still not good enough for me. I don't want to be waiting around for your patience to run out, or for some other dude to steal your attention."

Desiree gazed at him, then looked away suddenly. "I see."

"You are the way you are; I respect that. But who you are doesn't fit with who I am. I want a wife and kids and forever. And I need to be with someone who wants that, too. And you and I both know that's not you."

Finally conceding, Desiree nodded. "I guess."

They sat silently for a few moments. Roland was glad they had this little discussion, so he could finally close the door on this part of his life. His time with Desiree was fun, but it was over.

"So you...you're in love with Lovey?"

"Yeah." He looked at her. "I am."

"Even if being with her means still seeing me? We *are* best friends, you know."

"Doesn't matter."

"Maybe you should just make a clean break with somebody else," Desiree suggested, a hint of desperation in her voice. They both heard it. "Lovey might not even want to go there with you, after all this."

Shaking his head, Roland stood. It was time to get this woman out of his house. "Why don't you let me and Lovey worry about that. Have a good evening, Desiree."

Figuring there was nothing more she could say, she slowly stood and followed him to the door. He held it open, patiently waiting for the next stall tactic that he knew was coming.

She stood close to him. "One more round, for the road?"

"Nah."

Placing a hand on his chest, she leaned in closer. Her pride wouldn't just let her walk out the door without *something*. "A good-bye kiss, then?"

He gently removed her hand and looked right into her pleading eyes. "Accept the fact that I'm done and just leave, Desiree. Quit grabbing for scraps 'cause your ego can't take somebody walking away from *you*, for once."

Her mouth falling open slightly, Desiree turned and walked out quickly. His eyes held nothing else for her, other than the message that she was now just embarrassing herself.

As much as she tried to fight them, the tears were running down her face before she even got to her car.

Chapter 28

LOVEY WASN'T READY to talk to Roland or read his messages. She didn't want to hear anything about him and Desiree.

That didn't mean she didn't think about him, though. He was on her mind way more than she wanted him to be. Her heart missed him, despite everything that happened, and that only annoyed her. She would give anything to be able to just put him out of her mind altogether.

Taylor was still in the picture, and she sincerely enjoyed his company. One night, they went back to her apartment after having spent the day at the park, throwing the Frisbee and chasing each other around. Lovey hadn't laughed so much in weeks, and it felt wonderful to forget about everything for a while.

"I appreciate you not making fun of how I run, Taylor," Lovey giggled, handing him a bottle of water before joining him on the couch. "If this was a few years ago, you wouldn't have caught me so easily."

"You held your own pretty well. Though I'd like to think I'd still catch you, regardless."

"I think your super-long legs give you an unfair advantage."

Taylor laughed and slid an arm around her shoulder. "I gave you a head start, remember?"

"Yeah, you did. Still, though." Lovey grinned at him.

Taylor's smile faded into an enamored gaze. "Well, I couldn't let you get away, now could I?"

He leaned in, gently grabbing her chin before kissing her. Lovey closed her eyes, receiving him willingly. Their water bottles rolled to the floor as Taylor's hand slid to caress her face, and Lovey gently gripped his wrist as she turned her body towards his. He grabbed her waist, pulling her closer. Their kiss deepened as Lovey slid her arms around his neck, her hand gently resting on the back of his neck. She tried to just get lost in the moment and enjoy it, but her mind couldn't help comparing Taylor's kiss to Roland's.

Taylor began gently pushing Lovey onto her back with his body, and Lovey gently placed a hand against his chest, breaking the kiss.

"I'm sorry," Taylor immediately said. "Am I moving too fast?"

"I just don't want to rush things..."

"Of course. I totally understand." Taylor sat up, running a hand down his face. "I apologize."

"It's okay, really." Lovey gave him a reassuring smile. She gently squeezed his arm. "You're a great kisser, you know."

"Yeah?" Taylor smiled at her.

"Absolutely."

"Mind if I try to improve my grade?"

"You think you can?"

"Oh, that sounds like a challenge!" Taylor began tickling her, causing Lovey to shriek and giggle incessantly. She tried to crawl away from him and he gently tackled her on the floor, continuing the funny torture. After several moments, he abruptly leaned down and claimed her lips again, not being able to resist anymore. Lovey grabbed the sides of his face as she willingly kissed him back, somehow more receptive now than she had been just minutes before. Taylor rolled his body onto hers, and she let him.

"Please tell me if I'm going too far," he whispered between kisses.

"Let's just keep it right here." She sighed as he placed a soft kiss on her neck. "This is enough for now. Is that okay?"

"Of course." He moved his lips back to hers. "Whatever you want, love."

Lovey appreciated Taylor for not pushing or pressuring her, in that moment or during any of the times they spent together after that. As attracted as she was to him, there was something holding her back. She knew at some point she was going to have to address things with Roland, because as much as she might not want him to, he still occupied a good chunk of her thoughts and heart. She just wanted to be sure she was strong enough to handle whatever he was so eager to tell her.

Part of that included getting back to her old self, physically. A lot of her self-confidence had dissipated when she started putting on weight. And when she remembered the reason behind that—Desiree constantly sending her fattening desserts—it didn't do much to help her mood. She knew part of it was her fault because she succumbed to the temptation every time, but that's just what Desiree had counted on. Desiree knew sweets were Lovey's weakness, and had used it against her. Lovey was still trying to come to grips with that.

In the meantime, she was back in the gym, working out for an hour or so after work, and drinking her green smoothies again. She forbade herself from having any sweets and chugged water like it was going out of style. It felt nice to start being able to fit into her clothes again, and to hear Taylor and her coworkers comment on how she was slimming down. That was *one* thing she could have some control over.

THE DAY FINALLY CAME where Desiree called.

It had been three weeks since the pre-Valentine's Day party, and Lovey hadn't seen or spoken to Desiree at all since then. She didn't have much to say to her, even though she knew they would need to talk eventually. She wasn't going to be the one to initiate it, though. All through their friendship, she was always the one to break whenever they had disagreements, even if Desiree was the one in the wrong. Lovey just refused to do it this time, even if it meant they didn't talk again. That's just how fed up she was.

"Hey," Desiree greeted, somewhat tentatively.

"Hey."

"How've you been?"

"I've been great."

"Really?"

"You sound surprised."

"Honestly, yeah, I kinda am."

"What, did you think your sabotage efforts were going to leave me in some kind of deep depression?"

"Sabotage? What are you talking about?"

Lovey figured she wasn't going to own up to anything. Not that easily. "What can I do for you, Desiree?"

"I wanted to invite you to the day party I'm having this weekend at Café Circa. It's time we finally talked."

"I don't really think one of your parties is the place to do that."

"Maybe not, but I'm going to be tied up with stuff most of the weekend, and I don't want to keep putting it off."

"Well then it needs to happen some evening during the week or when the party is over. You've had more than enough time to work on what you're gonna say."

"Work on what I'm gonna say? You make it sound like I'm gonna try to con you or something. What's up with you? Why are you so snippy with me?"

"Never mind, Desiree. When you find time in your schedule to come talk to me here at my place, you let me know. Just make sure you call first."

"Okay, okay! How's tomorrow night?"

"Tomorrow night is fine. I should be home around six."

"Fine."

The next night, Desiree showed up at Lovey's apartment and was surprised to see Liz there, barefoot on the couch and giving her the evil eye.

"I didn't know she was going to be here," Desiree looked at Lovey almost accusingly.

Before Lovey could respond, Liz jumped up. "Yeah, well, I am. So?"

"*So* this is between me and Lovey. You don't need to be here, Liz."

"Don't tell me where I need to be, Desiree."

"What's up with this?" Desiree asked Lovey, pointing at Liz.

"I think it's past time I said some things to you myself," Liz spoke up, again beating Lovey to the punch. She moved closer to Desiree. "I've just been *waiting* for a chance to tell you about yourself. You're so full of shit it's not even funny. And you're not gonna keep screwing my sister over."

"Nobody's screwing anybody over. And you don't know anything about this so you need to mind your own business."

"Oh, see you must not know; if it has to do with Lovey, it *is* my business. Especially since I'm the one that had her back when you were putting some man over your friendship with her."

"Liz, you need to back up outta my face."

Stepping even closer, Liz glared menacingly at Desiree. "And what do you think you're gonna do about it if I don't?"

Desiree returned Liz's stare-down. "Lovey, girl, get your sister..."

"Why are you calling for her? You can't handle yourself?"

"I'm just trying to give you ample opportunity to come to your senses. 'Cause once you push me too far, that's gonna be it."

"You mean like this?" Liz bumped Desiree with her shoulder.

"Liz!" Lovey finally spoke up. She should've known letting Liz come over wasn't the best idea.

"Or *this*?" Liz shoved Desiree hard with both hands, sending her reeling back several steps.

Desiree looked shocked for a second, but she quickly charged back at Liz, ready to throw down. Lovey jumped between them, blocking her path.

"Hey, y'all cut it out!" she yelled, keeping them both at arm's length. "This isn't gonna get us anywhere! Liz, it'll be best if you go home. Desiree and I need to discuss things in private. I'll call you later."

Still glaring at Desiree, Liz nodded. "All right, I'll go. But don't you let her smooth-talk her way out of everything."

"I got it, Liz. Just go."

Lovey kept her body in between Liz and Desiree as Liz put her shoes back on and grabbed her keys and purse.

"Just say the word and I can come back," she told Lovey. "Love you."

"I love you, too."

Once Liz left, Desiree huffed, "What the hell was that? I didn't know this was gonna be some kind of ambush!"

Lovey just shook her head and moved back to the couch. "When I told her you were coming, she insisted on showing up and confronting you. In hindsight, I should've just waited until after your visit to tell her about it. But nobody was trying to ambush you."

"Maybe *you* weren't but she surely was!"

Sighing, Lovey shook her head. "Let it go, Desiree. You wanted to talk, so let's talk."

Calming herself, Desiree sat down on the couch. The confrontation with Liz made her forget how she had planned to kick things off.

"I know you probably expect me to make a bunch of excuses for how things are with us, but I'm not gonna do that," she proclaimed. "The whole situation with Roland...I know I didn't handle it well. I just got carried away with everything."

"So that's why you tried to sabotage me?" Lovey asked bluntly.

"I still don't like that word *sabotage*..."

"It doesn't matter if you *like* it or not, Desiree; let's call it what it is. Just admit it. When you came to my office with that big hunk of Mama Elyse's cake saying you wanted to bury the hatchet, that was a bold-faced lie. The whole point of that visit was to kick off your mission to fatten me up. And sadly, I fell for it headfirst."

"I..."

"You exploited my weakness under the guise of friendship. Constantly sending me sweets, buying me dresses that were too small, playing on my insecurities by telling me Roland doesn't like thick women, which probably isn't even true. You even encouraged me to get back with my two-timing ex. What did you do, hunt Evan down and tell him to call me?"

"No! I just happened to run into him at the store, I swear. But...I admit I did give him the impression that you were still interested in him."

"Did you mention anything about him to Roland?"

Desiree couldn't look at Lovey. "When he, um, he mentioned that he hadn't heard much from you and I said that you were back in touch with your ex..."

"Wow, Desiree."

"Look, I'm not proud of any of this," Desiree defended. "I know there's no excuse."

"No. There is absolutely no excuse."

"I just saw you and Roland getting so close and felt like y'all were leaving me out...I was jealous. And yes, I know I'm the one that encouraged you to spend time together. And yes, y'all tried to warn me that it could turn out like it did. But I had it in my head that Roland could never be as into you as he was into me. Clearly, I was wrong."

Lovey just looked at her.

"If it makes you feel any better, Roland dumped me," Desiree muttered, clearly not enjoying admitting such a thing. "Right after you sent that text saying you were done, he said he was done, too. He told me straight-up that he just wants you."

Her stomach clenched. "Really?"

"Yeah. He's in love with you."

"He said that?"

"That and more."

Lovey couldn't deny the jolt that shot through her upon hearing that. She didn't know what she wanted to do about it, but she loved hearing it.

"I see," she finally murmured, looking away.

"Lovey...I hope we can move past this. I really do miss you as my friend and want us to just put this whole mess behind us and move forward."

Slowly turning her disbelieving eyes back to Desiree, Lovey shook her head.

"Are you serious?" she marveled. "Just put this whole mess behind us and move forward? What makes you think we can do that after all this, Desiree? What makes you think I'd even want to be your friend after this?"

Desiree's jaw dropped. "Lovey, come on...I know I messed up, but-"

"No, Desiree, messing up would be ruining my favorite jeans or accidentally erasing all my episodes of *Black-ish*. This was not *messing up*. Everything you did, you did deliberately. You planned all of this to take me down, all for a man that you were trying to get away from months ago because things were getting too deep for you. Instead of talking to me, friend-to-friend and woman-to-woman, you turned this into some kind of contest that nobody really wins."

"I know, I was stupid! But that doesn't mean I don't still love you or want us to be friends, Lovey. We're like family! In a lot of ways, I'm closer to you than I am to my own sisters!"

"Yet I bet you've never done anything like this to any of them, have you?"

Desiree looked at her helplessly.

"You have *no* idea how much you've hurt me, Desiree," Lovey continued, a hand to her chest. The emotions began to make their way up to her eyes, and she didn't try to stop them. "I've seen you do this kind of thing to other people, but that was back in the day; I thought you outgrew this kind of childish crap. And even if you hadn't, I *never* thought you would do it to me. But apparently, I was foolish to think I was exempt if it involved something you wanted badly enough."

"Lovey," Desiree scooted a little closer to her on the couch. "I admit, I wasn't thinking, but-"

"And that's what makes all this even worse; you didn't think about the consequences of what you were doing. You weren't concerned about our friendship at all, or what you were doing to me. Really, I doubt you even considered what would happen if you *did* end up with Roland; how you would just end up right back where you were when all of this started, running from things when he wanted to move forward. All you could see was what you wanted in the moment, Desiree, no matter what it did to anyone else. I can't forget that."

A lone tear rolled down Desiree's cheek. She didn't try to hide or stop it.

"I don't even feel like I know you anymore, Desiree." Lovey's voice was strong as tears rolled down her own cheeks. "I've been a good friend to you since we were teenagers. I've respected you. I've kept your secrets. I've had your back. I've loved you unconditionally. You were like a sister to me. And all it took was a man you liked showing a little too much interest in me for you to throw all that away."

For the first time, Desiree began to feel actual shame for everything she did. "You really don't think you can forgive me for this?"

"I'm sure I'll be able to forgive you one day, but...I don't know if I can trust you again."

That hit Desiree like a punch in the face. She had clearly underestimated how deep her actions would cut Lovey, or how far she had pushed things. All along, she was so sure that Lovey would forgive her, even if she was mad at her for a while. But she might have wrecked things between them to the point where they couldn't be fixed.

"Lovey, I can make this up to you. It would kill me to lose you as a friend. I just...give me a chance to make things right."

"You can't make this one right, Desiree." Lovey's voice was sad. "Even if I *wanted* to forgive you right now and try to forget about it, I have to have more respect for myself than that. I've dealt with a lot from you, Desiree, but this...I can't do it this time. I can't justify it, I can't make excuses for you, I can't sweep it under the rug. You've simply gone too far this time. And I just need a break from you for a while."

Dejected, Desiree stood, knowing there was nothing more she could say. She couldn't believe things had gotten to this point. Her head was swimming as she started for the door, wishing this was some kind of bad dream.

"And even after all this," Lovey called out when Desiree's hand was on the doorknob, "You still have yet to say 'I'm sorry.'"

Desiree turned to her, embarrassed by the observation. She wanted to rectify that but knew it wouldn't mean anything to Lovey now.

"Some things never change." Lovey wiped her eyes. "Please lock the door behind you."

Feeling like the stupidest person alive, Desiree left.

Chapter 29

ROLAND HAD TO ADMIT that he hadn't expected Lovey to ignore him this long. It had been almost two months, and Roland was going crazy.

"You hurt her, man," E.J. reminded him. Roland was visiting his brother's house to watch some basketball, something he didn't get to do that much. Seeing his brother and sister-in-law Natalia together only made him kick himself harder for messing things up with Lovey. "You don't just get past something like that."

"I know, but how can I try to fix things if she won't talk to me?"

"This isn't really something you can fix, bro. It's all about whether she wants to forgive you or not. And even if she does, she might not give you another chance."

"Thanks, E.J."

"Hey, I'm just letting you know. You made her think she wasn't enough for you, despite the feelings you claimed to have for her. Doesn't help that the other woman was her best friend. Chances are, Lovey might just be done with you altogether."

Roland didn't want to think that. He didn't want to imagine his life without Lovey in it because he acted like a stupid adolescent for a few weeks.

Not bothering to leave another message that he was sure would go unanswered, he decided to just show up at her place. He couldn't resist. He missed Lovey and had to see her, even if it ended in her telling him to kiss his ass.

He pulled up to her apartment building, praying she was home. He tried to work out what he was going to say when he noticed a man who looked vaguely familiar step outside. When Lovey emerged behind him, Roland realized it was the guy she was at Barfly with at the pre-Valentine's Day party. He watched anxiously as Lovey stood there talking to the man, her arms hugged around herself against the chilly night air, slightly shifting her weight from side to side. Finally, the man hugged her, then placed a lingering kiss against her lips. Roland's jaw tightened, the sight infuriating him. He resisted the urge to run the guy down as he watched him walk to his car. Lovey stood there and waved as he drove off, then went back inside.

Roland had to gather himself. He hadn't been prepared to see that. Was Lovey dating this guy now? Were they a couple? Roland knew he had no right to feel upset, but he was. The only man Lovey needed to be with, in his mind, was him.

Knowing he'd get nowhere just sitting in the car stewing, he made himself open the door and get out. Hurrying to Lovey's door, he knocked harder than he probably needed to, adrenaline fueling him.

"Did you forget something?" he heard Lovey ask. She must not have checked the peephole because she swung open the door with a wide smile that faded when she saw Roland standing there.

"Hey, Lovey."

"Roland, what are you doing here?" She closed her sweater and folded her arms under her breasts.

"I had to see you. Can we please talk? It's been weeks."

"You can't put a time limit on my feelings, Roland. I had every intention of reaching out to you when I was ready."

"Well I'm here now; can I come in?"

Lovey just looked at him.

"I'm not trying to pressure you, I swear," Roland continued. "But this has been killing me, Lovey. Whatever comes of it, I just want to get everything out on the table. At the very least, I want to apologize to you to your face."

Looking away briefly, Lovey finally conceded. "Okay. Maybe we *should* go ahead and do this now. Come in."

Roland tried not to let her statement make him think the worst as he entered the apartment and closed the door behind him. He watched Lovey inch her way to the couch, and it hit him that he was actually there with her, finally. Unable to resist, he grabbed her and turned her to him, enveloping her in a tight hug. To his surprise, she didn't push him away; she only stiffened briefly before letting her body relax against him. He buried his face against her neck, inhaling that familiar lavender scent, enjoying being close to her again. His arms just kept tightening around her and hope surged through him when he felt her hug him back.

Eventually, she gently eased back and stepped away from him. Roland looked longingly at her, and she had to look away, her face flushing slightly.

"I need some water," she murmured, her hand gently touching her throat. "I'll be right back."

She turned and hurried to the kitchen. Roland couldn't resist following her, even though he knew her sudden thirst was nothing more than a temporary reprieve. Now that he was finally with her, he didn't want to be away from her, even if she was just in the next room.

"Lovey," he said as she retrieved a bottle of water from the refrigerator. "First and foremost, I am so, so sorry for everything. I can't even begin to express how stupid I was for agreeing to that shared relationship and everything that happened after it."

Taking a long swig of water, Lovey put the cap back on the bottle and set it aside. "Thank you for saying that."

"I'm not going to insult you by trying to make an excuse or justify anything," Roland continued. "The only thing I can offer is an explanation, and it's not even a great one."

"I'm listening."

"The last two women I fell for turned out to be the wrong ones. And this shared relationship was just a way to stall my falling for you, because I was scared of possibly getting it wrong again. I told myself two beautiful women going hard for me was flattering, even though I already knew who I wanted." He moved closer to her. "And that woman *wasn't* Desiree."

"But knowing that, you still went along with it," Lovey reminded him, inching away. "And not only that, you spent more time with her than you did with me. How do you think that made me feel?"

"I know, Lovey, and if I could go back and make the right decision, I would!" Roland slapped a hard hand to his chest. "I was stupid, I'll be the first to admit that!"

"Yes, you were!"

"And now I'm asking, damn near begging, for you to let me make it up to you!" Roland took another step towards her. Both of them were almost yelling, the emotions running sky-high. "If there is any good that came out of all of this, it's that it just made me realize how much I love you; being away from you has been *torture*, Lovey! As dramatic as that sounds, I mean it more than anything!"

Her breath hitching in her throat, Lovey took a tiny step away from him. "Desiree was my best friend, Roland! I can't forget about that!"

"I don't expect you to forget about it, baby, believe me," Roland insisted, finally closing the distance between them. His body trapped her against the counter, his arms bordering her body. "I'm fully aware that I'm gonna have to earn your trust back. I'm fully aware that I'm gonna have to work for your forgiveness. I'm fully aware that it's going to be a while before the hurt from what I did goes away, if it ever fully does." He held her face in his hands, thumbs stroking her cheeks as he looked into her doubtful eyes. "However long it takes, I want to do all of that. Please let me do that, Lovey..."

Lovey opened her mouth to speak, but nothing came out. She shook her head and started to gently push against him. "I don't know if I can, Roland. As much as I might want to..."

"Lovey, please listen to me, okay?" Roland briefly dropped his hands from her face but remained where he stood. "The night we kissed for the first time, I made a promise to myself that I was going to love you like you deserved to be loved. That I was going to be better for you than all those other dudes that dogged you in the past. Now, I know I've messed up. But the difference between me and them is that I *know* I made a mistake, and I'm here in your face humbling myself. Whatever it's gonna take to get you back..."

She wanted to stand strong and be firm, but the tears were stinging Lovey's eyes. It was another time she hated how emotional she got.

"I want to be with you more than anything, Lovey. But if nothing else, you at least know how sorry I am."

Everything in her wanted to push him away and tell him to get the hell out of her apartment. But she couldn't make herself say those words. Lovey could feel the sincerity and the remorse radiating off of Roland like heat from a furnace. Try as she might, she couldn't make herself ignore that.

"Roland, I..." She looked into his eyes, her thoughts bouncing against each other. "I..."

"What, baby?" Roland whispered, gently kissing her salty cheeks, her forehead, the tip of her nose. "Tell me what you want me to do and I'll do it."

Her hands inched up to grip his jacket. He leaned in even closer to her.

"I don't want to be a fool for you, Roland," she managed to say.

"I'm not trying to make a fool out of you, Lovey. I swear. *I'd* be the fool if I let you get away."

Momentarily closing her eyes, Lovey opened them to Roland's lips gently kissing hers. He waited for resistance and when she gave none, he kissed her again. They exchanged several brief nips before finally melting into each other, giving in to what they both yearned for.

Roland wrapped Lovey tightly in his arms, not being able to get close enough to her. Part of him kept expecting her to suddenly push him away and kick him out, not being able to get past his screw-up, but she didn't. She just held onto him as tightly as he was holding on to her, returning his urgent kisses.

After a long while, they slowly tapered off, their eyes on each other. Without a word, Lovey grabbed his hand and led him to her bedroom.

After kicking their shoes off, they sat on Lovey's bed, facing each other, and talked. They talked about everything that happened, including all of Desiree's indiscretions and the state of their friendship as a result. Roland felt terrible for having anything to do with breaking up a years-long friendship like he had.

"I am *so* sorry," he expressed, his voice anguished.

"I appreciate that, but you aren't the one who got dirty with it. That was all Desiree."

"Still, though. You two have been friends for years; I just hate that I came between y'all."

"It's probably a good thing, Roland. As much as it hurts, if something like this didn't happen now, it would have happened at some point. I needed to see what kind of person she is."

"It still blows my mind that she would do that stuff to you."

"Yeah. Mine, too."

"And for the record," Roland leaned forward, a flirtatious gleam in his eye. "I have absolutely no problem with thick women."

Blushing, Lovey bit her lip. "Good to know. I'm getting the extra weight off, though."

"Extra weight or not, it doesn't change anything. You're still bangin'. But your weight is meaningless, anyway; it's about the kind of person you are. And you're at the top of the ranks when it comes to that."

Lovey smiled, his words touching her. The night they had gone to Maggiano's, Lovey was insecure about her weight but Roland looked at her the same as he always had. He didn't treat her differently. There were no questions in his eyes about what might be going on with her. The problem was all in Lovey's head. So she hadn't helped things any in regards to the lack of time she and Roland were spending together, because there were several times she cancelled or turned down plans with him because she was worried about what he'd think of her weight. That hadn't occurred to her until that moment.

"Thank you, Roland. That means a lot, to hear that."

Wanting to be closer to her again, Roland moved over so he was sitting next to her. He picked up her hand and played with her soft fingers.

"So what's going to happen with us?" he finally asked.

Lovey inhaled a shaky breath. "I want to tell you to go home and let me think about things for a few days. I want to still be mad at you. But I'm not."

He looked at her, brows raised. "Really?"

"That's not to say I'm over it, but I can deal with your stupid decision better than I can deal with Desiree's malicious actions. And I believe you when you say you're truly sorry. With Desiree, I don't know what to believe. She never even really apologized."

Roland shook his head, not even surprised.

"And I know I should apologize for my part in all this, too-"

"Nope," Roland put a finger to her lips. "I'm not gonna let you do that. None of this is your fault, baby."

"I let my pride cloud my good judgment just because I was upset with Desiree."

"Maybe so, but still. You didn't mistreat either one of us. So don't try to make yourself be wrong, here."

She smiled, gazing into his handsome face. There was no denying how good it felt to be there with him. Part of her, a small part, questioned whether forgiving him was a good idea. It tried to conjure up the hurt she felt when Roland was spending so much time with Desiree, or when they were showing out in front of her on the dance floor at Barfly. As much as Lovey didn't enjoy thinking about those things, she truly felt she could get past them. The fact that Roland hadn't tried to make any excuses or expect her to just get over it because he acknowledged he was wrong went a long way with her.

And when it came right down to it, Lovey was in love with Roland, too. And she just didn't want to waste any more time.

Still, she said, "Roland, if there is *any* doubt in your mind that I'm the only woman you want to be with, please tell me now. I need for you to be absolutely sure-"

He stopped her words with a kiss, his hand brushing stray hairs from her face. Easing back, he looked right into her eyes. "I am absolutely, a hundred percent sure, Lovey. I got being stupid out of my system when I felt like I lost you. There's no way I'm going through that again."

"In that case," she kissed his palm before easing off the bed. "I'll be right back."

"Where are you going?"

She looked at him. "I need to speak to Taylor. I have to let him know I can't see him anymore. Preferably that's something I'd do in person, but that would mean I'd have to wait longer to finally make love to you. And I don't want to do that."

His eyes darkening, Roland bit his bottom lip seductively. "Make the damn phone call."

Acknowledgements

I'm so thankful to God, my family, and my readers and supporters. I appreciate all of you. There's not one part of your support that I take for granted.

Keep an eye out for a sequel to this story. Lovey, Desiree, and Roland aren't quite done yet. ☺

Thanks so much for reading! Hope it brought you at least a little enjoyment, which is my main goal, especially now.

If you liked this story, please consider leaving a review. And if you want to show *extra* love, share that you read it on social media! ☺

You can find me on Instagram and TikTok at @authorjessicaterry and on Twitter at @itsJessicaTerry. And don't forget to subscribe to my email list at www.jessicaterry.com.

Also by Jessica Terry

Some Like 'em *Thick*
It's All Right...Now
Not By a Long Shot
Get Right
Decisions and Consequences
Take One For the Team
When You Share Too Much
Backtalk
Emasculated
Restless
The Beginning of Again
Always and Nevers
She is Me

The Introvert Series

Did you love *Split By the Bell*? Then you should read *The Karma Call*[1] by Jessica Terry!

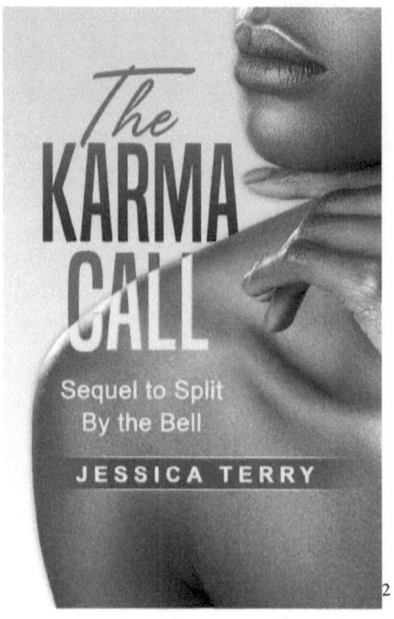

Desiree Mashburn did her dirt without thinking karma would eventually come calling. But screwing over her best friend to win a man's affections was apparently the final straw.Her life begins going from sweet to sour fast, and worst of all, she's lost the best friend she knows she'll ever have in Lovey Tate. Desiree aches to reconcile, but winning Lovey's trust back might be too tall of an order.Lovey finally has everything she's wanted in life, including Roland, the man she and Desiree battled over. But she

---

1. https://books2read.com/u/bo2d9Z

2. https://books2read.com/u/bo2d9Z

has her own issues, and can't help but question Desiree's motives. She misses her friend, but doesn't want to be a fool again.But when a painful part of Desiree's past resurfaces, she knows she needs Lovey more than ever. Can she win her trust back, or is it too little too late?

Read more at https://www.jessicaterry.com/.

About the Author

Jessica Terry caught the writing bug at a young age and loves little more than holing up at home in Douglasville, GA, cranking out contemporary novels. And eating.

Another thing she loves is interacting with her readers. Sign up for her email list and keep up to date with new releases at www.jessicaterry.com.

Read more at https://www.jessicaterry.com/.